STARDUST

GRACE WALKER

STARDUST

DEDICATION

Thank you to my wonderful family, who has always supported me.

In loving memory of Alex

PROLOUGE

King Zamir of the Embleck Army stood before two hologram projectors, examining the figures shown.

One showed a girl who looked to be in her very early teens with vivid red hair. The other showed a young teenage boy with deep green eyes.

"How are the subjects, Your Majesty?" Commander Ankor stepped into the dark room.

"The girl is enjoying her life in the desert," King Zamir deducted. "…and the boy is struggling through the events of high society."

"Are you sure these children can affect our takeover of the galaxy?" Ankor asked hesitantly.

"Yes," King Zamir snapped. "I know what I'm doing, *Commander.*" He emphasized the title, reminding Ankor of his position.

"Of course, Your Majesty." Ankor bowed low and

backed out of the room.

"Yes…" King Zamir stared at the holograms. "These children can greatly affect my reign." He stared at the boy. "His life is filled with so much sadness and pain."

In the hologram, an older woman approached the boy and began scolding him. The boy stared at his boots, looking even more miserable.

"Perfect," King Zamir hissed. "He is almost within my reach. Soon, I'll draw him entirely into my grasp. Then, nothing else can stand in my way."

King Zamir paused for a second to glance at the three-dimensional image of the girl. She was stroking a small animal in her lap and smiling.

"Unless she could oppose me…" King Zamir mused before shaking his head and chuckling, a truly terrifying sound.

"Not likely," he scoffed.

"After all, what's one little girl?"

CHAPTER 1

YEAR: 9017

"Come on in, Joffrey!" Anise Desson called from the lake, flipping her wet braids over her shoulder. "The water's great!"

Joffrey meowed in disagreement, lashing his long tail. Her pet kibit—an alien species with the body of a cat, but his back half was green and scaly—usually loved the water.

"Alright, alright."

The hot desert sun of Ceran beat down on Anise's skin, making her shoulders hot to the touch. She sank beneath the lake's surface, relishing the cool water.

Joffrey paced the edge of the lake, rattling his large, powerful bat-like wings that allowed him to fly through even the harshest desert storms. He stared distastefully at the water, meowing in displeasure.

Anise sighed and swam to the lake's edge, climbing onto the shore and accidentally splashing Joffrey with water. He hissed at her, shaking himself dry.

Anise pushed her wet hair back as her stomach tightened with hunger. "Well, since *someone* doesn't want to swim, why don't we go to the marketplace for dinner?" She picked up her cloak from the shore and shook the sand off before pinning it around her neck. "I'll race you there!"

Joffrey perked up and flapped his large wings, scattering the sand around him. He lifted into the air and flew off towards the marketplace.

"Hey, no head starts!" Anise shouted, racing after him.

Courtesy of the desert heat, Anise was nearly dry when she reached the marketplace entrance. Joffrey was sitting beside the entryway, grooming himself. When she slid over to him, he leaped up and into her arms.

"You win again." Anise scratched Joffrey behind his ears. "Now, we should go before the dinner hour is over!"

Anise pulled down her hood, running her fingers through

5

her twisted, damp hair. Although she wished she could leave it up, it would do no good. Her vibrant, dark red hair and vivid teal eyes stood out from the crowd of dark-haired and brown-eyed Ceranith, labeling her as an outside instantly. The people of Ceran didn't like outsiders, and Anise really couldn't blame them.

Ceran was a small planet, but her village was tiny—even on Ceran. Very few people—all native Ceranith—called the village home, purposefully avoiding contact with most of the outside galaxy.

The last time outsiders arrived; they were led by a man with red hair. His ship had the crest of the Embleck Army, an enemy to the galaxy. The man had stationed at least fifty soldiers on the planet and then left.

Even now, Embleck Army soldiers patrolled the marketplace, constantly eyeing anyone who stayed in one place too long, and often expecting free meals. Truthfully, everyone was afraid to refuse or call the Qor, the protectors of the galaxy.

Now the stain of the Embleck Army tainted Anise, who hadn't been well accepted even before then.

Anise sighed and headed into the marketplace with Joffrey close on her heels. The second she slipped past the archway entrance, she was enveloped by the sounds and scents of the Ceran marketplace.

People called out to one another, hurrying to get their items before sunset. Anise took a deep breath and savored the scents of food cooking: peppers, fresh bread, and cumin. It made her hungry, and she fingered the few coins in her purse.

On weekends she worked as a dishwasher at the Maroosh Inn, but they had been closed due to repairs, leaving her in a pinch.

Still, she was grateful for the work they had given her before. Nobody else was willing to hire the strange outsider girl. She knew the only reason they had hired her was that, as a dishwasher, no one had to speak to her.

A shriek yanked her from her thoughts, and Anise saw a hovercar heading straight for a small child. She snatched the boy, pulling him out of harm's way, with just a second to spare.

"Get out of the road, you little desert rats!" the man in the vehicle shouted.

"You should watch where you're going!" Anise shouted back.

"Filthy outsider." The man revved his engine, sending a cloud of sand over Anise as he sped off.

Anise stuck out her tongue, making a rude hand gesture at him as a woman came rushing up.

"Oh, Firon!" she exclaimed, taking the boy from Anise. "Thank you, thank you."

"Of course," Anise began. "I—"

The woman looked up, but she instantly dropped eye contact when she saw whom she was talking to. "Come along, Firon," she said coolly, sticking her nose in the air as she walked away, pulling the child behind her.

"You're welcome," Anise said to the empty air. The little boy waved, and Anise returned the gesture, another sigh escaping her as she continued deeper into the market.

The further Anise ventured into the villager, more of the people tried to avoid her. A woman holding the hands of two small children quickly crossed the street to avoid passing Anise. A group of young men leaning against a building moved away as they saw her coming. People looked away and made a point to avoid eye contact.

Anise kept her eyes on the ground, wishing there was a way to communicate that she wasn't a threat. She wasn't a curse, though the often superstitious Ceranith might disagree. It didn't matter how polite, quiet, and respectful she was—nothing ever changed.

And will it ever?

A few moments later, Anise passed by a group of

Embleck soldiers sitting around a table piled high with food. Joffrey meowed, pawing her cloak.

"Okay, okay. Traditional distracting maneuver," Anise whispered.

Joffrey crept over and leaped up onto the table. He yowled and flapped his wings, knocking over glasses of punch to spill across the table.

"Hey, you! Get away!" the soldiers exclaimed. Joffrey meowed, snatched a radio off the table, and dashed off.

"Get it!" shouted the soldiers as they threw back their chairs, racing after Joffrey.

Anise smirked. The plan worked every time. She strolled over to the table and picked up a plate of food that had yet to be touched.

After filling her canteen with ice water, Anise casually slid into a small alleyway. She gave a piercing whistle, and a moment later, Joffrey came racing back to her.

"Good job, sweetie." Anise kissed his head. "Dinner is served."

Anise broke off a chunk of bread and offered it to Joffrey. He ate all rapidly, then decided to busy himself with catching small sand crabs for the rest of his dinner.

Anise shrugged and ate the rest of the food in a flash. Once finished, she leaned over and peeked out of the alley. The marketplace was much emptier, and the soldiers had disappeared.

"Come on, Joffrey," Anise ordered, but he didn't budge. "Joffrey, let's go."

Joffrey looked annoyed to be pulled away from the dozens of crabs he could catch, but he still flew up and settled into Anise's arms.

Now the moons were high in the sky, shining silver light over the marketplace. The once bustling scene was almost silent at night. Anise strolled through the empty marketplace with Joffrey purring in her arms, enjoying the peace and quiet without the pressure of dozens of eyes on her.

They passed the marketplace entrance and continued through the red desert, the moons' light making Joffrey's wings and scales shimmer.

Finally, they reached the large turquoise-colored lake, and the small, strange house beside it.

Half of the house was small and boxlike, with a short round tower at the side made of tan sandstone crumbling at the edges. However, the left side of the house had crumbled due to a storm a long time ago, so Anise had to get creative. The other side of the house was the front of a small spaceship.

She'd found the remains in an old shipyard a few years ago. Most of the ships were in pieces, and she had used the front of one to make one side of her house. One ship was whole, but it needed many repairs, and she still missed a few vital pieces.

Anise shoved open the house's door and stepped inside the empty room. She wished she had someone to greet her at the door, but she had been alone for years.

But now this broken home became hers, and the tiny kibit kitten living in the ruins became her only friend.

"And we're doing well," Anise said to herself.

Joffrey leaped from her arms and raced down the hall into the tower room. Anise followed slowly. The tower room had no stairs or second floor, and she slept there on a small pallet bed.

"Thanks for the help with dinner." Anise scratched Joffrey's head as she opened her wardrobe, selecting her sleeping clothes.

Joffrey climbed on top of the bed Anise had made for him. She had used a tall pole and then molded another on, so Joffrey could use his prehensile tail to hang upside down, his favorite way to sleep.

"Good night, Joffrey," Anise murmured, settling down on her pallet. Joffrey meowed back, and she smiled before falling asleep.

11

CHAPTER 2

Before the sun rose, Anise slipped outside, wading into the lake, cool from the night.

"Better to get it over with," Anise reminded herself.

Closing her eyes, she dunked herself in the cool water, coming up for air with a shriek—a mixture of delight and the cold.

Joffrey sat on the lake's edge, grooming himself as Anise began her morning laps. She paused to watch the sunrise as the night sky changed from rich indigo to vibrant shades of red, yellow, and pink before settling on a shade of pale orange as she resumed her laps.

Now Joffrey jumped in the lake, swimming out to her, and meowing incessantly.

"What's up, buddy?" Anise stroked his head with one hand, treading water. "You seem antsy."

Joffrey hissed and took her braid in his mouth. Pulling on her, he started to swim for shore.

"Okay, okay." Anise swam with him and climbed up on the bank. "Now what, mister?"

Reaching down, she tried to pet Joffrey, but he hissed again and started toward their house.

"Well, I guess we're going home." Anise shouted after her pet, "I'll beat you there!"

Anise raced over the slippery red sand, skidding up beside Joffrey. He sat by the door, looking very pleased with himself.

"Alright, you might have won this time, but I'll get you later."

Anise took her towel off the rack and started drying her hair. As she did, she glanced at her calendar.

"You know, tonight is the start of the Sun Festival!" She bounced on her toes. "And you know what comes after." The Sun Festival was a week-long celebration in the middle of summer. And, every year on the day after, it was Anise's birthday.

Joffrey meowed in agreement and started fluffing his fur as

13

Anise began twisting her hair into double braids. She was careful to tuck the royal blue streak that ran through her hair on the underside of her braid. The blue was natural, and she couldn't dye it either.

"It's so strange," Anise said out loud. She had stood in this room and said the same thing hundreds of times but still had no answers.

Anise sighed and picked her favorite outfit: an olive green wrap top and light brown leggings. She carefully wrapped the top to cover her right shoulder and the strange marking she had on it.

On her upper right shoulder, she had a white marking of two star shapes, set slightly aside from the other. She didn't know what the marking meant or how she got it, but it had been there for as long as she could remember. Anise also pulled her short, brown cloak from the closet and a cream scarf to tie around her waist.

Once she was dressed, and while Joffrey was content, she carefully opened her small jewelry box. Inside were her two most prized possessions (other than Joffrey): a teardrop-shaped pendant of turquoise strung on a gold chain and a bracelet with round, turquoise beads. She had owned the necklace since she was a child, but the bracelet she had saved for and bought a year ago.

Anise took the necklace from the box and gently fastened it on. The only time she took it off was when she went swimming, and the weight had become a comfort. She also slipped the bracelet on her wrist and lightly tugged on her ever-present gold hoop earrings.

"Are you ready, Joffrey?" she asked, checking her reflection in her cracked mirror.

"Mrrow," said Joffrey.

"Perfect," said Anise. "Then let's go!"

The two of them left quickly, stopping only when Anise took a few coins from her purse, and Joffrey saw a crab that he decided had to be eaten that very minute. Once Anise had pulled him away, they were off to the Sun Festival.

Anise grinned as she entered the marketplace. The buildings were draped with golden streamers and colorful ribbons. Everyone dressed in brightly colored outfits, strolling among booths and stalls filled with food, jewelry, and an assortment of colorful clothes. Small children waved long sticks with bright ribbons tied to the ends. Music and laughter drifted through the air.

The Sun Festival was a week-long celebration to have fun, relax and be grateful for everything they had. It only happened once a year and only on Ceran and its sister planet, Sheera. Even the Embleck soldiers were more relaxed and often stayed in their hotel or joined in a few of the festivities.

Anise ducked past a large group of soldiers, eating what looked to be every type of food in the marketplace and chatting loudly. When they looked away, she took a cinnamon date roll and ate it as she continued.

Anise finished the small roll as she heard a shout behind her. She whipped around to see Joffrey leap onto the soldiers' table and snatch an entire fish filet before dashing into the crowds. The soldiers raced after him.

Anise whistled for Joffrey and ran off into the crowd. Shoving through dozens of people, she ducked into an alley and glanced around, trying to get her bearings. All the alleys connected, weaving behind and between buildings as a huge maze.

A moment later, Joffrey came bounding in, still munching on the last of the fish.

"You little scamp!" Anise knelt to look at him. "You almost got us caught! You know those guys hate thieves! If they caught us, they might—Joffrey? Joffrey, are you even listening to me?"

Joffrey, in fact, was *not* listening. Joffrey was busy licking fish off his paws.

Anise sighed. "I'll have to save the lecture, I guess." She peered out of the alley and saw the soldiers sifting through the crowds. "Let's head for town square through here. I...*think* I know the way."

Anise scooped up Joffrey and began through the maze. Joffrey leaped from her arms to catch a crab as she neared where she thought the town square was.

"Joffrey." Anise turned around, walking backward. "Come on!" She stepped back around a corner, turned around, and promptly crashed into a person.

"Ouch!" they both exclaimed as they tumbled to the sandy ground in a heap.

"Sorry," Anise mumbled, pushing herself up. As she turned around, preparing to race away, the person spoke.

"No, I'm sorry, Miss. It was completely my fault. Are you hurt?"

Anise paused. From the voice, she had determined the person was a boy. He had a crisp accent she had never heard before.

And besides that, she recognized the language he spoke as Starloth, the traditional language of the galaxy. Her robot parents had taught her both languages, but almost everyone here spoke Ceranith. His manners made her pause too. Most people told her to scat or to get out of the way.

"Miss?" The boy's voice interrupted her thought, and she finally spun around.

He was younger, she guessed about her age, with short, wavy blond hair that looked carefully styled.

"No, I'm fine," Anise replied in Starloth.

"Oh, you do speak Starloth." The boy looked relieved. "Everyone I've tried to talk with speaks something I can't understand at all, so I was afraid you couldn't understand me, and I'd have to try and apologize without speaking, which, you know, is very difficult."

Anise blinked at the torrent of words, trying to keep up. "I do speak Starloth," she said slowly. "But I'm not the best."

"You're doing great," the boy said, his voice genuine. "Even your pronunciation is great, and that's hard."

Anise smiled a touch. "Are you lost or something?"

"Oh!" The boy flushed, glancing around. "Yes, I guess so. I…I came for the festival but got turned around. Is it that obvious?"

"No, but most people don't just wander through alleyways," Anise pointed out.

"True." He drew a line in the sandy, red dirt with the toe of his boot.

Typically, Anise would've left long ago, but curiosity possessed her to stay. This boy was another outsider—just like she was. Realizing no one else was likely to help him, Anise made an offer.

"Do you need help finding the town square?"

The boy looked up with a surprised yet grateful expression. "I would greatly appreciate help, but only if I won't inconvenience you."

"It's no bother; that's where I was going anyway," Anise said.

"Thank you, Miss." He offered her a slight smile. "You're too kind."

"I'm happy to help." Anise nodded and started leading the way to the town square.

"May I ask your name?" the boy sped up to keep pace with her.

Anise paused. She decided against telling him her real name. She didn't know who this boy was. After all, he could be a thief or scoundrel, trying to exploit her. Although Anise knew she could defend herself if needed, she was still cautious.

Besides, after she ran away, she gave her name as Ree to anyone she met, just to be safe. Her robot mother had been named

RE-3835, so she used Ree as a small tribute to her.

"Or if you want, you could just give me something to call you. I understand an alias is often safer here," the boy added, and Anise glanced up from thinking.

"Thanks," she said. "You can call me Ree. Everyone does."

"Alright, Ree it is."

"And what's your name?" Anise asked.

The boy thought momentarily. "Well, I, too, would like to stay off the radar...so you can call me Roy."

"Great." They continued to walk in silence, though Anise couldn't resist peeking at him from the side. The clothing he wore was clearly high-quality, from his shined shoes to his canvas jacket and the silver ring on his middle finger.

What's someone like him doing here? Anise mused, shooting another look at the stranger. *If I were rich enough to afford those clothes, I wouldn't touch a place like this with a hundred-foot pole.*

Snapping from her thoughts, Anise brought them to the corner of an alley. "Right around the corner is the exit from here to the festival."

"Thank you for bringing me here," Roy said gratefully.

"No problem." Anise shrugged. "I guess I'll see you around?"

"Sure." Roy held out his hand, and she shook it. A warm flush crept up her neck, and she wondered why.

"Bye." Roy turned the corner and disappeared into the crowd. Anise watched him go and felt a strange sense that she had lost something.

"I'm being silly." Anise sighed. She glanced at Joffrey, who was sitting at her feet. "Come on."

Anise turned the corner, entering the crowd. She walked among the stalls but stayed on the outskirts of the festivities. It wasn't enjoyable to be at a party where she knew no one and no one was willing to talk to her.

For a half-hour, Anise walked around, pausing to listen to the music and watch the dancing. She leaned against the side of a building and stared at the ground. Closing her eyes, she imagined being part of the crowd, if only for this week.

In your dreams.

The soft crunch of footsteps broke through Anise's thoughts, and she opened her eyes to see another pair of shoes next to hers. Anise glanced up and saw Roy standing in front of her.

"Roy?" Anise shifted, confusion washing over her. "What is it?"

Roy offered her a hesitant smile. "Well, I—I was looking around, and I noticed pretty quickly that everybody's avoiding me like the plague. I don't know enough Ceranith to carry on a conversation. Then I saw it looked like you were in the same boat as me, so I thought I'd ask...why?"

"I suppose you were right." Anise shrugged. "No one wants to talk to me either. Outsiders aren't accepted here."

"Oh." Roy leaned against the building. "That does take some of the enjoyment out of it."

"Yeah," Anise agreed.

"Well…" Roy shifted, rubbing his thumbs over his fingertips in a nervous gesture. "Would you like to explore with me today? No pressure if you say no."

"I think that sounds wonderful." Anise grinned.

Roy mimicked her expression. "Okay, then let's go find some of whatever that amazing smell is coming from."

Anise laughed. "That's the saska. It's a dessert—" She broke off when she realized Roy was already at the stall.

Shaking her head, Anise went after him. When she reached him, he had two creamy dessert cups in his hands.

"Here." He handed her one.

"Oh. Is this for me?" Anise asked hesitantly.

"Yes, of course. As a thank you for helping me find my way." Roy smiled at her before tasting his dessert. "Oh my stars, this is incredible!"

Anise took a spoonful of her own. The sweet citrus pudding was ordinary on Ceran, but Anise had never tried one. "You're right."

The pair began to walk alongside the buildings that framed the town square, savoring the sweet, creamy saskas.

"So, Roy…" Anise began. "What brings you to this marketplace?"

Roy kept his gaze on the ground for a moment before glancing up at the pale orange sky. "I…just needed a break. I was out flying in my ship when I saw this place. It reminded me of somewhere I visited as a child. I figured I could use some happy memories about now, so here I am."

"I'm happy you picked here," Anise said. "Otherwise, I never would've bumped into you."

"I'm glad I came too."

The two of them strolled through the square, eating the last of their desserts when a band started to play a lively song.

People all over bustled to the center of the square to start the dancing. Roy glanced at them before turning to Anise.

"Would you like to dance?" He held out his hand.

"Sure." Anise accepted his hand and pulled him into the crowd. When the second tune started, everyone began dancing. Anise took both his hands and led him in the dance. It was a traditional Ceranith melody, one without sheet music that relied solely on the heavy beat.

"What's this choreography?" Roy asked, trying to keep up.

"I'm not sure there's whatever that is," Anise said. "It's just fun!"

"Okay?" Roy tried to follow her movements but instead stepped on her toes.

"I'm so sorry!" he exclaimed. "I'm afraid this is way out of my league. I can waltz, do almost every type of ballroom, and even tango a little, but I have no idea how to do this without injuring you."

Anise shrugged and pulled him away from the crowd. "No problem. Let's explore some more."

"I'd like that." Roy smiled and squeezed her hand.

Together they continued around the edges of the square.

Roy glanced around all the food stalls, then back at Anise. "Are you hungry?"

Anise bit her lip. "I can't pay—"

Roy cut her off with a wave of his hand. "Don't think about it. Tonight's my treat."

Anise bit her lip. "Are you sure?"

"Of course," Roy replied, as though it was nothing.

"Thank you very, very much."

"No problem." Roy echoed her. "Now we should get tasting!"

Anise and Roy started around the square again, this time stopping to try all the different types of food—spicy mushroom soup, lime and cumin vegetables, and dozens of desserts.

And it was only after their third dessert that Anise realized she still hadn't let go of Roy's hand.

"That was wonderful," Roy said.

"You bet!" Anise exclaimed. "I haven't had that much good food in a while."

"I've never had food that good!" Roy playfully bumped into her, and she lightly shoved him back.

A bird trilled loudly, and they both glanced up. The moons were starting to rise, and stars twinkled in the sky.

"I probably have to get home now," Roy said. "My ship's at the marketplace entrance."

"We're almost there." Anise tugged him forward, and they reached the entrance where a small spaceship was sitting right outside.

"I'd like to see you again." Roy turned to her. "May I come back to meet you? Please?"

"Of course." Anise blushed. "What about tomorrow at three? We can keep exploring the festival."

"Perfect." Roy grinned. Before Anise knew what he was doing, he had placed a small bag in her hands, turned, and climbed into his ship.

"See you tomorrow!" Roy called, closing the cockpit of the ship. Anise waved back as he took off.

When Roy's ship was swallowed up by the dusty atmosphere, Anise glanced down at what he had given her. It was the small bag that had held all of his coins. She opened it, and despite the dozens of things he'd bought, it was nearly full.

"This is enough to pay for at least two weeks' worth of food! Maybe even three!" Anise gasped.

"Meow," someone said in a condescending voice.

"Ah!" Anise jumped.

Joffrey sat at her feet, staring at her with disapproval.

"Joffrey, you scared me," Anise scolded. "Where did you go off to?"

Joffrey kept staring at her for a minute before turning and dashing off toward their house. Anise shook her head at her pet's antics and went after him.

CHAPTER 3

Anise bounced out of bed early the next morning. She made her pallet bed more cheerfully than usual and picked her second-best outfit: a pair of dark brown shorts and a matching top. She also pulled out her cream scarf and sighed when she saw it had yet another rip.

Winding it around her hips, Anise left the bedroom in search of Joffrey. He had been fussy since she left him yesterday, and she wanted to make amends.

"Joffrey! Here, kibit, kibit."

Joffrey emerged from under the small table and meowed at her.

"Hey, buddy. Look, are you going to pout there all day or come swimming with me?" Anise asked.

Joffrey hissed, dashed around her, and ran out the door. Anise followed him with a smile on her face. It was the perfect day to go swimming.

Anise and Joffrey spent the day in the lake, splashing in the water and swimming laps until late afternoon. Anise sighed contentedly and looked up at the pale orange sky. The sun was getting low, and Anise gasped—she'd promised to meet Roy in just a few minutes!

"Joffrey, I have to go! See you later!" Anise called as she clambered up the shore and raced to the marketplace.

She was almost dry by the time she arrived; only her hair was still damp. As she dashed to the entrance, she could see Roy leaning against his ship.

"Hello, Ree!" he called, his whole face lighting up when he saw her.

"I am so sorry to be late!" Anise panted. "I was swimming and completely lost track of time."

"No problem." Roy shrugged. "I just got here. Let's go now."

Anise grinned and followed him into the marketplace. Roy walked through the crowds, clearly with a destination in mind. Anise started to wonder where he was going when they reached the square. The dancers were about to start another song as Roy pulled her into the middle of it.

"Roy, what's this for?" Anise asked, just as the next song started. Roy took her hands and began leading her through the dance.

"Roy, how did you ever learn this?" Anise exclaimed in delight.

Roy grinned. "After I got home last night, I looked up proper Ceranith dances."

"That's…that's so sweet." Anise was touched. "Why, though?"

"I wanted to be able to dance with you." Roy dropped his eyes, spinning her around.

"Thank you," Anise said softly as they continued dancing.

A new song started, and Anise gave a small start.

"What is it?" Roy asked.

"Oh, this was a song that my parents used to sing to me when I was small," Anise said wistfully. "It's my favorite." She softly sang a few of the words: "*L'amor dura per sempre.*"

"You have an amazing voice," Roy told her.

"Thanks again." Anise smiled.

They danced in silence for a few songs, and finally, at sunset, they pulled away from the crowd.

"That was wonderful." Anise smiled at Roy.

"I'm so glad you enjoyed it." Roy smiled back. "May I walk you home?"

"Yes," Anise said slowly. "But I will warn you; there isn't a lot to walk to."

Roy sent her a slightly confused look but said, "No worries. I don't mind." He took her hand and exclaimed, "Lead the way!"

Anise did so, leading him across the desert. They chattered and laughed as they walked, but Anise quieted when they got close to her house. For some reason, she felt slightly nervous. She hadn't had anyone at her house…well…*ever*.

They slid down a large sand dune, and her house came into view. "Well, this is where I live," Anise said, opening the door. "It's not much."

Roy looked around the small room with its crumbling walls and the tiny portable stove tucked in a corner—the sandy floor and rickety table. And then he turned to her and smiled. "I think it's charming."

"Would you like something to drink?" Anise offered.

"Sure, if you have one." Roy carefully sat down at the table.

Anise started to put water through her filter when Roy asked, "Are your parents at home? I'd like to introduce myself."

"Oh." Anise paused and turned around. "Actually, I've been on my own for a while."

"Oh, stars." Roy clapped a hand over his mouth. "I am so sorry; I had no idea, sorry, sorry, sorry."

Anise chuckled. "It's fine."

"Do you mind if I ask what happened?"

"No, I don't mind. I had some robots that took care of me, but when I was eleven, they just short-circuited, and I've been on my own ever since."

"I'm sorry," Roy said. "How did you end up here?"

"Well, the robots were the only parents I've ever known, and I grew up in another village a few miles away. But, after they died, I didn't want to go to an orphanage, so I decided to leave."

Anise shrugged. "After I packed, I found someone who was coming here. I hitched a ride, and he left me in the marketplace. I ended up getting lost in the desert, but I found this house." She gestured around. "I fixed it up. Lived here ever since. But, since I look so different, I guess people are afraid I'm associated with the Embleck soldiers." She shot him a half-smile. "I'm not, by the way."

"Well, that's good. The Embleck Army is ruthless." Roy furrowed his brow in thought. "But were the robots always your parents? You're not a robot, are you?"

"No, I'm not a robot." Anise giggled and handed him the glass. "I guess whoever my real parents are…I guess they didn't want me."

"I find that hard to believe," Roy said. "You're an amazing person. Your parents would have to be crazy not to want you."

Anise blushed. "Thank you, Roy."

"I mean it." Roy smiled. "So," he changed the subject, "What do you like to do?"

"Well, I like to swim," Anise said, relieved to move away from the topic of her past. "There isn't a lot to do around here, so I spend most of my time in the lake."

"Cool!" Roy exclaimed. "It sounds fun."

"It is." Anise nodded. "It's also a great way to cool down in this heat."

"It is supremely hot." Roy fanned himself with his hand. "It rarely gets this hot where I live."

"It's only early summer. You should wait and visit in midsummer when it's one-hundred-seventeen!"

"Stars, no." Roy shook his head. "But I suppose I could visit, just to see you."

"I'd like that." Anise smiled. "If you want, we could go swimming tomorrow."

"I would…" Roy started slowly. "But I don't know how to."

"You can't swim?" Anise asked.

"No." Roy sighed. "It's embarrassing. I'm seventeen, and I can't swim, but I never learned. My parents mostly care about my academic education, not things like swimming."

"Oh." Anise furrowed her brow. "Well, if you want, I can teach you."

"Really?" Roy pushed back his chair, standing. "I would love that!"

"Of course!" Anise grinned. "Just bring some old clothes tomorrow, and we'll start lessons."

"Wow, thank you." Roy leaned over and hugged her. Anise stiffened slightly, and Roy jerked away. "Oh, sorry! I—I didn't mean to be presumptuous"

"No, you didn't upset me." Anise quickly assured him. "It's just…I haven't been hugged in years. Honestly, I haven't even had a friend in years."

"Oh." Roy glanced down. "Well…I haven't either. I'm glad we can be friends."

"Me too." Anise wrapped her arms around him, and he hugged her back.

Anise's heart fluctuated in her chest. The weight of Roy's arms around her…the warmth of his breath against the back of her neck…the tiny movement of his fingers against her back—her heartbeat raced, confused by the foreign sensations.

They held each other for just a second too long before pulling away. Roy left his arm around Anise's shoulders, and they walked out to his ship.

"Goodbye, Ree." Roy slowly pulled back and smiled at her as he climbed into his ship.

"Goodbye, Roy!" Anise waved as he flew off. As she turned to go back inside, she realized she couldn't stop smiling. Joffrey came and plopped down in front of her.

"Meooow," he said firmly.

"I have a friend," Anise said to him, ignoring his annoyance.

It was only now that Anise realized how much she missed having people to talk with and how lucky she was to have Roy in her life.

Early the next afternoon, Anise climbed up on top of her roof to watch for Roy. The hot summer wind blew across the desert, scattering sand.

Anise shielded her eyes with her hand, staring into the pale orange sky for Roy's ship. No ship appeared, though, so she leaned back and let the sun warm her skin.

A skittering sound made her turn her head as Joffrey flapped up on the roof.

"Hi, sweetie." Anise stroked his head. "I'm just waiting for Roy."

At Roy's name, Joffrey hissed and flattened his ears back on his head.

"Why won't you like Roy?" Anise asked her pet in

exasperation. "He's so nice."

"Meeerow," Joffrey said scornfully.

"Are you just jealous?" Anise asked. "You haven't had to share me in…ever."

A hesitant thought crept into Anise's mind. Maybe, just maybe, Joffrey knew something she didn't. She shook her head and shut down that thought. She didn't want to believe that Roy could have any ulterior motives.

Besides, what could anyone want with me, of all people?

Before Joffrey could agree or protest, a sudden wind whooshed past them as Roy's ship zipped into view and landed beside the lake.

"He's here!" Anise leaped up and climbed down the house. The second her feet hit the ground, she dashed to Roy's ship. He was getting out just as she reached him.

"Hi, Roy!" Anise smiled at him. Her expression shifted to confusion when she noticed what he was wearing. "I thought you were going to wear old clothes."

Roy tugged on the collar of his perfectly tailored shirt. The only thing that looked old about it was that it was slightly faded.

"Well," he bent over to take off his dress shoes. "This

was the best—worst—I could get. After any of our clothes get even slightly worn out, Mother tosses them. That means that about every year, we all get entirely new wardrobes. She manages to keep the tailors of the planet busy all year round, though."

"Okay, then." Anise was slightly stunned at the idea of getting an entirely new closet every year! The only time she got new clothes was when she couldn't stitch up the old ones anymore. "I hope she won't be angry about you getting them all wet."

"Oh, don't worry." Roy straightened up and smiled at her. "She won't care because I've been out of her house and sight for almost three days. That's kept her in a decent mood all this time."

"That's awful!" Anise exclaimed in disgust and horror. "No mother should be glad that her child is out of her sight. Especially since you're so sweet and…" she trailed off when she realized Roy was blushing and felt her face heat up.

"Um, are you ready for your first lesson?" Anise changed the subject quickly.

"Yes, definitely," Roy said and followed her to the edge of the lake.

"Okay, the first step is to get in about halfway and start moving your arms like this." Anise demonstrated how to move his arms and started into the lake.

Roy hesitantly stepped in after her. He carefully copied her movements as she watched.

"Perfect start," Anise said, pulling him farther into the water. "Now try it here."

Roy did try, but the second Anise let go of him, he promptly sank. Anise gasped and dove after him. She wrapped her arms around his waist and dragged them both up.

"Well, that was pathetic." Roy shook water droplets from his hair.

"No, it was a good start." Anise encouraged. "Now, do you think you could stay afloat if I let go?"

"I think so," Roy said.

Anise let go and struggled but managed to stay above water for a minute before sinking under. Anise grabbed his arm and helped him get his head above water. "That was good!"

"Thanks," Roy said, wiping the water from his eyes.

Anise let go of his arm but paused when she saw a dark bruise peeking out from under his shirt sleeve. "Oh, what happened to you?"

Roy glanced away from her. "It's nothing."

"Okay," Anise said hesitantly. She guessed by his reaction

39

that it wasn't "nothing," but she didn't press him. He obviously didn't want to talk about it.

Roy cleared his throat. "I'm ready to try again."

"Great, let's try this." Anise swam to the shore and dragged a small raft made from large palm leaves. She had used it when she learned to swim in this lake. "Here." she handed it to him, and he tried again, this time staying afloat.

"YAY!" Anise threw her arms in the air, splashing them with water. "You're getting the hang of this."

Anise continued the lessons throughout the afternoon, and by sunset, Roy could swim without the float and was getting better each time he tried.

"You're doing wonderful." Anise praised him when he came up for air.

"Thank you," Roy said. "I did have the best teacher."

Anise blushed at the compliment. "Well, you were a great pupil."

She treaded water, shooting a glance at Roy, "So…what's it like where you live?"

Roy, also treading water, paused and thought for a moment before answering. "I live on Karpolanix. It's a huge city, almost the entire planet. There's a neighborhood in the middle of the city with a huge wall around it. That's where we live." He looked thoughtful as he continued. "I live in a house with my parents and my older brother."

"Are you close with him?" Anise asked.

Roy chuckled bitterly. "No. I—he—no. No, definitely not."

"I'm sorry," Anise said softly. She wondered if Roy's brother had anything to do with his bruise, but she didn't ask.

"It's fine." Roy shrugged. "Someday, my life will change. I'll move out and buy a big house on the far edge of the city, somewhere away from all the noise. I'll have a family that I love and…and I'll be happy."

"That sounds perfect," Anise said. "I do believe you'll have all that."

"I hope so," Roy replied, and they smiled at each other. "What do you want for your future?"

Anise furrowed her brow for a moment. "I…I don't know. I never really thought about it."

"You've really never thought about your future life?" Roy asked.

"Well, I used to," Anise admitted. "But after my caretakers died, I was more focused on getting through each day. I guess I haven't really thought about it lately, though."

"Well, you could think about it now," Roy said. "What do you want in your future?"

Anise was silent for a moment as she pondered. "I think what you said sounds wonderful. I want…I want a family, people to love and who love me too."

"I don't think you'll have much trouble finding that," Roy said.

"I'm afraid I might," Anise admitted. "No one in this village will trust me. The Embleck Army has warped their view of outsiders too much."

"Then maybe you need to dream outside this village," Roy suggested. "If they can't see how amazing and kind you are, that's their loss."

"But even if I had a way to leave…where would I go?" Anise asked.

Roy glanced up at the sky and smiled a little. "I guess that's the beauty of being on your own. You could go anywhere. A pixel on a holomap, a place you've only seen holographs of—the options don't end."

Anise thought on that for a moment. "You're right. Maybe I should start dreaming again. If I don't, it's positive I won't get anywhere."

Roy's smile grew. "Exactly. So where would your dream place be?"

"I think I would want somewhere warm," Anise decided. "I don't like the cold. I want a place that's welcoming. Somewhere that has meaning."

"That sounds good," Roy said. "You know…if you wanted some help, someday, to get off this planet…I could help you."

"Thank you," Anise said sincerely. "But I do have a question for you."

"Go ahead," Roy said.

"Why me?"

"What do you mean?" Roy asked.

"I mean…why are you offering to help me so much? You've been so nice to me, and…I'm just not used to it," Anise finished, realizing how pathetic she sounded.

Roy swam over to Anise and gently took her hand. "That's exactly why I'm doing this." He glanced away for a moment. "I'm not used to it either. Back home…let's just say… I'm used to being treated like I don't really matter…and I know how awful that feels." Roy smiled, though it was bittersweet. "And I don't want anyone else to feel that way…especially a person like you."

Anise was surprised to feel tears pricking her eyes, and she blinked them away. "Thank you, Roy. I can't tell you how much your friendship means to me. I don't know how your family doesn't adore you."

Roy shrugged. "I just don't really fit in with them. But it's fine."

"It doesn't sound fine," Anise said gently.

"Maybe not," Roy admitted. "But it won't last forever."

Anise nodded slightly as she met Roy's eyes. He slowly reached out and tucked a strand of her wet hair behind her ear. Anise's heart began to beat rapidly. Roy opened his mouth to speak again, just as an enormous splash filled the lake.

Anise shrieked as water gushed in her mouth. She heard Roy coughing somewhere out of her vision. Anise wiped the water from her eyes as she scanned the lake for Roy. There he was, floating a few feet away.

"What was that?" Roy swam over to her.

"I have no idea," she said. "Maybe it was a—"

Anise's words cut off as a wet object flew at her face and knocked her under the water. She twisted away, but the thing grabbed her hair. She felt Roy grab her arm and pull her to the surface.

"What was *that*?" Roy exclaimed.

"I *still* have no idea," Anise countered, just as a small, furry head popped out of the water in front of her.

"Joffrey!" she said in shock. "You little rascal!"

"You know this…creature?" Roy asked.

"Yes." Anise sighed. "He's my pet."

"Okay…" Roy still looked slightly alarmed, but just then, a loud ringing sound came from inside his ship. "Oh, that's my comm." He sighed and swam to the edge of the lake.

"Comm?" Anise asked, following him.

"Yes." Roy scrambled out of the lake, shaking water from his hair. "It's short for Galactic Communicator. Everybody just calls them comms."

"Oh." Anise watched as Roy picked up the comm and held it up to his ear. The instant it was on, Anise could hear a voice on the other end start shouting. Roy jerked it away quickly, keeping it a few inches from his head. The longer he listened, his face continued to fall, his expression turning to stone.

"Okay, bye," he said finally and clicked it off. "That was my mother. She says that I have to come back to the house now. Apparently, they're hosting a dinner party tonight, and I have to be there, so no one thinks I've run off and become a delinquent." Roy made air quotes with his fingers and sighed. "She also said I have to be present more the next three days because she and Father are taking me to apply for some colleges, and they'll be attending parties that I also have to come to."

He sank down on the sand with a groan. "Agony."

Anise watched with sympathy and climbed out of the water, sitting beside him. "I'm sorry."

"It's fine," Roy said unconvincingly, staring into the distance. "It could be worse."

"Aren't you a little young for college?" Anise asked.

"I'm seventeen, but I finished school early, so technically, I could apply. Besides, this is one other opportunity for my parents to get rid of me. They wouldn't pass that up." He sighed again and stood up. "I have to go now, but can I see you tomorrow afternoon, even if it's just for a little while?"

"Sure." Anise smiled as he stepped into his ship. "Goodbye!"

"Goodbye," Roy responded. He closed the door and took off into the sky.

CHAPTER 4

The following afternoon, Anise waited for Roy at the marketplace entrance. He was fifteen minutes late, and Anise couldn't help being a little worried.

At that moment, Roy's ship soared down. Anise pulled up her scarf to cover her face as sand flew in every direction.

Roy jumped down from his ship and seemed surprised to see Anise standing there. "Oh, I'm so sorry. I didn't see you there, or I would have landed further away."

"It's no big deal," Anise said, dusting sand off herself. "I'm always covered in sand anyway."

"And sorry I'm late," Roy said as they started into the marketplace. "First, my mother wanted to speak with me, then my brother…detained me."

"It's fine," Anise said. "I'm just glad you're here now."

"Me too," Roy said.

Anise glanced behind Roy. "Uh oh."

"What?" Roy asked, trying to turn around.

"Trouble," Anise whispered, grabbing Roy's arm and tugging him into an alley.

"What is it?" Roy said as Anise led him through the alleyways.

"The Embleck soldiers were doing what they call a 'routine check,' which is basically their excuse to me sure no one is plotting against them."

"But why does that mean you can't walk through the marketplace?" Roy said.

"When you have a habit of stealing from the Embleck soldiers, it's a good idea to avoid them as often as possible," Anise said.

Roy laughed, sounding surprised. "That does make sense."

Anise led them out of the alley, and they were back at the marketplace entrance. "Why don't we go over to my house instead?"

"Good idea," Roy said.

They walked through the desert in silence for a minute before Roy spoke up.

"So, I'm guessing you've caused the Embleck Army a lot of trouble if you have to avoid them that carefully."

"I suppose." Anise shrugged. "I don't like them, so I don't have any problems stealing from them."

"I don't like them either," Roy said. "I've heard about what they've done, and it's...awful. I don't know how they even get people to join such a horrible organization."

"They probably offer power or wealth," Anise said. "That can be alluring for lots of people."

"Not me." Roy shuddered. "I can't imagine how miserable it must be to know you've traded your soul for power and wealth...knowing that you're part of such an evil organization must make a person wish they couldn't feel any emotion."

Anise was about to reply when Roy's comm buzzed.

"Oh no," Roy muttered as he pulled his comm from his pocket. "Hello?"

Anise winced as the same shrieking as before came over the comm. Roy looked annoyed.

"But you said—" Roy was cut off, and he closed his eyes for a moment. "Fine."

Roy hung up and glanced at Anise. "I'm sorry. They said I could have the afternoon, but Mother has apparently changed her mind. I'm going to have to hurry home."

"I'm sorry," Anise said. "Can you come back tomorrow?"

"Mother said if I leave the house tomorrow, I'll regret it for the rest of my life." Roy sighed. "And Cameron will make sure of it. But I can make it the day after. Does that work for you?"

"Sounds good," Anise said. "I'll see you then."

"Okay," Roy said. "I can find my way back. See you this weekend!"

"Bye," Anise said, already missing him.

The day without Roy passed by uneventfully. Anise spent

her mornings tinkering on her ship and afternoons swimming to stay cool.

Finally, the weekend arrived, which meant Roy was coming back, and she was turning seventeen.

Early on her birthday morning, Anise crept out quietly as not to wake up Joffrey. She stopped to admire the beautiful sunrise before going to work on her ship. It was early afternoon when the roar of a ship pierced the air.

Anise leaned out of the ship's engine crevice when she heard the ship land. "Hi, Roy!"

"Hi, Ree!" Roy practically leaped out of his ship and raced over to her. "I've missed you."

"And I've missed you." Anise wiped her hands off on a rag and said, "Would you like to come inside? I could use a drink."

"Thanks." Roy followed her inside the house. "So, how's the work on the ship going?"

"Not bad, but I'm missing the basic motivator and the light fuel. Until I find a way to get those, it'll never get off the ground." Anise took two glasses from the cabinet. "You're in luck." She grinned. "Today, I have something much better than water. Cerafruit lemonade, a Ceran specialty."

"Yum." Roy tasted the sweet drink. "What's the occasion?"

"Well." Anise took a large sip of her lemonade. "It's my seventeenth birthday."

"Your birthday?" Roy exclaimed. "Happy birthday! I hope I'm not interrupting any plans," he added.

"No, not at all." Anise shrugged. "Since I was eleven, I really haven't done anything special for my birthday."

"That is unacceptable," Roy said. "I would love to do something for you today. Since you don't have any plans, why don't I go pick up a few things and then come back here to get you?"

"Really, Roy, you don't have to do anything," Anise said, but Roy shook his head.

"I insist," he said, standing. "Can I pick you up a little before sunset?"

"Sure." Anise smiled. "Thank you."

"Don't mention it." Roy leaned in, gave her a quick hug, and returned to his ship.

Anise watched him from the window. She thought she saw him peek at the engine of her ship before climbing into his own. *Maybe I imagined it*, she thought. As she turned away from the window, Joffrey came bounding in.

"Hi, sweetie!" Anise cried, picking him up and spinning around. "I have a feeling that this is going to be a great birthday."

An hour before sunset, Anise left her ship and went inside to get dressed. She pulled a white dress from a box in the corner of her room.

It was her best outfit, one she wore very rarely. It had puffed short sleeves and a corseted top with a square neckline. The skirt was pleated and fell a few inches below her knees.

Anise put it on, relieved that it still fit. She twisted her hair into two mini buns on the top of her head but let the rest flow loose.

Just as Anise was slipping on her bracelet, she heard Roy's ship land outside.

"He's here!" she said and raced to the door. Joffrey, who had been sleeping on the table, glanced up at the noise.

Anise paused for a moment to touch her necklace before throwing open the door. She stepped out into the blinding sunlight just as Roy walked up. When he saw her, his eyes grew wide.

"Ree, you look beautiful," he said in awe. Taking his comm from his ship, he asked, "Do you want to take a holograph together?"

"Sure!" Anise said.

Roy stood beside her, and they both smiled.

Click!

"Perfect." Roy showed her the holograph before tucking the comm in his pocket. He offered her his hand. "Are you ready to go?"

"We're going in your ship?" Anise asked.

"Yes…unless you'd rather not. It would just be a long walk…"

"I'd love to!" Anise exclaimed. "I haven't been in a ship in forever. My robot parents taught me to fly—and yes, I know that eleven is underage," she added at Roy's shocked expression. "But I loved it."

"Okay then!" Roy helped her into the passenger seat and took the steering. "Let's go."

Anise held her breath as the ship rose into the sky. Her house shrank as they went higher. Roy pulled a lever, and they zipped forward.

"This is amazing!" Anise said as Roy let them glide over the desert. "Where are we going?"

"It's a surprise." Roy grinned at her.

For about ten minutes, they flew over the never-ending desert. Anise kept herself pressed against the window, peering out at the planet whooshing by.

Finally, in the distance, she could see a spot of color against the golden-red sand. There were green palm trees and what appeared to be water.

"What's that?" she asked.

"It's an oasis," Roy said. "I saw it when I was flying here the first time and thought it would be the perfect spot."

The ship landed on the outskirts of the oasis. Roy helped Anise down and took her hand.

"Close your eyes," he said, and Anise did so. She let him lead her through the trees. He slowed to a stop and softly said, "Okay, you can open them."

Anise's eyes flew open, and she gasped. She stood on the shores of a large lake much like her own. On the sand in front of her a bright blue blanket with a basket sitting in the center had been laid out.

"Oh, Roy! It's perfect!" she exclaimed and hugged him tightly. "Thank you!"

"You're welcome." Roy flushed. "I thought a birthday picnic might be something you would enjoy."

"I do! I really do!" Anise carefully sat down as Roy opened the basket and presented her with a plate that held a thick piece of bread topped with vegetables coated in a red sauce.

"Yum," she said. "What is it?"

"Oh, we call it pirafin. It's a classic dish where I live. I didn't know exactly what foods you like, but I was almost positive you would like this."

"Okay!" Anise took a large bite and instantly realized that Roy was right—and that he had excellent taste in food. "This is heavenly!"

"I'm glad."

They sat together and ate in silence. The sun had set, and only the light from Roy's ship kept them from complete darkness.

Once they had each finished the pirafin, Roy said, "I have one more treat."

He pulled two small dishes from the basket, and on each of them was a miniature cake. They were frosted in white with pale blue swirls that were slightly lopsided.

"Our housekeeper makes a wonderful cake," Roy handed her a dish. "I frosted them myself, so they may be a touch messy."

"That's so sweet!" Anise dug her fork into the cake and took a bite. "This is wonderful!"

When every last crumb had been eaten, Roy put the dishes back in the basket and put the basket in the ship. He leaned into the backseat and pulled out four packages, each wrapped in teal paper and tied with a large white ribbon.

"These are for you." He placed them in front of her, a pleased expression on his face. "Since you haven't had a birthday celebration in five years, I'm doing five years' worth of celebration."

"Roy, really, this was too much!" Anise said.

"Not at all. Go ahead." He gestured to the gifts.

Anise selected the first package and tore away the paper, revealing a carved wood box holding half a dozen teal ribbons.

"Oh, how lovely!"

"They're for your hair," Roy said softly.

"They're beautiful."

Anise then reached to open the second box. She pulled a large olive scarf from it.

"It's a special fabric," Roy said as she tried it on. "It'll protect your skin from harmful sun rays, but it won't make you hot."

"That's so thoughtful," Anise said in awe. It was large enough to wrap around her shoulders and protect them.

When Anise pulled open the third package, she was surprised to find a pair of light brown boots.

"Oh, Roy!" she jumped up, raced over to him, and hugged him tightly. "These are perfect!"

"I hoped they would be." Roy grinned. "Go ahead and open the last one."

Anise picked up the last box and nearly dropped it. *It must weigh a dozen pounds!*

Anise carefully opened it, having no idea what it could be. Lifting the lid, she peered inside.

Nestled in tissue paper were two small devices. For a second, Anise was confused, but she quickly realized what they were.

"The basic motivator and the light fuel for my ship!" Anise exclaimed. "Thank you so much, Roy!" She pulled them out of the box to admire. "They must've cost a fortune."

Roy shrugged. "You're worth it."

As Anise tucked them back in the box, he picked up the blanket and said, "I have one last gift, but I'm saving it for a little later."

"Okay," Anise said, pulling her new scarf around her. The sun was disappearing quickly, and a chill was setting in.

"Is it just me, or is it kind of cold for the desert?" Roy asked.

"It is cool," Anise agreed.

"I'm going to make a fire," Roy decided. He gathered a few branches and took a lighter from the basket.

In no time, a warm fire was blazing. Anise moved closer to warm her hands. "This is so much better."

"Definitely." Roy settled in beside her, and they watched as the last of the sunshine faded away.

A little while later, Roy stood up. "I want to show you something."

Anise stood quickly. "Now where are we going?"

Roy smiled mysteriously and took her hand. "Out." He leaned down and pulled a burning branch to use as a torch before leading her through the trees.

Confused, Anise followed him. She was starting to wonder what he was doing when they stepped through the branches and instantly were back in the desert, staring at the thousands of stars that lit the sky.

"Wow," Anise said. "I know these are the same stars I see back home, but out here, they seem so…magical."

"True." Roy stuck the torch in the sand. He laid out the blanket, and they both sat down. In silence, they watched the sky.

After a moment, Roy wrapped his arm around Anise's shoulders, and she leaned her head against his shoulder.

"Thank you for everything, Roy," she said softly. "This has been the perfect birthday. I'm…very lucky to have bumped into you."

"I think I'm the lucky one," Roy said. "This week has been the best of my life. The festival, the dancing, the swimming lessons…I never knew I could be this happy."

"Me either," she smiled.

"Ree," Roy turned to her. "I know we only met a week ago and we're young, and what I'm about to say is very forward, but I want to tell you how I feel."

"Please do." Anise bit her lip and hoped it was something good.

"I've been dreaming about my future and how I want it to change. But it always felt like it was missing something." His expression was soft as he said, "Now, I'm starting to realize when I look at my perfect future, I see you there with me." He peered at her face with his emerald green eyes. "What would you say to that?"

"I'd say…" Anise's heart fluttered. "I'd say that sounds perfect." She leaned in. "You suggested that I should start dreaming of my future again. I did…and now I can't imagine a future without you in it."

Roy's face lit up. He whispered, "I think I'm falling in love with you, Ree."

Anise sucked in her breath. "I think I'm falling in love with you too, Roy."

Roy smiled and leaned in closer. Anise leaned in too, her heart going triple time. Her face was only inches from Roy's. She closed the distance until she could almost feel his lips on hers when—

Abruptly, Roy was yanked backward. Anise leaped up just in time to see Joffrey with Roy's shirt in his mouth, pulling him back.

"JOFFREY!" Anise scolded. "Let him go!"

Joffrey let go with a hiss, and Anise glared at him. "I am so sorry."

"It's fine," Roy said and stepped closer to her, but Joffrey hissed.

"It's getting late, and I don't think he's going to leave us alone. Maybe I should bring you home."

"Alright." Anise nodded as she turned to Joffrey. "You, however, can fly on your own, mister."

Joffrey meowed indignantly, but Anise ignored him and led Roy back to the ship.

They both climbed in, beginning the flight home, when Roy said, "By the way, just before I left the house, Mother told me I need to stay around the house this week. She and Father are taking me to apply to more colleges and are having parties that I have to attend."

"Alright," Anise said.

"Also, I wanted you to have this." Without taking his eyes off the desert, Roy handed Anise a small comm. "It's my extra comm. My number's in there, so you can call me if you need to."

"Thanks." Anise tucked the comm in her dress pocket.

"Also," Roy said, "My last name is Lecru."

Anise decided to tell him her name. "My real name is—"

At that moment, Roy jerked on the ship's steering, and they shot towards the ground. Roy let the ship hover beside a large sand dune.

"What is it?" Anise whispered.

"There was an Embleck Army ship up there." Roy craned his neck around to see the sky. "They're everywhere around here."

"Unfortunately," Anise sighed.

"I think it's gone," Roy said and lifted the ship back into the air.

They reached Anise's house a few minutes later. Joffrey landed beside them and ran inside the house. Roy climbed out first and helped her out. He walked her to the door and said, "I almost forgot." He stepped over to the ship and took something from the back.

"Here." Roy handed her a flower unlike any that she had ever seen.

It was a huge, white rose. The petals were ruffled, and the edges were tinged with royal blue. "It's a galaxy rose," he told her. "They're the flower of the galaxy."

"It's gorgeous," Anise smiled. "Thank you again....for everything."

Roy quickly leaned in and kissed her cheek. "See you

next week."

Anise beamed. "See you next week."

Roy grinned back and got into his ship. She waved as he took off into the starry night sky.

Anise sighed with happiness and danced inside, spinning into her bedroom.

From the pile of boxes in the corner, Anise pulled a box that held her robot parents' old things. The instant she opened it, the scent of mechanic's oil filled the room and reminded her of her parents.

Anise dug through it, seeing bottles of oil, a few holographs of her as a small child, and some spare gears. She continued searching until she found what she needed.

"Aha!" Anise exclaimed and pulled out a large bottle that was filled with a clear liquid.

"Liquid glass," she read. Dozens of times, she had seen her robot parents use this to preserve something that was in danger of fading or being lost.

Anise found an old tray in the box and placed it on the table. She poured the liquid glass into the pan and dipped her rose in it. Carefully spinning the blossom, she coated the entire thing in the clear liquid. She pulled it out and hung it upside down from

Joffrey's bed.

"Merow," Joffrey said indignantly.

"Hush, you." Anise was still a touch cross at him for spoiling her moment with Roy. Joffrey stared at her pitifully, and she groaned.

"Fine, you can sleep with me, just while the rose dries, and just as long as you start being nice to Roy," Anise bargained.

Joffrey hissed but climbed on her bed anyway. It was only after she had gotten into bed as well that she realized Roy had never given her the fifth present.

Anise wondered what it could be. He had given her everything she could need, but her curiosity was piqued.

Settling into bed, Anise gave up trying to guess. She decided that he would probably bring it next week and, only moments later, fell asleep.

CHAPTER 5

Two days after Anise's birthday, she lounged at her table, finishing off the last of the cerafruit lemonade. She peeked outside at the sun and saw it was still early afternoon.

"Joffrey!" she called. "I'm going out for a walk in the marketplace. Are you coming?"

Joffrey meowed loudly and came skidding around the corner.

"Good boy." Anise stroked his back before heading out the door. She walked with a skip in her step out to her ship.

Thanks to Roy, the ship was running perfectly, and the lessons from her robot parents were still fresh in her mind. Her flying skills had improved significantly—especially now that she could properly reach the gas pedal.

Anise climbed into the pilot's seat and pulled the power lever.

The ship's engine rushed to a start, and she lifted it into the sky.

The joy that came with flying fizzed through Anise's chest—joy she gave Roy the credit for.

All too soon, she landed the ship outside the entrance after only five minutes of flying. She leaped out with Joffrey on her heels and strolled through the streets.

Unsure where she was going, Anise simply made her way along the outskirts of the streets and watched the activity. Even if she wasn't part of it, it was fun to watch.

As Anise walked along, she decided to see when the Maroosh Inn would be open again. She turned and hurried down to the large tall building. A sign on the door read, "Opening Soon."

"That's unhelpfully vague," Anise said to Joffrey and started to go back to the ship. However, the market was crowded with people, making the process unnecessarily slow.

With a sigh, Anise turned and decided to walk back to the entrance through the alleyways.

"Joffrey!" she called, and he came quickly. "Come on."

As soon as Anise turned the first corner and lost sight of the marketplace, an uneasy feeling crept up on her. It almost felt like someone was…watching her. She tugged her braid anxiously, but no one except for Joffrey was in sight.

Anise continued through the alley. "We're almost there." She turned a corner—and caught sight of four Embleck Army soldiers. Quickly, she turned around to go the other way, but three more soldiers had appeared right behind her.

"Hello," Anise said casually, hoping they would let her go on her way. "Can I help you?"

The soldiers glanced at each other and nodded. Anise took a step back and crashed into the four soldiers that had come closer. Two of them seized her arms, and she shrieked.

"Let go of me!" Anise tried to jerk away. Joffrey became frantic and leaped at the soldiers, biting, hissing, and clawing.

One soldier grabbed Joffrey and tied him up. The rest continued to struggle with Anise. She kicked one in the shin, elbowing another in the neck, but they refused to release her.

"What do you want with me? I haven't done anything!" Anise snapped, but the soldiers ignored her.

One soldier, who appeared to be the leader, said, "We just need to see if you are who *he* thinks you are."

"Who's he?" Anise asked as the leader walked closer

The leader smirked as another soldier pulled aside her cloak to see the marking on her arm. When the leader saw the marking, his smirk grew wider. "Truly perfect. Bring her."

Panic set in, making Anise head spin. The Embleck Army— everyone had heard the stories of what they did to prisoners—she was *dead*—

A blast of black light shot through the air and hit one of the soldiers holding her. He toppled to the ground, and Anise thrashed away from the other soldier. They started to reach for her, but she shrieked, "Stay away!"

To her shock, the soldiers' faces went slack, and they stepped away from her.

Acting purely on instinct, Anise snatched up Joffrey and ran out of the exit. The desert flew by as she fled, no destination in mind. The sand dunes shifted beneath her feet, and she stumbled to the ground. Anise remained there, trying to catch her breath as her body shook.

A moment later, she heard footsteps, and a pair of brown boots appeared in front of her. Anise looked up and saw the boots belonged to a man wearing a brown cloak.

"Hello, Miss Desson."

"How do you know my name?" Anise scrambled to her feet, clenching her hands into fists.

"I know many things about you," the man said. "I've been watching over you for some time."

"Well, *that's* not creepy at all," Anise said, preparing herself
for a fight. "I've never seen you before."

"I only check up on you a few times a year." The man
shrugged. "And I'm very good at never being seen. You didn't see
me when I shot the soldier."

"That was you?" Anise took a step back. "Listen, I'm telling
you now—I don't want any trouble. You can leave me alone, and we
can pretend this never happened."

"I'm afraid not," the man said.

"Then what do you want?" Anise snapped.

"I want to warn you," the man's expression abruptly turned
grave. "We are afraid this attack was only the start. They didn't get
you now, so they'll try again later."

"Why do they even want to capture me? Who is the 'he' they
were talking about? And who is *we*?" Anise nearly shouted.

"We are the Qor," the man said. "And the Embleck Army
wants to capture you because they know something that you don't.
Something I know."

"And what is that?"

"You aren't just an ordinary girl, Miss Desson. Did you see
what happened with those soldiers? You told them to stay away, and
they did. It wasn't their will."

"What are you saying?" Anise asked.

"I think it's quite clear."

"Then spell it out," Anise insisted.

"Mind control."

"Mind control?" Anise exclaimed, stepping back. "Now I know you're crazy. That isn't even possible!"

"I can assure you, Miss Desson, I am not crazy, and yes, mind control could be possible with you." The man seemed to see she was doubtful, so he added, "Because of the marking on your arm, the blue in your hair, and now this episode, I can deduct—you are one of the very, very few people who possess these powers."

"Okay…" Anise took a deep breath. "So, what should be done about this?"

"Come and join the Qor," the man told her. "Leave this place and come with me. We can keep you safe."

"Leave?" Anise was incredulous. "I can't just leave! I have a life here, a home!"

"I was afraid you might say that." The man shook his head. "Still, we cannot just leave you here; it's not safe. You must reconsider. I will return in a week, and we must make a decision."

"First, tell me more about these abilities."

"I cannot do that," the man said. "The information could be compromised."

Anise looked around them. "We are literately alone in the middle of the desert."

The man sighed. "The Embleck Army cannot discover this information. If you join the Qor, I can tell you more then."

"But—" Anise started, just as Joffrey yowled loudly. She turned around to find him still tied up. "Oh, baby!" She dropped to her knees and started untying him. "I'm so sorry I forgot you. You were so good!"

Once Joffrey was untied, Anise turned back to continue speaking to the man, but he was gone. She scanned the desert and just barely saw him in the distance, walking away.

"Wait, come back!" Anise leaped up and raced after him. He continued walking, ignorant of her. She slowly started to catch up, but when she slid down a sand dune, she saw him boarding a large ship.

"Wait!" Anise reached the ship just as it took off into the sky. She covered her face with her scarf as sand flew in every direction.

As the sand settled, Anise opened her eyes and looked around. The ship was gone, but she could see something nestled in the sand where it had been. Coughing, she carefully picked up the box and gasped.

On the lid of the box was the same symbol she had on her arm. Anise pulled open the box, and inside sat a single comm and a note that read, "In case of emergency."

"Well, great." Anise dropped her head into her hands and sighed heavily, her head spinning.

In less than half an hour, her entire life had been thrown in the air and shaken to bits—and she didn't know how it would land either.

Joffrey came up beside her and rubbed his furry little head against her arm. She smiled and picked him up.

"We may be about to hit a rough patch," Anise ruffled his ears. "But you'll be with me through it, won't you?"

Joffrey meowed affirmatively and licked her. After a moment, he leaped up and took her braid in his mouth, tugging her up.

"Okay, time to get back up." Anise pushed herself to her feet and asked, "Joffrey, do you know how to get us home? I'm afraid that I'm completely turned around."

"Meeow." Joffrey flapped his wings and headed east, so Anise followed him. Within a few minutes, the marketplace came into view.

"You little genius!" Anise kissed his nose. She saw her ship at the entrance and ran over.

Anise took her place in the pilot's seat while Joffrey settled into the passenger seat. She lifted the ship into the air and began to soar over the desert. After a few minutes, she felt herself start to relax. Flying was her way to unwind, and she really needed to unwind now.

"Hey, Joffrey." Anise began to get an idea. "What about taking the long way home?"

Joffrey bounced in his seat, and Anise grinned. "I agree."

Anise shifted the gear lever, putting the ship in racing mode. She shoved her foot onto the gas pedal, and the ship shot forward. The speedometer quickly rose to over two hundred. Anise laughed as Joffrey began purring, and she twisted the steering.

The ship began looping around, and she squealed. It had been years since she had raced, but it was perfect. When she lived with her robot parents, her human friend's brother took them both racing. She hadn't seen them since she had run away, but she could still race.

They continued to zoom over the desert until night. Finally, Anise steered the ship home. Their house came into view, and she slowed the ship down. She shifted the gear lever back to normal and landed the ship beside the lake.

"That was *fun!*" she exclaimed. "I still have it!"

Joffrey purred and dashed inside. Exhaustion set in quickly, and Anise followed him. She changed into her pajamas and sank onto her bed. Joffrey ran over and curled up in her lap.

"Good night, Joffrey." Anise settled down to sleep.

A few days after Anise's visit from the Qor, she continued keeping to herself. Part of her remained afraid to go to the marketplace after her encounter with the soldiers, but her food supply was running out.

On the plus side, Roy was visiting tomorrow. She wanted to ask him his opinion on what to do. He knew more about the Qor and Embleck Army than she did.

But Anise also wanted to see what he thought of the possibility of her powers. Part of her hoped he would say the man was crazy and she was perfectly normal…but the other part secretly wished he would tell her of other cases similar to this one and assure her it didn't make her a freak; it was just rare.

"It's too much to figure out now, though," Anise told herself. "Joffrey!" she shouted. "I'm taking the ship to the marketplace. We need food."

"Meowerrr," Joffrey said from on top of the table. "Merow."

"Let's go." Anise picked him up and went out to the ship. Dumping Joffrey in the passenger seat, she climbed into the pilot's seat and lifted the ship into the air.

"We're going on a little flight around the desert first," Anise said to Joffrey. "That way, if anyone is watching the house, they'll think we went for a joyride, but then we'll go to the market."

"Meeerooooow." Joffrey began licking his paws.

"I'm glad you agree."

They flew out over the desert, silently and quickly. After she had been flying for a few minutes, Anise realized that two ships were following her. She saw the symbol on the side was a large triangle with a smaller triangle on each side.

The Embleck Army symbol.

"Joffrey, we have company!" Anise shifted the ship into racing mode. She pulled the speed lever, and her ship shot forward. The ships chasing matched her speed, catching up.

Anise hit the speed harder, and she continued to go faster. She caught sight of a large dune and smirked.

"Joffrey, this is going to be too easy." Anise angled her ship at the dune and kept low.

She steered straight for the dune. At the last second, she pulled a lever, and the ship swept up. The first of her pursuers crashed straight into the dune, and she heard an explosion behind her. The second ship, however, also swept up and continued following her.

Anise hissed out a breath and tried to increase her speed, but the ship seemed to be at its max.

"Joffrey, can you do something helpful?" Anise exclaimed. "We're being chased by enemies, and you're bathing yourself!"

"Meeeeeeerow." Joffrey leaned under his seat and pulled out the box that she had found from the Qor.

"Good idea. Call the Qor on the comm," Anise said, swerving as the ship shot a bolt of black light at her.

Joffrey knocked the comm from the box and pressed the 'call' button with his paw. A moment later, a voice said, "Yes?"

"I—"

A blast hit the ship, and it rocked to the side. The comm landed underneath Joffrey, and the call was disconnected.

"Oh no." Anise tried to dodge again, but another blast hit the ship, making it rock.

The other ship continued firing. Anise pulled on the speed one more time, and her ship began to gain momentum.

"I think we can do it," Anise said, but just as she spoke, the other ship shot straight up. She wondered what it could be doing until it dove and swept down right in front of her.

Anise shrieked just as it fired a black bolt straight at her engine. It hit, and the entire ship shook and jerked. With that final blast, the Embleck ship took off into space.

"I don't have any control!" Anise gasped as she wrestled with the steering.

The ship shook like a leaf as she lowered it to twenty feet, fifteen feet—the ship began to jerk harder, and the windshield began to crack.

It's going to explode. Anise realized in numb horror. *I need a shield!*

Just as she thought this, a bright white light appeared around her and Joffrey—at the exact second, the entire ship exploded. Debris hit the light, and the sound of continuous explosions made Joffrey yowl. For a moment, it seemed as though the shield would protect them—

Anise screamed as the white light shattered, and she plummeted to the ground. Everything seemed to blur as she fell, and a moment later, she felt herself hit the ground as pain exploded across her entire body.

Vaguely, she could hear Joffrey meowing in distress. Anise dimly realized hundreds of sharp things were stabbing her right hand and arm just before she drifted into unconsciousness.

Slowly, light began to filter into Anise's eyes. She carefully opened them and groaned as a deep pain settled back into her body. Managing to lift her head, she glanced around.

She was lying in the middle of a vast area of wreckage and debris, and she could see that her left leg was bent in a way it definitely shouldn't be. Her left wrist was the same.

Anise slowly closed her eyes again, longing for dark unconsciousness when the pain in her right hand returned abruptly and worse than before. She barely managed to turn her head enough to see her hand, but what she saw made her nauseous.

Her entire right hand and wrist were full of hundreds of glass shards. Each of the cuts dripped blood, turning her hand red.

Anise swallowed hard and looked away. She tried to move enough to sit up, but it sent a wave of pain through her making her groan again.

The new pain made her dizzy, and she felt herself start to drift off again.

Just before her eyes closed, Anise barely heard the sound of a ship landing and, only seconds later, the thumps of running feet. A dark shape blocked the sunlight just as she fell unconscious. Again.

CHAPTER 6

Anise heard the rustle of fabric and the whisper of hushed voices. She shut her eyes tighter as a light shone into them.

"I think she's waking up," she heard a woman whisper.

"Finally," said a deeper voice, and Anise opened her eyes.

She lay on a hospital bed with an extremely tall man and an extremely short woman standing beside her, each dressed in scrubs.

"Hello, Miss Desson," the woman said. "I'm Doctor Bruin, and this is my nurse, Patrick."

"Hey." Patrick saluted her with two fingers.

"Where am I?" Anise managed. Her voice felt abrasive against her dry throat, and her voice sounded rough and scratchy.

"Oh, don't worry, sweet," Doctor Bruin said. "You're in the Qor's infirmary. Some of our members found your shipwreck and brought you here."

"Oh," Anise said. "Thank you for saving me. I—wait, where's Joffrey?" She tried to sit up, but Nurse Patrick gently pushed her back down.

"Don't sit up. You need to take it easy," Patrick insisted. "I assume Joffrey is the kibit. He's fine."

"Oh, thank the stars." Anise gave a sigh of relief. "Can I see him, please?"

"Sure, he's right over here," Patrick walked across the room to a small pet bed. "We tried to take him somewhere else, but he went crazy. He's been sitting by you most of the time." He placed Joffrey on Anise's cot.

"Joffrey!" Anise exclaimed. Joffrey leaped into her arms and purred while rubbing his head against her.

"Isn't that nice?" Doctor Bruin said to Patrick, who nodded with misty eyes.

"It's precious," Patrick said.

"Um, if I may," Anise asked. "How long have we been here?"

"Two weeks," said Doctor Bruin. When she saw Anise's horrified expression, she added, "We kept you sedated through the worst parts. You broke a lot of bones, so it was important for you to stay still so your bones could heal properly."

"Oh." Anise didn't know what else to say until a realization hit her. "I have to make a call—now. Ugh, but my stuff is back at the house."

Patrick picked up a small box and placed it on the bed next to her. "Here. We had some people go and get your things." He took her comm from the box and handed it to her.

"How did you know where I live?" Anise asked, disturbed.

"One of our members knew," Patrick said. "He said he's been looking out for you."

"Oh." Anise pushed aside the discomfort, typing in Roy's number. The comm rang, but eventually, the ringing stopped.

"I guess he couldn't get it," Anise said, trying again. She heard it ring for a full minute before a woman's sharp nasal voice answered, "Yes?"

"Hello, may I speak to a Roy Lecru, please?"

"There is no one here by that name," the woman said.

"Oh, right." Anise realized Roy was not his real name. "Do you have a boy living there who's seventeen with blond hair?"

"I only have one son who is twenty-one with dark hair," the woman snapped. "That is all. Don't bother to call again."

Click! Anise put down the comm. "She hung up…and he's not there. He must have given me the wrong number by accident, which means I can't contact him. Oh, Patrick, can you see if you can find something about the Lecru family? Please?"

Patrick and Doctor Bruin both stared at her as though she was crazy.

"What?" Anise asked. "Is there something wrong with the name Lecru?"

Patrick snorted, and Doctor Bruin elbowed him in the ribs.

"What am I missing here?" Anise asked.

"The Lecru family is…well, they have a reputation," Doctor Bruin explained. "It was just surprising for you to ask about them."

"Oh," Anise said, not quite understanding. "Can you still look up the Lecru family? Please?"

"Of course," Patrick said and quickly began tapping on his comm. After a moment, he said, "It says that there's only one Lecru family, and they only have one son under the name of Cameron Lecru, who is twenty-one."

"Where is Roy?" Anise thought aloud. "It's like he just vanished."

"Well, there's no death record for him, so maybe…could you have hallucinated him?"

"No, I'm wearing the scarf and ribbons he gave me," Anise protested, but even as she spoke, doubt weighed heavy on her chest.

Could I have really hallucinated everything? Am I really that lonely? Or crazy?

"Well, on the bright side, I've been looking at these tests, and your bones are almost perfect," Doctor Bruin said.

"Can I get up soon?"

"Yes, you can start now." Doctor Bruin said. "Your bones responded well to our remedy, and they are healed enough that you should start moving." She turned to leave before turning right back around and sitting on the edge of the bed.

"There is one more thing," she said. "We ran your DNA through our system after we found you, and…we found a close match."

"You mean I have family here?" Anise breathed.

"Yes," Doctor Bruin smiled. "He's a very nice young man, and ever since we told him, he's been asking to see you as soon as you were awake."

"I want to meet him too." Anise sat up. "Can I start trying to move?"

"Sure, I'll go get some things we could use and be right back." Doctor Bruin left.

"Here," Patrick started unwrapping one bandage on her left hand and wrist but paused. "By the way, I think I should warn you. When they brought you in, your hands were more damaged than the rest of you, so we had to use some metal to hold everything together." He picked up a parcel from the table beside them. "I got these for you, just in case you wanted them."

"Okay," Anise said uneasily. "Please finish unwrapping."

Patrick nodded and slowly unwrapped the rest of the cloth. Anise almost gasped when she saw her left hand. Half a dozen gold rings had been set variously into the skin of her fingers, and a large band in her wrist.

Anise took a deep breath as Patrick finished her right hand and almost gasped again. Her right hand had only had three rings, but the entire back of her hand and wrist were covered in thin, jagged scars that matched the shapes of the shattered glass.

"I was afraid that this would upset you," Patrick said. "It would upset me, so I got you the gloves."

He handed her the parcel. With shaky fingers, Anise opened it to reveal a pair of soft, light brown gloves that came up over her wrist. She glanced at her hands again and almost choked as the memories of the shipwreck came rushing back. Falling. Pain. The horrible stabbing feeling in her hand, blood everywhere—

"Miss Desson!"

Anise sucked in a breath as she fell out of the flashback. Patrick was rubbing her shoulders and gently saying, "It's okay, you're here, you're safe."

"Thank you," Anise said shakily and picked up the gloves. She silently slipped them on and wiggled her fingers. "That feels good."

"Perfect," Patrick said understandingly. "Let's stand you up." He helped Anise get to her feet. She wobbled a little, but with him supporting her, she was able to walk around the room.

"Good job," Patrick encouraged. "We have a strengthening elixir that should give you a boost."

Anise took the elixir and walked around the room again, this time alone. She was on her third time around when Doctor Bruin came back in.

"Miss Desson, how does walking feel?" she asked.

"Good." Anise jogged around to demonstrate.

"Well, do you feel up to meeting with your relative today?" Doctor Bruin questioned.

"Yes!" Anise gave a tiny jump and said, "I'm ready now!"

"Patrick, take Miss Desson to the private library, and I'll go get Mr. Desson."

"His last name is Desson too?" Anise said in shock. "How close could this relative be? A cousin?"

"Probably," Patrick said as they left. "This way."

Patrick led Anise through various halls until they reached a room with large double doors. Inside were large windows, and the walls were covered in bookshelves.

Patrick helped Anise sit on a window seat, checked if she was okay, then left.

"I'm so excited," Anise said to the empty room. She peered out the window, and she could see a large shipyard where people were washing, repairing, and landing ships. She was watching one man struggling with an engine just as the double doors opened, and a young man stepped in. He scanned the room, but his face took on a shocked expression when he saw her.

"Are...are you Anise Desson?" he barely said.

"Yes...are you a Mr. Desson?" she stood and walked over to him.

"Yes." He stared at her. "You're really here. Finally."

He reached out to embrace her, and Anise gave a start. "I'm sorry, but we haven't been properly introduced. Can I get your name?" she asked.

Realization dawned on the man's face, and he said, "Oh, I'm sorry. I forgot that you probably wouldn't remember me." He looked at her lovingly. "I've been looking for you for twelve years. I just can't believe it's really you."

"Okay, but who are you?" Anise asked. "My cousin, my—"

"Brother," the man said softly. "I'm your brother, Caiden."

"My brother?" Anise breathed. "My brother, Caiden…wait." Blurry memories began to surface in her mind, and she gasped.

"Cay," she realized. "That's what I called you. I do remember you!"

Joy broke on Caiden's face as Anise threw herself into his arms. He returned her embrace, warm and comforting.

"I've missed you, more than you could know," Caiden told her. "It's been quite a long time. I can't believe my baby sister is all grown up. Last time I saw you, you were only four."

"Really?" Now that Anise was really looking, she could start to see the resemblance between them. They had the same eye shape, and the slope of her nose was very close to his. He had warm, soft

90

brown eyes that made her feel safe, just like they had done when she was a child. His dark, chestnut hair didn't match hers, but she could still see that they were obviously related.

"Yes, and ever since I read the letter, I've been able to search for you properly." Caiden led her to sit down on the window seat again.

"What letter?" Anise asked.

"Didn't you have robot parents?" Caiden asked.

"Yes, but they short-circuited and died when I was eleven. I've been living alone since," Anise replied.

"Oh no…I'm so sorry." Caiden sighed. "On each of our sixteenth birthdays, our robot parents were supposed to give us a letter that explained everything. Why we were sent away, what happened, all of that."

"Wait, what do you mean 'we were sent away'? I thought that nobody wanted me, so I was just dropped off on Ceran," Anise said.

"Oh, not at all!" Caiden wrapped an arm around her shoulders. "Mom and Dad love us both! Let me explain."

"Dad was on the planetary council of Veraconix—" Caiden broke off when he saw the confused expression on Anise's face. He began to explain. "Each of the planets has a council of seven. That's called the planetary council. The head of each planetary council is on the Galactic Council. They make the laws and government. Understand?"

Anise nodded, so he continued. "Anyway, Dad was on the planetary council of Veraconix, which is our capital planet, and so he had a high position in the galaxy. When the Embleck Army started attacking council members, Dad began to worry about us. So, he made arrangements for us to go into hiding separately to keep us safe."

"Mom left a month before everyone else. She thought Dad was being paranoid, but she still left. A few weeks later, we received a letter that said she wanted a divorce. She had met someone else and didn't want to have to worry about going into hiding with us. She never liked being in the center of all the politics."

Caiden sighed a touch. "Dad agreed, obviously. The divorce was completed very, very fast, and we lost contact. A few days later, there was another attack, so Dad decided that we needed to leave. He sent me to Xicarinoth and you to Ceran, I guess. I didn't know where you were, and I still don't know where he is." He turned to Anise and saw her eyes were misty.

"Hey, what is it?"

"I know it's silly," Anise sniffed. "But when you've lived your life thinking nobody cares about you…it feels really good to know that someone does."

"That's not silly," Caiden reassured her. "I'm just sorry you had to live like that."

Just as he finished speaking, Doctor Bruin came into the room. "So, have you two gotten acquainted?"

"Yes," Anise grinned. "This is my brother."

"Oh, wonderful!" Doctor Bruin said. "It's time for you to come back to the infirmary. We want to monitor you tonight, and tomorrow Councilor Indu wants to see you."

"Wow, Indu." Caiden explained to Anise, "The Qor also has a council that takes care of military matters."

"Why does he want to meet with me?" Anise asked.

"He didn't say." Doctor Bruin shrugged. "Come along."

After a night of sleeping in the infirmary, Anise fidgeted in a chair outside an office, waiting to see Councilor Indu. She twisted her fingers and tugged on her new gloves, getting used to the feeling of fabric covering her skin.

"Miss Desson?" a voice called from inside the office. Anise stood, and the door slid open. Inside, a man with dark, graying hair stood at the window.

"Yes?" Anise asked.

The man turned around, and Anise inhaled sharply. "You!"

"Ah, Miss Desson, very good to see you again." He smiled. "I'm glad I can properly introduce myself. I am Councilor Indu of the Qor."

"Nice to see you." Anise tried to regain her composure. "Again."

"Indeed," Councilor Indu replied. "I do apologize for my odd behavior. You must understand; there are Embleck spies everywhere, and I am a valuable target for the enemy. However, you were important enough to risk it."

"How did you find me?" Anise queried. "Actually, how do you know who I am?"

Councilor Indu thought a moment, a brief, bittersweet smile crossing his face. "I knew your family. Your father, specifically. I was the best man at his wedding. He was like a brother to me."

"Oh?" Anise fought a spark of hope. "Do you know where he is now?"

"I'm afraid not," Councilor Indu admitted. "He's been in hiding for many years. Safety concerns, you know."

"Of course." Anise nodded, tamping down her unreasonable disappointment. "I'm sorry to be abrupt, but…why did you want to see me?"

"Well, first, I wanted to check on you. I heard you were in a nasty accident."

"Yes, though I'm fine now," Anise answered. "The infirmary is incredible at what they do."

"We have the best here," Councilor Indu said proudly.

Anise kept her expression polite. If the Councilor had information about her, she still wanted it.

"Well then." Councilor Indu clapped his hands together. "I suppose you want to continue our conversation from the desert."

"Yes, please," Anise said quickly, hoping she didn't come across too eager.

"First, I must tell you this: now that the Embleck Army is aware of your location, it will not be safe for you to return to Ceran."

"Where else am I supposed to go?" Anise asked, worry creeping into her tone. "I—I don't have anyone who will take me in."

"I would be honored to give you a place here," Councilor Indu said. "As a favor to your father. The Qor is always accepting new applications."

"I'm not sure…" Anise began.

"I did the same for your brother," Councilor Indu told her. "He's found satisfaction with his life here. I truly believe you could do the same. You can stay here with your brother, where it's safe."

Anise tugged her gloves, turning over thoughts in her mind. It wasn't like she had any other options. If she couldn't return to Ceran… "Is that really my only choice?"

"I could apply you to a university instead," Councilor Indu offered. "You could stay at school full time and further your education."

What education? Anise scoffed internally.

"However, there are many strict requirements. You might have to study for an extended period of time before being accepted."

"I…I see." Anise didn't have much hope in a university. She'd never had any formal schooling. Her robot parents had taught her what she needed to survive…but advanced studies had never been important to her.

"You could study, learn, and get a high-level job," Councilor Indu continued. "Work a traditional job in a city office, and build a life for yourself there."

"No, I…" Anise shook her head. "I'm not interested. I want to stay here with my brother."

"So you'll join the Qor?"

"I will," Anise agreed. "But only after you tell me more about my abilities."

"Very well," Councilor Indu said. "We went to the sight of your accident, and there appeared to be broken pieces of light scattered through the wreckage. Do you have any idea where it came from?"

"No, not at all. When I was in the ship, I thought that I needed a shield, and that…*thing* appeared." Anise furrowed her brow, recalling the event. "It was almost…a shield?"

"I see." Councilor Indu scanned the heavily filled bookshelf against the wall. "I've studied this topic for many years and believe my guess is correct. It was a shield, one you created."

"How?" Anise asked. "I have no idea—"

"Your power must draw on a certain energy field to create shields. The same energy you used to control the minds of the Embleck soldiers."

"How does that work?"

"I am not entirely certain, but I want to test a theory." He held out his hands to Anise, palms up. "Place your hands on mine. Now, focus on your powers."

Anise did as he instructed. She closed her eyes and concentrated, searching for any semblance of a feeling like her powers. Slowly, she became aware of a steady hum racing through her body.

"I can feel a…humming?"

"Alright, now enhance that hum." Councilor Indu closed his eyes as well. "Feel it in the air, racing through the galaxy. A source of power, pulling at you."

Anise frowned, unable to sense anything as significant as he described. Just as she was about to say no, a tiny glimmer of power touched her consciousness. It was more than a glimmer—now an endless expanse of silver energy shimmering behind her closed eyes.

"I—I think I feel it!"

"Excellent." Councilor Indu stepped back and opened his eyes. "It appears my theory was correct."

Anise also opened her eyes, severing her connection to the energy field. "What theory?"

Councilor Indu beamed. "Your powers are connected to stardust and feed off of star energy. That's why your force fields are unbreakable! Star energy is the most powerful in the galaxy. The tiniest amount is used in ship light fuel so they can travel at lightspeed."

"I have a connection to the most powerful force in the galaxy?" Anise said in disbelief. "And I can use that power?"

"Yes," Councilor Indu admitted, though he looked worried. "Though using this power is not without consequences. Channeling this much power can be extremely draining if overused."

"Understood," Anise said. "But…why can I only do this now? I never could do this before."

"I believe they were triggered when you were in a life-or-death moment. You needed a shield, so your subconscious triggered the ability as a survival instinct. The same thing happened with the mind control. You were in a life-or-death situation, and the ability was activated."

"I've never heard of anything like this before," Anise said doubtfully.

"You wouldn't," Councilor Indu conceded. "Anyone with these powers would want to keep it a secret—and you should also."

"Why?"

"The only known case of powers like yours is King Zamir of the Embleck Army. If people knew you had these abilities, they might assume you are affiliated with him and the Embleck Army."

"Good reason," Anise admitted. "That makes sense. Thank you for that information."

"Of course." He patted her shoulder and opened the door. "Come directly to me anytime you have more questions."

"Thank you, sir." Anise nodded before leaving the office. Caiden had offered to meet her in the private library after the meeting.

After asking one of the passing soldiers for help, Anise found the library. Caiden stood before the large, ceiling-high windows, his back to her.

Anise approached him, calling, "Hello!"

Caiden turned around and smiled when he saw her. "Hey, Anise. Come see this."

Anise peered out the window, her eyes widening. Dozens of ships flew through the air, twisting and weaving between each other.

A deep longing to be in the sky pulled at Anise's chest.. "What are they doing?"

"Test flights." Caiden watched the ships intently. "Someday, I'll be in charge of a fleet of ships."

"Really?" Anise watched.

"Yeah. I'll be a ship commander." Caiden's eyes followed the ships. "One of these days…"

"I'm joining the Qor as well," Anise told him. "We can serve together."

"I'm happy to hear it." Caiden wrapped his arm around her. "It's a good life, Anise. And we'll be together."

Anise rested her head against his arm. "I'm so glad I found you."

"I'm glad I found you, too."

For the first time in what seemed like forever, Anise felt like she was home. *I wish I could tell Roy about this*, Anise thought wistfully.

Roy, I hope that wherever you are, you're as happy as I am.

CHAPTER 7

YEAR: 9026

"Hey, Commander! Wait up!"

Anise Desson turned around to Keisha running after her. "Keisha, how long are you going to keep calling me that?" She grinned at her friend. "It's been six months since my promotion."

"I don't know, maybe FOREVER." Keisha threw an arm around her shoulder. "It's worth celebrating."

"True," Anise agreed, unable to hide her grin.

"So, what's up?" Keisha asked, throwing her colorful scarf over her shoulder.

"I have a meeting with Councilor Indu," Anise replied. "Then lunch with Caiden."

"Good luck," Keisha said. "I'm going to polish my ship. Can we meet up later?"

"Sure!" Anise waved as Keisha left. She continued down the hallway and saw Caiden standing by one of the large windows lining the hall.

"Hey!" Anise walked up beside him.

Caiden jumped, seeming startled to see her. "Oh, Anise. Where are you off to?"

"A meeting." Anise shrugged. "What about you?"

"Just watching the people working in the shipyard," Caiden said.

"Sounds…fun," Anise said half-heartedly.

"I know, boring," Caiden said teasingly. "Now, you should scoot. You don't want to be late."

"Alright. I'll see you at lunch." Anise sighed a little as she walked away. Over the years, she'd learned Caiden liked to watch the world go by. Sometimes he would sit in the cantina and watch the people for hours.

103

Anise hated to watch the world go by; she wanted to go with it! She wanted to fly her ship, race with Joffrey, or take a day trip to somewhere she'd never been.

Not that the idea of going it by myself is appealing, Anise grumbled to herself. She did adore Caiden, but he had no desire to experience the things she did. He wanted to play life safe.

Anise pushed aside a prickling of resentment. The years on base living a structured life hadn't quashed her desire for something...more in her life. A change in her days that were similar to every other day.

Or something worth changing for.

Anise sighed again as she pulled away from her thoughts and approached Councilor Indu's office door. She knocked on the door before smoothening her uniform.

"Enter," Councilor Indu called.

Anise pushed open the door and stepped inside. "Hello, Sir."

"Hello, Commander Desson." He stood from his desk and shook her hand. "How are you?"

"I'm doing well, thank you."

"Good, good...how are things going with your powers?"

"Very well," Anise said excitedly. "I've been testing making shields in unique shapes. Look, I can make a sword." She swirled her hands through the air and created a sword of sparkling white light.

"Fantastic!" Councilor Indu clapped his hands together.

"I've also made progress with learning to heal," Anise added hopefully. "It's not easy, but I'm improving."

"Excellent. Healing is one of the most important abilities you have," Indu reminded her. "It is vital you know how to use it well."

"Is that what you wanted to talk to me about today?" Anise let the sword fade away.

"No, not entirely." Councilor Indu sat back down, and Anise followed his lead. "I wanted to discuss a problem with you."

"Alright," Anise said. "What kind of a problem?"

"You have been doing very well with your training, and your abilities give you an advantage. I've decided I want to assign you to a very important mission. You would have your team with you, of course."

"Thank you, Sir," Anise said. "What is it?"

"One of our bases on another planet sent out a robot with a piece of information that may be crucial to us. Unfortunately, the robot's navigational system had a short, and it crash-landed on Redoridia. It is necessary to find it before the Embleck Army does."

"Of course." Anise nodded. "I accept."

"I must add a warning," Councilor Indu said solemnly. "We have received frequent reports about High Commander Monroy leading troops on that planet. It's almost entirely forest, but the Embleck Army is frequenting it."

As he spoke, Councilor Indu pulled a small holo-projector from his desk and set it in front of her. He pressed a button, and a 3D hologram appeared above it, slowly rotating. Anise leaned closer. The hologram showed a tall man wearing the black uniform of the Embleck Army and a mask that covered the lower half of his face.

"Who is that?" Anise asked.

Councilor Indu frowned at the projection. "High Commander Monroy of the Embleck Army. He works very closely with King Zamir, and must be eliminated. I am counting on you. Your powers will give you an advantage that no one else has."

"I'll eliminate him," Anise promised.

"Good." Councilor Indu handed her the projector and said, "That is all. I'll see you tomorrow for the assignment."

Anise left the office but paused outside the door. She stared at the slowly rotating hologram. "Watch out, High Commander Monroy. I'm coming for you."

CHAPTER 8

High Commander Liam Monroy strolled briskly through the halls of the Embleck Palace. He had a meeting with King Zamir of the Embleck Army—and if there was one thing you didn't want to be with King Zamir, it was late.

Liam shot a quick glance at his wrist comm, checking the time. A dozen messages instantly blinked over his screen, the words melting into each other. Scribbles of black writing stood out against the bright screen, far too hazy to read.

The effects of yet another sleepless night seemed to be settling in nicely; with clear vision as the first causality. Liam dashed a gloved hand over his eyes, allowing for a moment of focus before the words blurred away again.

Liam winced, picking up his pace. He'd memorized the time it took to reach the throne room from his quarters on the nearby base after years serving the Embleck Army. However, the…incident that morning had stripped more time than expected, leaving him a few minutes short.

Briefly, Liam's thoughts flashed to the dream that'd filled the few minutes of sleep allowed to him. Images of the place he'd once called home drifted through this mind, clearer than the world currently around him.

Despite the nine years he'd gone without setting foot on the planet where he'd once resided, the clarity never left—much to Liam's grievance.

The scenes playing before his eyes left Liam unsettled, thus throwing off his minute-by-minute schedule. Now he'd have to make up for lost time or risk the wrath of his leader.

As Liam continued through the dark, shining Embleck halls, he passed a group of soldiers, standing together and talking. They all wore the black uniform of the Embleck Army, their helmets dangling loosely from their hands.

The hard shell of a mask covering the lower half of Liam's face bit into his skin, constraining his jaw. He stifled a prickle of envy at the lower ranked soldiers, knowing he should feel grateful for his rank. The title of high commander placed Liam above almost every position.

Yet there was something about the freedom that came with being a nobody—simply another Embleck soldier; another cog in the great machine—creating the longing Liam tried to ignore.

When had he last been a nobody? Liam scoured his memories, a faint echo of a headache pulsing through his temples. One faint recollection brushed his mind…

"Sir." The soldiers quickly put their helmets back on, saluting Liam as he walked by.

Snapping from his thoughts, Liam acknowledged them with a quick nod, noticing the way their hands trembled as they saluted.

Igniting fear in people wasn't something Liam had exactly aspired for—it had just *happened* with time and rank. Not to mention his favor with King Zamir…

Walking further into the base, Liam entered another hall—one far less inviting. Shadows dripped from every corner; the temperature icy cold. Liam resisted the urge to shiver, even in his heavy black cloak. His eyes darted to the dark regions of the hall, where shadows seemed to slink down from the corners of the high ceilings, lingering around him.

Despite being alone, Liam couldn't shake the feeling that someone—or something—hovered right behind him. But every time he looked over his shoulder to check, the hall remained empty.

Shaking off the sensation of a clawed hand on his shoulder, Liam raised his fist, knocking on the tall double doors of the throne room. His sharp knock echoed through the dim hallway, and a moment passed before it was met with the low, gravelly voice of King Zamir.

"Come in, High Commander Monroy."

The doors swung open, and Liam stepped into the presence of King Zamir. He walked up to the raised dais, stopping before it as he glanced up at the black throne.

King Zamir stared down at him, his eyes obscured by the low pointed swoop of his mask. In one hand, he held a staff of almost black wood, with a blood-red crystal set at the top that seemed to drain the light from the room.

Liam bowed low, and a slight smile crept across King Zamir's face, revealing slightly pointed teeth.

"You may rise, High Commander Monroy."

Liam bowed his head in acknowledgment, returning to his statue-like posture and keeping his eyes lowered, staring at his scuffed black boots. *I should make an appointment to have them cleaned*, Liam mused begrudgingly. The Embleck Army demanded perfection—he'd get a sound scolding if he left them like this. *Wait. I meant to do that a month ago, didn't I? Or...last year?*

"Monroy."

"Apologies, Your Majesty," Liam said. "You requested my presence?"

"Yes," King Zamir hissed. "I require your expert skills."

"Sir?"

"My spies have reported that a Qor robot has crashed on Redoridia. You will go with a group, and you will find it before the Qor soldiers do."

"Of course, Your Majesty."

"One of their best, Commander Desson, will be leading their search. She is an opponent that needs to be eliminated."

"Of course, Your Majesty," Liam repeated, keeping his gaze low. "How else may I assist you?"

"I've brought it, Your Majesty," an imposing man with greying hair called as he entered the room carrying a wrapped parcel.

"Ah, High Commander Ankor," King Zamir rasped. "Good."

Liam frowned under his mask at the sight of High Commander Ankor, King Zamir's right-hand man. He despised Liam—a fact not helped by King Zamir always paying Liam special attention—almost favoring him.

"Hello, *High Commander Monroy*," High Commander Ankor sneered at him.

Liam offered a vague tilt of his head in Ankor's general direction. "Anything else I may assist with, Your Majesty?"

Ankor's face reddened with offence, but King Zamir ignored this, taking the wrapped parcel from Ankor with bony gloved fingers. "High Commander Ankor has brought a dose of your elixir for you to take."

Liam's eyes darted up, and he quickly lowered his vision again. Rubbing his thumbs over his fingertips, Liam spoke in a low tone. "Your Majesty...I believe I've had my dose this month."

"My schedule has changed." Zamir's voice vibrated with the note of an unspoken threat. "You have a protest?"

"No, Your Majesty," Liam managed through a clenched jaw.

"You should have respect for His Majesty," Ankor snapped.

"Apologies," Liam inclined his head to King Zamir. He knew better than to argue. "May I go now?"

"You may." Zamir gestured toward Ankor. "Give it to him."

High Commander Ankor thrust the parcel at Liam vehemently while giving him an evil look. Liam shifted, letting his right-hand rest on his ray gun while taking the parcel with the other.

"Thank you, Your Majesty." Liam bowed to King Zamir and purposefully ignored Ankor before turning. He kept an even pace as he approached the door, feeling Zamir and Ankor's gaze burning into his back.

The double doors closed behind him, and Liam dropped his polite expression. Resentment washed over him in droves as he stared at the wrapped parcel he held.

Since when did Ankor have authority over me? Liam strode through the dark hall, ignoring the darkness tugging at his cloak and the cold wind rippling through his hair. *We're equal in rank—he should be consulting me, not treating me like a cadet.*

Entering the expansive Embleck hangar, Liam scanned the ships, their forms melting against the backdrop of glistening stars

"Can I be of any assistance to you, High Commander Monroy?"

Liam flinched, his hand flying to his sword hilt before he recognized the distorted face of the hangar manger. He blinked roughly, though his vision remained blurred.

"Just prepare my ship, Ashford," Liam ordered, pinching the bridge of his nose, a headache already forming.

The hangar manager nodded and rushed off. Liam subtly rubbed a hand over his eyes, hoping it would clear his vision long enough to walk up the ramp of his ship.

"Right over here, High Commander." Ashford popped up out of nowhere, once again startling Liam.

Relieved that his vision had cleared, at least somewhat, Liam followed as they passed dozens of Embleck ships. Out of the corner of his eye, Liam noted most of the ship mechanics and pilots pause what they were doing to stare wide-eyed.

As one of the highest-ranked people in the Embleck Army, Liam *could* understand their staring, but the sensation of dozens of people watching made him uncomfortable. Finally, they approached his large private ship, where the pilot waited.

"Is there anything else, High Commander?" the hangar manager asked, his entire body nearly vibrating with nervous energy.

"No, that's all," Liam said briskly. "Thank you, Ashford."

Ashford nodded, stepping back with a bow as Liam boarded his ship. The large door slid closed behind him with a hiss, and Liam took his seat, set back from the pilot and copilot's chairs. The android pilot swiveled its chair around, lifeless vision sensors locked on Liam.

"Back to residential base." Liam sank down in his chair, allowing the parcel in his hand to slip to the floor with a *cling*.

The engines hummed faintly as the ship lifted into the air, soaring into the darkness. Liam barely saw the stars, nor the asteroid belt as the ship left the atmosphere, jumping to lightspeed.

Soon, the silence of the ship took over, and Liam faded into his mind. Fractured images rubbed at his consciousness—places he hadn't been in years, things he'd destroyed, people he'd met—one person in particular.

"We're approaching the base, High Commander."

Liam inhaled deeply as he returned to the world of the living, cringing at the bright interior lights of the ship. He leaned over to dim them, though even the lower setting burned at his eyes.

Giving up, Liam glanced out one of the large windows, his vision once again blurry. Even so, he could make out the largest base of the Embleck Army. It hung in the middle of space, just outside Nockalore's atmosphere, rivaling the size of the moons it orbited alongside.

The pilot transmitted Liam's code to the base and received landing clearance. A few minutes later, the ship landed smoothly in the hangar. Standing, Liam picked up the parcel and quickly disembarked.

Liam kept his gaze straight ahead as he exited the hangar, resisting the urge to look back at the eyes he felt staring after him. He strolled through the halls quickly, noting the way each person he passed glanced up at him.

Half-heartedly, Liam entertained the idea of making an order that forbade people from looking at him, but eventually decided against it. Finally, he reached the upper halls where his quarters were located, along with those of other high-ranking officers.

Catching sight of his door, Liam reached up and jerked off his mask. Instant relief washed over him, as he felt able to breathe properly again.

"Oh, Liam! It's been a while since I've seen you around here."

Freezing, Liam bit back a sigh. There was only one person here who would call him by his first name, and he'd been hoping to avoid her.

Liam turned around. "I was here last week, Commander Darleva."

Commander Sandra Darleva stepped closer, smiling in a way that could be considered enchanting. "Oh. Well, it felt much longer. I was beginning to miss you."

Liam raised an eyebrow. "Miss me?" *It's not that she misses me, it's that she wants something. Wouldn't be the first time either.*

"Yes, of course." Sandra stepped even closer, and Liam took a step back. "I was hoping you'd return soon. I heard about how you'd discovered a Qor base and recovered a compass of theirs."

"It was a map," Liam pointed out blankly.

"Oh, well, whatever it was, it sounded wonderful, and I just wanted to congratulate you." Sandra batted her eyelashes.

"You could have sent a message," Liam suggested hopefully. "I have a comm."

"I wanted to tell you in person," Sandra said with wide eyes, as though she was shocked Liam would even suggest such a thing. She stepped forward and took his arm.

"Well, you've told me now. If you don't mind, I better be going," Liam tried, hoping for a quick escape. In the past months, Sandra had developed a quite unwanted infatuation with him, much to Liam's deep confusion.

"So soon?" Sandra said, her voice full of articulated dismay.

I wonder if she ever had a career in theater, Liam mused. "Yes, I'm afraid so. I've had a busy morning, and quite the headache."

"You wouldn't like any company?" Sandra suggested, sliding up to him.

Liam bit back a sigh. He didn't keep the company of *anyone*—especially no one in the Embleck circle. "No, thank you."

"Oh, Liam, some of us are going to this lovely event on Nockalore tomorrow night. Why don't you join us?" Sandra asked, practically hanging on Liam's arm.

Liam tried to extract his arm from her grasp, but she held tightly. He hated to be rude....but she didn't seem to be taking the hint. "Commander Darleva?"

"Yes, Liam?" Sandra's voice carried the smug note of someone about to get what they wanted.

Liam gripped the doorknob to his room. "It looks like you stepped in paint. Your boot is black."

Sandra let go of Liam's arm, glancing down at her boots with an irritated expression. "Oh no—wait, of course, my boot is black! So is my other one. It's the *uniform* color."

"Oh, sorry for the mistake," Liam said, unlocking his door.

"But wait, what about tomorrow?" Sandra exclaimed, her expression petulant.

"Sorry, I think I'll have a headache then." Liam stepped inside. "Goodbye."

Quickly, Liam closed the door, but he still heard the sound of Sandra's offended scoff.

With a sigh, Liam leaned his back against the door as the sound of Sandra's heeled boots faded. His escape had definitely not been graceful, but hopefully, it would discourage Sandra.

Why, of all men, did she have to pick me? Liam wondered dully. Of course, the answer was clear—his rank. At least, it was the only answer Liam consider. He'd encountered Commander Darleva a time or two while on the Embleck base. Quite a few years older than himself, Sandra had hovered around meetings with Zamir and Ankor, eyeing Liam in a way he hadn't noticed until recently. Her intense interest remained recent—roughly since the death of the distinguished commander she'd been seen with constantly.

Now alone with his thoughts, Liam sighed heavily, staring down at the bottle in his hand. Tossing his mask on the bed, he trudged across the room and set the bottle on the dresser with a *clank.*

Bracing his palms on the dresser, Liam peered at his reflection in the wall mirror. Short, wavy blond hair, with a natural royal blue streak through it. Shadowed, dark green eyes. A few faint lines barely creased his forehead as he frowned at his reflection. He looked tired, to his annoyance. Not that he'd admit it to himself.

Liam glanced away from his unwelcome reflection, his eyes falling on the bottle sitting next to a picture of a young woman standing next to a younger version of himself.

Wistfully, Liam rested his chin in his hands and leaned against the dresser, staring at the picture. The memory of that day seemed like a short eternity ago. Sunlight shone through the girl's red hair, illuminating it like fire. They both beamed, and the girl's head rested against his.

Liam eyed his image's smile critically, knowing he hadn't smiled like that since the day the holograph had been taken.

"Ree," Liam whispered. "I miss you." Nine years blurred her face, but he still remembered their time—especially their meeting, when she had crashed into him, knocking them both to the ground— the first moment he'd fallen in love with her.

Liam closed his eyes, remembering the smile on her face as she told him, "See you next week."

It had been the last thing she ever said to him.

Something twisted deep in Liam's chest, tightening his lungs. Vague words flickered through his mind—*shipwreck…parts malfunction…dead…*

I didn't even know your real name. Liam traced his thumb over the holograph projector frame. *And yet I…I killed you. If I had checked those pieces…but I didn't, and…and now you're gone.*

The knot in his lungs burned his throat, and Liam bit his lip, although he felt no sadness. *Enough,* he ordered himself. *Self-pity won't bring her back or change that it's your fault—won't change that you're a monster. Accept the truth.*

Forcing himself to turn away, Liam picked up the bottle from the dresser. The dark grey liquid sloshed in the bottle, making his stomach turn.

After Ree's death, King Zamir offered him a potion that would remove his ability to feel sadness. Liam accepted it, of course, no questions asked. Anything to strip him of the soul-encompassing grief numbing his mind.

Biting back a flicker of uncertainty, Liam uncorked the bottle. He hesitated only a second before tilting the bottle up and swallowing the elixir.

Liam seized the edge of the dresser as the room began to spin. Any emotion drained from his body as a dull ache settled into his bones. The floor seemed to tilt sideways, and Liam stumbled over to the bed, flopping down face-first.

I hate myself. I hate my life. Liam groaned, pulling a pillow over his head.

The second he did, the constant humming sound that filled his mind became louder. For as long as he could remember, he had heard a humming sound in the back of his mind. It was clear, sweet, and never-ending. It had faded at times but never stopped. He didn't mind. It was almost comforting, except for now. Now, it was louder than usual and made his head ache.

Liam groaned again, removing the pillow. The humming quieted a bit, and he closed his eyes until he finally fell asleep.

CHAPTER 9

Anise sat on her bed, polishing her sword while Joffrey watched. "It's been too long since I polished this thing. The hilt is dull."

"Meoooowwwrr," Joffrey said disapprovingly.

Anise finally finished her sword and reached for her ray gun. She had to clean it once a week and make sure everything was working.

Quickly, Anise cleaned the knob that changed the ray's settings. Her ray gun was a standard model, which meant it had two settings—the first being a stun ray, blue in color. The second was the standard white energy rays that she usually used in battle.

Anise glanced up and caught a glimpse of the time. "Oh stars, I'm going to be late!" The team Councilor Indu had assembled would be waiting if she didn't hurry.

Anise leaped up from the bed, sheathed her sword, and gave Joffrey a quick kiss. "Be good until I'm back, okay?"

Joffrey mowed in agreement as Anise closed the door behind her. She hurried through the base, heading for the hangar when a voice stopped her.

"Commander Desson!" Anise turned around and saw High Councilor Mills approaching her.

"High Councilor Mills." Anise saluted him. High Councilor Mills was the head of the Qor's council. Rarely seen outside his office, Anise wondered what had brought him here.

"Hello, Commander." He nodded. "Are you about to leave with your team?"

"Yes, Sir," Anise said. "May I assist you?"

"I just wanted to make sure you are prepared for this mission." High Councilor Mills glanced around before saying in a hushed tone, "And I wanted to know, how are the ability training sessions with Councilor Indu going?"

"Oh, I...wasn't aware you knew about those," Anise said, somewhat surprised. "Councilor Indu said it was important to keep them private."

"Yes, that is true, but I know *everything* that goes on around here," High Councilor Mills reminded her. "It's part of the role."

"Of course, Sir," Anise said.

"There was something I wanted to inform you of," the High Councilor continued. "I have good reason to believe that someone here is leaking information to the Embleck Army."

Anise stared blankly for a moment, processing. "A traitor?"

"Possibly."

Anise swallowed hard. "Thank you for telling me, Sir. But...*why* are you telling *me* this?"

"It is important for our leaders to take advanced cautionary measures in this time," he said. "Especially for you. If someone from the other side discovered you had such extraordinary powers, they would make you their number one target. It would put you in much more danger."

"I'll be careful," Anise promised.

"Good. Carry on," the Councilor ordered. Anise saluted, turning and heading toward the hangar.

"Oh, Commander?"

Anise turned as he said, "Make sure you get that robot. What is inside is vital and irreplaceable."

"Yes, Sir." Anise saluted him again as she stepped out the door. "You can count on me."

"I know I can." His voice drifted through the door as Anise took a deep breath and went to the Qor ship.

"NO!" Liam jerked upright, throwing out his hand—

Only to realize she was gone, and he'd awoken alone in his room. Liam slowly curled his fingers into a loose fist, clinging to the sensation of her hand in his.

Liam pulled his knees up to his chest, resting his forehead against them as his frantic heartbeat slowly calmed. The frequent nightmares since he had joined the Embleck Army had never gotten easier.

Ree. Liam closed his eyes again, lying back down. The nausea and pain accompanying the elixir had faded slightly, but his vision remained blurry. A soft knock sounded through the room, dragging him from his thoughts.

"Come in," Liam called, still lying face down, muffling his voice.

"Sir?" A young man with dark brown hair stepped into the room. Upon seeing Liam laid out, he asked, "Sir, are you alright?"

Liam forced himself to sit up and acknowledge Commander Brendon, his right-hand man and the closest thing he had to a friend. They'd joined the Embleck Army as teenagers, becoming close over the years.

"High Commander?"

"Yes, sorry." Liam shook his head and tried to fix his hair. "What is it?"

"King Zamir has ordered that we leave for Redoridia right away," Brendon informed him.

Liam sighed, pushing himself off the bed. "Fine. I have to get ready. I'll meet you all in five."

"Yes, High Commander."

Liam strolled into the hangar of the base, keeping his expression measured as he felt eyes on him instantly. Through his limited vision, he could make out High Commander Ankor and Commander Brendon already standing by the ship, as well as a large assembly of androids. However, the two young men standing behind Brendon were unfamiliar.

Liam stopped in front of Brendon, nodding towards the newcomers. "Who are these two?"

"Cadets Deven and Andrew," Brendon explained. "Zamir personally requested for them to come."

"I see," Liam noted how they shrank slightly when they saw him. "Nice to meet you, boys."

"It is an honor to meet you, Sir," Deven said, awe in his voice as he saluted. Andrew followed suit, remaining silent.

Liam inclined his head in response as they boarded the ship.

"To Redoridia," High Commander Ankor ordered the pilot.

Taking a seat off to the side, Liam pondered Zamir's warning about Commander Desson. For Zamir to personally warn him meant this commander was a severe threat—one that needed to be eliminated quickly. Zamir would be counting on him thanks to his…unique advantage.

Liam rested his fingers on the hilt of his sword, feeling dark energy hum through the hilt to his hand. All those years ago, Zamir had told him he possessed great power. All he had to do was let Zamir activate it. Not that Liam ever wanted power—but Zamir wouldn't take no for an answer.

Allowing his powers to be activated wasn't something Liam regretted…but it stripped him of another layer of normality, pulling him further from…

Humanity. The word echoed clearly through Liam's mind.

Liam bit back a sigh as he summoned his powers, reaching out to touch the minds of the others in the ship. Their mental voices and thoughts drifted through his own mind—Devan, excited to be here; Andrew excited to be with Devan, who he considered to be a brother, as Liam learned. Brendon, of course, alternated worrying about Liam and planning scouting strategy. And Ankor, as usual, pondered ways to eliminate Liam while making it look like an accident.

Satisfied, Liam retracted him powers, the voices quieting until his was left with only his own. He rubbed his thumb over the sword hilt, feeling the similar power contained inside. The sword possessed the key to the other half of his power. With a slice of the sword, Liam could create a tear in the universe—a portal to anywhere he'd seen clear enough to picture.

Liam shifted in his seat, feeling Ankor's eyes on him. Silently, he wished he could teleport to the forest, but he hadn't seen it before—not to mention the confusion it could create.

Zamir had warned him that no one could know of his power, as it would create too many enemies. Liam didn't mind the secrecy, as it kept any more attention off himself.

"We're about to land now, High Commander," the pilot called. The ship lowered through the thick canopy, touching down in the forest.

High Commander Ankor disembarked first, shooting Liam a nasty scowl. Liam ignored him, walking down the ramp with Brendon at his side. The androids followed them, standing in formation.

"Start searching," Liam commanded, an ache settling into his skull.

The androids accepted his order, moving to sweep the forest for the missing Qor robot. Vaguely, Liam watched the process. Everything seemed to be correct—Liam's eyes caught on a rustle in the thick jungle plants. With the lack of any breeze, something living had to create that movement.

Liam placed his hand on the hilt of his sword, activating his mind reading abilities. Instantly, he was hit with the mental voices of his squadron, but further away he heard the quiet thoughts of at least a dozen minds.

With a subtle gesture from Liam, Brendon hurried over. "Sir?"

"We have company." Liam discreetly motioned to the bushes. "Qor, I believe."

Brendon nodded. "Shall I give the order?"

Liam watched another faint movement. "Yes."

Brendon drew his ray gun. "In those bushes, open fire!"

Immediately, the androids halted searching and activated the ray guns set into their skeletal arms. They blasted the foliage to pieces, but revealed no Qor soldiers. Liam drew his ray gun. Something—

"Your aim is a little off."

Liam whipped around, his gaze instantly locking on a young woman with red hair and wearing a Qor uniform as she stepped out of the bushes *behind them*. She spun a ray gun casually, her vibrant eyes meeting his.

A sharp slice of an emotion Liam didn't recognize cut through his chest. Why did breathing seem a strain?

The woman winked, making a gesture behind her. A dozen Qor soldiers rose from the foliage, opening fire on the Embleck androids. Liam remained frozen in place, his hand loosely gripping his ray gun.

"Sir?" Brendon shouted.

"Return fire," Liam ordered, snapping back into the present.

The Embleck androids returned fire, though their slow reflexes gave the Qor soldiers an advantage. Liam struggled to pull his mind together—for the first time in years, he was unsure of the best strategic move.

The sound of a ray gun being cocked snapped Liam from his thoughts as he caught sight of a Qor soldier pointing his ray gun at Brendon's back.

"Look out!" Liam drew his sword, barely blocking the shot. It reflected off his blade, leaving Brendin unharmed.

"Thank you, Sir." Brendon's wide eyes and pale skin conveyed his shock.

"Of course." Liam ducked his head, turning back to the battle. It was time to move

Liam surveyed the battle in front of him when a sudden movement caught his attention. Devan, the cadet, lifting a red ray gun to aim at Commander Desson.

With a twinge of unknown regret, Liam realized he wouldn't have to worry about Commander Desson anymore. Embleck death rays caused instant fatalities.

Devan pulled the trigger, and the blood red ray struck Commander Desson in the side. Her sword fell to the ground as she dropped to one knee, pressing a hand to her ribs.

At the exact moment, a stabbing pain cut through Liam's side. Stunned, he pressed a hand to the spot, but the pain quickly ebbed.

"Sir, are you alright?" Brendon asked.

"Yes, of course," Liam managed, his mind spinning. *What's wrong with me?* "Is—"

Liam's words broke off as he saw Commander Desson…stand up. She shouldn't be alive, but..he watched as she slowly get to her feet and picked up her sword with her left hand still pressed to her side before lunging for a nearby android.

*Okay, **now** might be a good time to worry about her.*

CHAPTER 10

Anise heard the sizzle of the ray a second before it hit her. Pain struck her so hard that she stumbled forward as the world seemed to dissolve, and she briefly wondered if she had been struck by lightning.

For a moment Anise stood, stunned, until the clang of her sword hitting the ground pulled her back.

Realizing she only had a second before the ray's power overtook her, Anise dropped to one knee and laid her hand over her side. She activated her healing abilities, beginning to heal the wound. There wasn't time to fully heal it—not here.

Once the blood stopped flowing, Anise took a deep breath and stood, reaching for her sword and lunging for the android behind her. A series of strikes, and it fell to the ground in pieces.

Anise dove into the underbrush of the jungle and took a deep breath, carefully assessing the damage to herself and wincing when her fingers hit the wound. Her entire left side burned like a thousand suns. As much as she wanted to stay hidden in the bushes, she knew her team needed her.

Taking another deep breath, Anise pulled her hand away. Councilor Indu had been correct that the ability was draining, and she rarely used it. Already, she could tell she'd have to continue pulling energy constantly to keep her injury sealed. She needed to get to a medic, quickly...but there was a mission at hand.

She had promised Councilor Indu. *I'll get rid of him.*

Anise glared through the thick jungle vegetation at High Commander Monroy, deflecting shots away from his human squadron.

Well, now's the perfect time. Keeping low, Anise crept through the jungle foliage. She pulled the ray gun from her belt and raised it, biting back a gasp as the movement sent a spark of pain through her side.

Ignoring the sharp burning sensation, Anise once again raised, aimed for his face and fired.

High Commander Monroy apparently possess inhuman reflexes, managing to jerk out of the way with the laser bullet barely grazing his face. He lifted a hand and felt the tiny droplets of blood on his cheek.

Anise quickly pulled back, retreating into the forest as she internally berated herself. Monroy scanned the bushes, quickly catching sight of her.

Stumbling to her feet, Anise bolted deeper into the forest despite the stabbing pain in her side. A moment later, she slowed, realizing she couldn't run forever.

Pulling an extra surge of energy to herself, Anise whipped around and raised her sword as High Commander Monroy broke through the trees.

"Looking for me?"

Monroy twirled his sword. "Actually, yes."

"Perfect." Anise aimed a slice across his face, but he blocked it effortlessly.

Anise caught her breath, lifting her sword again. "It is a privilege to fight the greatest weapon of the Embleck Army."

The mask covering his face hid his expression, but Anise thought he flinched. "Weapon?"

Anise took the opportunity and swung at his head. Monroy casually blocked the strike before stabbing at her leg. Anise quickly

135

blocked the hit and returned with a strike of her own, only to gasp as a bolt of pain coursed through her.

"You know, I'm not sure this is a fair fight," High Commander Monroy said. "But it does make things easier for me."

Anise scowled and pulled more energy into herself, ignoring the slight dizziness that came with it. She struck out again, this time coming only inches from his head. High Commander Monroy dodged, though less than before.

"Well, maybe things are more even than I thought." he said. "It is unfortunate, the way you brushed off the ray. It semes I'll have to deal with you myself."

"You horrible, murderous creature!" Anise growled and attacked him again, just missing. "When I get a half a chance, I'll, I'll…"

"You'll what? Slice me in half?"

"I could," Anise replied, nicking his arm.

"Throw me in a black hole?" he suggested.

"That would get rid of you."

"Feed me to a livotic?" High Commander Monroy swung his sword, cutting her leg.

"Ugh!" Anise growled. "Stop adding ideas to my list, scum!"

Anise blocked his next strike before aiming for his shoulder. Her blade cut a deep gash over his shoulder, ripping through his cloak and created a long gash. He winced in pain and stumbled back, clutching the wound.

Catching sight of the red already staining his skin, Anise saw her opportunity and struck out again.

High Commander Monroy raised his sword in defense, but Anise could tell it took more effort. He had been cut on his right shoulder, so it was impossible to use his sword without worsening the injury.

Anise carefully ducked his next swing, noting it was weaker. She twisted behind him, swing her sword again and striking him in the head with the flat of the blade. The sword did as she intended, knocking him out before he could react.

This works out well. Anise raised her sword, pressing the tip against the base of his skull.

Do it.

Do it now.

Why aren't you doing it?

Anise adjusted her grip on the sword hilt. Every logical option involved killing him—the man who served the evil Embleck Army and found favor with King Zamir.

137

But yet, something, some *tiny* voice in the back of Anise's mind, screamed at her that she'd regret this for the rest of her life.

Anise growled in frustration with herself, deciding it didn't matter. The safety of the galaxy was worth any regret she'd feel. She placed her hand at the top of the hilt, about to push it down—

A shout derailed her train of thought. Anise glanced up—the Embleck Army soldiers were starting to retreat, heading in her direction.

Sheathing her sword, Anise turned and dashed into the forest as the soldiers came crashing through the bushes. She wove her way through the trees, trying to recall which direction Caiden and the others were.

Abruptly, a flash of light struck Anise in the eye—reflected light. Anise took a small step back, shifting until she caught sight of a glimmer under a bush.

Dropping to her knees, she peered into the bush. Underneath the branches laid a small, silver, round robot, emblazed with the Qor symbol.

Yes! Anise pulled it out, the movement sending another shot of pain through her, and she doubled over. Exhaustion from using the energy field started to set in rapidly.

Anise let go of her connection to the field and quickly picked up the robot. Her slapstick healing began to fade, and she could see a bloodstain appearing on her jacket.

Picking up her pace, Anise hurried in the direction she hoped her team was. After a few tense minutes, she caught sight of the Qor ship through the thick trees. Faintly, she could hear Caiden and Keisha calling her name.

"I'm here!" Anise called as she stumbled into the clearing. "I've got it."

"Anise!" Caiden raced over to her. "You found it!"

"Yeah." Anise handed him the bot, swaying on her feet.

"What's wrong?"

"I got hit with a death ray," she mumbled, and Caiden grabbed her arm.

"A death ray?! We have to get you to a medic."

"I'm fine, really…" Anise protested weakly as Caiden pulled her aboard the ship.

Liam awoke to the sound of voices. He groaned and opened his eyes slowly. "What happened?"

"Oh, thank the stars." Brendon leaned over him. "We were starting to think you were dead."

"No, not quite." Liam touched his aching head.

"Good," Brendon said. "As for what happened, we found you in the forest in pretty bad shape. You lost a lot of blood."

"Argh—yeah, I remember now." Liam reached for his shoulder. "Commander Desson was…more skilled than I anticipated." *And I was distracted.*

"Don't worry. The medic said you'd feel normal in a day or two."

Liam sat up, doubting the medic's credibility. "King Zamir was right, though. Commander Desson is very skilled."

"True. She is known well. We'll make a plan about how to eliminate her."

"The problem is that I—" Liam broke off, a memory hitting him like a flash of lightning. Commander Desson's teal eyes glistened in his mind, reminding him of an evening under the Ceran stars—

"Sir, are you okay?" Brendon looked worried.

"Yes, I'm fine." Liam struggled to collect himself. It was impossible. Ree had been dead for nine years. He couldn't hope…

"I need to speak with King Zamir."

"Actually, His Majesty ordered your immediate presence," Brendon reported.

"Perfect." Liam stood, hesitating as the world spun. Collecting himself, he nodded to Brendon before exiting the infirmary, striding through the halls until he reached Zamir's throne room.

"Enter, Monroy."

Liam thrust the doors open, his pace quick as he approached the dais and gave a short bow. "You asked to see me, Your Majesty?"

"Yes." King Zamir stared down, beckoning him closer. "I heard there was a little incident with a certain Commander Desson."

"Oh, yes, Your Majesty." Liam debated if he should say anything. "She caught me off guard in battle. It was my error."

Zamir waved a hand. "No, no. I believe there is something else on your mind."

Liam shifted uneasily. "I thought…well, Commander Desson resembles…Ree. I…I wondered if she…she survived?" He felt hope rise in his chest and tried to fight it down. "I can see the resemblance perfectly."

King Zamir went silent, his expression thoughtful. "I knew you would wonder that."

"And?"

"*And*…there will be no further questions." King Zamir raised his staff, the red jewel beginning to glow. Liam jerked away, but abruptly the world faded to black.

CHAPTER 11

Slowly, Liam drifted awake, finding himself in his own bed with Brendon standing over him.

"It's about time!" Brendon said. "Are you just going to continue getting yourself knocked out often, or should I keep my hopes up?"

"I hope not." Liam rubbed his head, which ached fiercely. "What happened?"

"You blacked out during your meeting with King Zamir. Head trauma, he said."

"Oh?" Liam sat up, his mind fuzzy. "I don't remember a meeting with King Zamir."

Brendon shrugged. "Weird. All I know is that when I was dragging you around the base for the second time this week, you were mumbling about a Ree."

"Oh."

"Who is Ree, again?" Brendon asked.

"She was a friend," Liam said softly. "A very long time ago, that is."

"Ah...did you love her?"

"What?" Liam exclaimed.

"When you talk about her, you look dreamy," Brendon said with a straight face.

"I do not!" Liam said indigently. "But...I did love her, yes. She was so kind, and she had the most gorgeous red hair and—" Liam broke off when he realized he couldn't picture Ree's face or remember her eye color. "What's wrong with me? I can't remember her!"

"Don't panic," Brendon said soothingly. "Take a deep breath."

Liam glanced to his dresser, his heart picking up pace. The holograph had vanished from its place. What had happened? Why couldn't he remember Ree—or what had happened after he'd returned from the forest?

Brendon rubbed Liam's shoulder. "It'll be okay. I'm sure it'll come back to you soon. You did recently have a head injury. That often causes temporary amnesia."

"Right, right." Liam felt his panic start to cease. "I'll remember soon…I hope so anyway."

Glancing at her wrist comm, Anise winced at the time as she hurried to High Councilor Mills' office and knocked on the door.

"Come on in."

Anise cracked open the door and stepped inside. "Councilor Mills, I brought you the bot." She placed it on his desk.

"Thank you very much." High Councilor Mills smiled at her. "We are very grateful to you."

"It was my honor to assist the Qor," Anise replied.

"I heard you were injured," he mentioned, worry in his eyes. "Is everything alright?"

"I was, but it's…minor." Anise glanced at the closed door. "My abilities…helped."

"Of course." Mills nodded. "I'm pleased to hear it. You are invaluable to us, Commander."

"Thank you, Sir."

"That is all," Mills decided. "Have a pleasant afternoon."

"You as well." Anise bowed slightly before exiting the office. She strolled down the hall, knocking on Councilor Indu's office door.

"Come in."

The door slid open, and Anise stepped inside. Councilor Indu smiled at her, taking a seat. "Ah, Commander Desson. Please sit."

Anise sat in one of the plush chairs across from him. "You said you had an assignment for me?"

"Yes, I do," Councilor Indu confirmed. "As you know, our base on the planet of Eranook recently suffered an attack from the Embleck Army."

"I did hear about that. Was anyone hurt?" Anise shifted in her chair, wondering what this had to do with her.

"A few people were, but they were mainly targeting this." The Councilor pulled up a hologram of a small rectangular device.

"It's a coordinates map of our largest facilities. During the attack, they stole this, and I believe they took it to their own base near the planet of Nockalore." He sighed heavily. "Fortunately, it has an advanced lock on it, but we must retrieve it before they discover the code. If they do, they will have our bases in the palm of their hand."

Anise examined the hologram. "And the assignment is to infiltrate the base and steal it back?"

"Precisely. Of course, you will select a few members of your team to accompany you."

He leaned forward in his chair. "I'm sure you know that this mission would be more dangerous than most. If you get caught, it's unlikely to receive our interference."

"I understand." Anise nodded. "I'll still take it. But I don't want to bring anyone. I couldn't put my team members in that kind of danger."

Councilor Indu nodded. "I do understand your concerns, but I very much doubt that your brother will want you to go alone. Besides, it's a difficult mission to take on alone."

Anise sank in her seat slightly. "You're probably right. I'll select a few people."

Councilor Indu sat back with a grin. "Splendid. You will be providing a great service to the Qor. Now, time is of the essence here. We'll send your squad out tomorrow morning."

"Yes, Sir." Anise stood, shook his hand, and left the office.

"Anise?"

Anise turned in surprise. "Oh, Caiden. I wasn't expecting you."

"Keisha said you had a meeting with Indu for an assignment," Caiden said.

"I did," Anise agreed.

"So, what did he want?"

"He had a job for me. I head out tomorrow."

"A job doing what?"

"I'm going to retrieve a stolen map from one of the Embleck Army's bases."

Caiden's face became a mask of horror. "He wants you to sneak onto an Embleck Army's base?"

"Yes." Anise let him hang for a moment before adding, "And you can come with me. If you want."

"Oh, good." He looked relieved but only for a moment. "I'd still feel better if it was me going instead of you."

"Cay," Anise sighed. "I'll be fine. Trust me; I know what I'm doing. I need to go pick the team members that will join me."

"Okay," he sighed. "Want some help?"

"Sure," Anise accepted as they continued down the hall.

CHAPTER 12

The following morning, Anise scanned her selected squadron: Caiden, his best friend Tyler, Tyler's cousin, Keisha, and another of her team members, Lydia.

The fabric of Anise's forged Embleck seemed cold against her skin. Each of her team members wore the same, and the sight sent a shiver up Anise's spine.

Anise shifted anxiously, doubts running through her mind. *What if I'm not qualified to do this? What if I fail? What if we get caught?*

Behind them, a small shuttle landed, and one of her team members leaped out. "Here you go, Commander. One Embleck Army shuttle, as ordered."

Anise pulled herself form the depressive fog of worry, mustering up a smile. "Wow, Jack, this is wonderful! How did you all manage it?"

"We lifted a ship from the repair shop on Carnos. When you arrive, it'll be just like you're bringing it back. No one should be suspicious."

"Thanks again, Jack." Anise shook his hand and climbed aboard with her team members right behind her.

"Okay, Tyler, take the controls. Everyone else down to the cargo hold."

The ship rocked and rose, taking off into space as they filed into the small, dark room lined with large wall compartments. Anise turned, addressing her team. "Alright, everyone. I have a map that Councilor Indu provided, so I'll be navigating. Once I get us up to the third floor, Lydia and Keisha will trick the guards away from the navigational room. After recovering the map, we'll take the ship down to Nockalore's surface, and rendezvous with a Qor ship."

"After we get off the base, we'll stay in the forest until our ship comes?" Lydia confirmed.

"Yes," Anise said. "If we can't get to the forest, there are escape pods we can use. If something happens to me, Caiden is in charge."

Anise paused. "And if we get captured...there's nothing that can be done. So, on that cheerful ending note, we're probably

151

in Embleck territory. Everyone select a compartment and get in. Be as quiet as possible. Got it?"

Her team nodded and began climbing into each compartment.

Caiden tapped her on the shoulder. "There's one compartment that's large enough for two. Want to share?"

"Sure."

Anise climbed in after Caiden, closing the compartment door. Anise stared at Caiden's face inches from hers. He was pale, even in the darkness, worry vibrating off of him.

"Is everything okay?" Anise whispered. "If you're worried about today, it'll be fine."

"I'm not really worried about if we can complete the mission; I just…I just don't want to risk anything happening to you."

Anise sighed again and leaned against him. She wished she could tell him about her powers so maybe he would worry less, but Councilor Indu had warned her that if anyone knew, it would put her and them in danger.

"Don't worry about me. You can't focus on me all your life. I'll be fine."

"I know, I know. But I'm your big brother. Isn't it my job

to worry about you?"

"I thought the big brother's job was to be absolutely exasperating and to annoy your little sister endlessly," Anise said thoughtfully and wrinkled her nose at him. "You do a pretty good job at that."

"Ha ha, very funny." Caiden grinned, shoving her with his shoulder, and she pushed him back.

"We're approaching the Embleck hangar." Tyler's voice came through the room again. "Prepare for landing."

The room went dead silent as the ship slowly landed. Tyler came down and silently ushered everyone out.

Anise scanned the Embleck shipyard. Technicians and pilots alike hurried around, ignoring Anise and her crew as they disembarked.

Holding her breath, Anise led her crew through the shipyard, trying to stay near the outskirts in hopes of not being asked for identification. They slipped around ship after ship, finally reaching the large elevator.

Anise pulled a stolen key card from her pocket and slid it into the slot. The elevator doors opened, and her crew shuffled in. Anise hit the button for the third floor, and the elevator began to rise.

Tapping her toe on the floor, Anise eyed the buttons lighting up as they rose. The doors chimed, sliding open.

Anise peeked out of the elevator—and immediately jerked her head back in when she saw a group of Embleck soldiers walking down the hall, straight for the elevator.

"Quick, press the button for another floor!" Anise whispered, and Lydia pressed the button for the fourth floor.

The elevator rose up, and a moment later, the doors opened. This time the hall was empty.

Faking confidence she didn't feel, Anise led her team down the hall. She glanced around a corner and saw a group of Embleck soldiers talking with each other.

"There are some soldiers over there, and they're not leaving anytime soon. Time for Plan B."

Tyler sighed. "Well, you know a mission's going well when you have to change to Plan B before you even get to use Plan A."

"What's Plan B?" Caiden whispered, ignoring Tyler.

"That." Anise pointed up at a large air vent on the wall. "Lydia, see if you can hack into the system and shut down the vents on these floors. They'll notice, but not right away. We should have enough time."

Lydia pulled out a small hacking device and began tapping. A tense few seconds later, she smiled and said, "I've got it. Hurry, I'm not sure when they'll find out."

"Cay, help me up," Anise instructed.

Caiden lifted Anise up onto his shoulders. Anise reached into her pocket and pulled out a small electric screwdriver.

Anise carefully took off the vent's coverings and looked inside. "Alright, we're good. Come on."

With a boost from Caiden, Anise climbed up inside the vents and reached down to help Keisha and Lydia as the boys lifted them up. Quickly, the girls helped pull the boys up, and Tyler placed the cover back over the vent.

The group carefully crawled through the vents until Lydia called softly, "Stop! There's a vent opening right here that will leave us near the navigational center."

"Perfect." Anise caught sight of the vent, leaning down to peer through

No Embleck soldiers were visible, so Anise carefully removed the vent covering. She tucked it back in the vent and leaped down.

The landing jarred Anise's ankles, and she rolled them, making sure she could walk before giving the all-clear. Caiden and Tyler lowered the girls down before jumping down. Anise gestured them forward as they crept down the halls.

Anise stopped at the corner and leaned around. The door at the end of the hall was where they needed to be, and it was, guarded by two Embleck soldiers. The symbol on the door matched the Embleck code for *navigational center*, exactly as High Councilor Mills had said it would.

"Lydia, Keisha, your turn," Anise whispered.

Tense, Anise watched as the girls approached the guards at the door and began making a complicated series of hand gestures to signal it was time for the changing of the guard. If they made one movement wrong, the guards could sound the alarm.

They finished the movements, and after an agonizing second, the guards at the door gave a quick, sharp nod and marched away.

Lydia and Keisha took their places, and Lydia snapped her fingers, signaling to Anise that the coast was clear.

"You all stay here," Anise whispered. She pulled out the code Councilor Indu had given her to unlock the door and crept over. She ducked behind Lydia and typed in the code. With a soft click, the doors slid open.

Anise slipped inside and glanced around. The empty

room was full of giant screens with maps displayed across them, and a glass tray with a lid and lock, full of hard drives. She tip-toed over and scanned them but didn't recognize the map she needed.

Time was ticking, and worry started creeping up on Anise. She had to find this drive and get out before she got her whole team caught. Sooner or later, the guards would realize their mistake, or someone would come in and find her.

Anise caught herself starting to panic. She took a deep breath and squared her shoulders.

You can do this, Anise told herself. *Just breathe and think.* She examined the room more carefully and caught sight of a blank screen with another locked box beside it.

Yes. Anise pulled a special hairpin from her hair. It was specially designed to deactivate digital locks.

Anise carefully inserted the pin into the lock, which fritzed and deactivated. She reached inside and took the drive before creeping back to the door.

Darting across the hall back to her team, Anise waved Keisha and Lydia over.

"I got it!" Anise exclaimed quietly.

"Good job!" Tyler whispered, and Caiden gave her a hug.

"Time to go." Anise pressed a button on her comm, alerting the Qor that they'd found the map.

Trying to act casual, Anise and her team strolled down the halls. Anise peeked down the next hall before gesturing for her team to follow her.

"Something's wrong," Caiden worried aloud. "There should be more guards, or traps or *something.*"

"Don't worry," Lydia touched his arm, and Anise noted the slight flush of her brother's face.

Anise grinned, fully intending to tease her brother once they'd returned safely. Abruptly, a shrill alarm echoed through the base, and her team collectively jolted.

"Don't run, try to act natural," Anise ordered, picking up her pace. "The escape pods are on this floor. Let's go."

A group of Embleck soldiers slid around the corner, raising weapons at them. Anise whipped out her pistol, shooting the soldiers as the rest of her squadron did the same.

The last Embleck soldier collapsed, and Anise shoved her pistol back in her belt. "Go, go!"

As they tore through the halls, the sound of pursuit became louder. Anise skidded to a stop, an idea hitting her. "Everybody go! I'll catch up!"

The second her teammates were out of sight, the Embleck Army's guards ran around the corner. Anise reached out her ability and latched onto their minds.

Black out.

The guards dropped to the ground, and Anise bolted, quickly catching up with her team. The alarm continued to ring as Anise heard more Embleck soldiers approaching. She held the map tight against her chest—it would get back to the Qor, no matter what.

Anise's breath came quick, and each movement sent a bolt of pain through her leg where she had broken it in her shipwreck all those years ago.

A spark of hope flared in Anise's chest as she caught sight of the escape pods—maybe they could escape after all—

At that moment, dozens of guards appeared around the corner behind them. Anise stopped a second to catch her breath. There was no way they could escape like this. It would take too long to launch the escape pod, and the guards could turn off the launch, trapping them all.

Anise made a split-second decision.

"Everyone in," Anise ordered, and her team followed her instruction. She shoved the drive into Caiden's hands and slammed down the launch button. The door shut, leaving her alone on the base.

"Wait, Anise, what are you doing?" Caiden pressed his hands against the glass door.

Anise placed a light kiss on the glass. "Love you."

"NO, wait!" Caiden shouted. A robot reached for the deactivate launch button, and Anise sliced its claw arm off just as the pod launched.

Drained, Anise's power wouldn't activate. She raised her sword, but she was only one person against an army—swiftly captured, handcuffed, and led to the dungeon with her head held high.

CHAPTER 13

Liam sat on the edge of his bed, reading a book—well, *trying* to read a book. However, he had read the same paragraph three times and still didn't understand what was happening in it.

Something distracted Liam, and he couldn't seem to focus. His hum had shifted to a higher, faster pace, and since it had shifted, he felt off.

Liam sighed and slammed the book shut. The sound was strangely refreshing, so he opened it and slammed it shut repeatedly.

In the process of doing this a sixth time, Brendon burst through the doors. Liam glanced up to see an urgent expression on his friend's face, which quickly morphed into confusion.

"Why are you opening and closing that book, Sir?"

Liam flushed and shut the book quietly, placing it on the table. "Never mind why. What's so urgent that you had to interrupt my...reading."

Brendon straightened, his expression neutral. "The guards captured Commander Desson."

Liam shot to his feet, book slamming forgotten. "How? Was there anyone else?"

"She was here with the other Commander Desson and a few people. They managed to steal back their map."

Liam blinked. "The other Commander Desson? Is she married?"

Brendon tilted his head to the side. "Why is *that* the first question you're asking?"

"It—it's not. No reason."

"Well, no. Our reports say that they are siblings."

"I see." Liam shook his head as his hum increased in volume.

"High Commander Ankor is already waiting for you at the interrogation room. We're both supposed to be there now."

"Very well. I'll get my mask and meet you there."

Brendon nodded and dashed off.

Liam donned his half-mask and nodded to the guards who slid the interrogation room's doors open. He stepped into the room with High Commander Ankor and Brendon close on his heels.

For a moment, no one said anything, allowing Liam to examine Commander Desson.

Pinned against the wall in a metal contraption, bruised and bloody, she still held her head high. They briefly locked eyes before Liam turned away. She stared at them with fire in her expression and finally spoke.

"I suppose you have come for my interrogation," she said in a bored tone.

Despite her being the enemy, Liam had to admire her bravery. "And I suppose you're correct."

Liam took a step closer and saw her draw away slightly. No one else seemed to notice, but he took a step back anyway.

"Don't worry." Liam closed his eyes so he could read her

163

mind. "This will only take a moment."

Liam concentrated and reached out for her mind…only to find silence. He furrowed his brow. No, that was impossible. Surely, he'd be able to read her mind. He pulled harder but heard nothing.

Using all his power, Liam dug down as deep as he could and faintly heard the words *hard drive*.

"So, Commander." Liam's mind spun as he tried to pull himself together. "You came here for your precious hard drive."

She tossed her unraveling braids. "And what if I did?"

"Perhaps we should use some more physical methods to influence her," High Commander Ankor whispered to Liam.

"No."

"No?" Ankor repeated.

"I'm not going to let you torture her." Liam rubbed his temples against the headache that was forming.

"What are you talking about?" Ankor hissed. "How else do you expect an answer?"

Liam bit back a sigh. He didn't know why…but Ankor wouldn't hurt her. Not if he had any say in it.

"Didn't anyone teach you blockheads that whispering is

rude?" Commander Desson said haughtily.

Brendon smirked behind his hand, but High Commander Ankor didn't find the remark amusing.

"That's it," he said. "Tell us how you got on this base, how your team got away, and what you came for, or you shall regret it!"

Commander Desson rolled her eyes. "Who let him out of his cradle? Don't you people know the afternoon is ideal napping time for whiny children?"

Brendon snorted and chuckled quietly. High Commander Ankor turned red and took a step closer to Desson.

Liam rubbed his head harder. Sighing, he gave up on her, and instead, he addressed High Commander Ankor.

"There were others with her. Do we have any of them?"

"They all somehow escaped," Ankor said. "And *she* won't tell us how."

Liam was curious how five people had infiltrated the base, four had escaped, yet they managed to capture the best one. However, he didn't bother to question the fact. It wouldn't change anything now.

"Well, we may have lost the map, but now we have a living girl who's seen it." High Commander Ankor stepped closer to her. "Tell us where the Qor's bases are, or face the consequences."

"No," Commander Desson snapped.

"WHAT?" Ankor boomed. "What was that?"

"I will not tell you anything. Ever. Doesn't matter what you do. I let a bunch of Embleck brats take over the galaxy."

"Brats?" Liam arched an eyebrow.

"Yes, brats." Commander Desson met Liam's eyes as though daring him to argue with her. "You're all a bunch of selfish brats who are trying to take over everything just to make up for the lack of, well—anything—in your lives when really you'll never find it."

High Commander Ankor's face became redder and redder as she spoke, while Brendon looked slightly ashamed.

"And you know what?" Commander Desson leaned forward, dropping her voice as though about to share a secret. "That thing that you'll never find is called happiness." She leaned back, looking satisfied. "You know, that good, warm feeling you get in your heart... Oh, wait! You don't have those, my mistake. You people wouldn't know what happiness was if it slapped you in the face. All you heartless, brainless idiots—"

High Commander Ankor backhanded her across the face at her remark. Liam opened his mouth to protest but quickly snapped it shut. He noticed Brendon had tightened his hands into fists. *She is the enemy,* Liam reminded himself.

"You foolish, incompetent girl! Tell me where the hard drive was taken right now!"

Commander Desson turned her head to High Commander Ankor and spat in his face. Everyone stood still for a single second before High Commander Ankor growled and lunged for her.

However, this time, Liam stepped between them. "That will be all, High Commander."

He took Ankor by the arm and began escorting him to the door. Brendon followed, but Liam could've sworn Brendon mouthed *sorry* to Desson before leaving.

"What was that?" Liam hissed at High Commander Ankor once they were in the hallway.

"But she—"

"That was unnecessary," Liam interrupted. "Next time, I will perform the interrogation alone."

High Commander Ankor turned red and stalked off. Liam sighed, his headache only worsening as his left for his rooms.

Long after the base lights were off, Liam laid across the foot of his bed, wide awake. The rapid pace of his hum kept him awake, along with fractured memories he couldn't quite picture.

Impulsively, Liam sat up and pulled on his heavy cloak and reached for his mask. He put it on reluctantly, standing and grabbing a little something that might give him the upper hand.

Liam raised his sword and sliced down, creating a portal. *Without Ankor, I'll be able to convince her to talk.*

Sheathing his sword, Liam stepped through. Black lights swirled around him as he took another step, appearing outside the prison doors. He snapped his fingers to close the portal and knocked on the door.

An annoyed guard opened the door, but his expression quickly changed to fear when he saw who stood outside.

"High Commander Monroy!" The guard gave a quick bow.

"That's alright." Liam stepped inside. "I'm here to interrogate Commander Desson."

"Yes, Sir." The guard handed him a set of keys. "Last door down."

"Thank you." Liam took the keys and set off down the hall.

"Oh, um, High Commander, Sir?" The guard called after him.

Liam turned around. "What?"

"Well, you see, High Commander Ankor was able to recover a syringe of what appeared to be a poisonous substance from the prisoner and—"

"When was High Commander Ankor with the prisoner?" Liam interrupted sharply. "I was supposed to be in charge of all interrogations of this prisoner."

"Oh, I…I suppose it must have been when they returned her to the prison?" The guard said this more as a question. "I'm sorry, Sir, I just was supposed to warn you. She's a lot more dangerous than she looks, if you ask me."

"Thank you for the information." Liam turned and started back down the hall. *You have no idea.*

Liam approached to the final door, took a deep breath,

and unlocked it before stepping inside. No he stood in a small, narrow room with a door on the other end: the lobby room for the prison cell. Liam walked over to the other door and peered inside through the small, barred window.

Commander Desson sat on the floor, her back against the wall with her head hanging limply.

Liam heard a sniffle from her, followed by a quiet choking sound. She was crying, he realized, and instantly felt like an idiot for not realizing sooner. It was hard to believe this was the girl who had yelled at all of them. Now she just looked so small.

Her tears grew louder, and Liam felt his stomach ache at the sound. Guilt surged through him, and he started to leave when she looked up.

"Oh. It's you." She used her gloved fingertips to wipe away the last of her tears and stared up at him with the same fire in her face, despite her shivering.

Liam hesitantly unlocked the door and stepped inside the cell. "It's me." He took a step closer to her.

Commander Desson stood up and lunged for him, struggling against her chains. Liam jerked away, slamming back against the door.

The cell filled with a clanking sound as Commander

Desson's chains stopped her from reaching any further. Liam kept his back pressed against the door warily. She leaned forward, glaring at him with the intensity of a thousand suns.

Liam was quite positive she would have liked to throw him in the sun at that moment…yet his heart seemed to beat faster. Somehow, her intense teal eyes seemed almost familiar.

Realizing she couldn't reach him, Commander Desson sighed and said, "Great, what do you want now?" She crossed her arms. "Have you come to try and pry the secrets of the Qor from me, like that other guy?"

Liam had been in the room for less than thirty seconds, and somehow, she had already caught him off guard. "Wait, what other guy?"

"You know, the other guy. Kinda has a face like a weasel biting into a lemon."

"Oh, you mean High Commander Ankor," Liam realized. No one else in the Embleck Army could match up to that description.

"Yeah, him." Commander Desson casually waved her hand. "He doesn't make very good company."

"What was he doing down here?" Liam asked her.

Commander Desson scoffed. "Why should I tell you anything?"

"Because I have something you want." Liam unhooked his secret weapon—a canteen—from his belt and held it up to show her as he took a slow step forward.

"What is it, poison?" Commander Desson said sarcastically. "Cause if it is, I don't want it."

"No, it's not poison," Liam said, taking another step. "It's water."

Commander Desson gave a little jerk as though she was about to try to pry it away from him. "Okay, so if it's non-poison water, why are you offering it to me...and what do I have to do to get it?"

Liam looked into her teal eyes, wondering if it was possible he had seen them before. "You just have to tell me precisely what High Commander Ankor wanted with you. Tell me exactly what he did, and this whole thing is yours."

"That's not too hard." Commander Desson was staring at the canteen he still held. "I haven't had water all day."

"It can be all yours," Liam said. "Plus—" he reached into his pocket and pulled out something else. "—this too."

Commander Desson's eyes widened at what he held. "A protein bar."

"You can have both of these if you tell me about Ankor

and just a few other things," Liam coaxed.

Commander Desson eyed him suspiciously. "Why are you offering me this? What is so important about this Ankor that you're offering a prisoner food and water?"

"I need to know for...reasons you wouldn't understand," Liam said. In truth, he wanted to know why Ankor was so interested in this particular girl. If there was valuable information he could get her to share, it would please King Zamir and give him a one-up against Ankor.

And, if he was really, really honest with himself—which he wasn't—something in him wanted to offer Commander Desson some relief.

"Tell me all about Ankor, and the canteen is yours. Answer a few other questions, and the food is yours too."

"...Fine," Commander Desson said. "What all do you want to know?"

"From start to finish of when Ankor was here," Liam said.

Commander Desson sighed. "Alright. Well, he came down here with two other soldiers and dragged me into this little room. They tied me to the chair and started asking questions about the Qor. The Ankor guy had this case with him—"

"What kind of case?" Liam interrupted.

"It was a little bigger than my hand, and it was black. It had all these little tools in it."

Liam nodded. He had a lot of experience with prisoners and interrogation, so he knew what case she meant. It held many small tools and a recording device. Liam was often at interrogations so he could use his powers. Another officer would try to extract information from the prisoner while Liam would slip into their mind and pick out the answers he needed.

"Anyway," Commander Desson said. "He started taking out tools. There was this little stick with a handle and a sharp metal end. He kept poking me with that, and I called him a few things in return."

Now that Liam's eyes had adjusted to the dark a little, he could see what she meant. There were tiny dots of dried blood on the tender skin beside her nose, the corner of her eye, and her temples.

"After that, there were some eye drops that burned, and when I still didn't answer, he yelled a lot." Commander Desson looked like she was recalling the event. "Oh, and when I still wouldn't talk, he brought out this little device. I think I was supposed to be intimidated, but it just looked like an eyelash curler, so it wasn't as frightening as he had hoped, I think. It did have spikes, though, so definitely not a regular eyelash curler.

More like an eyelash curler of doom or something."

Liam, who had no idea what an eyelash curler looked like—or even was—just nodded. "I see. Was that all?"

"Well, after he was done using that—which took a long time—somebody called his comm. He answered all worried, and the other soldiers brought me back here, but they got my syringe away from me before I could make any use of it. "

Liam nodded, moving on to his next question. "One of the guards said you had a syringe. What was in it? Poison?"

"…Yes. I had a syringe of it hidden," Commander Desson admitted. "Just in case. Is that all?"

"Alright." Liam handed her the water canteen.

Commander Desson accepted it and stepped away from him until her back was against the wall. She sank to the floor and immediately began drinking.

Liam watched as she drank at least half of it without stopping. Finally, she put it down and stared at him.

"You said you had more questions. What are they?"

Liam shifted from crouching to sitting and removed his heavy cloak, dropping it beside him. "Well, I guess my next question is this: do all Qor members carry poison with them?"

Commander Desson dropped eye contact. "I…I can't tell you that."

"Why not?" Liam asked, confused. Why was keeping that secret so important?

"Because it could jeopardize the Qor's future," Commander Desson snapped. "And I wouldn't do that, not even for a three-course meal and freedom."

"It won't hurt anything," Liam said.

"It could," Commander Desson retorted. "You might as well go."

"I'm not done quite yet," Liam said. "I still have questions."

"Like what?" Commander Desson frowned.

"Like…how did you get the ship you used to sneak onto this base?"

"Well…I guess telling you won't hurt. It was taken from your base." Commander Desson snorted. "You don't have very good security."

"That's odd," Liam mused. "I haven't seen any reports about a missing ship."

"I told you, the security was lacking. They probably

didn't even know we stole it."

"Still, that's odd." Liam mentally filed that away and moved on to his next question. "Where is your team taking that hard drive?"

Commander Desson actually laughed. "You really think I would tell you that?"

"No," Liam admitted. "But it was worth a shot."

"Actually…" Commander Desson leaned forward. "I'll make you a deal. You tell me two things I need to know, and I'll answer your earlier question about the poison."

"I thought I was trying to get info from you, not the other way around," Liam raised an eyebrow. "You might make a good Embleck Army interrogator."

"Oh, don't try to be charming." Commander Desson rolled her eyes.

Liam coughed a little, glad his mask hid his sudden flush. "I wasn't being charming; I was proposing an idea."

"Charmingly," Commander Desson pointed out. "Deal or no deal?"

"Deal," Liam said. "What do you need to know?"

"A Qor base on Eranook was attacked, but no one knew

where it was. How did you find it?"

"His Majesty King Zamir told me about it," Liam said. "He was the only one who knew where it was."

Commander Desson was silent for a moment. "Alright."

"Now, tell me, do all Qor members carry poison?"

"I don't know about everyone," Commander Desson wouldn't meet his eyes. "I brought one because I knew the risks of this assignment."

"We once captured a spy who had a poison syringe as well as another we couldn't identify. What was it, and do all spies carry it and the poison?" Liam asked.

"I don't know about spy gear," Commander Desson said. "I don't know any spies. But I wouldn't be surprised if they had the poison too."

"Why, though?" Liam pressed. "Why would they carry one syringe? That won't work against all of us."

"It's not for you; it's for them!" Commander Desson exclaimed. "Because they know if a spy gets caught, they'll be killed anyway, so they might as well make it easy. Besides, you can't betray the Qor if you can't speak."

"Oh," Liam whispered.

He privately resolved not to tell King Zamir about that. He didn't like the idea of taking the only escape from the spies, most of whom were innocent people. And something in Liam was deeply disturbed by the fact that he was probably one of the people the Qor soldiers were most warned about.

Liam knew he was feared throughout the galaxy…but for some reason, that fact didn't seem like an accomplishment.

When did it ever feel like an accomplishment? Liam wondered. For some reason, he didn't feel like being feared was a good thing…even though King Zamir constantly told him it was.

"And anyway," Commander Desson said quietly. "If you don't use it on yourself…you get a shot at one Embleck soldier." She stared up at him, a cold darkness in her teal eyes. "When I came on this base…I knew I wanted my shot to be at you."

Liam looked at her for a second, slightly disturbed by the hate in her eyes—but more disturbed that those eyes still seemed familiar. He noticed he was staring and quickly took on a casual position before shrugging. "Yeah, I get that kind of thing a lot—comes with the role."

Commander Desson seemed confused for a moment. The expression quickly faded, though, and was replaced with loathing. For a split second, Liam felt guilty, but it evaporated quickly.

"Is that all?" Commander Desson asked tersely.

"Not quite." Liam snapped back to the present as he stood up and started to pace. "You snuck in here with four other people and stole back your hard drive. You were captured while everyone else escaped. You—" he paused mid-pacing. "You took my cloak."

Commander Desson leaned against the wall with Liam's cloak wrapped around her, her expression annoyed. "It's freezing down here, and my chains let me reach it." She shook her chains at him. "I'm from the desert. I don't like the cold."

"Well, you look very cozy." Liam forced sarcasm into his voice because she did look cozy and warm and *perfect*. He shook his head and tried to regain his composure. "The colors of the Embleck Army look good on you." He put a confident expression on and hoped it looked real. Commander Desson's face took on a disgusted expression.

"I'd rather freeze, thank you." She shoved the cloak away and instantly started shivering again.

Liam picked up his cloak and knelt down beside her again. "Okay, last question. How did your team escape when you got captured? I probably shouldn't tell you this, but you're often referred to as one of the best around here. Your capture doesn't make sense."

Commander Desson sighed heavily. "I'm only telling you to get it over with…and so I don't have to talk to that other idiot again. Besides, I guess it won't hurt anything." She lifted her head to look him in the eyes. "I stayed behind to fight off the guards so they could escape."

Liam was silent with shock. No matter how hard he tried not to be, he was amazed by this girl.

"You sacrificed yourself for your team?" he asked.

"Yes."

"I see…" Liam swallowed hard. Commander Desson was willing to die for her cause—her squadron, even.

Did he have anything in this galaxy he'd sacrifice himself for? Certainly not the Embleck Army…he didn't have any family to love…

A girl long dead. You've wanted to die for her for nine years.

"Alright, are you satisfied now?" Commander Desson asked.

Liam pulled himself back to the present. "Yes, you've been most helpful." He pulled out the protein bar and handed it to her. "Here."

Commander Desson took it, careful not to let her gloved hand touch his own. She ripped the wrapper open and began to eat it.

Once she finished, she glanced up at him disdainfully. "So, are you just going to stay here all night, or are you going to go back to whatever evil things you pass the time with?"

"I—um—well—I'll be leaving now that I have my information," Liam stuttered.

"Oh, wonderful," Commander Desson said. "Now, if you will excuse me, I'm going to sleep."

"Of course." Liam nodded and stepped away. He glanced back at her shivering on the floor and felt another stab of sympathy.

Liam walked back over and laid his cloak in front of her. Commander Desson stared up at him with confusion.

"Here. I know you don't want it, but it gets colder at night." Now, Liam wasn't positive that was the truth, but he needed some excuse so she would take it. She just kept staring at him, so he turned away and left.

As Liam locked the door, he glanced back to see her reach for the cloak.

CHAPTER 14

Anise jolted awake with a loud clang, followed by a torrent of foreign words. Squeezing her eyes closed, she rolled over, wishing this was only a nightmare. Despite the discomfort of the prison, she had slept well due to sheer exhaustion.

Now that she was awake, though, worries flooded her mind, and she sat up. Anise pulled High Commander Monroy's cloak tighter around herself. The warm, heavy cloak, for some strange reason, comforted her.

Anise pulled it up higher to cover her nose and inhaled the slight scent of ash and something else...but she couldn't figure out what.

Abruptly, a faint humming sound filled the air, sounding as though it was right outside her cell door.

"Is something there?" Anise called, not really expecting a

response.

"Hello." High Commander Monroy stepped inside. "Sorry, I didn't mean to frighten you."

"It's fine," Anise managed, her pulse racing.

High Commander Monroy nodded slightly.

Anise glanced behind him, but there weren't any guards with him. Reaching out with her mind control, she searched for something—anything—to take control of. Monroy's presence was simply void—hollow and cold.

"Did you want something?" she finally asked him.

"Oh, yes." He seemed to snap out of a trance. "They will be here momentarily, so I came to fetch my cloak and canteen."

"Sure." Anise handed him the cloak and canteen, which he accepted with a soft thank you.

"I need to go." He turned to leave. "I'll see you soon."

"Wait." Anise realized what he had just said. "Why will I see you soon?"

"You're being taken to another base," Monroy said as he closed the door behind him.

"Well, great." Anise rubbed her temples, causing her chains to clank loudly.

Outside the door, the sound of many heavy footsteps echoed down the hall outside her cell.

"Oh well." Anise sighed again and stood up just as a dozen guards marched into her cell.

"Hey," she made the halfhearted greeting, but none of them responded.

Two of them unchained her from the wall and replaced the chains with handcuffs. Once they finished this process, one guard motioned to someone outside the door, and a tall, dark-haired man stepped inside. It took her a moment to realize he was one of the men who had been at her interrogation, the one who had apologized. He stood silently, running his eyes over her.

"It's time to go," he announced finally. "Come on. We have to meet High Commander Monroy on time."

The soldiers shoved her forward roughly, causing her to stumble.

"Hey!" the man snapped. "There is no reason to be rough with her."

Anise glanced at him. "Thanks," she whispered as they started walking again.

"Of course. I know this is all scary for you. I might as well make it easier."

"How did you know?"

"Experience." He sighed. "Don't worry too much. High Commander Monroy won't hurt you."

"Really?" Anise arched an eyebrow, doubtful.

"Yes." He nodded. "He may be intimidating, but I call him a friend. I know he wouldn't."

Anise felt a tiny spark of hope at that. "Thank you. What may I call you?"

He paused a moment as though calculating what he should reveal. "Technically, I'm Commander Grant, but you may call me Brendon."

"Thank you, Brendon." Anise smiled the faintest bit, and he returned it with a nod as they continued.

Liam paced in his room, energy vibrating through his body. His mind replayed his conversation with Commander

Desson over and over.

A sharp knock at the door drew him from his thoughts. "Come in."

High Commander Ankor stepped inside, an expression of barely concealed disgust on his face. "Monroy.

"Ah, High Commander!" Liam pasted on a fake smile. "What can I do for you?"

"King Zamir wants *you* to take Commander Desson to another base," High Commander Ankor ordered. "Alone."

Instant objections flooded Liam's mind. "Why alone? No guards? That doesn't make sense."

"*You* do not need that information," High Commander Ankor snapped. "You just need to do as your King orders you."

Liam ground his teeth together. "Anything else?"

"Indeed." High Commander Ankor had a nasty smile on his face as he handed Liam a small bottle full of thick, gray liquid. Liam's expression sank when he recognized it. "King Zamir has asked me to deliver this to you."

"I'm sorry, but that looks like my emotions elixir." Liam took the bottle with the tips of his gloved fingers.

"It is." The smile hadn't left High Commander Ankor's face. "King Zamir requests you to take another now."

"I took a dose yesterday!" Liam protested.

"Shall we discuss this with King Zamir?" High Commander Ankor asked, and Liam sighed heavily.

"No." Liam pulled out the cork and swallowed the contents in one sip. He shoved the cork back in as all emotion drained from his body, instant nausea settling in.

"Perfect." High Commander Ankor took the bottle and left, slamming the door behind him.

Liam moaned as the room began to spin, and he stumbled to his bed, flopping down face first. Several minutes passed before there was another knock on the door.

"Enter," Liam groaned.

Brendon pushed the door open, his eyes going to Liam, lying on his bed with his head buried in his pillow. Brendon raised an eyebrow, taking a step closer. "Ummm...how are you doing, Sir?"

Liam sighed, lifting his head. "Well, let me just say this: if the entire base blew up right now, my life would be greatly improved. As long as I was on said base, anyway."

Brendon's sigh echoed Liam's. "Sir, you can't say that

every single time I ask how you are."

"I've been telling you that for nine years now, haven't I?" Liam replied, offering Brendon a tired smirk. "I see no reason why it won't work for the next nine years. Not that I'll live that long," he added as an afterthought.

Brendon just stared at him sadly.

"Alright, what did you need?" Liam asked, sitting up and wincing when his head began to pound. "My head is killing me."

"I'm sorry, Sir, but we have the prisoner and are ready to leave."

"Oh…fine." A deep irritation settled in Liam's chest, something he suspected could be a side-effect of the potion.

Reluctantly, Liam stood and started to leave when he noticed Brendon giving him a strange look.

"What?" Liam asked roughly. "What's the look for?"

"You aren't wearing your mask," Brendon remarked.

"Who cares?" Liam snapped, instantly regretting it when he saw hurt flash across Brendon's face.

"I'm sorry," Liam sighed. "I just took my potion and—"

"Never mind." Brendon held up his hand. "I get it. Can you walk to the ship?"

Liam took another few steps, testing himself. The dizziness accompanying the movement made the room waver before his eyes. Carefully, he his mask from his dresser and put it on.

"Yeeess." He drew the word out. "I'm perfectly fine."

"I doubt it," Brendon muttered but didn't protest further.

"Come on," Liam ordered and started out before promptly crashing into the doorframe.

"Are you sure you're fine?" Brendon checked.

"Yes," Liam said and stepped out the door.

A dozen Embleck soldiers led Anise down the hallway, keeping her in the middle so she had nowhere to run. However, Commander Brendon had left to fetch High Commander Monroy.

I wonder... Anise reached out with her mind control, latching onto each of the soldiers' minds. "Tell me which one of you has the keys to these cuffs."

One soldier answered in a monotone. "I do."

"Then unlock these things already," Anise demanded.

The soldier did so, freeing her wrists. Anise spun around, ducking through the other Embleck soldiers and bolting down the hall.

The Embleck base acted as a maze, and Anise had no idea where she was going. She needed to find the escape pods, but she had no idea what floor she was currently on, nor where they might be.

For now, all that mattered was hiding. Anise ducked around a corner—

High Commander Monroy halted in the middle of the hall, eye widening as he caught sight of her. Behind him, the hall split into two—one of them Anise's key to freedom.

Anise swallowed hard, stepping out from behind the corner. High Commander Monroy simply stood and stared at her for a long moment. He wore his mask, but Anise could see his expression creased in…pain?

Finally, Monroy seemed to recognize the situation at the exact moment Anise made her move.

Anise dashed past High Commander Monroy's, spinning around him. He remained frozen for a split second before reaching for her.

"Wait!"

Panic tightened Anise's lungs as she felt his fingers brush her wrist. She expected him to heave her back, but his touch felt surprisingly gentle. His fingers wrapped around her wrist, but as Anise jerked away, her turquoise bracelet slipped off in his hand.

"My bracelet!" Anise started to reach for it but thought better, turned, and ran.

Anise paused only a second at the fork of the hall before picking the left hallway. She darted a quick glance over her shoulder, catching sight of Commander Monroy, staring down at the bracelet in his hand.

CHAPTER 15

Frozen, Liam stood in the middle of the hallway, dizzy and aching from his emotion elixir. Commander Desson had disappeared a few seconds ago, the sound of her footsteps fading away.

Liam glanced down at the bracelet in his hand. The smooth, round turquoise beads seemed familiar, and he rubbed his thumb over them.

Where have I seen these before? Liam wondered as a dozen Embleck soldiers ran up to him.

"Sir, where did she go?" the captain asked.

Liam stared at the bracelet. Some strange emotion rose in his chest, he felt a flicker of memory not quite there.

"Sir?" the captain insisted.

Liam looked up at the two hallways. He could almost sense Commander Desson down the left hallway.

"Right," Liam said softly. "She went right."

The soldiers raced off down the right hall, leaving Liam standing alone with the bracelet. A moment later, he slipped the bracelet into his pocket and continued to his ship.

Anise shifted from foot to foot as she waited in the hangar. Halfway down the hallway, she'd run into a group of soldiers, and she had been no match without a weapon. Now, she was currently surrounded by at least twenty guards and again handcuffed.

"So, who are we waiting for?" Anise asked the guards, and they all sighed. She guessed she was the most inquisitive prisoner they'd ever had, and it seemed to exasperate them.

"We are waiting for High Commander Monroy of the Embleck Armies to come and take care of you so we can go on break," one of the guards responded.

"Oh," Anise said. "You know, you could leave me here and go on break early."

All of the guards scoffed in unison. "That will not happen."

"Oh well. It was worth a try."

As Anise shifted her feet again, Commander Brendon entered the hangar. Seeing her, he smiled slightly, stepping over to her. "Just a touch longer. My High Commander will be here soon."

At that moment, a loud alert sounded, and a soldier by the door announced: "High Commander Monroy of the Embleck Army!"

High Commander Monroy entered the room, and Anise eyed him suspiciously. A glaze covered his eyes, though the rest of his expression remained obscured by his mask. He walked down the stairs slowly, occasionally jerking his hands as though he was afraid of falling.

Very strange.

Finally, Monroy reached the hangar and stopped a few feet in front of her. "Thank you, gentlemen, but I can take her now."

The guards nodded, saluting High Commander Monroy before they left. Brendon leaned in to whisper to Monroy, but Anise could hear what he was saying.

"Are you sure you want to take her there alone? Why don't you bring some guards?"

High Commander Monroy shook his head but then clutched it tightly. "No, King Zamir told me to take her alone."

"Why would he say that?" Brendon hissed.

"I don't know. He just said it would have better results," High Commander Monroy whispered harshly.

"Fine," Commander Brendon sighed and gestured to the ship. "After you, High Commander."

Monroy nodded and started towards the ship. He made it up those steps without incident. However, when he reached the door, he walked straight into the doorframe.

Anise snorted.

Monroy shook it off and carefully stepped inside but hit his head on the top of the doorframe. Muttering a foreign curse, he ducked, disappearing into the ship.

Commander Brendon sighed heavily before taking Anise's arm gently and leading her inside.

Definitely very, very strange.

Commander Brendon released her arm, hooking her handcuffs to the wall before dropping her bag on the far corner of the ship.

Anise sighed and glanced downward, but a small sparkle caught her eye. Her hairpin!

Brendon must've dropped it, she realized, snatching it off the floor and concealing it in her hand. It would do her no good now, but later…later, it might be useful.

Anise glanced around the ship. It was small enough that she could touch both the side walls at once. To her dismay, the control panel and steering were out of her reach.

Commander Brendon stepped off the ship, leaving her alone with High Commander Monroy. Anise tensed slightly, but he ignored her and went to the controls.

The ship rocked as it lifted into the sky, and Monroy typed coordinates into the control panel. Once they were in the air, he put the ship on autopilot and sank into one of the chairs with a heavy sigh. He glanced up at her with tired eyes.

"Sorry. I'm not used to using the autopilot."

"I can tell," Anise said, perhaps unjustly. To be fair, she struggled with the autopilot on larger ships as well—not that she'd admit it to him.

High Commander Monroy cocked his head at her as a button on the ship's dash lit up, casting light onto his face. Anise peered closer in the dim light, noticing his deep emerald eyes.

Anise furrowed her brow as she thought. She was almost positive she had seen those eyes before. *Maybe not. It's not like he's the only person in the galaxy with green eyes.*

The light continued flashing, and High Commander Monroy pressed a few buttons on the dash. A moment later, to Anise's surprise, he reached up and jerked off his mask. It fell to the floor with a clatter as he ran a gloved hand over his face.

Anise found herself staring at him, stunned at the difference without his mask. He had a handsome face with a slightly upturned nose and full lips.

Scolding herself for allowing a single positive thought about him, Anise pulled her eyes away. A vague sensation of familiarity drifted over her.

Anise glanced up, her eyes meeting his, and for a moment, she knew him.

Abruptly, the entire ship jerked wildly, tossing Anise across the floor and throwing High Commander Monroy across the dash.

He shot back to his feet and slammed down a button as the ship rocked again.

"What was that?" Anise exclaimed as the ship continued to rock.

"Qor ships. They're firing at us." He pulled hard on the controls. "Hang on!"

The ship jerked and swooped down, heading for the planet Redoridia. A moment later, they cut through the atmosphere, and Anise watched the trees whizzing by beneath them.

A blast struck the ship, throwing Anise into High Commander Monroy. Another shot hit, and they were both tossed into the wall. Anise met Monroy's wide...dazzlingly green eyes, flecked with gold and amber.

Shut up about his eyes!

Monroy twisted away from her, the stunned expression on his face fading. As he brushed past her, Anise recognized the sweet scent of his cloak as the same in his hair.

Why in the galaxy would I ever notice that?

Another blast rocked the ship, and Monroy stumbled to the control panel. While he was occupied, Anise pulled out her hairpin and began picking her handcuffs. With a soft click, they unlocked.

Anise dropped the handcuffs and dove for her bag. Inside, she found all her belongings, including her sword, strapped to the outside. Her fingers fumbled as she jerked it free. The sharp *clang* of the blade striking the floor caused Monroy to spin around.

"What are you doing?" he snapped, pulling free his own sword.

"I'm stopping you from hurting the Qor," she returned. "And you're in my way."

Anise raised her sword and slashed at him. He drew back and returned striking. A continuation of their battle in the forest ensued as the ship rocked.

Dodging a strike, Anise decided she had to end this battle—quickly. The ship wouldn't hold together much longer at this rate—if Monroy won their battle, he'd be able to destroy the Qor ships in an instant. An impulsive idea struck Anise, and she made her move.

High Commander Monroy struck at her, and she ducked, sliding under his arm. In one swift movement, she twisted around and stabbed her sword through the control panel and the engine underneath.

"What did you do?" Monroy exclaimed as the ship began to sputter and shake.

"I stopped you from hurting the Qor," Anise replied as

the engine sputtered, shivered, and stopped. She attempted to activate her powers to create a shield—but nothing happened.

They locked eyes as the ship began to freefall toward the planet's surface. Anise screamed for all it was worth, while Monroy remained completely silent.

They tumbled faster and faster, crashing into each other. Anise was thrown against the window, catching sight of the treetops just a few feet away.

"Brace yourself!" she shouted as the ship hit the trees, then the ground and everything went black.

CHAPTER 16

Liam awoke to light beaming into his eyes. He winced as his head began to throb.

With a groan, Liam sat up, clutching his head when the movement made it worse. He glanced around at the rubble surrounding him. The ship was a few feet away, at least half of it missing.

"Well, that's fantastic." Liam pushed himself to his feet, trying to ignore the ache that settled into each of his muscles. On the bright side, the effects of his potion seemed to have worn off. He could see straight again and was only a touch dizzy, but he guessed that was from the crash.

"Commander Desson." Liam braced himself on a piece of the ship, scanning the wreckage for her. "COMMANDER DESSON!"

"I'm here." Her voice drifted from the other side of the ship, and she came into view as she sat up. "And you're alive," she remarked, frowning at him.

"Don't sound so disappointed," Liam said.

Commander Desson took in the wreckage. "What now?"

"I guess we're going to walk to the base. I doubt we can fix the ship any faster."

"I'm not going anywhere with you," Commander Desson snapped.

"I think you will."

"Is that a threat?" Commander Desson crossed her arms.

"No, I just think it's a much better idea," Liam said. "It will increase our survival chances. Plus, you don't have anywhere else to go."

"Well…fine." Commander Desson groaned, rubbing her shoulder before panic flashed across her face. "Where's my bag?"

"I don't know, look around," Liam said, reaching for his own bag where it peeked out of the wreckage. Catching sight of Commander Desson's sword, he picked it up, placing it in his bag.

"Really helpful," she sighed.

As Commander Desson looked for her bag in the ruins of the ship, Liam froze. He held still and waited, sensing a tremor running through the ground.

"Look out!" Liam shouted, grabbing Desson and her newfound bag. He jerked them both away from the ship as it exploded in a wave of fire, showering them in debris.

The smoke soon faded, leaving them with Liam's arms wrapped around Commander Desson, surrounded by the remains of the ship.

Abruptly, Desson realized their proximity, quickly twisting away and punching Liam in the shoulder, disgust written across her face. "HOW DARE YOU PLACE YOUR MURDEROUS HANDS ON ME!"

"MURDEROUS? *MURDEROUS?* I JUST SAVED YOUR LIFE, YOU UNGRATEFUL LITTLE PEST!"

"ONLY BECAUSE YOU WANT TO TAKE ME BACK TO YOUR BASE TO INTERROGATE ME MORE, YOU EVIL MORON!"

Liam stared, incredulous. "ISN'T THAT BETTER THAN BEING DEAD?"

"NOT REALLY!" Commander Desson stepped further

away and began to dust herself off rapidly as though his touch had contaminated her.

Liam bit back a retort and reached into his bag, pulling out a spare pair of handcuffs.

"What do you think you're doing?" Desson snapped as Liam took hold of her wrist and locked one of the cuffs around it before locking the other one around his.

"I'm making sure you won't run off," Liam replied as he pocketed the key.

"Oh yes, make sure I don't run off and leap into one of the dozens of ships around here and fly off. Very important," Commander Desson said sarcastically.

Liam ignored her. "We need to get moving. The nearest base on this planet is at least a three days walk."

"Fine. Let's get moving, Monroy," Desson said, throwing her bag over her shoulder.

"It's High Commander Monroy," Liam stated in annoyance. He might not enjoy serving the Embleck Armies, but he took his position of high commander as an honor.

"I will address you as Monroy because I do not serve your side, nor will I ever. Therefore, you are not *my* high commander," Commander Desson snapped, giving him a nasty look. She turned around and stalked off, pulling him after her.

"Okay, okay. Monroy is fine," Liam said, hurrying to catch up, so she wouldn't pull on him.

"Good." She sent him a strange expression, missing the dip in the ground and tripped. Liam nearly fell as well but managed to grab her arm and pull them both up.

"Didn't I already tell you to keep your murderous hands off of me?" she grumbled and jerked her arm from his grasp.

"Sorry," Liam replied automatically.

Commander Desson shot him another odd look but continued walking. After a few minutes, she took a small green bottle from her bag and drank half the contents.

"What's that?"

"It removes aches and bruises from exterior trauma, like a ship crash." She paused a moment and offered, "You can have some if you like."

"…Thank you." Liam accepted the bottle and raised it to his lips but stopped midway. "Don't you need more?"

"No, I already took my dose." She said begrudgingly. "You might as well take it too. Besides, if you're in pain, you may slow us down."

Liam started to take it but stopped again.

"What now?" Commander Desson looked exasperated.

"Didn't you drink out of this bottle already?"

"Stars, just drink it already!"

Liam did as she said, relaxing slightly as his aches and pains seemed to fade away. He handed her the empty bottle, which she stuffed back into her bag. "Thanks."

"Sure," she responded and flashed him a quick smile.

Liam felt his face heat up, and he glanced away. *What's wrong with me? I haven't felt anything close to this...since I started taking my elixir.*

Curious, Liam reached out with his powers, touching her mind. A whisper brushed the edge of his mind, but he still couldn't get a clear connection. *It's like she's...immune to my abilities?*

"Come on!" Liam snapped back to reality and found Commander Desson tugging on him. She couldn't go any further without him while they were cuffed together.

"Sorry." Liam caught up, allowing her to continue.

"You know, for an evil robot weapon, you sure do say sorry a lot." Commander Desson smirked.

"I am not a robot!" Liam exclaimed. *Why would she say that?*

"Of course, my bad." Commander Desson stood up straighter, made her face completely blank, and said loudly, but without any emotion: "You there, do this and that. Kill those things. Move faster."

Liam winced. "Do I really sound like that?"

"Let's just say I pride myself on doing an excellent imitation of you."

They continued the walk in silence, giving Liam time to think. *I can't believe I actually sound like that. No wonder she called me a robot.*

"You must have some tiny, miserable version of a heart, though, since you shoved Brendon away before he got shot." Commander Desson's voice cut through his train of thought.

"He's a friend." Liam shrugged. "Wait, how do you know Brendon's name?"

"Will you punish him if I tell you how?" she asked, placing a hand on her hip.

"No, of course not!" Liam said. "I told you, he's a friend."

"Well then... he told me." Desson stared defiantly at him.

"That's strange," he muttered. *Why would Brendon do that?*

Commander Desson seemed to be waiting for more explanation, but when none was given, she shrugged and started walking again, faster than before, and Liam rushed after her.

It wasn't until the sun had set and the forest was bathed in moonlight that Liam and Commander Desson finally stopped to rest. Liam's muscled ached, both from the crash and the endless walking.

"Here." Liam took Desson's wrist, unlocking the handcuff on her wrist.

"It's about time." Commander Desson pulled her hand away, rubbing her wrist.

"And here." Liam offered her the hilt of her sword.

Commander Desson stared at him as though he was insane. "Why are you giving me this?"

Liam stared back at her. "Why wouldn't I?"

Commander Desson tilted her head to the side. "Because you know I'm an enemy. One that dislikes you, particularly."

Liam shrugged. "I don't know what's in this jungle. I wouldn't leave you without a way to protect yourself. Besides, if you really wanted me dead, you would have killed me in the forest."

Commander Desson's expression changed from suspicion to surprise. "How…"

"How what?" Liam asked as he started searching for some leaves to use as a bed.

"How can you say that so calmly?" Commander Desson asked, sheathing her sword.

"I suppose because it's true."

Commander Desson seemed surprised again. "I suppose."

Liam pulled some large leaves to use as a bed for himself while Commander Desson watched.

"Wait." Reaching into her bag, she pulled out a large fabric square.

"What's that?"

"It's a blanket." Desson rolled her eyes and shook it out.

When it was unfurled, it was large enough to fit at least two people. "You can share with me."

Now Liam stared as though she was crazy. "Why are you offering?"

"You saved me from the explosion." Desson didn't seem happy to admit it. "It's the least I can do."

Liam rubbed his fingers over his wrist, uncertain how to react. "Thank you."

"Do me a favor and grab the white sack from my bag," Commander Desson ordered, and Liam did so. She took it from him and removed a roll from inside. "I packed enough for two."

"Thank you again." Liam accepted it, and the two sat down for their small meal. Once the last rolls were gone, Commander Desson stood and brushed away breadcrumbs.

"I'm going to bed now." She lifted an eyebrow, staring at him warily. "Coming?"

"Alright." Liam stood, remaining a few feet away. Commander Desson watched him as she lowered himself to sit on the far edge of the blanket.

Liam could sense the nerves in her body language—she clearly still considered him a threat.

Liam stepped closer, slowly sitting on the edge of the

blanket furthest from her. "Listen…I know we're enemies, and I'm not expecting you to…trust me or anything."

Commander Desson drummed her slim, gloved fingers on her leg. "Go on."

Liam shifted. "You don't have to trust me, but you can trust that I won't hurt you. We're in this together, and I have no reason to want you dead."

"I'm an enemy of your army," Desson pointed out. "That's enough for most."

"Not for me." Liam propped himself up on his elbow. "You can sleep. I promise I won't hurt you."

"And you're not afraid of me killing you in your sleep?" Desson asked, her tone calculating.

Liam shrugged. *Not the worst way to go.*

Commander Desson glanced at the sword lying beside her. "Well…thank you."

"No need to thank me." Liam rested his head on his arm, lying on his side and facing away from her. "Good night."

"Night," Desson replied, only somewhat begrudgingly.

Liam awoke to the sound of breathing filling the darkness. He waited for it to fade as nightmares usually did, but this time it didn't.

Panic seized Liam as he realized that he wasn't alone. He heard a soft moan from behind him, and something warm touched his side.

Hesitating for only a moment, Liam reached for his sword lying beside him. He wrapped his fingers around the hilt, rolled over, swung his sword down…

…and stopped it mere inches from Commander Desson's sleeping face.

Liam froze in horror, slowly pulling the blade back and dropping it behind him. He let out a sigh of relief but paused in confusion. Why did he care about her at all?

The bright moonlight filtered through the trees, casting shadows on Desson's sleeping face. She looked…*angelic*, laying in the moonlight with her red hair fanned out around her face. The red wisps seemed to glow, giving her an unhuman aura, and something caught in Liam's chest.

Look at yourself. Liam scoffed at himself. *A monster admiring an angel.*

No way. He couldn't care anything for her. Even admiring her led him down an unwelcoming path. They were on opposite sides, so that was the end of that. Nothing more could ever happen. With a heavy sigh, Liam dropped his head and drifted back to sleep.

CHAPTER 17

The sound of chirps and leaves rustling pulled Liam from sleep, a stark change from the beeping alarm sounding through his room, usually long after he had already awoken.

Liam sat up, disoriented. The bright sunlight proved it was already morning—when had he last slept through the entire night?

Light filtered through the trees, giving the forest a golden glow. Liam raked a hand through his hair, glancing behind him. The blanket was empty, and a quick scan of the trees didn't reveal Commander Desson.

Liam quickly got to his feet, adrenaline setting in. Desson's bag still sat beside the blanket—if she'd attempted to escape, she would've brought it.

A faint sound caught Liam's attention, drawing him into the forest. As he followed the sound, it cleared into the voice of

Commander Desson.

Who would she be talking to? Liam wondered. *If she has a communication device…*

Liam stopped at the edge of a small clearing, his eyes locking on Commander Desson, sitting beside a shimmering pool of water. Relief washed over Liam—relief he immediately shut down.

Commander Desson's voice drifted through the trees as she softly sang. The lyrics were in a different language, but the melody seemed familiar.

Stepping forward, Liam crossed his arms and leaned his shoulder against the tree, listening. Desson's voice certainly wasn't perfect, but something about it pulled at his chest, a feeling of comfort settling over him.

Commander Desson tossed her hair over her shoulder, and Liam noticed it was dripping wet. She combed her fingers through it, finishing her song, and silence fell over the forest.

Liam barely breathed, uncertain how he could avoid scaring her. Desson sighed heavily before standing and twisting the water from her hair.

With a soft huff, Desson turned, locking eyes with him. She jolted, pressing a hand to her chest. "What are you doing?"

"Looking at you," Liam said vaguely, distracted by the glistening droplets of water dripping from her waist-length hair. The sunlight highlighted the gold in her dark red hair, shimmering with water.

"Uh huh…" Desson raised an eyebrow. "Looking *for* me?"

"That's what I said."

Desson pressed her lips together, struggling to fight off a smirk. "Yeah, sure."

Liam glanced up, uncertain at her amusement. "What?"

Desson shook her head, her lips turned up. "Why were you looking…*for* me?"

"I…didn't know where you were." Liam dragged his attention from her hair. "It's pretty self-explanatory."

"Oh, right." Desson gestured around them. "Well, here I am."

"What are you doing out here?"

"Washing my hair, genius." She shook her head, spraying him with water droplets. "It needed it. Now I'm just trying to detangle it enough for a braid."

"Can I help?" Liam instantly wondered where the offer had come from—what was he thinking?

"How are you expecting to help me?" Desson asked, crossing

her arms.

"Can I just try?" Liam asked.

Desson hesitated a moment before nodding. Warily, she turned around, darting him a look over her shoulder.

Liam swallowed hard and stepped forward, gently wrapping is fingers around a lock of her hair. Water seeped through his gloves, but Liam barely noticed.

Carefully pulling apart her tangled locks, Liam began dividing her hair into three sections, unable to quit wondering if it felt as soft and silky as he imagined it would.

Liam twisted a section around his finger, abruptly freezing. His heart skipped a beat as sunlight shone off a single lock of royal blue hair…the same color as his own.

"Is something wrong?"

Liam pulled himself back into the present, noting the way his fingers began to tremble. "No…no, it's fine."

So what? She dyes her hair. It's nothing, Liam told himself as he resumed, trying to shake the strange feeling creeping over him.

"Done," Liam said a moment later, handing her the end of the braid.

Commander Desson took her braid, an impressed expression

on her face. "Where did you learn to do this?"

Liam shrugged, a memory flashing through his mind. "My younger cousin, Tiffany. She was always asking me to play salon with her. She'd style my hair, and all her dolls. Anyway, she wanted to be the salon customer, so I learned how to braid her hair."

Commander Desson remained silent for a moment. "That's very...sweet of you."

"It was nothing." Liam stepped back. "Let's get moving. We have a long way to go."

"Right." Desson dropped eye contact. "I'll go grab my bag."

Liam nodded, watching as she disappeared into the trees. An odd ache thrummed through his chest as he waited for a moment before following her.

Anise stumbled to a stop at the edge of a swampy lake,

shooting a glance at Monroy. While Anise struggled to catch her breath, he seemed unphased, staring out over the lake with no emotion.

"I guess we'll have to swim it." Anise knelt and started rearranging the contents of her bag so she could fit her boots in.

"Swim?" High Commander Monroy sounded incredulous. "Can't we just walk around?"

"We could, but it would add another day on. I don't even know where it ends." Anise glanced up at him. "Why? Can't you swim? Or are you afraid of water?"

A red tint crept up his neck. "I can swim, and I'm not afraid."

Anise waited for more explanation, but he offered none, staring at the water with a closed expression. With a sigh, she pulled off her boots and tucked them into her bag. "Here, give me your boots."

"Why?"

"My bag is water-proofed. Trust me; you don't want to walk around with waterlogged boots and wet clothes sticking to you."

"Fine."

Anise placed them in her bag and shrugged off her vest,

dropping it in before she tucked the small dagger from the bag into her belt. Thankfully, the Embleck soldiers hadn't confiscated anything in her bag before the crash.

Anise tied back her hair, and High Commander Monroy handed her some bunched fabric. She glanced up in confusion, instantly realizing it was his shirt.

"You—I—what are you doing?" Anise stammered, noting it took her a minute to pry her gaze away.

Monroy's voice sounded almost shy, though Anise detected a hint of humor. "You said it yourself. I don't want to walk around with wet clothes all day."

"Don't use my own words against me," Anise reprimanded him as she stood. "I wasn't expecting *your shirt.*"

Monroy shrugged, crossing his arms over his bare chest. "I didn't want it getting wet."

Anise mentally scolded herself for being dismayed at his concealing gesture as she hefted her bag over her shoulder. She turned away from him and began wading into the lake.

Warm water soaked into the fabric of her forged Embleck uniform, and Anise wrinkled her nose. She took another step, only to slip on the algae-coated bottom.

High Commander Monroy lunged forward, his arm encircling her waist and pulling her up. Anise gripped Monroy's arm, her back pressed against his chest. Her pulse raced, and she reminded herself it was only from the near fall.

Anise glanced over her shoulder, meeting Monroy's emerald eyes. He quickly looked away, a notable flush creeping up his neck.

"Thank you," Anise said, her voice an octave softer than she meant it to be.

Monroy nodded before realizing their close proximity and quickly releasing her. Anise inhaled a shallow breath to calm her rapid heartbeat as she continued into the lake.

"What, no scolding about my murderous hands?" Monroy's teasing expression sent an odd sensation over Anise's skin, and she fought back a laugh.

"Not since you saved me from falling into the lake," Anise replied, unable to resist a smirk.

"The same lake we're about to swim through?"

"Why, are you disappointed? I suppose I could scold you anyway if you wanted me to."

"No, I'm good."

The ground dropped off, forcing Anise to swim. She shot a glance at Monroy, noting the lack of emotion on his face. A soft, warm object brushed across her foot, and Anise froze.

"Did you feel something?"

Monroy blinked, coming out of a daze. "What?"

"Never mind." Anise continued to swim, feeling something wrap around her ankle.

"Monroy!" Anise hissed. "There's something touching me."

"Probably just a fish," Monroy said, his voice cutting off as a giant tentacle rose out of the water. "Or not."

"Swim!" Anise shouted as they started for shore.

Anise glanced behind her, freezing as a giant tentacle wrapped around High Commander Monroy and dragged him under the water. Without thinking, Anise dove after him.

Cracking her eyes open, Anise saw the tentacles belonged to a massive creature with dozens of tentacles. The murky water prevented her from fully seeing the creature, or Monroy.

Anise shot to the surface, inhaled deeply, and sunk back under the water. She caught sight of Monroy, struggling against the tentacle wrapped around his throat without much success.

Quickly, Anise jerked her small knife free from her belt, stabbing the tentacle nearest to her. It twisted, and the tentacle around Monroy's neck loosened.

Monroy pulled free of the creature and swam toward the surface, his eyes still closed. Anise followed him, her lungs burning for air.

Anise's head broke the surface of the water just as she felt a tentacle wrap around her ankle, dragging her under the water. Anise struggled, the arm holding her knife pinned to her side.

Beside her, Monroy had another tentacle wrapped around him, but now his head lolled on his shoulders. Panic set in strong, and Anise managed to pull one arm free. She quickly switched the dagger to her free hand and stabbed through the tentacle.

A low rumble filled the water as the creature released them. Anise threw an arm around his chest and kicked as hard as she could, dragging them both up.

Anise broke the water's surface with a gasp, sucking in a lungful of sweet air as she lifted Monroy's head above water. He remained unconscious, and Anise realized her choice: leave him behind or—

With a deep breath, Anise shifting to a backstroke so she could keep an arm around Monroy and hold his head above water.

Carrying another person and swimming without one arm instantly drained Anise, but she refused to consider any other option.

As they neared the shore, Anise's limbs began to shake as she briefly wondered if she'd be able to make it. Monroy hadn't moved, and she couldn't help worrying it was already too late.

After what seemed to be eternity, Anise's feet touched the shore, and she adjusted her grip on Monroy, dragging them both to shore.

Anise collapsed on the bank, pillowing her head on her arm. Every muscle in her body ached, and her lungs burned from the effort. *I made it.*

Catching her breath, Anise forced herself to sit up. Monroy hadn't moved from where she'd dropping him on the edge, still unconscious.

Anise inched over to him, checking for a pulse. A faint pressure beat against her fingers, but it seemed slow. *I wonder if I could heal him...*

Hesitating, Anise glanced over Monroy's face. She'd never tried to heal anyone but herself—certainly not her enemies.

But you need him, Anise reasoned with herself. *He knows where an Embleck base it—maybe you can steal a ship from there and escape. You need him alive for that.*

Decided, Anise lightly placed her fingers on the definition of his ribcage, opening her powers. A warm feeling enveloped her, flowing through her fingers.

After a moment, Anise pulled her hand back, the warmth fading. A second or two passed, and doubt settled in. *Maybe it only works on me. Maybe I didn't do enough. Maybe—*

Abruptly, Monroy choked, rolling onto his side as he spat out a mouthful of lake water.

Relief washed over Anise as Monroy continued to cough, his body wracked with spasms. He was alive. *I healed him.*

Monroy pushed himself into a seated position as he finished coughing, glancing up at her with red eyes.

"What happened?" he asked, his voice rough.

"We were attacked by a giant creature with tentacles, and you almost drowned," Anise managed, exhaustion slightly slurring her words.

"Oh." Monroy coughed again, wiping his hand over his lips. "You saved me?"

"Yeah." Anise pulled her knees up to her chest. "I need my navigator."

"Of course." Monroy shook his head, spraying water droplets around them. "Are you okay?"

"I can barely keep my eyes open," Anise said as she laid down, resting her head on her arm. "I need a rest. Just…one… minute…"

CHAPTER 18

Liam jolted awake, disoriented. He sat up, glancing around as he tried to recall how he'd gotten here. The rippling lake drew his attention as memories flashed through his mind.

Glancing beside him, Liam's eyes locked on Commander Desson. She lay on the shore, sound asleep.

The sensation of her arm around him broke through Liam's consciousness. *She saved me.*

Why?

Liam glanced at her again, questions swirling through his mind. The peaceful expression on her face tugged at something in his chest, drawing him in.

Commander Desson truly had an aura around her, one sending an odd buzz through Liam's veins. She seemed to radiate light, peace, goodness, purity—free of all the hatred, resentment, and misery that consumed most people Liam met. Her presence itself was bright, warming…almost inhumanly so.

Angel. The word echoed through Liam's mind, and he braced his hand on the ground, unable to look away. It fit, and the realization sent a tiny spark of an unknown emotion through Liam. *If she's an angel, what am I?*

A monster.

Liam winced slightly, recognizing the truth. Desson shifted in her sleep, a faint smile pulling at her lips.

Stars, she's beautiful.

Shocked at his thoughts, Liam tore his gaze away from her. His breath came quick as his mind spun. *What are you thinking? Have you lost your mind? Monsters don't admire angels.*

Even if she is beautiful.

Commander Desson shifted again, her eyes fluttering open. She glanced around, dazed, until she caught sight of him.

The half-asleep on Desson's face shifted when their eyes met—and she smiled. A genuine, warm, barely-awake smile that made Liam's heart skip a beat.

"Hi." Her soft voice, tainted with sleep, sent Liam's pulse

racing.

With a groan, she sat up and interlocked her fingers, stretching her arms over her head as she arched her back. Liam forced himself to stare at the lake, intensely ignoring the sight in his peripheral vision.

Desson sighed as she relaxed, turning to face him. "You okay?"

"Yeah." Liam's voice held a rough note which he quickly corrected. "Yeah, I'm fine. Thanks."

Desson nodded, though she shot him an odd look before turning away and reaching into her bag. "Here's your boots and shirt."

Liam accepted the items, putting on his boots and pulling on his shirt as he stood, though he left it unbuttoned. Commander Desson stood as well, scanning the sky.

"We still have a few hours before sundown." She threw her bag over her shoulder, starting into the trees. "Let's go, Monroy."

"It's Liam."

Desson stopped, turning back to him with surprise written across her face. "What?"

"My name's Liam." Liam rubbed his fingers against the

palms of his hands, trying to quell the strange sensation in his chest. "After you saved my life, well…just thought I'd tell you."

"Liam." Desson offered him a half-smile. "My name's Anise."

"Nice to meet you, Anise." Liam offered her his hand.

Desson laughed lightly as she reached out and shook his hand. "You as well. Now, let's get moving…Liam."

Liam pulled his thoughts together as she started into the forest, and he followed. She paused, waiting on him to catch up. Once he did, they resumed walking.

After a few minutes, Liam noticed Anise glancing at him out of the corner of her eye. "Is something wrong?"

"Oh. I…I just noticed that." she drew her finger from her right shoulder to her left hip, mimicking his scar. "How did it happen?"

Liam shoved down the memory trying to break through. "An…altercation with my brother."

"Oh." She didn't say anything for a moment. "Sorry, I shouldn't have asked."

"It's fine," Liam said. "I don't mind. It was…a long time ago."

Anise nodded slightly. "Were you ever…close with him?"

Liam shook his head. "He was older than me, and we didn't live the same lifestyle. It…wasn't exactly a shock."

"I see," Anise said, though it seemed like she didn't.

Silence fell as they walked. Liam glanced up at the sky, noting the lack of sunlight. "Looks like it may rain."

"I hope so," Anise said, a slight bounce in her step. "Maybe it would cool off some."

"We're barely dry from the lake," Liam reminded her.

At that moment, a rumble of thunder echoed through the forest, and raindrops began splashing down around them.

"Great." Liam sighed.

Anise threw her head back, spreading her arms as the raindrops landed on her. Liam watched her, bemused. "What are you doing?"

"Enjoying the rain!" Anise replied as though it was obvious.

"Okay…"

"Come on, try it!"

"I'm okay," Liam said. "We need to keep moving."

Anise rolled her eyes, but followed, splashing in the accumulating puddles and touching the large plant leaves with the raindrops scattered on them.

"Why do you like the rain so much?" Liam asked, raking his wet hair out of his face.

"It never rained where I come from, so I like to enjoy it when I can," Anise explained, using her sleeve to wipe raindrops from her eyes. "Besides, it's—"

Her words cut off as a leaf full of water above them tipped, the contents spilling over her head

Liam fought back the urge to laugh. "Did you enjoy *that*?"

Anise grinned, pushing her dripping wet hair out of her face. "Yes!"

Liam shook his head, unable to hold back a slight smile. "I don't think we'll enjoy it as much if it rains all night."

"Oh, don't worry." To Liam's shock, she reached down, taking his gloved hand in her own and picking up her pace. "Just enjoy it. If you can't be happy at the small things in life, what's the point of living?"

Liam glanced at her, seeing the true happiness in her

eyes—at nothing more than rain! Such a simple joy...one Liam couldn't recall feeling since his childhood.

If you can't be happy at the small things in life, what's the point of living?

I wish I knew.

By the time the sun dipped below the horizon, the rain had slowed to the occasional droplet, and they stopped in a small clearing to make camp for the night. Anise found some small berries she insisted were safe, so they made a fire and sat down to eat.

Liam eyed the berries in her outstretched hand doubtfully. "Are you sure they're safe?"

Anise sighed. "If they weren't, would I be eating them?"

Liam considered this and relented, accepting a few of the berries.

"You should eat more than that," Anise said, offering him

more. "Aren't you starving?"

Liam shrugged. "I'm fine."

Anise shook her head as she continued eating. Liam watched the flames flicker, his thoughts locked on the woman next to him. The sight of the blue streak in her hair held his attention, and he couldn't shake the feeling that it meant…*something*.

"You look thoughtful." Anise's voice broke Liam's concentration. "What's on your mind?"

"Nothing," Liam answered automatically.

"That expression is too thoughtful for nothing," Anise said. "Come on, let's hear it."

Liam pulled his thoughts from the coincidence of her hair, and instead asked, "When did you join the Qor?"

"When I was seventeen," she replied. "I couldn't enlist until eighteen, but I helped as a ship mechanic until I could officially join."

"Your parents didn't mind you working on a Qor base?"

"They weren't really part of the picture," Anise admitted. "One of the councilors took me in after I had a…particularly nasty shipwreck. He thought it would be good experience for me."

Liam nodded, uncertain what to say. "Considering your success, I suppose he was right."

"He was," Anise agreed. A moment passed before she spoke. "Now I have a question for you."

"What's that?"

"What made you join the Embleck Army?"

Liam forced his expression to remain neutral. "Why do you ask that?"

Anise shrugged. "You don't seem the Embleck type. What made you join them?

Memories pulsed at the back of Liam's mind. "I realized I belong with them."

Anise rested her chin in her hand, staring at him. "Why do you say that?"

Liam turned his gaze back to the fire. "I wasn't close with my family. But there was a girl...the kindest person I've ever met. She'd lived a hard life, but it didn't break her. We became friends, and in just a few days, I...couldn't imagine a life without her."

Anise shifted closer to him. "Is that bad?"

Liam briefly closed his eyes. "It wasn't at first. She had

this…project she was working on, and I brought her some pieces. There was an accident—a parts malfunction. My fault." Liam steeled himself, forcing his words. "She *died*. It was completely my fault. I…I killed her. I killed my best friend and the only person I've ever loved."

Anise placed her hand on his shoulder. "I'm so sorry."

Liam shook his head. "Don't be sorry for me. It was *my fault*. And if that doesn't make me worthy of the Embleck Army…I don't know what would."

"It doesn't sound like your fault," Anise said. "How could you have predicted a part malfunctioning?"

"She'd be alive today if I'd never met her," Liam said, his voice rough. "That alone puts her death on me."

Anise went silent for a moment. "How did you actually join the Embleck Army?"

"After I found out, I just…walked. Ended up at the shipyard. An Embleck officer approached me and offered me a life." Liam shook his head. "I was young—foolish. Blinded from the grief. I couldn't stay where I was anymore. Couldn't live a normal life knowing what I'd done. The Embleck Army is where someone like me belongs."

Liam bit back a sliver of pain as he recalled. "I packed a bag, then pretended to sleep. Someone opened my door—I thought it was my father, checking on me."

"And it wasn't?" Anise's voice held a note of sympathy.

"No." Liam kept his voice emotionless. "It was my brother, standing over me with a kitchen knife. I didn't move out of the way fast enough." He rubbed the scar across his chest.

"My brother had followed me—told me he knew where I had been and that I was a traitor. He said this was the opportunity he had been waiting for to finally get rid of me. When I tried to explain, he wouldn't listen. I managed to knock him out, grabbed my bag, and ran."

Liam couldn't look at Anise, unwilling to see the horrified, disgusted expression he was sure she had. Anise removed her hand from his shoulder and to Liam's shock, placed her hand over his.

"Do you ever…" Anise's voice held none of the disgust Liam expected. "Do you ever wish you hadn't joined them in the first place?"

Liam darted a quick glance at her expression. It seemed fairly neutral, a hint of curiosity showing through. He'd asked himself the question before…but never admitted the answer.

"Maybe…sometimes." Liam realized what he was saying. "Wait—no. I mean no."

The flames reflected in Anise's eyes, and Liam thought he caught a glimmer of sympathy.

"I guess that's the long answer," Liam said, feeling strangely vulnerable. "I probably shouldn't have said all of that."

"It's okay," Anise said, her voice quiet. "Sometimes, it's easier to talk to someone you don't really know."

"I guess so." Liam met her eyes, teal mixed with the gold of the fire. She smiled slightly, glancing back at the fire.

Liam shifted, abruptly hit with déjà vu. The jungle seemed to fade away, and a silent desert took its place. Stars filled the sky, their light reflected in Anise's eyes. Her form was fuzzy, but the brilliant color of her eyes remained clear.

A warm feeling spread through Liam's chest as he shifted closer to her—

The scene snapped back into reality. The desert vanished, and the stars disappeared behind the jungle's canopy. The fire crackled, and Anise's form came into focus.

Anise didn't seem to have noticed his lapse of presence as she gazed into the fire, her hand still over his own.

Liam's mind spun, and he quickly stood. "It's getting late. We should get some rest."

Anise seemed momentarily surprised, but she nodded.

"You're right. And…I'm glad you told me."

Liam remained still as Anise stood, gently touching his arm with her gloved fingers. "And for the record? You shouldn't blame yourself for what happened. It wasn't your fault."

"Thank you for…saying that," Liam said quietly. He couldn't keep from blaming himself—his actions led to Ree's death. But the knowledge that Anise didn't blame him…it touched something in his chest.

"Of course." Before Liam knew what was happening, Anise wrapped her arm around his shoulder, giving him a side hug. Almost as quickly as it happened, she pulled away.

Liam tried to keep the shock off his face as Anise pulled the blanket out of her bag, laying it out on the damp ground. She glanced back at him over her shoulder. "Coming?"

"Yeah…" Liam swallowed hard. "I'm coming."

Anise settled on her side, and Liam laid with his back to her, trying to slow his racing heart.

"Good night, Liam."

"Good night, Anise."

The sharp screech of a jungle animal cut through the night, and Anise jerked awake with a gasp. She watched a dark shape leap from one tree to another before disappearing.

Anise waited a tense moment to see if the creature would return. The canopy remained clear, the forest silent.

"No...don't."

Anise jumped, sitting bolt upright. Her eyes darted around the dark forest before she recognized it was Monroy—no, Liam—talking in his sleep.

"Please, don't..."

Anise leaned over him, noting the pained expression on his face, even in sleep.

He must be having a nightmare. Anise felt her heart go out to him. After her shipwreck, she'd suffered frequent nightmares that had thankfully faded a few years ago.

241

"Please, don't make me...*please*..."

Anise furrowed her brow. It sounded as though he was begging with someone, but it made no sense. *Who in this galaxy could make him do anything?*

Liam inhaled sharply, his voice strangled. "No! No, don't!"

Anise shoved her hesitations away, reaching out and laying her hand over his. "Shh. You're okay."

Liam shifted slightly but didn't wake up. Anise laid back down, her hand still resting on his. After a moment, Liam's face relaxed, and his breathing slowed back to a normal speed.

Anise began to doze off when a few minutes later, Liam began talking again. Sitting up again, Anise placed her hand on his shoulder and leaned in closer.

"Don't, please—no, stop!"

Anise practically threw herself back into a sleeping position as Liam jerked awake. Keeping her eyes open a sliver, Anise faked sleep as she watched.

Liam looked around frantically as though searching for something. He sighed heavily, shaking his head. Anise laid perfectly still as he glanced at his hand in hers.

"Oh…" Liam hesitated a moment before beginning to pull his hand back.

Anise tightened her grip slightly. Liam halted, slowly relaxing his hand before laying back down. Anise waited until his breathing evened into sleep before inching closer, closing her eyes, and drifting off to sleep.

CHAPTER 19

Liam slowly awoke to sunshine streaming through the trees. The haze of sleep still hovered around him as he pulled the woman in his arms closer.

Wait—WHAT?

Liam's eyes flew open, his eyes locking on Anise's sleeping face. Her body nestled against his as she slept, an arm loosely wrapped around him.

Well, this is awkward. Liam allowed his gaze to linger on her face, realizing it didn't feel awkward. It felt…*peaceful.* Comforting—the way he'd always imagined *home* would feel. wasn't.

Why her?

Of all the women in the galaxy, it was Anise stranded in

the jungle with him. It was Anise who smiled in her sleep, sending a warm sensation through his heart. Liam wracked his memories, trying to recall if he'd ever felt *anything* for a woman since Ree.

The clear answer of *no* echoed through his mind.

A *Qor soldier*. After *nine* years, he'd developed *affection* for a *Qor* soldier.

Why do you do this to yourself? Liam asked as he removed his arms from around Anise and rolled over, putting some distance between them. *Do you enjoy suffering? You have to cut this off now. No emotions. No affection.*

His movement woke Anise, and she opened her eyes, glancing at him. "Good morning."

"Morning," Liam replied.

Anise scanned the trees. "How much longer until we reach the base?"

"Not too long. I think we should get there sometime to— what are you doing?"

Anise stood, approaching one of the large trees and removing her boots. "Getting some breakfast."

"Breakfast?" Liam repeated as she braced her foot on a branch and began climbing the tree.

"I noticed these rain melons last night," Anise called down. "After all the rain yesterday, they should be perfect."

The tree rustled, and a melon dropped, hitting the ground. It shattered, splattering everything with light blue juice.

"Catch!" Anise called.

Liam stepped forward, neatly catching the melon, followed by another.

"Got them," Liam called up, setting the melons on the ground.

"Thanks!" Anise tested a branch with one foot. It appeared sturdy, but when she put both feet on it, it snapped with a loud *crack*.

"Anise!" Liam lunged forward, barely catching her in his arms.

Anise clung to his neck, her eyes wide. "Stars. Thank you, Liam."

"No thanks necessary." Liam held her a moment longer before slowly lowering her to the ground.

Anise removed her arms from around his neck as a faint red crept over her face. She turned, immediately tripping over her bag.

Liam grasped her hand, but her glove slipped free. Quickly, he took hold of her upper arm as Anise righted herself.

"Thanks again." Anise shook her head. "I'm not usually this clumsy."

"No problem." Liam released her arm, offering her glove.

Anise reached for it with her bare hand, only to abruptly jerk it back—but not before Liam saw why she wore the gloves. Her right hand was covered in jagged scars with metal rings set into a few of her fingers.

Without making eye contact, Anise took her glove, quickly tugging it back on. Liam remained silent as they gathered up the surviving melons and sat around the cold fire circle.

Anise shifted. "I guess there's no use in pretending you didn't see that."

"See what?"

Anise glanced up in confusion before realization dawned on her face. A tiny smile crossed her face. "Thank you."

Liam returned the gesture. "Of course."

"Here." Anise moved beside him, showing how to crack open the fist-sized melons. She pulled it apart, revealing the sweet, blue fruit.

Liam cracked his lightly on the ground. It fractured with a spray of blue juice. Anise let out a short laugh as Liam wiped the juice from his eyes. The sound made a warm feeling wash through Liam,

Making a second attempt, Liam cracked harder. The melon broke it half with another splash, and Anise laughed again.

Liam couldn't keep from smiling. Anise's laughter was musical—a sound he'd never tire of hearing.

"There you go," Anise said, laughter still coloring her voice.

They finished breakfast and collected their bags before beginning to walk again. Silence fell over the forest as they kept a quick pace.

Anise glanced at him as they walked. "Do you know where I'll be going after we get to this base?"

Liam hesitated. "No, I'm afraid not."

"Oh." Anise went silent for a moment. "I guess after this, we won't see each other again."

"No, we won't." Liam's breath caught as a sharp pain cut through his chest. "We're on opposite sides—enemies."

"Right." Anise nodded firmly. "Enemies. But I don't know if we will be much longer."

Liam turned to her. "What?"

"Embleck prisons are known for frequent fatalities." For some reason, Anise didn't seem worried as she said it.

"No," Liam said without meaning it. "You'll be fine. I promise."

Anise raised an eyebrow, doubt coloring her voice. "Really?"

"Really." Liam would appeal to King Zamir. Surely, there could be a benefit to using her as a hostage for their map or something else of the sort. He didn't like the idea, but at least she would get home.

"That's...kind of you." Anise's voice pulled Liam from his thoughts.

Liam adjusted his gloves. "It's nothing. We're enemies. I just...don't want you to die."

Anise smiled slightly. "Pretty low standard, I'm afraid."

"It's odd for an enemy," Liam pointed out.

"True. But you know...I think we're odd enemies."

CHAPTER 20

As the sun rose higher, so did the temperature. The humidity made the air feel heavy, and Anise wished for cooling rain. She removed her jacket, shoving it into her bag.

Liam had removed his shirt, instead wearing a black vest from his bag. Anise blamed the warm feeling in her chest on the heat. Sunlight shone down through the trees, playing off the gold in his wavy blond hair, as well as the—

Blue. Anise's eyes widened. Liam had a hint of dark blue in his hair. She gasped, and he glanced at her with a bemused expression.

"Is everything okay?" Liam asked.

Anise nodded silently. Surely it was nothing. He dyed it—maybe it was a cultural thing. Coincidental, certainly…even though it matched the blue in her hair perfectly.

How didn't I notice that earlier? Anise asked herself, trying to keep from staring.

Liam stepped behind her as they passed a large tree, switching to walk on her right side. Anise glanced at him, instantly shock sweeping over her. On Liam's upper left arm, he had a black marking of a circle with two stars in it.

Anise grasped Liam's arm, stopping him and gesturing to the marking. "What's that?"

"This? I'm not sure." Liam twisted his arm around to get a better look. "I've had it for as long as I can remember. I don't know what it is."

"I have the same one," Anise whispered, touching her own mark.

Liam went pale. "You...what?"

Anise met his eyes, her mind racing. *I wonder if he has powers too.*

"Do you have powers too?"

Anise couldn't speak, demonstrating instead. She held up her hand and created a force field around the two of them. Liam's expression changed to wonder, and he stepped over to the edge of her shield, reaching out to touch it.

"No, wait—" Anise started, breaking off when his fingers

went straight through it. "How?"

Liam glanced at her before stepping completely through her shield. "Does that normally happen?"

"No," Anise said, stunned.

"Is that your only power?" Liam asked as he stepped back through, and she shook her head.

"I can also control minds," Anise said with a casual wave of her hand. Liam expression shifted, and she smirked.

"Don't worry, I can't control yours." She added, watching him relax slightly. "Not that I didn't try. What about you?"

"I can *read* minds," Liam said eagerly. "But not yours. I can also make portals using my sword."

Anise paused. "If you can make portals, why haven't you gotten us out of this jungle?"

Liam sighed. "It has to be my sword—the one from Zamir. This is just a temporary one. The one I need is having a fault in the hilt repaired."

"Great timing." Anise quipped. "But seriously…what's going on? We both have the same marking, the same blue streak, and abilities that work on everyone except each other."

"I've never met anyone my powers wouldn't work on,"

Liam admitted.

"Me either," Anise said. "The day you came into the prison, I was trying to control your mind the whole time, but it wouldn't work."

This is so freaky. Liam's voice sounded slightly echoey as he spoke.

"I agree."

"With what?" Liam asked in confusion.

"You said this was freaky, and I agreed."

"I didn't say anything." Liam's voice held a note of worry.

"But I heard you," Anise pressed. *Did I imagine it?*

"Maybe." Liam shrugged.

"I didn't say anything!" Anise exclaimed.

"It's almost like…reading your mind…" Liam began, his expression thoughtful. "But instead of me seeing your mind, you're putting your thoughts in mine."

"Like…a transmission?" Anise suggested.

"Yes!" Liam agreed. "How are you doing that?"

"I don't know!" Anise said. "It's just happening!"

"Okay, okay." Liam crossed his arms, pondering. "Does anything feel...different when you're doing it?"

"Well...we were connecting over our powers," Anise thought aloud. "Maybe that created some kind of...thread."

"Possibly." Liam drummed his fingers on his arm, a motion Anise found strangely attractive. "How do we control this *thread* then?"

Anise closed her eyes, focusing on the energy of her powers. Faintly, she felt a hum hovering just outside of her consciousness.

Reaching out, Anise touched the presence, feeling it envelope her thoughts. Liam jolted, his head whipping up.

"What?"

"I can hear you." Liam touched his temple, wonder in his eyes. "It's like you're in my head."

Anise released the presence, feeling it slip away. "And now?"

"I can't hear anything." Liam resumed drumming his fingers. "Wait—my..." Abruptly, he flushed, halting his fingers.

Anise stared at him in confusion for a moment before realizing she'd allowed her mind to brush the outside energy. Heat crept up her neck as it dawned on her—*he heard me.*

Playing dumb, Anise jerked her thoughts away from the outside. "What?"

"Nothing." Liam's face conveyed what Anise suspected. "How are you doing this?"

"It's like there's a presence…near my mind, but not in it. When I touch it, you can hear my thoughts."

Liam uncrossed his arms, nodding. "Okay. I'll try that."

Anise held her breath with anticipation, waiting. She watched as Liam concentrated, faintly scrunching his nose. Anise found it adorable—*wait, no. He's your enemy, remember?*

L'amor dura per sempre.

Anise's breath caught Liam glanced up at her, an innocent expression on his face. "Did it work?"

Unable to speak, Anise stared at Liam. Liam, with his…*blond* hair…knew the words to her favorite song. A memory flickered through her mind, blurred by the years: Roy, spinning her in the town square of the tiny Ceran village she'd called home as she sang that exact lyric—her favorite one.

There's no way. Anise pinched her wrist, forcing herself to be reasonable. *Roy isn't the only blond guy out there. You can't even picture his face properly! Besides, there's no records he ever existed! He probably lived unregistered on a mercenary ship or something, and his entire life story was something he made up. What color were his eyes anyway? They weren't green—right?*

"Anise?"

Anise snapped back to the present. Liam stared at her expectantly. "Did I do it right?"

"Oh…yeah. Yeah, you did." Anise tried to keep her voice even. "Where…where did you learn that song?"

"My family lived on Ceran, so I heard it a lot. It's a traditional song there, right?"

"Yeah…it is." Anise swallowed hard. *Roy didn't live on Ceran. He didn't know the song. Plus, he didn't have the blue streak in his hair—or the marking on his arm! And Roy's eyes were…blue? Brown? They couldn't have been green…*

"So…" Liam shifted his weight. "What are we going to do about this?"

"I…I don't know," Anise said, forcibly dismissing any idea that Liam and Roy were related in any way. "But I want to know more. You're the only person I've ever met that…well, that has *anything* that resembles my…condition."

"I agree. We need to figure out why we're connected like this—and preferably how it works."

"But how?" Anise pressed. "We're supposed to be mortal

enemies. We can't exactly meet up every Thursday for drinks and research!"

"Well..." Liam began, a slight smirk playing over his face. "Maybe we could be...part-time enemies?"

Anise opened her mouth to protest but paused. "Part-time enemies," she mused. "I like that."

"We can figure out details later. For now, we can agree to figure this out together." Liam held out his hand. "Part-time enemies?"

Anise accepted Liam's handshake. "Part-time enemies."

The trees began to clear ahead, and a large fortress could be seen through the trees. Liam put his finger to his lips and peered through the jungle.

"The base is in the valley at the bottom of this hill," Liam whispered to Anise over his shoulder.

"Why are we whispering?" Anise hissed, peering over his shoulder. Her eyes lit up when she caught sight of the vast shipyard.

"Because soldiers are trained to attack at the sign of a threat, and they may assume we're a threat."

"Right." A strange expression passed over Anise's face, and Liam turned back to look at the base. "Liam, are all the ships kept activated?"

"I think so," Liam muttered, not really paying attention. *How do I get into view without them attacking us?*

"Do the ships have tracking devices?"

"No, they don't. We don't want people hacking into the system and finding out where all our ships are," Liam explained, barely hearing his own words.

"Perfect."

Liam whipped around at the sound of a sword being unsheathed. Anise raised her sword, no emotion on her face.

"What are you doing?" Liam drew his own sword, settling into stance.

"I'm sorry." Anise struck for his leg, and Liam quickly blocked it.

Anise pulled her sword up before he could block it, and Liam realized she'd faked the hit, forcing him to leave his torso and head unprotected.

Taking advantage of his stance, Anise slammed the hilt of her sword into his head before shoving him back.

Stunned, Liam stumbled as the world reeled before his eyes. His back collided with a tree, and he went to a knee, trying to gain control of his spinning vision. The jungle foliage crashed as Anise fled, vanishing into the greenery.

Liam staggered to his feet as the world tilted. Using the tress for support, he started down the hill, coming into view of the Embleck soldiers.

A sharp pain shot through Liam's temples and he clutched his head, slowly lowering himself to sit back on his heels as the ground seemed to move like water.

Voices shouted, and Liam closed his eyes as pain pulsed through his skull. A moment later, he felt a hand on his shoulder, shaking him.

"It's High Commander Monroy!"

Opening his eyes, Liam waited as the world sharpened into focus, allowing him to make out Brendon's face.

"Brendon?"

"Sir, what happened?" Brendon exclaimed. "Where have you been?"

A roar filled the air as ship took off at top speed, blasting them all with a gust of hot wind.

"What was that?"

"*Who* was that?"

Liam glanced up, a slight smile crossing his face. "Anise."

"What? What's 'a niece'? Who's niece?" Brendon shook him. "He's delirious. Let's get him to the infirmary."

"What about that ship?" a soldier exclaimed.

The question snapped Liam into focus. "Leave it," he ordered. "Take me inside."

The soldiers nodded, and Brendon pulled him upright. Liam looked back, but the ship was long gone. Still, he couldn't erase his smile as Brendon helped him inside.

Anise pulled the stolen ship's lever, clearing the planet Coradon's atmosphere. She already had contacted her base and been cleared for landing, despite being in an Embleck ship.

Soon, Anise landed the ship, beyond relieved to be home. She leaped out, scanning the shipyard.

"It's Commander Desson! She's alive!" Anise heard Tyler's shout of joy, and spun around.

"Tyler!" she exclaimed as he raced to her and hugged her tightly.

"We were so worried about you!" Tyler exclaimed, pulling back. "When you were captured, that was bad enough, but our pilots reported that you had been in a ship crash with High Commander Monroy. Everyone thought…well, never mind. Caiden will be so relieved."

Anise winced. "How is he?"

"He's a mess." Tyler pursed his lips. "He's been doing

his assignments listlessly, he talks in a monotone, and he's missed lunch with Keisha and me all week."

Anise sighed. "Has he been blaming himself?"

"That too." Tyler shook his head. "The Council hasn't made an announcement yet or hosted a service. They were going to give it a week."

"I need to find him."

"He's in there," Tyler said. "He just stepped inside to get something."

"Tyler, what's all the shouting for? We have to…" Caiden stepped outside and froze when he saw who was standing next to Tyler.

"Hi, Cay."

"Anise," Caiden whispered. They ran to each other and collided in a tight embrace. "You're alive! Are you okay?"

"I'm fine," she promised, taking his hand.

"Did Monroy hurt you?" Caiden's face darkened. "If he did—"

"No, no, no." Anise shook her head. "He didn't lay a hand on me." *Other than to save me from falling on my face a few times.*

"Thank the stars." Caiden hugged her again. "Is there anything you need?"

"Just something to eat." Anise quipped. "And probably something other than this uniform. I prefer the Qor colors."

"No problem." Caiden threw his arm around Anise's shoulders. "Hey guys!" he called as they went inside. "Guess who's back!"

CHAPTER 21

"It's so nice to have a real meal," Anise said to Caiden as they left the base's cafeteria. "I really needed something other than rolls and melons."

"I'm just glad you're home." Caiden wrapped his arm around her shoulders. "I was so worried."

"I know—and I'm glad to *be* home. But this proves I can take care of myself," Anise reminded him for the hundredth time. "I get being worried, but you can see I'm fine."

"Okay, okay." Caiden slowed as they approached her room. "I'm going to bed. I couldn't sleep while you were gone, and I'm exhausted."

"Alright." Anise unlocked her door. "See you later?"

"See you later." Caiden strolled back down the hall.

Anise slipped into her room, fumbling in the dark for the light switch as a skidding sound caught her ears. The light clicked on just as Joffrey bolted at her from under the bed.

"Hi, Joffrey!" Anise scooped up her pet and cuddled him close. "I missed you!"

"Meoowwww!" Joffrey purred and nuzzled her.

Anise smiled, stroking his back as she walked around the room, collecting some clean clothes. She'd spent all evening with Caiden, Keisha, Tyler, and Lydia in cantina. Now it was a few minutes past midnight, and she needed to relax.

Joffrey jumped from her arms and flew up onto the bed. Shaking her head, Anise left him there and turned on the bathwater, making sure to lock the door.

The last time she had left the door unlocked, Joffrey had decided to jump in the tub with her, resulting in chasing a wet kibit around her room with soap in her hair.

"Finally." Anise stripped off her dirty, sweaty Embleck uniform, and tossed it on the floor. deciding she'd never wear it again. *Maybe I'll stop by Ceran for one of the bonfires.*

Anise stepped into the warm water and felt her muscles relax instantly. She sighed in contentment and sank deeper into the warm water of the tub. Walking through the jungle for almost three days had made her feel positively grimy, and swimming through a slimy lake definitely *did not* count as a bath.

Thinking about the lake brought Anise's mind to Liam. Her perception of him had changed drastically in the past three days. She'd seen a different side of him—one she almost...*liked.*

Anise wondered if she had been too quick to trust him. But for some reason, it felt as though she already knew him. He had been sweet, and it confused her. Besides, he had been someone to talk to.

Truthfully, although Anise adored Caiden, Keisha, and Tyler, she couldn't help but feel...lonely. Spending time with Liam had changed something, and now she felt *different.*

"Oh well." Anise washed herself thoroughly, finally beginning to feel clean again. She ducked her head under the faucet so she could rinse her hair when she heard a voice.

Anise?

Anise took her head out of the running water, listening closer.

Anise, can you hear me?

Liam, Anise realized, relieved she wasn't hearing things.

Am I doing this right?

Once second, Anise tried transmitting, ducking back

under the water. She didn't really want to talk to him yet—after all, she *had* clocked him in the head. What did you say after that?

Liam's voice silenced as Anise finished rinsing her hair and stepped out of the tub. Wrapping her bathrobe around her, she started to work through the tangles in her hair. A moment later, a humming noise filled the room.

Anise opened the door to her room, expecting Joffrey in mischief. He laid on the bed asleep, and confusion settled over Anise as she turned back to the mirror.

Abruptly, a swirling black portal formed in the middle of her bedroom. Anise's eyes went wide as Liam stepped out of it, his back to her.

Anise adjusted her robe and checked her hair, waiting for Liam to notice her.

"Where—" Liam started as he turned around. He immediately closed his eyes when he saw her, red tinting his face. "Sorry, sorry! I had no idea."

Anise resisted the urge to laugh at his clear embarrassment. "It's fine, see?" She tucked her gloveless hands into her robe sleeves right before he opened his eyes.

Liam glanced at her. "I didn't mean to scare you, but when I didn't get a response…"

"Oh...I guess I did it wrong," Anise said. "What's up?"

"Well...I wanted to make sure you escaped.' Liam scanned the room. "I assume you're okay?"

"Yeah, I made it home," Anise replied, oddly touched by his concern.

"When you didn't reply, I was afraid you'd been captured again." Liam still avoided her eyes.

Anise's gaze traveled to his head, and she could faintly see a bruise spreading from under his hair. Liam saw her looking, and his hand traveled to the spot.

"How's your head?" Anise asked hesitantly.

"No big deal." Liam shrugged.

An awkward silence filled the room. Anise shifted "is there...anything else?"

"Oh, yeah." Liam perked up slightly. "The Galactic Records Hall on Veraconix. If there is any information about...whatever we have, it should be there. They have old books, new books, and digital records."

"So...should we make a trip?" Anise asked.

"I think so," Liam said. "It's open all night."

"Wait—tonight? It's nearly one!"

"Oh. Right." Liam ducked his head. "I forget most people are asleep by now."

"You're not?" Anise said, stunned.

Liam shrugged again. "I…don't really sleep anymore."

"Oh." Anise twisted her robe sleeve. "Well, I'm not too tired."

"Are you sure?" Liam said. "I can wait, it's fine."

"No, let's go now," Anise decided. "It should be less crowded, and I don't know if you can walk around in public."

"Not really," Liam admitted. "Night is probably better."

"Let me change really quick," Anise said, closing the bathroom door. She pulled her damp hair up, put on her clothes, slipped on a clean pair of gloves, and stepped out.

"Ready?" Liam asked.

"I am, but you may need to make a few adjustments," Anise said. "Just take off these badges, the symbol pin and…" she gave him a once over. "Let's lose the cloak."

"Better?" Liam set his badges on her dresser as she laid the cloak over a chair.

"Yes, much better," Anise said.

"I wonder if I could teleport us there," Liam began. "Usually, I can't bring anyone with me, but I'm curious if you could come."

"I'm willing to try," Anise decided.

Liam slashed his sword through the air, and a swirling portal appeared before them. Turning to Anise, he held out his hand. "Are you ready?"

Anise placed her gloved hand inside his own. "Yes."

"Let's go," Liam said as pulled them both inside the portal.

Anise glanced around in amazement. She stood in the middle of space, surrounded by colorful. nebulas and silver sparkles filling the dark emptiness.

Tightening her grip on Liam's hand, Anise closed her eyes as they took another step. When she opened them, they stood in front of the Galactic Records Hall.

"It worked!" Anise said happily.

"That's useful." Liam glanced around. "Shall we go now?"

Anise led the way inside, passing only a few people. They received an odd look or two, but Anise forced herself to look straight ahead, ignoring everyone else.

"Everything we need should be in here." Anise pulled the door open and stepped inside.

The records hall was breathtaking. Bookshelves lined the walls all the way up to the domed glass ceiling, revealing the night sky, any stars hidden by the city lights. One wall had a long desk along it, and individual desks were scattered around the room. The scent of old books and another slightly metallic scent flooded the room.

"Where do we even start?" Liam asked, his eyes locked on the brimming bookshelves.

"Let's try the digital records first," Anise decided. "We can search anything that relates to telepathic connections, powers, or unique stars, or anything about the star symbol

"Good idea," Liam said as the two of them selected computers next to each other. Silence fell over the room with only the shuffle of books and occasional *screech* of a chair against the floor.

Anise scanned an article, her eyes lighting up. "This might be something. It says that the ancient Xorayn Empire had a symbol that resembles stars, but there's no picture."

"Is there any record of it anywhere else?" Liam asked.

Anise read over the article. "Yes—there's a book here, and it has one of the only known records of this symbol."

Liam oushed back his chair. "Let's go. It'll be in the history section, right?"

"Right." Anise switched off her computer and followed. They reached the history section and began checking the spines of the books.

"I could spend the rest of my life here," Liam said, lightly running his fingers over the books. "Easily."

"Live and die in a library?" Anise joked. "I don't think I could do it."

Liam nodded, looking thoughtful. "Doesn't sound bad to me."

"I'd get lonely," Anise said, pulling out a book. "Look, this must be it."

Liam left the bookshelf, reading over her shoulder. "Yeah, I'd guess."

The symbol of the Xoryan Empire had been burned into the thick leather book cover—the same symbol marking each of them.

"It's our symbol." Liam stepped back, crossing his arms. "Why do we have the Xoryan symbol on our arms? The empire's been dead for thousands of years."

"I don't have a clue." Anise thumbed through the book.

"It's all written in Xoryan runes. There's nothing I can read."

Liam sighed. "At least we know what it is, right? It's so late—I'm sure you're exhausted."

Anise shook her head, even as she felt the energy slowly draining from her body. "I…well…yeah."

"Come on, let's get you home," Liam said, placing his hand on her shoulder as they walked to the exit.

"I should check on Joffrey anyway," Anise mentioned, hoping he hadn't shredding anything while she was gone.

Liam stopped short. "Joffrey?"

"Yes, Joffrey," Anise said. "He doesn't like it when I leave him alone."

"Oh…of course." Liam resumed walking. Anise wondered what had caused him to stop.

They exited the building, and glanced around. After determining the courtyard was empty, Liam unsheathed his sword and created a portal They both stepped through, appearing in Anise's room.

"Joffrey!" Anise called. He'd vanished from his spot under the bed. "I hope he didn't get into my closet again."

Liam choked. "Pardon?"

"It was a disaster last time," Anise said, opening the closet door, relieved that it was empty. "He's probably under the bed."

Liam's eyes had gone wide, and he stared at her as though she was crazy. Anise dropped to the floor and stuck her head under the bed, but it was empty.

"Joffrey, come out!" Anise said firmly. "I want you to meet Liam."

Liam backed toward the door. "Maybe I should just go," he said, just as a loud skittering noise came from behind the bathroom door.

"Great, he locked himself in the bathroom again." Anise opened the door, ignoring Liam's alarmed expression, and Joffrey came racing out. "This is Joffrey."

"Oh!" Istant relief washed over Liam's face. "Joffrey is your pet."

"Yes, what did you think he was? A chair?"

"No, I thought…never mind." Liam knelt down. "Hi, Joffrey."

Joffrey flattened his ears against his head and hissed at Liam.

"Joffrey!" Anise scolded. "Be nice." She couldn't help

thinking of the one other person Joffrey had instantly disliked: Roy.

"I'll be going now," Liam said as Joffrey swiped at his ankles. "See you soon?"

"Sure, I—oh! Don't forget these." Anise handed him his cloak and badges.

"Thanks." Liam shot her a quick smile and stepped through a portal, instantly vanishing.

Joffrey hissed loudly at where the portal had been. Anise absently stroked him. The way Liam smiled at her…it seemed so familiar.

Roy. Anise couldn't keep the name from echoing through her mind. *No, you already decided it wasn't him! You're just projecting because you've wondered about Roy for nine years. You want confirmation that you're not crazy and he actually existed in the first place.*

Anise set Joffrey down, picking up her comm. Bypassing the code, she sank onto her bed, searching through the Qor's public records.

Lecru. The result showed three members of the Lecru dynasty—an older man and women, and their son—Cameron Lecru, who bore barely any resemblance to Roy.

No record. Anise clicked off her comm, a strange mixture of disappointment and relief filling her. A tiny part of her wished he was Roy—being able to connect with him after all the years would have been wonderful.

But if he was Roy…Anise stood up and walked around the room, processing. She thought back to what he'd imagined for his life, and her heart ached faintly. Could Roy have changed that much?

It doesn't matter—it's not him, Anise told herself firmly. She turned off her light and collapsed into bed, instantly asleep.

CHAPTER 22

Liam paced through the small library of the Embleck base. He'd spent his free morning searching for any information on the Xoryan Empire, but it turned out quite difficult. Not that there was a lack of information, but very few people knew how to translate the runes, leaving most records in the Xoryan runes.

I wonder if Anise has any new information. Liam activated his powers, reaching for the energy field around them.

Anise? Are you there?

A moment passed before Anise's slightly accented voice floated into his mind. *Yes, I am. What's up?*

I wanted to discuss the situation with you, Liam transmitted. *Somewhere neutral, preferably.*

Sure, Anise replied. *What about the lake in the jungle?*

The lake I almost drowned it? Liam teased.

No repeats. Humor colored Anise's voice. *I'll take my ship and leave now.*

I'll do the same.

See you then.

You too. Liam broke off the connection, leaving his quarters and hurrying down to the shipyard.

Liam deployed his ship's landing gear, setting it on the shoreline. He lifted the hatch and jumped down, his boots sinking slightly in the wet sand. Scanning the trees, Liam walked along the edge of the lake. "Hello?"

The jungle rustled, and Anise emerged from the trees. "I'm here."

"Perfect," Liam began. "I—"

Liam broke off as a movement caught his eye. The foliage

across the lake shook as a dozen Embleck soldiers stepped out, each with a ray gun trained on Anise.

"You—" Anise jerked, glaring at Liam with fire burning in her eyes. "I should never have trusted you!"

"I—" Liam halted as Anise closed her eyes, and a second later, the Embleck soldiers collapsed.

Liam inhaled sharply as Anise spun around, whipping her ray gun from her belt and aiming at his head.

"Drop your sword." Anise's voice held no emotion, her expression cold.

Liam did as she ordered, unsheathing his sword and dropping it before kicking it out of reach. Anise kept her pistol trained on him the entire time, unwavering.

"Don't move." Anise took a step back, retreating into the forest.

"Anise—" Liam stepped forward, freezing as the *crack* and sizzle of a ray gun echoed through the forest. The tree behind him smoked, a blacked mark on the trunk.

"That was a warning." Anise's voice shook, ever so slightly. "Move again, and I won't miss."

"Listen, I didn't plan this!"

"Oh really?" Anise stopped moving back. "Then why are *your soldiers* here?"

"I don't know," Liam said honestly.

Anise tightened her finger on the trigger. "Yeah, right—traitor."

A flash of light struck Liam in the chest, and the world seemed to slow. He stumbled back, ice spreading through his veins. Anise's ray gun flashed in the sunlight as she turned and vanished into the forest.

Liam's knees hit the ground as the world darkened and he faded into unconsciousness.

Bright light shone into Liam's eyes, only to be blocked by Brendon.

"Again? Seriously?"

"How—what—" Liam sat up, recognizing the Embleck

infirmary with shock. "How am I alive?"

"You were shot with a stun ray," Brendon said. "They're not usually lethal."

A stun ray. Liam's mind spun. *She could've killed me— but she didn't.*

Why?

"What...happened?" Liam asked.

"I don't know," Brendon reminded him. "Ankor said the ambush Zamir ordered on Commander Desson failed, and you were injured. That's all I've heard."

Liam clenched his jaw. How did King Zamir and Ankor know about his meeting with Anise? There shouldn't have been any way Liam knew of—but he *did* know he'd just ruined the small amount of trust she'd given him.

"High Commander, Sir?" A soldier entered the infirmary room, anxiety dripping off him. "King Zamir has asked to see you."

"Fine. I'm coming."

The soldier practically leaped out of Liam's way as he stormed out of the infirmary, ignoring Brendon's protests about "rest" and "stun wounds qualifying as a serious injury."

Liam rapped on the throne room doors, fury brimming in

his chest.

"Enter."

Liam shoved open the doors, stalking up to the dais. He kept his expression in check, suppressing his urge to confront his ruler.

"Monroy." Zamir's voice held no trace of emotion. "Has she been captured?"

Liam forced himself to answer calmly. "No, Your Majesty."

"Hmm." Zamir drummed his fingers on the armrest of the throne. "Perhaps failure is the result of attempting this on your own."

Zamir's voice held a concerning tone, but Liam dismissed it, anger pulsing through him. *Control. It's better if that's what he thinks. You don't want him suspecting there was any other reason you were with Anise. Leave it be.*

"Yes, Your Majesty," Liam ground out through gritted teeth.

"Despite this... failure, I have news for you."

"Yes?"

"Your Majesty, are you—" High Commander Ankor stepped into the room, instantly scowling at Liam. "I didn't realize you were…busy"

"I am informing Monroy that General Gaveren has been…removed from his position." King Zamir turned his head to Liam. "His role is now yours."

Liam's anger shifted to shock. High Commander Ankor let out his breath in a hiss, glaring at Liam with pure hatred.

*If looks could kill…*Liam shot a glance at Ankor. "What happened to Gaveren?"

"He has been disposed of," King Zamir said, his note offering no room for discussion. "You will replace him."

"Thank you, Your Majesty," Liam replied numbly.

King Zamir selected a badge from the armrest of his throne, carelessly tossing it to Liam. Liam caught the badge, his eyes running it. He was a general now—one of the most powerful roles in the Embleck Army.

And he didn't want it.

"That is all, General Monroy," Zamir ordered. "Ankor and I have much to discuss."

"Yes, Your Majesty." Liam offered a shallow bow before leaving, feeling Ankor's hateful glare burning through him.

CHAPTER 23

Anise berated herself as she landed her ship in the Qor shipyard, fury burning through her body. *You should've known better than to trust an enemy! Just because he smiled at you? Come on, Anise!*

Leaving her ship, Anise stormed inside the base, her jaw clenched so hard it hurt.

"Commander Desson!"

Anise stopped, forcing a pleasant expression on her face as she saw Councilor Indu approaching. "Hello, Councilor."

"Is something wrong?" Indu asked, worry clouding his expression. "You look unwell."

Anise inhaled slowly. "I alone in the forest and attacked by Embleck soldiers."

Councilor Indu scanned her for injuries, his expression intense. "Are you alright?"

"I'm fine." Anise said, bitterness in her voice.

"Why don't we step into my office for a moment?" Councilor Indu abruptly changed the subject. "I have something I wish to discuss with you."

"Of course, Sir."

Anise followed Councilor Indu to his office, uncertainty washing over her. Once inside, Councilor Indu locked the door and gestured to a chair in front of his desk. "Have a seat."

The grave tone to Indu's voice prompted Anise to sit without question.

Councilor Indu sank into the chair behind his desk. "I suppose Councilor Mills told you about his fear that there is a traitor here."

Anise fingered her necklace, the events in the forest leaving her mind. "Yes, he did tell me."

Councilor Indu nodded. "Before, I assumed he was worrying needlessly. But now, after this attack, I fear he may be right. How else would the Embleck Army know you were in the jungle?"

Anise swallowed hard. She knew exactly how they had found her, but she couldn't tell Indu that. Instead, she asked him, "Is this incident the only reason you believe that?"

"No," Councilor Indu admitted reluctantly. "I thought it was coincidental, but now…" he trailed off and sighed again. "Just last week, we sent a team to patrol the jungle, and they found hundreds of Embleck soldiers waiting for them. And about a month ago, a squadron was sent to examine Embleck activity in a small village. When they tried to return and report, their ship was destroyed, and they were lucky to escape alive."

"Do you have any more information about the identity of the traitor?"

"No," Councilor Indu said. "But if there is a traitor, we have more to fear than just one person."

"What do you mean?" Anise asked.

"Where there's one, there's another," Councilor Indu said. "Problems like this often come in twos."

"Are you saying there may be *two* traitors here?" Anise asked, her unease rising by the second.

"I'm saying I haven't ruled out that possibility," Councilor Indu said solemnly. "I'm also afraid the traitor must be highly ranked. They have access to top clearance only information. Either they're an expert hacker, or this traitor has been here a very long time."

Anise pressed a hand against her stomach. A traitor—or two—had access to all their records? That could very well be the edge the Embleck Army needed to defeat the Qor and seize the galaxy.

"There is one other thing." Councilor Indu leaned forward. "The traitor knows the Qor Council's security code. They got into our records without tripping the alarm."

Anise inhaled sharply. "Are—are you implying that you think one of the councilors is the traitor?"

"I fear it may be true," Councilor Indu said grimly. "I fear it may be one you know."

Anise sat silent, shocked at what he was implying. "High Councilor Mills?"

Councilor Indu nodded.

"But he was the one who first told me about the traitor!" she argued. "Why would he tell me if he was the traitor? Wouldn't it just raise suspicion?"

"Not if he thought that telling you would throw the suspicion off him," Councilor Indu said gently. "Like how you are trying to defend him now."

Anise sat back, fear prickling at her chest. The High Councilor—a traitor. It was almost impossible enough to believe.

"But if he is the traitor," Anise began slowly. "Then he knows about my powers."

Councilor Indu nodded again. "I am afraid you may be hurt. Please take extra caution. I watched over you for many years while you were on Ceran, and I think of you as a daughter. It would break my heart to see you hurt."

Despite the grave situation, Anise felt a warm feeling spread through her at his words. "I will try, Sir."

"That is all I can ask of you," Councilor Indu said, looking relieved. "Avoid High Councilor Mills when you can, and come to me if you need anything."

"Thank you," Anise said gratefully.

"And please know I am doing all I can to recover any evidence to find who the traitor truly is. After all, it may not be the High Councilor, and I pray it is not. Still, I want you to be cautious, just in case."

"I will be," Anise promised.

"In fact," Councilor Indu added. "I have one of your squad members, Jack, assisting with attempting to trace the person who got into our records."

"Jack is a technology whiz, and I consider him a good friend," Anise said. "We don't often connect, but I trust he'll do his best for the Qor."

"He is indeed a genius," Councilor Indu said. "I do have one last question, and then you may go."

"Yes, Sir?"

"Was Monroy who attacked you?"

Anise shifted, uncomfortable. "He was there."

"I was afraid of that." Councilor Indu steepled his fingers on his desk. "Monroy is King Zamir's right-hand man. If he's found out about your powers, he may take a special interest in you. Zamir assigns him to the highest classed assignments, and I believe you would technically qualify."

"I suppose so," Anise said, trying not to picture Liam's face.

"That is all I had to say," Councilor Indu said. "As long as you're truly alright?"

"I am," Anise confirmed.

"Then that's all that matters." Councilor Indu stood and opened the door for her. "Let me know if you need anything else."

"Thank you, Sir."

Liam drummed his fingers on his desk, staring at the badge laying before him.

General. The title sounded abrasive to his ears—proof of his service to the Embleck Army.

An image of Anise flickered through Liam's mind, and he bit back a sigh. It had been a week since the attack in the jungle, and he hadn't spoken to her since.

Not that Liam would blame her if she never spoke to him again. He'd lost the trust she'd gifted him with, and it was unlikely she'd ever return it.

Liam glanced at his sword on the table. If he could talk to Anise…explain the truth. After learning about their connection, Liam couldn't fathom letting it go this easily. Pushing back his chair, Liam stood and lifted his sword.

Show me Anise Desson.

A small portal warped open, a blurred image in its center.

Anise stood alone in a small, dark room, surrounded by file cabinets. A few boxes were scattered about the room, each overflowing with file cases.

Now would be the perfect time to talk with her. Liam hesitated, spinning his sword in his hand absently. Teleporting to her without warning wasn't a mistake he wanted to make again—but what if they never spoke again?

If Anise refused to have anything to do with him after knowing the truth…Liam would accept it. But the idea of her believing that he'd betrayed her—it ripped at something in Liam's chest.

I have to tell her.

Activating his powers, Liam enhanced the portal, took a deep breath, and stepped through.

Anise spun around, her eyes going wide. Anger flushed her face, and she stepped back, clenching her fists. Liam closed his portal, abruptly deciding he should have rehearsed something—anything—to say.

"What are you doing here?" Anise snapped, her eyes flashing.

"I wanted to talk with you," Liam began, his voice quiet. "Please, let me explain—"

Anise cut him off, drawing her sword. "Why should I? You betrayed me!"

"We made a deal, and I wouldn't go back on my word," Liam said, his eyes locked on Anise's sword. "I didn't come to fight. I wanted you to know the truth."

Anise hesitated before steeling her expression and striking at him. Liam jerked his sword up to block her blade as Anise continued lashing at him.

"Anise, I don't want to fight you!" Liam dodged another strike. "Can—"

"If you didn't want to fight, you wouldn't be with the Embleck Army!" Anise yelled. "You wouldn't have to fight if you weren't part of an evil army trying to take over the galaxy! Don't you know what they're doing—what you're doing? They're destroying civilizations, killing innocent people—and you're part of that!"

"I know exactly what they're doing—you think I don't? know, and I hate it! I hate what they're doing, and I hate that I'm part of it!" Liam's raised voice betrayed his slipping composure. "It's killing me, but I don't have a choice anymore!"

Liam jerked his sword to his side to block a strike, realizing too late Anise had faked, causing him to leave himself completely vulnerable. Anise stabbed at his side, and Liam froze.

They briefly met each other's eyes, and Liam's eyes darted to Anise's blade, pressed against his side. She could've used it as an end strike…but hadn't.

Liam's sword clattered loudly to the floor. A stunned expression crossed her face, and she slowly withdrew her sword.

"I don't have a choice anymore," Liam said, his voice soft. "Not when I'm fighting for the Embleck Army. But I have a choice fighting you now." Liam locked eyes with her. "I won't. You can kill me now, if you wish. I'm not going to fight you."

Anise stepped back, some of the anger fading from her expression. "Why? Why should I trust you? Why should I believe you didn't betray me?"

"If I wanted to hurt you, I would have already. I had ample opportunity. But I promised your safety—promised I wouldn't hurt you."

"That was when we were stranded," Anise argued.

"My promise didn't have an expiration date." Liam watched the emotions wavering in her eyes. "And now I'm laying down my weapon. No harm will come to you by my hand."

Anise closed her eyes. "I want to believe you. But…Liam…you're an Embleck officer. That's—that's not easy to forget!"

"Trust me—I know," Liam said quietly. "If there's anything I can do to prove I mean what I'm saying…"

"Answer this honestly." Anise opened her eyes, full of intensity. "If you have no loyalty for the Embleck Army—why haven't you left?"

Liam resisted the urge to smile, amusement coloring his voice. "I don't have anything worth dying for."

Anise's expression flickered. "Dying for?"

"The Embleck Army is service for life. You serve until you meet death."

"Couldn't you run?"

"Sure," Liam admitted. "You could desert. But if you're caught—and you will be caught—you'll be killed, and not mercifully."

Closed emotions played over Anise's face. "So…death is the only freedom. You have to choose between the hand of the enemy or the hand of the army you serve."

"If I chose to die to escape the Embleck Army, it wouldn't be by their hand." Liam rubbed his fingers over his wrist. "I have better methods."

A foreign emotion flashed over Anise's face, and she set her sword on a box.

Liam offered her a half smile. "Running and dying to experience only a few weeks, months—even a year—of what? There's nothing for me in this world."

"How do you know that?" Anise's boots clicked on the floor as she stepped around a box, stopping an arm's reach from him. "Second chances are everything if you look."

Liam shrugged one shoulder. "Second chances aren't for people like me. I accepted that a long time ago."

"Maybe not for people like you," Anise said softly. "But there could be one for *you*."

Liam shifted, something in his soul twisting sharply. *No—you know better. There's nothing for you here. Nothing worth living for, nothing worth dying for.*

"I...I believe you."

Liam's head snapped up. "What?"

"I believe you." Anise shrugged, unaware of the hope that flooded Liam's chest at her words. "I think you're telling the truth about the ambush."

"Anise, I—thank you." Liam inclined his head to her. "It's an honor."

"It's a second chance," Anise said, a smile tugging at her lips.

Before Liam could reply, a woman's voice drifted from the cracked doorway.

"Anise, are you in here?"

Anise grabbed Liam's arm. "Go, quick!"

The door swung open, and a young woman with dark skin and curly black hair stepped inside. She did a double take, her eyes locked on Liam. "Anise...who's this?"

"Oh, well...Keisha." Anise tugged at her gloves. "This...this is my...my new boyfriend, Liam."

Wait, what? Liam quickly caught his expression of confusion. He wrapped his arm around Anise's shoulders, smiling at Keisha.

"Oh. Oh, wonderful!" Keisha seemed baffled, but it shifted to excitement as she turned to Liam. "It's so good to see her socializing like this."

"Keisha," Anise hissed, her face flushing.

"You're a lucky guy," Keisha said, twirling her oversized scarf around her finger. "Anise is the best."

"She really is," Liam said, glancing at Anise.

Anise's blush deepened, and she coughed. "Yes—well—Liam is stationed on another base, but he he's off-duty today."

"How sweet," Keisha said. "I don't want to interrupt your special time. Can we meet up later, Anise?"

"Sure," Anise agreed, unable to meet her friend's eyes.

"Bye then!" Keisha's coral pink scarf swished as she swept out the door.

"Bye." Anise covered her face with her hands. "Oh my stars. I'm so sorry about the…boyfriend thing."

"It's not a problem," Liam said. "I'm sure…this would be hard to explain."

Anise nodded. "It…yeah, it would be."

Liam abrupted realized he still had his arm around Anise and quickly stepped away. "Well, I don't want to stay and jeopardize this any further."

"Good idea." Anise shifted her weight, her face still tinted red. "I'll be in touch, okay?"

"Of course." Liam picked up his sword and created a portal. "Oh, Anise?"

"Yes?"

"Thank you again. I won't break your trust again—not for anything in this galaxy."

A slight smile tugged at Anise's lips. "I know."

CHAPTER 24

Anise couldn't keep a slight smile off her face as she carefully closed the storage room behind her. She turned around and gasped, nearly colliding with Keisha.

"Keisha! What are you doing?"

Keisha grasped Anise's arm, silently pulling her through the hallways until they reached Anise's room.

"Hey—hey—what's going on?" Anise protested.

Keisha gestured to the door, and Anise unlocked it. Practically dragging her inside, Keisha locked the door behind them and turned to Anise.

"Keisha, what's wrong?"

"Oh please, Anise! It's not like you don't know!"

298

"Know what?"

Keisha rolled her eyes. "I'm not brain dead. Or blind. I saw those Embleck Army badges and the symbol on the *Embleck Army uniform* just as well as you did."

"I—I—" Anise stuttered.

"Is he threatening you?" Keisha placed her hands on her hips. "Or is this involvement voluntary?"

"He's...he's not threatening me."

Keisha arched an eyebrow; leaning to the side. "Oh, and look here." She walked over to the dresser, bent over, and picked something up.

"An Embleck Army badge! And who's it made out to?" Keisha held up the badge and shook it at Anise. "You're talking with *High Commander Monroy?*"

Anise held out her hand, and Keisha dropped the badge in her hand. Anise winced, clearly seeing Liam's name. "I promise, I didn't tell him anything—"

"Oh, I'm not worried about that," Keisha interrupted. "I'm *worried* that my best friend talking with first, the enemy. Second, oh, I don't know—someone trying to kill her? And someone she's trying to kill? That seems logical, right?!"

"I..."

"So, tell me." Keisha crossed her arms. "How does one end up dating their arch-enemy?"

"We're not dating." Anise found her voice. "We're just...talking. It's... mutually beneficial."

"Uh-huh." Keisha looked over her coral-pink fingernails. "Right...that look he gave you was totally just friendly."

"Wait...what look?"

"You mean you didn't notice the adoration mixed with maybe a touch of pure, undying love on his face?"

"That was just for show," Anise protested.

"Yeah, maybe, but when I peeked through the door after, he still looked like that." Keisha flopped down on Anise's armchair. "So yeah, sure. It's *mutually beneficial*."

"Keisha, I..." Anise sighed. "I can't explain it all right now. I just need you to trust me and my judgment."

"But how do you know he's trustworthy? That this isn't just a ruse? Or is...whatever this is something you only want to believe?"

"I trust he won't hurt me," Anise said finally. "That's all I have right now."

Keisha sighed, shaking her head. "I think you've gone a little mad…but I trust you. And if you trust Monroy…I'll accept that. *I don't trust him yet, though!*"

"Thank you," Anise sighed in relief. "That's all I needed to hear."

Keisha hugged her, and Anise returned the embrace.

"I have to get going," Keisha said, reluctantly pulling away. "But let's have dinner together, okay?"

Anise smiled. "I'd love that."

Keisha pulled her back in for one last hug before she turned and left with a swish of her scarf.

Anise felt her expression slip away, worry swirling in her chest. What if Keisha was right? What if she was blinding herself because she *wanted* to believe Liam?

It doesn't matter, Anise reminded herself. *You're just working with him to figure out this connection—and that's all. Keisha was exaggerating on the "look of undying love." Besides…Liam doesn't have to know.*

Guilt crept over Anise at her thoughts, but she shoved it down, turning back to the records shelf with a sigh.

Liam reached into the energy field, hoping to hear Anise's voice, but received only silence. It had been three days since they'd last spoken, and he'd been trying to make contact with her all day.

Anise? Liam tried again. He sighed heavily when he received no response. Again.

Besides receiving no responses, Liam's hum was off too. It was higher pitched than usual, wavering oddly. It was driving him insane—but how could he turn off something inside his own head?

Liam?

Liam breathed a sigh of relief. *I'm here.*

Anise's mental voice sounded strangely emotionless. *What's up?*

I was worried about you. Can I teleport over there?

Alright.

Liam created a portal and stepped into what appeared to be the back corner of a restaurant. He glanced around, but the room was nearly empty.

After the lack of screaming assured Liam no one had seen, he turned around, catching sight of Anise sitting at a small booth in the corner.

Liam stepped over to her, glancing over her. A red flush tinted her cheeks, and her eyes were red. Hesitantly, Liam took a seat beside her. "Anise, is everything okay?"

"Yes...I'm fine," Anise mumbled.

Now that Liam was closer to her, he could see that wasn't the case. He could feel the heat radiating off her arm where it touched his, despite her violent shivering.

"You don't look fine," Liam said gently. Recalling what his father had done when he was unwell, he ripped off his glove and pressed the back of his hand to her head.

The heat of her skin against his couldn't be a good sign. "Anise, I think you have a fever."

"Really?" Anise murmured, and a second later, slumped against his shoulder.

"Stars." Liam shifted around, carefully taking Anise's

unconscious body into his arms before standing.

This is a problem. Liam looked at Anise's flushed face, worry churning in his chest. She needed help, but he had no idea where to take her.

Liam readjusted Anise in his arms so he was supporting her head better, and left the restaurant. He walked through a series of identical empty hallways, hoping he would find someone to help.

"Hey!" A woman's voice shouted. It was Keisha, the girl that had seen them the other day. "What are you doing? What's wrong with Anise?"

"I think she has a fever," Liam said, shifting Anise so Keisha could check her forehead. "Can you help?"

Keisha pulled back her hand, a dismayed expression on her face. "Yes, I can. Follow me."

Keisha set off down the hall, and Liam followed her. She led them up a set of stairs and down another corridor.

"Get me her key card," Keisha ordered him as they turned a corner and came to a door.

Liam rather awkwardly adjusted Anise and reached into her pocket, pulling out a flat card. "This?"

Keisha nodded, taking it from him. She swiped it across

the door lock and led them inside.

"Put her down." Keisha went straight to a cabinet on the wall and searched through it. Liam carefully laid Anise on her bed and took off her shoes.

Keisha handed him a vial and two cold cloths. "She needs a capful of this stuff and the cloth on her forehead. Use the other for her face. I'm really late for an appointment, so can you take care of it?"

"I—are you sure?" Liam asked as he accepted the items.

"I think so…" Keisha's expression shifted as she finished. "High Commander Liam Monroy."

"Uh…" Liam's heartbeat jumped up as he tried to think of a quick excuse.

"I know who you are. Anise told me the truth after I saw you two." Keisha said, narrowing her eyes. "You better be careful with her. If you betray her…I won't hunt you down, but I'll hand her all the weaponry she wants."

"That won't be necessary," Liam said. "Thank for your assistance.

"I'll be back to check on her later." With that, Keisha turned around in a swish of her scarf and left.

Liam quickly turned his attention to Anise. He poured the

capful of liquid in her mouth and laid the cloth on her forehead while using the other to bathe her neck. Moments later, Anise slowly opened her eyes.

"What's going on?" she rasped and reached up to remove the cloth from her head.

"You're fine." Liam gently moved her hand away. "You have a fever, but Keisha and I are taking care of it."

"If I'm sick, you need to stay away," Anise managed, her voice dry.

"I'm staying to take care of you." Liam stood up and walked over to the small kitchen area. "Now, where do you keep your glasses?"

Anise pointed to a cabinet. Liam took the glass and filled it with cold water. He handed it to Anise, who accepted gratefully.

"Thank you," she whispered.

"No problem. Do you need anything else?"

"Can you make sure Joffrey has food in his bowl?" Anise gestured to a bowl sitting on the floor. "His food is in that bottom cabinet."

"Sure." Liam got the food bag and poured some into the near-empty bowl.

"Meerooooow."

Liam glanced up, seeing Joffrey had appeared beside the food bowl.

"Meeerroow," Joffrey said disapprovingly.

"Joffrey, behave," Anise called, immediately breaking into a coughing fit.

Joffrey hissed at Liam and ran over to Anise's bed. With a flying leap, he landed on her feet. There, he curled up and, with one last scornful look at Liam, fell asleep.

"I don't think he likes me much," Liam stated.

Anise chucked through her coughing. "Yeah—I think you're—right."

"What else can I get you?" Liam inquired after she had stopped coughing.

"Can I have some more water, my comm, and that book?" Anise indicated a book sitting on her dresser.

Liam brought the things to her. "Planets of the Galaxy?"

"It has holographs for every planet. I haven't gotten to travel much, so this is the next best thing." Anise opened the book, pointing to the holograph of a dog-eared page. "This is my favorite."

The holograph was of a beautiful ocean sunset from Keylamay. The stunning blue water reflected the bright colors of the sunset, gold, pink, and lavender.

"It is beautiful," Liam said.

Anise gently ran her finger over the page. "I've always wanted to see the ocean myself, but I guess I've never gotten around to it."

"Why not?"

"I've been busy training here," Anise began, pausing to cough again. "And besides, I don't have anybody that would go with me. I'd be happy to see it on my own, but it's better with someone else."

"I would take you to the ocean," Liam said, instantly stunned by the offer. "If that's not too forward."

"It's not too forward; it's nice." Anise smiled sleepily, then yawned.

"I think you need to go to sleep," Liam said quickly. "You have to rest if you want to get your strength back up."

"I know." Anise yawned again. "I'll go to sleep now."

"Good." Liam turned off the light. "Sweet dreams."

"Thank you, Liam," Anise whispered.

"What are friends for?" Liam smiled at her and created a portal home.

Anise sat in front of her mirror, finishing braiding her hair. It had taken a few days, but she'd finally recovered from her illness. Liam had transmitted and checked on her each day, a fact that made Anise's heart beat a little faster if she thought about it for too long.

A knock on the door pulled Anise from her thoughts. "Coming!"

"Hi, Anise." Caiden stepped inside her room. "How are you feeling?"

"Much better, thanks." Anise closed the door behind him. "How can I help you this morning?"

Caiden sat on the edge of her bed. "I had a question for you."

"Yes?" Anise tied off her braid with a scarf.

"Who's Liam?"

Anise whipped around, quickly trying to act casual. "How do you know about him?"

Caiden shrugged. "The other day, when we were at lunch and Keisha called. I overheard you say, 'No, not with Liam, with Caiden.' I was just…curious about who he was."

"Oh." Anise twisted the end of her braid in her fingers. "Well, Liam is from another base, and we… we're kind of…together?"

"Like…dating?"

"Maybe?"

"If he breaks your heart, I can beat him up for you," Caiden offered. "After you do, of course."

"Thanks," Anise laughed, relieved her brother didn't seem too upset. "But that hopefully won't be necessary."

"Good." Caiden stood up. "Well, I just wanted to check, so now I'll be off. When can I meet this guy?"

"Oh…I don't know," Anise said quickly. "He's very busy. Lots of important assignments and all that."

"I'll accept that for now." Caiden kissed her cheek on his way out. "Bye."

"Bye." The second he was gone, Anise let out a sigh of relief. *That was close.*

Now that her thoughts were on Liam, Anise decided to contact him and thank him again for everything he had done. *Liam?*

Hi, Anise. His crisp accent did something strange to Anise's core, and she internally scolded herself.

Is it possible for me to see you for a minute?

Um…yes. I'll make you a portal.

Anise waited, and a moment later, a swirling portal appeared. Taking a deep breath, she stepped through, appearing in an Embleck suite.

Liam dissolved the portal and sent her a smile, his expression tired. "Hi."

"Hi." Anise examined his face, noting the red flush over his skin. "Liam, are you sick?"

"I—" Liam started but broke off as he started coughing.

"Oh, I'm sorry." Anise shook her head. "I knew she shouldn't have been around me.'

"It's—fine." Liam managed to say between coughing. "I told Zamir I needed to take the day off, and he didn't protest."

"Well, I insist you get in bed now," Anise ordered. "You have to rest while you can. I'll get you some medicine."

"I can handle it; you should go home," Liam said, his voice rough.

"I'm taking care of you, just like you did for me," Anise said. "No arguments."

"But—"

"None. Into bed."

"Fine, fine." Liam pulled off his boots and dropped them beside the dresser. "But how are you going to get home if I don't make the portal?"

"I think I can work your sword," Anise said. "If you can go through my shields, I bet I can use your teleportation. Now, bed."

"Okay." Liam sank onto the edge of his bed, his skin paling despite the red across his cheeks.

"Much better." Anise pulled the blankets back. "What can I get you? A book you're reading, maybe?"

"I think I have a book of battle plans on the dresser."

Anise rolled her eyes. "Battle plans do not count as a book."

Liam shrugged. "Zamir doesn't approve of books."

What monster doesn't approve of books? "Sit back, alright? Rest. Where can I get you some water?"

"I have some glasses in that cabinet."

Anise opened the cabinet, quickly finding the glasses. But it was the small vial beside them that caught her attention. Anise picked it up, and the dark grey liquid inside sloshed unnaturally.

"What's this?" Anise held up the vial.

Liam winced, beginning to cough. "That's—my emotion—elixir."

Anise's eyes darted to the bottle. "What?"

Liam managed to get himself under control. "I take the elixir to…dull my emotions. It started after my friend died…and I've been taking it ever since."

Anise stared at him, a strange sense of horror creeping over her. "You—you mean that this removes your—your *emotions?*"

"Yes…" Liam said slowly. "But I don't think the last dose worked properly."

Liam broke into another coughing fit, leaving Anise standing shellstruck. She stared at the bottle in her hand, feeling tainted—as though the evil nature of the contents seeped through the glass.

Shaking off the icy claws around her heart, Anise handed Liam the glass of water. "I'm glad it didn't. Not being able to feel…can't be good for you." *Isn't that an understatement.*

Liam took a drink, his voice quiet and strained. "I…didn't mind too much then."

Anise turned back to the cabinets, feeling sick herself at the thought of Liam at only seventeen having his human rights stolen away from him.

They've taken his ability to feel. Anise's blood ran cold. *Stripped him of his books, his freedom, his emotions—what's next, his soul?*

Unless they already have it.

Anise shivered, going back to the cabinet and looking to see if it held any fever medicine. After a few minutes of searching, she still couldn't find what she needed.

Liam had fallen silent, and Anise hoped it meant he'd fallen asleep. She glanced back at him, stunned to see he was still awake. His head rested back on the headboard with his eyes barely open.

"My head hurts."

Anise approached him, noting he looked much worse than he had a few minutes ago. Anise pressed her hand against his forehead, feeling it burning with fever.

"Do you have any medicine around here?" Anise asked. "Or at least a cold cloth?"

Liam's eyes were half-closed, and he shook his head.

"Liam?" Anise pressed, but he didn't respond, his head limp.

Anise bit her lip before untying the scarf from the end of her braid. She turned on the cold water and wet her scarf thoroughly as her hair began to slip from its braid and fall around her face.

Tucking her hair behind her ear, Anise returned to Liam. He seemed to be awakening, mumbling to himself.

Anise swiped her scarf across his forehead, and for some strange reason, she found herself looking at his lips. *Watch it, Desson. Don't get any ideas.*

A few moments later, Liam opened his eyes. Anise continued to bathe his face and neck, and he glanced up at her.

Liam's fever-glazed eyes met hers, and a warm, genuine smile spread across his face. "Anise?"

"I'm here," Anise said softly.

Liam's smile grew at the sound of her voice. Abruptly, his expression became confused.

"What's wrong?" Anise asked.

Liam tilted his head to the side, examining her face. "When did I kiss you?"

Anise felt heat race up her neck, face, and ears. "N-no—no. You never kissed me."

Liam frowned slightly. "I should have. I remember almost kissing you."

Anise blinked, stunned. "When?"

"In the jungle…and the…oasis." Liam seemed to be struggling to remember what he was talking about.

Anise felt a chill run down her spine. *The oasis?* Memories of the oasis picnic she'd had with Roy flashed through her mind, but her thoughts quickly shifted to the other place he'd mentioned.

"What do you mean—the jungle?"

"Back when we were stranded." Liam's gaze travelled to her lips. "I'd still like to kiss you."

Anise couldn't keep the surprised expression off her face, but Liam didn't seem to notice it. "I—I think it's the fever talking now," she said with an awkward laugh.

"Maybe," Liam conceded, his eyes glassy.

Truthfully, Anise realized that if Liam had tried to kiss her, she wouldn't have objected—and the though frightened her. *Anise, what are you thinking? He's supposed to be your enemy—you shouldn't be thinking about kissing him!*

Anise leaned over and continued bathing Liam's flushed skin to distract herself from her thoughts.

Liam reached up and fingered her hair falling over her shoulder. Anise froze, her eyes locking with his. The tenderness in Liam's eyes was unmistakable, mixed with the daze of his fever.

Anise barely breathed as Liam brushed the back of his fingers across her cheek, his expression filled with reverence.

"You're so beautiful," he whispered. "Exactly like an angel."

Anise's heart beat triple time. *The fever must be making him talk more than he probably wants to. If he was a little more coherent, he wouldn't be saying any of these things.* She imagined how embarrassed he would be if he figured out what he had said.

But even if he didn't have the fever, would he think those things and just not say them?

"Thank you," Anise said finally. "Oh, I just remembered," she exclaimed, distracting herself from the fire burning her cheeks.

Anise dug into her jacket pocket, pulling out a small bottle filled with round tablets. "This is my fever medicine. I forgot I had it in this jacket from when I had my fever. Open your mouth."

Liam did, and Anise gave him the medicine "Hold it under your tongue. It should help you start feeling better pretty quickly."

"I hope so." Sleep faintly slurred Liam's words. "Thank you for taking care of me. It's…it's been a long time since…anyone cared."

"You're welcome," Anise replied softly. "You…you should go sleep. Get some rest."

"Okay." Liam closed his eyes.

Anise turned off the light and sank down in a chair by the window. She'd had Caiden, Keisha, Tyler, Jack—plenty of people to take care of her…and Liam had no one.

Not no one. I'm here now. Anise scanned around the room. Liam had no personal items anywhere; it could be anyone's room.

Liam's breathing became slow and steady, signaling sleep. Anise stood and picked up his sword from its hook on the wall.

Quietly, Anise tiptoed over to Liam's bed, gazing down at him. His soft…innocent...expression pulled at Anise's heart. A lock of his blond hair fell over his face, obscuring one eye. Anise leaned down and lightly brushed Liam's hair from his face.

An unexpected wave of tenderness surged through Anise, and next thing she knew, she gently pressed a kiss to Liam's cheek.

Stunned with herself, Anise lingered there for a second longer than she wanted to, simply savoring the tingling sensation on her lips.

Abruptly, Anise stood, slashing his sword through the air while thinking of home. In a flash, a swirling portal was created. Anise set the sword back on the dresser and stepped through the portal without looking back.

However, she left a little too quickly to see Liam open his eyes, a smile tugging at his lips.

CHAPTER 25

The next morning, Liam awoke to his alarm beeping shrilly. He groaned and opened his eyes, only to have his vision obscured by pure white.

Alarmed, Liam reached up and yanked off whatever it was before turning off the alarm.

Liam glanced around his room, then down at the fabric in his hand. It was a white scarf that was slightly damp. Abruptly, Liam remembered Anise putting him to bed and giving him something for his fever.

The images were blurry, and his memory seemed to be fading in and out. Even so, he did remember Anise being there.

She took care of me. Liam hesitantly touched the scarf. It was such a strange idea, having someone who cared about him.

A blurry scene drifted into his mind: Anise standing beside his bed, telling him *I think it's the fever talking now.*

Oh, stars. Liam dropped his face into his hands, dreading what he could have told her.

Liam? Anise's transmitted voice startled Liam, and he jolted.

Hi, Anise

How are you feeling?

Better.

Can you make me a portal?

Okay. A rush of worry hit Liam as he stood and picked up his sword. He hoped Anise wasn't going to arrive and reveal he had confessed undying love for her or something equally embarrassing.

Liam created the portal, waiting tensely until Anise stepped through the portal. "Oh, you look much better today."

"Do I?" Liam said, his mind abruptly blank.

"Yes, much better." Anise stepped forward and placed her hand on his forehead. Liam's eyes widened in surprise, but he didn't pull away.

"Your fever is gone too," Anise said and removed her hand. "That's good, especially since it was so high yesterday."

"It was?" Liam internally cursed his sudden inability to speak properly.

"Yeah, a little," Anise said this lightly as if trying not to worry him. "Yesterday, you were a little...out of it with fever."

Liam felt his face slowly flushing red. "I didn't...uh...say anything embarrassing...did I?"

Anise hesitated for a second, and Liam fervently hoped her silence didn't mean he had rambled on about her beauty or told her that he loved her.

Which, at this point, Liam worried wouldn't be too far from the truth.

"No, nothing embarrassing at all. Just mumbling about something or the other."

Liam let out a small sigh of relief.

"You were very thankful for my helping you," Anise said, and her expression...soft? "And you were very...sweet."

Something about the way she said sweet made Liam suspicious she wasn't telling him everything— but he decided he'd rather not know.

Something had shifted in Anise's eyes—something that hadn't been there before. A tenderness that Liam's heart beat faster.

"Well, thank you again," Liam said finally.

"Of course," Anise said, glancing away. "I probably should get going now."

"Alright," Liam accepted. "Oh, I think this must be yours."

Anise accepted the scarf he offered her, tucking it in her pocket. "It is, thank you."

"Hopefully, we can see each other again soon," Liam said softly.

Anise smiled. "I'd like that."

Liam created her a portal. "Bye."

"Bye." Anise waved as she stepped through.

Liam stared at the spot she had been standing in as another piece of his memory fell into place. Anise, leaning over and kissing his cheek.

*What in the galaxy did I say to her? W*hatever he had said seemed to be having a positive effect, though.

"What am I doing?" Liam raked a hand through his hair. He shouldn't be hoping Anise might be feeling the same way he was.

They couldn't be together unless he left the Embleck Army, or she left the Qor. Anise would never leave the Qor—and Liam didn't want her to. But he couldn't leave the Embleck Army without putting her in danger.

Liam aimed his sword at the android's battery core, winning the strike. The training droid powered off, and Liam sheathed his sword as he saw Brendon approaching him.

"Sir, King Zamir wishes to see you, Sir," Brendon reported.

"Again?" Liam asked in annoyance. "He never used to see me this often."

"Sorry." Brendon shrugged. "I'm just the messenger. He's waiting for you in the lab."

"I know it's not your fault." Liam bit back a sigh, leaving the training room.

Navigating the Embleck halls, Liam found the lab, and knocked loudly, taking out his annoyance on the door.

"You don't have to break the door down."

Liam scowled, stepping inside. The lab walls were covered in shelving, each shelf brimming with various elixir bottles. High Commander Ankor examined the shelves, turning when he heard Liam.

King Zamir stood beside a table, and he lifted his head as Liam approached.

"Greetings, Your Majesty." Liam bowed.

"Hello, Monroy," King Zamir hissed. "I haven't had a chance to ask about Commander Desson. How is her *removal* going?"

Liam's heartbeat jumped up, and he rubbed his fingers against the palms of his hands, his mind racing.

"You are nervous," King Zamir said, staring at Liam's hands.

Liam forced his hands to be still. "I...I..." he stuttered, trying to come up with some plausible lie.

"Yes?"

"I didn't want to admit the truth," Liam said finally. "I can't read her mind or teleport to her unless I know her exact location. It—it makes it nearly impossible to find her."

"I see..." Zamir nodded "Nevertheless, I hope you are not having any...temptations to leave our side."

"Never, Your Majesty," Liam lied. "My loyalty lies with you, always."

"Of course," King Zamir said. "Now that is settled…we have something for you."

High Commander Ankor looked unbearably smug as he handed King Zamir a tiny bottle filled with black liquid.

"This is for you to try." King Zamir's voice held a note of satisfaction. "Take it now."

"Must I?" Liam glanced at the bottle. Something about the liquid looked wrong, and a heavy sensation settled in his chest. "I'd rather not."

"You must," King Zamir demanded, and Liam reluctantly picked up the bottle.

Taking a deep breath, Liam uncorked the bottle and slowly lifted it, pouring the liquid down his throat. For a moment, nothing happened.

Abruptly, Liam began to feel warm, but it quickly shifted to hot. His blood seemed to be boiling, and spots appeared before his eyes.

Fire burned through his whole body, and sharp needles of pain shot through him. His heartbeat thumped and wavered strangely in his ears.

Liam clutched his chest as his heart tightened, and for a single moment, he felt as though he was falling. As abruptly as it started, the heat and pain stopped.

Something was very, very wrong.

Or maybe it's right. Liam's voice sounded hollow, and his head was cloudy as he pulled himself up.

"What are you?" King Zamir's voice broke through the fog.

"Ready to serve." Liam heard his voice as though it was far away.

"Good…Commander Desson is alone. Kill her."

"Yes, Your Majesty." Liam heard himself say. A tiny voice in the back of his mind wondered how King Zamir knew she was alone and an even tinier voice screamed that he couldn't hurt Commander Desson.

Of course I can. She must be removed.

"Now," King Zamir ordered.

"Yes, Your Majesty." Liam slashed open a portal and stepped through.

Commander Desson whipped around when she saw him, her expression relaxing. "Oh, Liam, what are you doing here? We didn't have a meeting."

Liam gave a start. How did she know his name?

Never mind. Liam raised his sword, pointing it at her. The voice in his mind screamed at him to stop, but he ignored it.

"Liam, what are you doing?" Fear flashed across Commander Desson's face as she pulled free her own sword.

"Removing an enemy," he snapped. He stabbed at her, and she dodged.

Liam continued to strike at her as she ducked away. She blocked his strikes but didn't attack. Something about fighting her was very wrong—pain ripped through his chest, though not from her blade.

Aiming a perfect strike, Liam knocked her sword from her hand, sending it spiraling across the floor. Desson reached for her ray gun, but Liam struck at her arm before she could reach it.

"Liam, please!" Desson shouted. Leaning back to avoid a stab, she stumbled and fell backward.

Liam raised his sword above her just as she threw a shield of white light at him. It passed right through his body—and something changed.

Cold ice flooded Liam's veins, his skin crawling. His heartbeat slowed and steadied to normal as the tiny voice came rushing in and filled his mind. Everything he had just done hit him like a bullet to the chest, and he staggered on his feet, hearing his sword *clang* against the floor.

"Liam?" Anise's voice shook. Liam glanced up and saw her backed up against the wall, pointing a ray gun at his head.

"Anise…" Liam's voice sounded hoarse and raw in his ears.

"Liam, what was that?" Anise whispered, the ray gun in her hand trembling.

"I don't know." Liam shakily stepped away from her. "I…I took a new elixir from Zamir…maybe…"

"What was it for?"

"He didn't tell me," Liam said. "I…I can't remember what happened after I took it. Wait…he did mention…you."

"Do you think…that elixir was because Zamir wanted you to…kill me?"

Liam rubbed his head, struggling to remember anything else. "I…it would make sense." He darted a look at her, his eyes instantly locking on a red stain appearing on her shirt. "Did…did I do that?"

Anise quickly covered her arm. "Don't worry about it."

Liam's mind spun, fear cold in his chest. Zamir had caused him to attack Anise with nothing more than an elixir...he'd drawn blood...*I'd have killed her if not for the way her shield reversed the elixir.*

Anise stepped forward, placing her hand on his arm. "Listen, I—"

Liam jerked away, holding out his hands as he backed up. "No—no, you have to stay away."

"Liam..." Anise's hand fell to her side, a distressed expression on her face.

"Don't touch me, please." Liam took another step back. "The potion's effects could come back. Just...I have to go."

"Okay." Anise wrapped her arms. "See you later?"

"Maybe." Liam refused to her eyes as he created a portal home.

CHAPTER 26

The next day Liam awoke with a throbbing headache. A sense of hollowness settled into him as he numbly completed his daily assignments.

I would've killed Anise. How didn't I realize?

Liam? Anise's voice pierced Liam's mind, and he shook his head harshly.

Please talk to me.

Yes?

Hi...are you okay?

I'm fine.

Good. Anise's voice held a note of doubt. *I'd like to meet up.*

I don't know. Liam shifted. He couldn't see Anise—what if

the elixir's effects returned? *I have an assignment to pick up some items from our Tironlay base.*

I'll meet you nearby, then.

Liam flinched. *No, Anise. Tironlay is Embleck territory—it's not safe.*

I've been on Tironlay before, Anise protested. *I've been to the base there.*

I can't. Liam swallowed hard. *Maybe later.*

Liam, if this is about—

Liam cut off the connection, blocking out her words. Truthfully, it took all of his self-control not to teleport to her...but he had to stay away.

If the potion's effects came back and he hurt her or worse...Liam wouldn't be able to live with himself.

"Sir, the ship is about to leave." Brendon appeared at the door.

"Fine." Liam donned his mask and followed Brendon to the ship.

Soon, the ship landed in the hangar of the Tironlay base. Liam disembarked, scanning the brimming shipyard. "I'm going to take a walk."

"A walk, Sir?" The office sounded baffled.

"Yes." Liam nodded. "You take the others and pick up the package for Zamir. I'll be back.

Without waiting for a response, Liam turned and left the hangar, venturing out into the rocky landscape.

Once out of sight, Liam removed his mask and dropped it beside a rock. The air was heavy with mist, and he could feel the tiny droplets of water settling on his face.

Feeling a faint sense of freedom, Liam traversed the rough terrain, hiking up the steep slant of the land. Giant boulders acted as hiding places, leaving Liam with the feeling that someone was watching him.

Brushing it aside, Liam continued, taking the last steps until he reached the top of the cliff. A narrow peninsula reached past the cliff face, and he walked out on it, stopping near the edge.

Wind whipped through Liam's hair as he scanned his surroundings. From the edge of a cliff, he could see tall, foreboding mountains, dangerously sheer cliffs, and far in the distance, a glint of sunlight off the lake. Liam glanced over the edge of the cliff, unable to see the ground through the heavy mist.

Liam stepped forward until the tips of his boots hung over the edge of the cliff. He peered down into the misty nothingness, wondering how far down the ground was.

The cliffs were the perfect place to think, and Liam allowed his mind to slip away. He couldn't risk Anise...but he also couldn't help longing to see her.

For a moment, Liam allowed himself to wonder what would happen if he left the Embleck Army.

We would both die, that's what. If he defected, the Embleck Army would kill him for it, and if he was with Anise...they would kill her too.

I'm already responsible for the death of the first woman I loved. I can't be responsible for another.

Wait. Liam caught his thoughts. *Love? Surely, I love Ree...but when did I start thinking about Anise like that?*

Do...I really...love her? It's been so long since I felt...anything...especially like this. I don't even know. The last time I felt even close to this was...when I was with Ree.

*But this...what I feel for Anise...*Liam raked his fingers through his hair. *This is a different feeling—deeper and stronger...something...unfamiliar.*

Liam sighed and scuffed his boot heel across the peninsula's edge, sending the small rocks falling down into the mist.

A faint sound caught Liam's attention, pulsing at the back of his mind. His hum quivered, shifting up an octave.

Liam spun around, his boot catching on a rock. He wavered, trying to regain his balance.

"Liam!" A hand grabbed his arm, hauling him back.

Liam stumbled at the force, falling beside—"Anise?"

Anise stared at him, her eyes wide. "What in the galaxy are you doing?"

"I—I was looking at the mountains," Liam stammered. "What are you doing here?"

"I knew you were upset about what happened, so I wanted to talk." Anise gripped his arm, worry on her face. "But you were acting elusive. And after what you said…I got worried…and Tironlay is known for its cliffs…" Anise trailed off.

"Oh." Liam glanced back at the mountains in the distance, then to Anise's hand around his arm. "I'm sorry, I shouldn't have—"

"No!" Anise shook her head violently. "Don't apologize. I need you to trust that it'll be okay. Don't take that potion again, and everything will be fine. I can take care of myself; better now that I know what could be going on."

"I do trust you," Liam said softly. "I know you can take care of yourself. I just…I don't want to hurt you."

"I get it." A moment passed before Anise rested her head on

his shoulder.

Liam held his breath as his heartbeat picked up. Anise's body nestled against his, and her arm slipped around his waist. Slowly, he allowed himself to relax, savoring the sensation.

"This is nice," Anise said, her voice quiet.

"It is."

Anise tilted her head, her eyes drawn to his new badge. "You're…you're a general now?"

"I…am," Liam said slowly.

"Well…congratulations," Anise said hesitantly.

"Thank you." Liam couldn't help but feel like his promotion wasn't something to be proud of, but he remained quiet.

They sat together for a moment longer before Anise shifted, glancing behind them. "Aren't your soldiers going to be looking for you?"

"Maybe." Liam held her just a smidge tighter.

"I…I should go. Before anyone comes looking for you." Anise pulled away, standing.

Liam got to his feet, wishing her words weren't true. "You're right. Transmit if you need anything, okay?"

"I will." Anise smiled gently. "Bye."

Liam watched her as she picked her way among the rocks and disappeared into the mist. A sense of loneliness and longing filled him.

You're just hurting yourself. You can't have feelings for her, and you know it.

Liam took one last look at the dark mountains before turning away and trudging back to the ship.

Anise carefully slipped through the rocky terrain, keeping her senses alert for any sign of Embleck soldiers following her. A voice caught her attention, and she spun around.

"Commander Desson!"

Anise placed her hand on the hilt of her sword as Commander Brendon racing towards her. "What are you doing here?"

Brendon skidded up beside her. "I hadn't seen you since you were in that shipwreck, so I wanted to see if you were okay."

Anise lifted an eyebrow. "You do? But I'm an enemy."

"I know," Brendon admitted. "But you're also really...nice—and a friend of General Monroy's."

"I'm not his friend," Anise said quickly.

"Oh, please." Brendon rolled his eyes. "I saw you two up on the cliffs. The only reason you two wouldn't be called friends is if you're more than friends."

"Oh." Anise felt herself flush. "Are you going to tell the Emblecks?"

"Of course not!" Brendon sounded offended. "I am loyal to my general over anyone else."

"By the way," Anise started. "Back when I was being held by the Army, you told me that Liam wouldn't hurt me. What made you say that?"

Brendon glanced at his boots. "Years ago...Liam and I were sweeping an Embleck territory forest...and we were supposed to eliminate anyone we found. There were three children playing in a clearing. Liam started over to them...and I was dreading what would happen."

Brendon cleared his throat. "Liam asked the kids where

their parents were, and brought them back. He warned them all to leave…and he wasn't supposed to do that…I realized he isn't a bad person. And…I knew he wouldn't hurt you either."

"You were right," Anise said softly. "He didn't."

Brendon smiled. "Called it. As long as you're okay, I have to get back before anyone notices I'm gone."

"Okay," Anise said. "And thank you."

"For what?"

"For telling me about the real Liam."

"Sure." Brendon gave her a short bow before turning and racing back into the mist.

Anise watched him go before continuing toward her ship, her mind turning her conversation with Brendon. More and more, Liam seemed like a good person in a bad situation.

Seeing Liam standing beside that cliff today…it had sent a bolt of fear straight into Anise's heart, forcing her to realize that she…she cared for him.

And how much it would hurt to lose him.

What are you doing? Why him, of all the people in the galaxy, it's him I'm—

Anise shut down her thoughts instantly. *No—no. You*

can't start thinking about him like that!

"Ugh." Anise buried her face in her hands. "Why?"

Obviously, Anise received no answer. Honestly, she wasn't even sure what she was asking.

What am I going to do? And if there's a chance he could be Roy...no, you decided it wasn't possible. Besides...Roy would have recognized me. There's no reason for him not to...

Right?

CHAPTER 27

Liam reclined back in his chair, pausing a moment from his book. A sense of…peace settled over him. He glanced up at the domed glass ceiling of the Galactic Records Hall, savoring the deep blue sky. It felt incredible to be away from the dark Embleck base and in the bright, airy room of the hall.

How long had it been since he'd simply enjoyed a book and the sunlight? Liam shook his head. It had to have been before he joined the Embleck Army. How could he have neglected one of his favorite hobbies for this long?

Liam cocked his head to the side, the soft music drifting through the hall catching his attention. It sounded familiar…

Ree's song.

The second Liam thought of her Ree, a bolt of sadness and pain shot through his chest. To his shock, tears filled his eyes, each beat of his heart painful.

What in the galaxy? Liam's throat ached, and he felt something drip down his cheek. He brushed his gloved fingers over his face and numbly realized he was crying.

Liam hadn't cried for Ree since the day he'd discovered her death. On that day, he had locked himself in his room and cried until his chest had ached, and he hadn't a single tear left. But the next day, King Zamir had given him his emotion elixir, and he hadn't cried about...*anything* since.

Standing, Liam created a portal home. He appeared into his room, instantly collapsing across his bed as the tears finally escaped.

Abruptly, the tears vanished, and his grief ebbed. Liam shook his head in confusion, only for the sadness to break over him like a wave. A minute later, it vanished again, returning almost immediately.

Liam swiped a hand over his eyes as the tears continued to flow. Grief...sadness...he hadn't felt it this deeply in years. It ripped through his soul, drawing him back to the day Ree had died.

Finally, the grief slowly trickled away, his tears fading. Liam sat up, disjointed and more than a little disturbed.

Standing, Liam trudged over to the window, strangely

unsteady on his feet. The stars filled the space around the base hovering above Nockalore, making Liam feel small.

Liam looked out at the sparkling lights as another bolt of grief hit him. He sank into a chair beside the window, knocking his bag from the jungle onto the floor.

The bag clinked as it hit the floor, and Liam's attention locked on the sound. Reaching down, Liam picked up the bag, curiosity filling him. He felt around inside, trying to figure out what had made the sound.

Liam's fingers brushed something cool and smooth, and he grasped the object. *What in the galaxy?*

A moment later, Liam had his answer as he pulled a bracelet with turquoise beads out of the bag.

Oh. Liam held the bracelet up to the light, examining it closer. *This must be Anise's. I put it in my bag before we left, but I guess I forgot about it.*

Liam dropped the bag beside the chair and stood before the window as his thoughts drifted to Anise. She was an enemy to the Embleck Army....but now...he couldn't think of her as his enemy.

More than that, I can't deny I have feelings for her. I...I just can't do anything about it. We're on opposite sides—nothing could ever come from this.

Besides, there's no way she feels the same. This thought sent a pang through Liam. *You can't forget that. Angels don't fall in love with monsters...like me.*

Almost subconsciously, Liam lightly pressed the beads against his lips. The bracelet made something flicker in the back of his memories, but he couldn't quite place it...

A faded, blurry image floated through Liam's mind: holding Ree's hand in the marketplace...and the turquoise beaded bracelet around her wrist.

How does Anise have the same bracelet?!

A loud knock jolted Liam from his thoughts. He quickly tucked the bracelet into his pocket and opened the door. Brendon braced his hand against the doorframe, panting as though he had been sprinting.

"Brendon?" Liam asked.

Brendon practically leaped inside, slamming the door. "Quick, you have to do something!"

"About what?"

"High Commander Ankor is on his way here now! They're preparing to ambush Commander Desson while she's scouting in the forest!"

"Oh, stars," Liam whispered. "Wait—how do you know

about Anise?"

"Doesn't matter, you just have to—"

Someone else knocked at the door. Liam and Brendon jumped as High Commander Ankor opened the door.

"Monroy, you need to come with us. King's orders," Ankor snapped and left.

Liam and Brendon shot worried looks at each other as they followed Ankor. Liam tried to transmit to Anise, but she wasn't responding. He could have used his new rank to dismiss Ankor's orders…but it was Zamir who had instructed him.

As the ship soared through space, Liam continued transmitting to Anise, but received no response. The ship soon landed in a dense forest, and disembarked. Ankor gestured for Liam to follow him as he tried one last time to transmit.

ANISE?

What's wrong? Anise's worried voice finally entered his mind.

Relief surged through Liam. It wasn't too late—he could warn her. *There's Embleck soldiers tracking you. I'm with them, but—*

A woman's shriek echoed through the forest. Liam jerked his head up and caught a glimpse of Anise through the trees, surrounded by Embleck soldiers. Liam bolted forward, forcing himself to stop before reaching Anise. Ankor appeared at his side as his worry grew.

Anise stood in a small clearing, her sword pointing at them. "Don't move a step closer."

What should I do? Liam asked her.

Don't blow our cover; I can handle this.

"Attack," High Commander Ankor ordered the soldiers. "Monroy, come over here."

Liam allowed High Commander Ankor to pull him a few steps away, his eyes locked on Anise.

Ankor took out a bottle from his pocket. "Take this—now."

Fear shot through Liam at the sight of the horrible black liquid inside the bottle. No—*no*, he couldn't.

"Zamir's orders."

Liam warred with himself desperately. If he refused...it could reveal Anise and his friendship, which would lead to their deaths. But if he didn't...

Ankor shoved the bottle into his hands, and Liam gripped it tightly. Anise struck down the last Embleck soldier, her eyes instantly flying to the potion bottle in Liam's hand. Instantly, all color faded from her face, and his hum jumped up, becoming frantic and high-pitched.

It was at that moment Liam realized his hum represented …Anise. When she was happy, the hum was clear and soft. But when she was scared, it became frantic. Liam almost wished he hadn't figured it out because now he could tell that Anise was...terrified.

It took all Liam's self-control not to throw the bottle in Ankor's face. The only thing stopping him was the knowledge that if he did, he'd be shot about sixteen times in two seconds, and Anise would be next.

"Take it," Ankor hissed.

A rustling sound filled the air, and Keisha burst from the jungle foliage, with two Qor soldiers right behind her.

"Anise!"

What are we going to do? I can't mind control them! Anise transmitted frantically.

I don't think we have any options. Liam responded. *I...I can't...I'm sorry.*

I know. Anise looked deeply pained.

No mercy, Anise. Liam met her eyes as he lifted the

bottle. *Promise me.*

Liam—

Liam swallowed half of the contents, bracing for the heat and pain...but nothing happened. The elixir didn't affect him this time—but now what?

Glancing at Brendon from the corner of his eye, Liam noted his obvious agitation. Against his own rules—and for lack of a better plan—Liam opened his powers to Brendon's mind.

You numbskull, fake them out already!

Oh. Liam raised his sword, striking at Anise. She blocked his strike, fear shining in her eyes.

Liam locked eyes with Anise as he dodged a strike. *So...you have any plans this weekend?*

Liam? Hope flickered in Anise's eyes.

It's me, Liam offered her a half smile. *Promise.*

Thank the stars! I—I don't know what to do here!

I have an idea. In a minute, we'll pretend that we're each injured. We can have our teams bring us back to our own ships, and it'll be like this never happened.

Good idea. Quick, line up with me so we can "stab" each other.

Perfect. Liam carefully moved so he and Anise were directly facing, continuing to trade strikes.

Here we go.

Liam twisted his sword so it slid under Anise's jacket, barely touching her side. She retaliated, stabbing at his ribs.

If Liam had remained still, Anise's sword would've barely grazed him. Instead, he stepped to the right, allowing her sword to rip into his side.

Liam didn't have to fake his gasp of pain as he stumbled backward, dropping his sword. Anise dramatically clutched her side and fell to the ground.

Good acting.

Liam realized that Anise didn't know he had actually been stabbed. *You too.* He tried to keep any hint of pain from his mental voice.

It almost seemed... Anise raised her head as Keisha and the boys raced to her, eyes locked on the red stain appearing on Liam's shirt. *Is that real?*

Yes?

Liam, why would you do that? Anise exclaimed as one of the boys scooped her up.

The Embleck Army won't tolerate any weaknesses. Any injury for me had to be real.

Why didn't you tell me that? Anise was almost out of Liam's sight.

It's fine. Liam allowed Brendon to hoist him to his feet. *It was worth it because you're safe.*

A moment passed. *Thank you.*

Anise's mental voice was warm with gratitude…and Liam wondered if there was something else there too.

You're welcome.

"Are you alright, Sir?" Brendon asked.

"More or less," Liam said through gritted teeth. The injury wasn't too deep, and with a dose or two of healing elixir, he would be fine.

"Good." Brendon wrapped Liam's arm around his shoulders.

"Brendon," Liam whispered. "How…how did you know that the potion wouldn't work?"

Brendon smirked as he helped Liam inside. "You know, water and black dye work wonders."

CHAPTER 28

Liam strode down the hall, deep in thought. He passed a group of soldiers leading a man in handcuffs—

Shock hit Liam as he did a double-take. "Brendon—hey you, stop!"

The soldiers froze, turning to him with fear in their eyes. "Sir?"

"What is the meaning of this?" Liam snapped.

"King's orders, General," one of the guards stammered.

"Liam, don't," Brendon whispered. "Just don't."

Liam stood, rooted in confusion. The guards quickly turned and led Brendon away. Liam hesitated for a moment before he turned on his heel and marched to King Zamir's throne room.

For the first time that Liam could remember, the doors to the throne room were wide open, and soldiers rushed around. Someone was shouting over the din, but no one was listening.

Liam shoved through the room until he stumbled into High Commander Ankor. He gripped Ankor on the shoulder, turning him around. "What's going on?"

"None of your business," Ankor snapped sharply, twisting away.

Frustrated, Liam shoved through the crowd, approaching King Zamir's throne. A dozen of the highest ranking officers surrounded him as they gestured to a holomap hovering above a table.

Liam walked up to the throne. "Sir—"

Without looking up, Zamir waved him away, continuing to speak with the other officers. A wave of anger crashed over Liam, but he refrained from showing it. He turned and pushed his way through the crowded room, finally reaching the hall and returning to his quarters.

Soon the lights of the base dimmed as night fell. Liam sat awake, watching the clock on his comm until it clicked over to the curfew—meaning the halls of the base would be empty, with the exception of the nightly patrols.

Liam stood and lifted his sword, creating a portal to

the only place Brendon could be: the prison.

Liam crept through the prison halls, scanning each cell. As he reached the end of the hall, the cells were empty, and he almost moved on to the next level. Something moved in the darkness of the last cell, and Liam approached.

"Brendon?"

"General Monroy?" Brendon stood from the undersized cot, shock evident in his voice.

"Brendon, why in the galaxy are you down here?" Liam pulled his cloak a little tighter against the chill filling the room.

"I...accidentally—" Brendon made air quotes. "—dropped a hairpin that Commander Desson used to escape back when she was captured. Someone played back the security footage, I suppose."

"What's with the air quotes?"

"It...uh...wasn't *exactly* an accident?"

"Wait. You—" Liam dropped his voice to a hushed whisper. "You helped her escape?"

"Yeah..."

"Brendon!" Liam whispered, stunned. "I—what possessed you to do that?"

"I wasn't about to let her be interrogated by the officers on that base," Brendon retorted. "The only joy in their lives is inflicting suffering. I didn't want to put her through that."

"I...I can't believe it," Liam said quietly, deeply grateful Anise had escaped from the jungle. "I thought you'd be loyal to the Embleck Army over a stranger you'd never met."

"Loyalty to the Embleck Army isn't all it's cracked up to be," Brendon replied, reclining back on his cot.

Liam shot a glance down the corridor before leaning in and whispering, "Do...do you ever think about...leaving?"

Brendon shot to his feet, gripping Liam's wrist through the bars. "Are—are you thinking of defecting?"

"Yes...no..." Liam swallowed hard. "But do you ever? Think about it, I mean."

Brendon sighed, releasing Liam. "Of course. But...I haven't ever planned on it. I follow you."

"Liam cocked his head to the side.

"When you saved me from the fire, I swore my loyalty to you. I intend to keep my promise."

"You know that as a part of the Embleck Army, you're supposed to be loyal to them, not just to me," Liam said.

"Sir, my loyalties do not lie with the Embleck Army; my loyalties lie with you. I am indebted to you, and where you go, I will follow."

A warmth filled Liam's chest at Brendon's words. "Thank you, Brendon. I don't know what I did to deserve you, but your friendship means the galaxy to me. I just don't want you to stay out of loyalty."

"I feel the same, Sir. Your companionship here is everything." Brendon returned his smile. "And I will not be leaving without you, General."

"Deserting means certain death…" Liam said softly. "But…if I ever find a way to leave…I'll get you out too."

"I'll look forward to it," Brendon replied.

Liam fought back a sudden desire to break Brendon out and simply leave, escaping into the night. Brendon talked as though that day would actually come…but Liam reminded himself it was impossible.

Please, Liam prayed silently. *Please, help me find a way to free Brendon from this nightmare—a way he can be safe…before it's too late for me to do anything. I—I know I can't survive this life much longer…please let me help him escape while I'm still alive.*

"So, what are we going to do about a particular commander you have feelings for?"

Liam snapped back into the present, an instant flush heating his face. "What?"

"Oh, please. I see the way you look when you talk about her," Brendon said. "So, what *are* you going to do?"

"Um…I'm not sure."

"Why don't you just tell her that you have feelings for her already?" Brendon said with a cheeky grin.

"I—I can't just do that!"

"Or you could go all in—tell her you're *madly* in love with her and want to run away to the Forgotten Isles of Norra! That works too."

Liam choked. "No, it doesn't!"

"*Why not?*" Brendon asked, exasperated.

"I…I wouldn't ask her to give up her entire life and leave behind all her family and friends for me." Liam shrugged one shoulder. "I wouldn't ask her to make that choice. No matter what."

"Wow." Brendon sat back, staring at Liam as though he had never seen him before. "You…you really do love her."

Liam simply sighed and leaned his head against the wall.

"So, what *are* you going to do?" Brendon probed.

"I…" Liam rubbed his fingers over his wrist. "I'm not going to tell her anything."

"*What?*" Brendon exclaimed. "Are you crazy? It's clear she feels something for you!"

Liam hesitated a moment. "No...no, there's no way."

She—she couldn't have any feelings for me. I'm a monster, remember?

"Liam, you're my best friend, but sometimes I swear your life's purpose is driving me crazy."

"Among a few other things," Liam said with a slight smile.

Brendon sighed, shaking his head. "You are impossible, Sir."

"You know it." Liam pushed off the wall. "I'll go talk to King Zamir. You'll be out by morning."

"Thank you, Sir," Brendon said as he laid down on the cot.

Liam turned to go but paused and glanced back at Brendon. "Brendon…what would've happened to Commander Desson if she had been taken to the other base?"

Brendon sat up, looking wary. "Why?"

"I want to know. What would have happened?"

"Well, um… I'm not sure you want to know, given your fondness for her," Brendon said gently.

"My imagination is producing enough terrible ideas as it is," Liam argued. "Just tell me."

"Torture," Brendon said bluntly. "Until they received all the information they could. And once they were done with her…well…"

Liam flinched. "I…"

"It's standard protocol for Qor prisoners," Brendon said, abruptly noting the horrified expression on Liam's face. "You *did* know that it's standard protocol…right?"

"I did not," Liam said quietly. *How didn't I know that?*

"I see," Brendon said slowly. "Well…I…I'm going to get some rest, okay?"

"Of—of course. I'll see you tomorrow." Liam created a portal, appearing back in his room. His mind spun as he walked to the window, watching the thousands of stars glittering in the night sky.

How did I ever end up in a place like this?

Liam gasped and sat straight up in bed, drenched in a cold sweat. He sharply inhaled a deep breath and then another, glancing around the room to make sure he was alone and the breathing he'd heard was only in his imagination.

Slowly, Liam's heartbeat returned to normal as he realized he'd had another nightmare. He bit back a groan—this was the ninth nightmare he'd had, and the week wasn't yet half over.

Falling onto his back, Liam stared at the ceiling. Sleep was something that came rarely—he'd been able to fall asleep once that night, and it was unlikely it would happen again.

The second he closed his eyes, the events of the nightmare started replaying. Liam's eyes flew open, and he rubbed a hand over his face, trying to forget the sickening scene.

With a sigh, Liam swung his legs around, placing his feet on the cold floor. He stood, grabbing his shirt and a jacket as he headed for the door, pausing only a moment to put on his sword belt.

Liam strolled down the dim halls, lit only by faint starlight, and he shivered in the chilly air. The sound of voices ahead caused him to slow his pace, listening.

King Zamir…and High Commander Ankor, speaking in hused tones. Liam remained perfectly still, his attention catching when he heard his name—they were talking about him.

Liam hesitated only a moment before he started after them. The voices became louder as he approached, though the words were hard to make out.

Carefully, Liam leaned around the corner, watching as King Zamir and Ankor disappeared into King Zamir's private office. They shut the door behind them, blocking off all sound.

Liam quickly drew his sword and created a portal. He stepped through and appeared in the small, dark closet of the office where he could hear every word.

"…elixir is the only thing keeping him on our side."

"Surely not," High Commander Ankor replied.

Liam's heartbeat picked up, adrenaline rushing through him. *The elixir…keeping me on their side?*

"The effects of the emotion elixir are essential to his loyalty," Zamir hissed. "It strips his ability to feel the emotions of happiness, peace, contentment, or *love*. Once they are gone, the elixir can fuel resentment and bitterness. If he could truly *feel,* he would be overcome with the grief and guilt for what he's done, pulling his loyalty from us.

"Of course, Sir," High Commander Ankor said. "I must admit, when you brought the boy in as your cadet, I did believe you'd gone mad. But Monroy has proved to be a valuable asset."

"Why else would I bring him here?" King Zamir scoffed. "I knew of his powers and how to trigger them. The abilities he possesses make him a powerful *weapon.*"

Liam inhaled sharply. *Anise was right. I—I'm nothing but a weapon to them...a pawn in their war. How was I so blind?*

"I have yet to discover what is causing the elixir's effects to be burned away so quickly," Zamir said, anger vibrating his tone. "But I will discover and put an end to it. For now, we will continue the increasing frequency of the doses."

"Yes, Your Majesty," Ankor said as they left the office, closing the door behind them.

Liam realized his jaw was clenched so hard it hurt, and he took a deep breath. Now he knew the truth.

Here, he was only a weapon waiting to be used. With a flash of pain, Liam realized...unless he deserted...there was nothing he could do about it.

The lights of the base had long come on, but Liam still lay across the bed, his face buried in his pillow. The hours had passed agonizingly slow, his mind turning over the conversation he'd heard.

Nothing but a weapon.

"Sir?" The door cracked open. "Are you up?"

"No," Liam groaned.

"Perfect." Brendon stepped inside, closing the door behind him. "Thank you for speaking with Zamir."

"What? Oh, sure." Liam vaguely recalled sending a message to Zamir about Brendon after he'd returned from his room.

"I brought your mask." Brendon offered it to him. "The smoke filter has been repaired."

Liam sighed. "Thanks."

"Of course." Brendon set the mask on the table.

Liam stared at it for a moment as an idea began to form. "Brendon, is there some way we could have that mask analyzed? You know to...check its functions?"

"I suppose," Brendon said. "I could probably do it if I had a holo-scanner."

Liam sat up. "I have one in that drawer."

Brendon took it out and began scanning the mask. "Okay...it has all the basic functions, smoke and toxin filtration, and...huh. This is strange."

"What?"

"Well, it has a vaporizing compartment."

"What—what would be the purpose of that?" Liam asked, already forming an idea.

"I suppose you could use it for a healing elixir or something," Brendon guessed. "Anything you wanted to user to breathe in instead of an injection or anything."

Brendon kept analyzing the mask, but Liam's mind faded away. King Zamir had always ordered him to wear the mask, insisting it was of vital importance. Now, Liam knew why

Zamir had instructed him, as always, to wear the mask when transporting Anise...but he'd taken it off midway through the flight. *If I had left it on...he would have activated the vaporizer. That's why there were no guards! He wanted me to kill Anise without any interference from the Embleck soldiers.*

"Sir?" Brendon's voice broke in. "Are you alright?"

"Yes," Liam lied. "Thank you, but that will be all."

"Of course." Brendon bowed and left.

CHAPTER 29

Anise awoke early, practically bouncing out of bed. "Good morning, Joffrey!"

Joffrey meowed from his place on the floor. Anise scooped him up and pressed a kiss onto his furry head. "Guess what today is!"

Anise raced through getting dressed, picking her favorite white blouse with a pair of soft brown pants. She was in the process of twisting her hair into a braid crown when someone knocked on her door.

"Happy birthday to my favorite little sister!" Caiden exclaimed as he stepped inside.

"I'm your only little sister," Anise reminded him playfully.

"Well, this must be for you." Caiden handed her a brightly

wrapped package with a bow.

"Thank you." Anise tore through the paper. "Oh, Cay! *Photos of the Galaxy, Volume II!* I love it."

"I'm glad." Caiden smiled at her. "So, what are your plans for the day?"

"I asked Keisha, Tyler, and Jack to lunch with us," Anise said.

"Do you have any plans for tonight?" Caiden glanced around the room.

"Uh…not really," Anise said.

"Alright."

"Why? Is something wrong?"

"No…" Caiden tugged on his shirt collar. "But…Lydia asked me out to dinner. She didn't know it was your birthday, so I told her I'd have to check. Would you mind if I went with Lydia?"

"I wouldn't mind at all!" Anise said with a grin. "I'd be thrilled, honestly."

"I guess I'll call her." Caiden beamed.

"Good idea," Anise said. "See you at lunch?"

"Absolutely." Caiden was already pulling out his comm as he

left.

Anise pinned down the end of her braid, beyond happy that her brother was finally going out with Lydia, whom she suspected he'd liked for years now.

Guess it'll be a quiet evening at home for me. Anise fingered her turquoise necklace. *Unless…I wonder if Liam…*

Impulsively, Anise reached into the energy field. *Liam?*

Hi! Is everything okay?

Yeah, I…I just had a question. Would you mind teleporting over here for a second?

Not at all. A swirling portal appeared, and Liam stepped into the room. "Hello again."

"Hi," Anise said, her eyes going to his ribs. "How's your injury?"

"I'm fine," Liam said quickly. "The Embleck medics are good at what they do. What was it you wanted to ask me?"

"I…" Anise abruptly felt slightly shy and internally winced. "I was wondering if you could…slip away for a little and…spend some time with me tonight?"

Surprise flashed over Liam's expression, a hesitant smile on his lips. "Yeah…yeah, I can definitely do that. Any…special reason?"

Anise fiddled with the hem of her glove. "It's not a big deal. Just my birthday, and I'll…be on my own this evening."

"On your own?" Liam shook his head. "Unacceptable."

"Well, my brother has a date." Anise shrugged. "I don't mind. Besides…then I can spend some time with you."

Liam's expression seemed almost shy. "You have any place that isn't too public in mind?"

"Not yet."

"Wait—I have an idea. Can I pick you up around seven?"

"Perfect," Anise said, feeling herself flush faintly. "See you then?"

"See you then." Liam offered her a quick salute before stepping through his portal.

Anise bounced on her toes, a sense of excitement filling her. She opened the door, only to nearly collde with Keisha.

"Anise!" Keisha crashed into her with a hug. "Happy birthday!"

"Thank you!" Anise exclaimed.

"What's the big birthday plan?" Keisha asked cheeriliy.

"We'll have lunch, of course…and Liam's going to pick me up tonight."

"Ooooh, ANISE!" Keisha grinned. "You're blushing!"

"I am not," Anise protested.

"If you're going to be meeting him, we should get you a new dress! It'll be my birthday present to you."

"Oh, Keisha, that's very sweet, but I couldn't expect you to—"

"Nonsense!" Keisha exclaimed. "Anyway, Granddad just sent me my allowance. I've been just dying to go shopping, and this will be perfect."

"If you really insist…"

"Oh yes, I definitely insist." Keisha linked arms with Anise and practically dragged her down to the shipyard.

"Move over, Joffrey." Anise shooed him away from

where her new dress lay out on the bed. After a morning of shopping and being dragged across the mall by Keisha, Anise had finally found the perfect dress.

It was a soft, bright teal color that matched her eyes perfectly. The sleeveless had hundreds of tiny, clear crystals scattered across it, making her glitter when she moved. The teal sash around her waist was tied in a large bow in the back, an the pleated skirt fell past her ankles.

At Keisha's insistence, Anise now also had a pair of sparkly silver heels. Keisha had sworn that this brand was the most comfortable heels ever made.

Carefully, Anise picked up the dress and slipped into it. The smooth fabric swished as it fell down around her. Anise tied the sash into a loose bow with only slight difficulty and checked her reflection in the mirror.

"It's beautiful." Anise admired her reflection.

"Meeow." Joffrey stared at her approvingly.

Anise twisted half of her hair up and let the other half fall down her back. She tugged out a lock, tucked it back up, and pulled it loose again. She left it loose and checked the clock.

He should be here soon. For some reason, she was almost nervous. Excited—but nervous.

A small part of her mind couldn't help thinking about her seventeenth birthday celebration with Roy, but Anise tried to forget about it.

"Meoow." Joffrey rolled around on the bed.

Anise slipped on her new heels and glanced back at her reflection. The dress was perfect, the heels were perfect, but her gaze traveled to her brown gloves. She seldom took them off, even now, years after her wreck, because when she didn't wear them, people often stared or asked questions.

"Meoow." Joffrey leaped off the bed and came up beside her.

"Hi, sweet." Anise frowned at her reflection in thought.

Joffrey looked at her for a moment. Abruptly, he jumped up and grabbed hold of her glove.

"Joffrey!" Anise wiggled her fingers loose before Joffrey could bite them.

"Meeoow." Joffrey yanked until her glove had slipped off completely. Pleased, he raced under the bed with his prize.

"Joffrey!" Anise cried in exasperation.

Frustrated, Anise glanced back at the mirror. Startlingly…she liked her appearance without the gloves. Hesitantly, Anise tugged off her other glove and laid it on the dresser.

Anise took one last look at her reflection and picked up her large silver shawl just as a hum filled the air and a swirling portal appeared.

Liam stepped into the room, instantly halting when he caught sight of her. His eyes widened, his expression softening as he gazed at her.

"Wow."

"What do you think?" Anise asked, feeling strangely shy.

"I...I think it's lovely." Liam met her eyes, the same shyness she felt reflected in his. "Happy birthday, Anise."

"Thank you." Anise hid her fingers in her long skirt. "So...where are we going?"

"It's a surprise." Liam created another portal before holding out his hand. "Are you ready?"

"Yes." Hesitantly, Anise placed her bare hand in his gloved one.

"You're not wearing your gloves," Liam commented, his eyes on her hand.

Anise felt a hint of embarrassment. "Do you mind?"

A stunned expression crossed Liam's face. "Of course

not." Slowly, he raised her hand to his lips, lightly kissing the back of her fingers. "I think you're beautiful, with or without them."

Anise flushed red, her face burning. "Thank you."

"Close your eyes," Liam said, pulling her toward the portal.

Anise closed her eyes, allowing Liam to lead her through the portal. The heels of her shoes clicked against a tile floor as she stepped out of the portal.

"You can open them now."

Anise opened her eyes with a gasp. They stood in the center of a huge ballroom with a paned glass dome ceiling and a glistening chandelier hung from it. The floors were royal blue tiles; the walls a glossy white.

"Liam, where are we?"

"I'm not exactly sure what this place used to be." Liam scanned the room. "I found it on patrol a few years ago...and I knew it would be away from either of our sides."

"It's beautiful," Anise said quietly.

Liam pulled out his comm, and a moment later, soft music filled the room. He set his comm down before tugging off the black gloves he always wore.

Turning, Liam held out his hand to Anise.

"May I have this dance?"

"You may." Anise placed her hand in his. A warm shiver raced over her skin. The last time she'd held hands without any gloves had been with R—*no, don't think about him.* The sensation was strange and foreign…but not unwelcome.

For a moment, they both remained still, each experiencing the feeling for the first time. Anise finally found her voice and spoke.

"I'm afraid I don't know the traditional dances," she admitted. "I've never learned."

"Don't worry." Liam guided her hand to rest on his shoulder. "I'll teach you."

Delicately, Liam placed his hand on her upper back and took her other hand as he began leading her through the steps of the dance. Anise stared at her feet so she could see the steps, stiffly following Liam's movements.

"You can relax," Liam whispered in her ear. "It's okay if you miss a step. There's no one else here."

Yeah, that's part of why I'm nervous! Anise thought to herself. *This…just the two of us—it feels…romantic! And I'm trying not to have feelings for you!*

Too late for that, a voice in the back of her mind mocked.

Shut up, Anise scolded. *Just because it's true doesn't mean it has to be said.*

"You seem lost in thought."

Anise pulled herself back to the present. "No, just concentrating. This style of dance is new."

"You're doing great so far," Liam said as the song ended. "Oh, I almost forgot." He released her, reaching into his pocket and offering her a small box.

"Liam, you didn't have to," Anise began.

"I wanted to." Liam shrugged.

"Thank you." Anise accepted the box and carefully opened it.

Inside laid a beautiful bracelet, each stone a different shade of pale blue, green, and aqua, with a few opaque white stones as well. The starlight glimmered off the bracelet, and Anise brushed the stones with her fingers.

"The stones are polished sea glass."

"Oh..." Anise gently lifted the bracelet. "Oh, Liam, it's gorgeous. Thank you!"

Impulsively, Anise hugged Liam. He froze for a moment

before lightly returning the embrace.

"I'm happy you like it," Liam said softly. "I know how much you wanted to see the ocean…and since I won't be able to take you there… this was the closest I could get."

"I…I love it," Anise replied.

They were both silent for a moment, lost in fantasies of things that could never be. Liam abruptly pulled back, breaking the silence. "Would you like another dance?"

"Sounds perfect," Anise said, slipping the bracelet on her wrist.

The music that began immediately caught Anise's attention. "This is Ceranish music."

"You said you were from Ceran, so I wanted you to have a taste of home."

"That's so…so sweet," Anise said.

"It's been a while since I've practiced this dance," Liam admitted as he took her hand.

"I don't mind leading," Anise said as they began the steps. "Besides. There's no one else here to see."

Liam offered her a smile as the music lifted, and they spun across the floor. To Anise's delight, Liam kept up easily through both the upbeat Ceranish songs. Soon, the music faded to a slow, lyrical melody, and they stood a little closer as they danced.

Anise glanced at Liam, noting the depth of emotion in his eyes as they met hers. "Now who's lost in thought?"

"I'm not," Liam murmured.

"I beg to differ."

"I'm just…admiring."

Anise looked around the ballroom. "It is stunning."

"I wasn't talking about the room," Liam replied, his gaze locked on…her.

Anise turned back to him, feeling herself flush. "The…night sky, then?"

"Stars, Anise," Liam whispered. "I mean *you*. You're *gorgeous*."

Anise's flush deepened. "Me?"

"Yes, you." Liam gently tucked a curl behind her ear, his voice shy. "I think you're the most beautiful woman in the galaxy."

"Thank you…" Anise replied finally, glancing up at Liam's emerald eyes. "Thank you so much for… everything."

Liam nodded, his gaze traveling to her lips. "You're welcome."

Maybe it was the moonlight or Liam's shy, tender expression—Anise didn't know what prompted her to take the last step forward and close the distance between them.

Anise brushed her lips against his, only the faintest contact sending shivers over her skin. Liam flinched, shock spreading over his expression. His eyes met hers before darting back to her lips.

"Anise...are you sure *you* want to do this?" Liam whispered hoarsely. "It—it could be dangerous for you and..."

Lightly, Anise placed her finger over his lips. "Yes."

At her reassurance, a tentative smile broke out on Liam's face. He bit his lip before leaning in, allowing Anise to close the gap.

Anise placed her arms around Liam's neck, erasing the last of the distance as she pressed her lips against his. Liam wrapped his arms around her waist, pulling her body close to his.

Liam's kiss felt soft and slightly hesitant, which Anise found endearing. She deepened the kiss, running her fingers through his short, wavy blond hair and savoring the feeling of his lips against hers.

Anise's heartbeat pulsed in her ears as Liam buried his hand in her hair, cupping the nape of her neck as his other hand held her waist. She gripped the front of his jacket, wishing she wouldn't ever have to let him go.

All too soon, Liam broke the kiss with a soft, quavering sigh. Anise rested her forehead against his, gazing into his eyes shing with...love.

"I think I'm dreaming," Liam whispered, his cheeks flushed.

Anise ran the pad of her thumb over his full lower lip. "I hope not."

Liam gently caught her wrist, pressing a kiss to the palm of her hand. "Kiss me again. Please."

"Well..." Anise drew the word out, watching his expression. "Since you asked so sweetly. How could I say no to that?"

A grin twitched on Liam's lips. "I'm hoping you can't."

Anise laughed, pulling him in for another tender kiss. Liam's hands found her hair again as he ran his fingers through her loose red waves. Anise grasped his jacket collar, briefly wondering how she'd let this happen before pushing those thoughts away. It didn't matter now. All that mattered was Liam.

When they broke apart, Liam met her eyes. "Would you like to go out to the balcony and look at the stars?"

Anise nodded, taking Liam's hand. Together, they walked out to the large balcony, taking a seat on a stone bench near the railing. Anise tilted her head back, gazing up at the stars. "They're so beautiful."

"They are." Liam ran his thumb over the back of her hand.

Sitting under the stars with Liam's arm around her and her head resting on his shoulder, Anise's heart filled with a warm, steady kind of happiness. The position, however, made her thoughts drift to her birthday celebration with Roy, and she felt a stab of guilt.

How am I doing this? There's—there's a chance he's...Roy. Besides, he's still grieving the first woman he loved. And we can't ever be together...I don't want to hurt him!

"Liam," Anise said aloud. "I know this is an odd question...but can you tell me about her?"

Liam turned to her in confusion. "Her? What are you talking about?"

"The woman you told me about in the jungle." Anise shifted. "The...the one you loved. I wanted to...hear about her."

"Well…" Liam furrowed his brow. "What do you want to know?"

"Just…anything about her." Anise swallowed hard. "Like…what was her name?"

"Her name was Ree," Liam said quietly. "At least, that's what I called her. We both kept our real names a secret—she was Ree, and I said my name was Roy. You know, since the last name I planned on using was Monroy."

"Planned on using?" Anise choked out, her voice stifled by a rush of emotions.

"I didn't want my family name all my life, so I decided to change my last name to my grandparents' last name: Monroy." Liam glanced at her uncertainly. "Is…that all you wanted to know?"

Anise's mind spun. Liam—Liam was Roy. Her best friend she'd almost fallen in love with. The same Roy who had given her hope for a better future and pulled her from the all-encompassing *loneliness* she'd felt.

What about his dreams for a happy life and a family? Anise's heart ached for him. *How did he fall this far?*

"Liam, I—I have something to tell you."

"Yes?"

"Do…do you remember when I told you that I was in a shipwreck before I joined the?"

"Yes." Liam's confused expression was returning.

"That was nine years ago." Anise stared at her scarred hands. "On…Ceran."

"Ree…her shipwreck was on Ceran," Liam said, processing.

More conformation, At first he called it an accident…and now I know it was a shipwreck. My shipwreck. "And a week or two before my—her wreck…I met a boy in the marketplace."

"Are you trying to tell me that you're dating somebody else?"

"No, no, not at all," Anise assured him. "When I met that boy, he didn't tell me his real name. Just that I could call him Roy." Anise paused, meeting Liam's wide emerald eyes. "And I told him to call me Ree."

Liam inhaled sharply. "Are you saying…"

"I'm saying…that I'm Ree." Anise offered him a half-smile

Emotions flashed across Liam's face as recognition dawned. "Wait…*Ree?*"

Anise nodded.

"I—Anise—" Liam grasped her hand, his gaze locked on her face as tears filled his eyes. "I—I'm so—s-sorry about the ship parts; I—I didn't know. I should have checked the pieces for malfunctions—can you ever forgive me?"

Anise wrapped her arms around Liam, pulling him into a tight hug, feeling his body shaking. "There's nothing to forgive, Liam."

"But—what—what about the pieces malfunctioning and causing your wreck?" Liam managed, his voice strained with emotion.

Anise took his hands gently. "It…wasn't your fault. The ship parts were perfect. I was attacked. That's why the ship crashed."

Liam dragged the back of his hand across his eyes. "Attacked?"

"The Embleck Army attacked my ship and destroyed it. If my powers hadn't saved me…I wouldn't be alive now."

"The—the Embleck Army tried to kill you? For no reason?" Liam asked, his voice catching.

"Well…not exactly no reason. The soldiers grabbed me in the marketplace, saying they knew who I was. They said 'he' wanted me and tried to drag me off. One of the Qor councilors rescued me. My wreck was only a few days later."

Liam looked on the verge of a panic attack. "I...I had no idea. I came back...I guess the day after your wreck. You weren't home, and I—I waited for almost an hour. I checked the village, then returned to the lake...I was so worried something had...had happened to you."

Anise placed her hand on Liam's shoulder, seeing he was clearly on the edge of breaking down. "There was an...an Embleck soldier there when I returned. He told me about your wreck."

A tear slipped down Liam's cheek. "He—he told me it was a malfunction in the ship parts...told me it was my fault. I was...I don't even know. *Heartbroken...*"

Anise cupped his cheek in her hand, and Liam looked at her with shining eyes. "I thought you were dead...I thought it was my fault."

Liam's voice broke, and he buried his face in his hands. Anise moved closer and wrapped her arms around him tightly.

"It's okay," Anise whispered, holding him close. "You can cry. I know how much you're hurting."

A choked sob escaped Liam's chest, and he buried his face in the crook of her neck. Anise gently stroked his hair as he struggled to fight back his sobs, his entire body shaking.

"Liam, I'm so sorry." Anise kissed his head. "It wasn't your fault, I promise."

Liam glanced up, tears slipping down his face. "Are—are you sure?"

"Absolutely." Anise wiped the tears from his cheeks. "You don't have to carry that guilt anymore."

Liam dragged his sleeve over his eyes. "I—I'm sorry, I didn't mean to break down like that. I just—" his voice caught. "I've missed you...so *so* much...I can't believe you're here...with me...*alive.*"

"Don't apologize." Anise hugged him close. "I missed you too. More than I even knew."

"Thank you," Liam whispered, pulling back. He swiped his sleeves over his eyes, shook his head, and turned to her with a shaky smile. "Seeing you is...incredible. And look at you! A commander of the Qor. You got off Ceran, Ree—Anise. I'm so happy for you."

Anise smiled faintly. *And you're an Embleck general. How am I supposed to be happy about that.* "I'm so...so glad we reconnected."

"Me too." Liam brushed away the last of his tears.

"But...I have to ask...why didn't you ever contact me?"

"I called the number you gave me, but the woman said she only had one son," Anise said, remembering the devastation she'd felt after realizing she had no way to contact him.

"Oh...that must have been my mother. If I'd already left, she probably decided to pretend I never existed."

"I wish I could have contacted you sooner." *Maybe then you wouldn't be an Embleck soldier.*

Anise leaned against Liam, looking up at the stars. "This reminds me of my seventeenth birthday."

"You're right." Liam abruptly sat up. "I never gave you the last gift!"

"Oh, I didn't mind," Anise said quickly. "Out of curiosity...what was it?"

Liam glanced down. "I...I still have it. I think it would be easier for me to just give it to you."

"Okay..." Anise said hesitantly, wondering what could make him look so nervous.

"I'll be right back." Liam created a portal and stepped in. Only a moment later, he reappeared and a tiny, round box in her hands, wrapped in faded teal paper and tied with a white bow.

Slowly, Anise unwrapped the paper. With slightly trembling fingers, she pried off the lid and gasped. Laying in the box was a small gold ring. The band twisted into a small heart at the top and had a tiny turquoise jewel.

"It's a promise ring," Liam whispered.

"*Oh...*" A pain shot through Anise as she looked at the ring. What would have happened if she'd received the ring nine years ago? She would have accepted, of course. They could have married...had children...the life they'd both always wanted.

And now we're on opposite sides of a war.

"It's beautiful," Anise said, offering the box back to Liam.

"You should keep it." Liam took the ring from the box, holding out his hand for Anise's.

Anise placed her hand in his, and Liam slipped the ring on the middle finger of her left hand. "It can't be a promise of engagement now..."

Anise nodded. "R-right."

"But." Liam lifted her hand to his lips, kissing her palm. "Keep it as a different promise."

"A promise of what?"

Liam looked at her, a deep pain hidden his eyes. "Do you really want to know?"

"Yes," Anise whispered.

"Keep it as a promise…that I never stopped loving you." Sadness tinged Liam's smile as he met her eyes.

Anise threw her arms around Liam's neck, pulling him close as she kissed him. Liam kissed her back for a moment, then pulled away.

"Do you want to go dance again? Liven the mood?"

Anise forced away the ache in her chest, offering Liam a bright smile. "Of course."

It was past midnight when Anise and Liam stepped from a portal and appeared in Anise's room. Anise turned to Liam with a smile. "Thank you for such a wonderful night."

"I should be thanking you," Liam said softly. "This is the

best day I've had in...a while."

"Oh!" Anise exclaimed, spinning around. "I just remembered; hold on."

Anise raced over to her closet and pulled out a large box. She dug around until she found what she was looking for.

"Look at this." Anise held out the galaxy rose Liam had given her all those years ago. The glass had protected it, preserving the fresh blossom.

Liam gently touched a glass-encased petal. "You kept it."

"I did." Anise kissed his cheek, and he pulled her into a real kiss.

When they separated a moment later, Liam gently tucked back a lock of her hair. "Actually, I have something of yours." He reached into his pocket and held out—

"Oh, my bracelet!" Anise accepted it gratefully. "Thank you."

"Of course," Liam said a little shyly. "I'm sorry I didn't think to bring it sooner. I'll...I'll see you later?"

"Definitely," Anise promised.

Liam took her hand, kissing the back of it. "Good night, Anise."

"Good night, Liam." Anise waited until Liam had stepped through his portal before quietly squealing and throwing herself on the bed.

"Meeeoow." Joffrey crawled out from under the bed.

"Oh, Joffrey!" Anise exclaimed. "I just had the best night of my life."

"Merow." Joffrey flopped down beside her, bored.

"Oh, it was perfect. The music, the stars, and Joffrey, I *kissed* him." Anise sighed. "It was...magically."

"Merooow," Joffrey said disdainfully.

"I know *you* don't like kissing, but *I,* on the other hand—" Anise broke off mid-sentence. "Why am I explaining this to you? You're a kibit."

"Me*row*." Joffrey stuck his tail straight in the air and stalked over to his bed.

Anise rolled her eyes as she set the rose on her dresser and changed into her nightclothes. She settled into bed and switched off the light, falling asleep with a smile on her lips.

CHAPTER 30

Liam lay on his bed, staring up at the ceiling. His mind replayed the events of the previous night as he remembered the feeling of Anise's soft lips pressed against his, and her hand on the back of his neck as she held him close.

A smile crossed his lips, something akin to peace settling over him. The moment had been perfect—something he'd treasure for rest of his life.

And then he discovered she was...Ree.

The torrent of emotions had felt suffocating—but finally he'd settled on joy, the sort that filled the hollow void in his chest with warmth. After all, he found that his first love he'd never forgotten was alive—and the same woman he'd fallen for now.

I...I love her. Liam rolled over, his mind spinning as he envisioned their first kiss. *I love Anise. I'm in love with a Qor commander.*

How did I let this happen? I didn't think I'd ever love anyone other than Ree. Well...I guess I don't. But I loved Anise before I found out she's Ree.

Liam thought back to their conversation, his mind locking on one element—Anise said the Embleck Army had attacked her, destroying her ship...but the Embleck soldier he'd encountered said it had been an accident.

They lied to me. I'm sure it was Zamir's orders. The sympathetic act he put on was exactly that: an act. An act that was another piece of the scheme King Zamir concocted to convince me to join the Embleck Army.

But why was it so important that I joined? Why was it so important they were willing to kill Anise—who they had to know was the other side of the link? Were my powers really worth her life?

Standing, Liam began to pace, struggling for any memories that could help...but there was nothing.

In fact, the lack of memories from the time right after he joined the Embleck Army was worrying. The days seemed to blur, and Liam couldn't remember a single clear thing from the first...five or six *years* after he had joined the Embleck Army?

That can't be right, Liam thought...but found it was. Even so, it seemed as though he didn't even have nine years of memories.

Taking his sword from its place on the dresser, Liam left his room with a destination in mind—the records room. *Maybe they'll be some explanation about this there—or at least some information or events I should be able to remember.*

Liam glanced around the corner and saw two guards standing at the doors. He shoved his shoulders back and stalked down the hall.

"General Monroy," one guard said in a slightly awed yet slightly afraid tone.

"How can we assist you?" the other guard asked.

"I require entrance to the records room," Liam demanded.

"I don't know, Sir…" the first guard said slowly. "Only King Zamir is supposed to see them."

"I was sent by King Zamir," Liam snapped, playing on their fear. "Let me in, or I'll have you removed from your posts."

"Yes, Sir." Both guards stepped aside, and Liam entered the records room.

The doors slid shut behind him, and Liam glanced around the room. The room was entirely shelves filled with record books, and a large computer screen covered part of the wall.

Liam examined the spines of the books, hoping for a history record—possibly one of all his assignments—until he abruptly stopped at a particularly intriguing book title.

Erasures.

Liam pulled the book off the shelf and began flipping through the pages. Each page listed the name of an Embleck soldier, most of whom Liam didn't know, and most only had one entry under their name. But, a moment later, Liam's eyes caught on a name he did know.

Commander Brendon Grant.

Liam ran his eyes down the page.

Name: Commander Brendon Grant.

Cause of erasure: discovered private information.

Cause of erasure: classed memory involving Liam Monroy.

Liam stared at the page. Brendon had been…erased—whatever that meant—because he knew something about…Liam.

Shifting his weight, Liam flipped the page again and froze at the name typed across the top.

Liam Monroy.

In a daze, Liam skimmed the page.

Cause of erasure: restricted memory regained

Cause of erasure: post-mission complications

Cause of erasure: teenage memory regained

Cause of erasure: discovered private shipwreck information

Cause of erasure: defied orders of King Zamir

Liam stared at the page, a sick feeling churning in his stomach. He slowly flipped ahead, the nausea only growing worse as the pages labeled with his name went on. Although most people only had one page, Liam had nine.

Nine full pages, the same number of years he had served the Embleck Army.

All at once, a memory hit Liam. A blurred image of a red jewel glowing as dark, cold feeling washed through him.

Liam dropped the book as though it was tainted, stumbling back.

"Are you alright, Sir?" one of the guards at the door called.

Liam struggled to get his rising panic attack under control. "Yes—yes, I'm fine."

Liam stared at the book, lying on the floor, still open to the last page of his...*erasures*. He had hoped the term referenced hard drives or something equally boring...but that clearly wasn't the case.

They were exactly what Liam had feared they were…and perfectly explained why he didn't have nine years of memories.

King Zamir's been erasing my memories. That's—that's why I can't remember most of my missions…and that must be why Brendon told me I had a meeting with King Zamir I can't remember!

Abruptly, a scene appeared in Liam's mind. He'd gone to King Zamir…and asked if Commander Desson could be Ree.

I did recognize her! I knew she was the same person! And he…he made me forget.

"Sir, do you need anything?" one of the door guards called, sounding a little impatient.

"No, I'm almost through," Liam replied, forcing his voice to be steady.

Liam carefully picked up the book and put it back on the shelf, noticing how his hands shook. He walked across the small room to the computer that held all the digital records.

With his fingers trembling, Liam typed the date of Anise's crash into the computer. One transmission blinked up, and Liam clicked on in. Instantly, the voice of King Zamir filled the room.

"Is it done, Ankor?"

Ankor's voice crackled with static as he spoke. "Yes, Sir. The girl's ship has crashed."

"Good...was there anything unusual at the site?"

"The pilot who crashed the ship did say he saw a...circle of white...light?"

King Zamir was silent for a moment. "That is a new development. Well, it won't change anything."

The record ended, and Liam stared numbly. Another record caught his eye. The date was the day after Anise's crash.

Liam clicked on it.

King Zamir's voice spoke. "Did the boy come to find her?"

Ankor's transmission sounded glitchy. "Yes, and I did as you said. I informed him of her death in a shipwreck and how he was at fault."

"How did he take it?"

Ankor's voice was smug. "He took it horribly...exactly like we hoped."

"Perfect," King Zamir said with a chuckle. "Just think...all these years, monitoring him, influencing him...it all led here."

"It is finally coming together, Your Majesty."

"I will be at the shipyard, waiting for him," King Zamir said. "Ready the elixir for when I return."

"Yes, Your Majesty."

The transmission ended, and Liam numbly switched it off. He had the final piece of information he needed to complete the puzzle.

King Zamir has been manipulating me...since I was a child. He was trying to force me into the Embleck Army. The numb sensation began to flicker, giving way to a deep rage. *He almost killed Anise because of it—I spent nine years mourning and believing myself at fault. I almost didn't survive the grief...*

Liam abruptly stood, storming out of the records room, and past the startled guards. He didn't bother to knock at the throne room; he shoved the doors open and stepped inside, letting them slam behind him.

"Ah, Monroy." King Zamir didn't sound surprised. "What is it?"

"You liar," Liam hissed.

"Me?" King Zamir sounded amused.

"You tried to kill Ree!" Liam accused him, seething. "You knew her death would cause me to join your side! You tricked me into taking your *elixir* so you could use me as your weapon."

Zamir raised an eyebrow. "Oh, did I?"

Liam's body shook with fury. "You've been lying to me and wiping my memories, so I'm just your loyal weapon! You tried to force me to kill my best friend—what kind of a monster are you?"

King Zamir remained silent for a long moment. "So...I see you found the records room. I should've destroyed it long ago."

"You're despicable," Liam snapped.

A sharp jab in his back followed by an electric shock halted Liam's next words. "He's also your king, Monroy, and you should treat him as such," High Commander Ankor said sharply.

"Quite right, High Commander." King Zamir said pleasantly before his expression turned ice cold. "Kneel."

Anger flashed through Liam. "Never again."

King Zamir seemed mildly surprised. "Hmm. That's interesting. He didn't refuse last time."

Liam's blood to ran cold. "Last time?"

"Surely you can figure it out," Ankor said smugly. "You can't remember discovering this, time and time again?"

Liam instantly berated himself—how didn't he guess that? He knew King Zamir had erased his memories ...but he didn't realize he'd known before.

"Yes," Ankor gloated, striking Liam another painful shock. "I suppose you think you can resist. But you can't. This rebellion is only temporary—shall we call it a *glitch* in your programming?"

"Our *brave little weapon* thinks he has somehow gained the strength and courage to stand against us." King Zamir drummed his fingers on the arm of the throne. "How amusing."

Ankor once again jabbed Liam in the ribs with his shock ray. Liam bit his lip until he tasted blood. "Maybe I have a reason to have courage now."

"I'm telling you for the last time," King Zamir warned. "Kneel, fool."

"Never." Liam straightened his shoulders and met King Zamir's icy eyes for the first time.

"Very well." Zamir raised his staff.

A bolt of shadow struck Liam in the chest, sending him to his knees. Pain exploded over his entire body, and he struggled to breathe. "You...evil..."

"Correct once again." King Zamir smirked and shot another blast at Liam.

Liam collapsed on the floor, convulsing. The shadows tore through his body in the form of icy cold agony.

King Zamir seemed almost pleased as he watched his prized pupil writhing on the floor. Ankor walked up to the dais, chuckling.

Liam fought to breathe, a task that was suddenly difficult. Footsteps approached him, and Liam barely managed to raise his head, instantly staring into the eyes of King Zamir.

"It is a shame," King Zamir said. "If you had only *stayed* my loyal weapon, I wouldn't have to do this."

Liam tried to pull away, but he could barely move. The jewel of King Zamir's scepter touched Liam's forehead, and he faded away into dark, merciful unconsciousness.

Liam awoke to his entire body throbbing. Spots appeared before his eyes, and he winced.

"Okay, I thought we were through with all this *let's get knocked out so Brendon has to drag me to the infirmary* business." Brendon leaned over Liam.

"I thought so too," Liam groaned.

"Then why in the galaxy does this keep happening?" Brendon asked.

Panic crashed over Liam like a wave, remembering King Zamir's scepter touching his forehead. *Wait…I still can remember! But how?*

Liam sat up, his mind spinning. He remembered everything—finding the records, the book of memory wipes, defying King Zamir…only to have his memories erased all over again. The memories were slightly blurred—like water spilled over a picture—but he had them.

"I don't know," Liam replied. "I'll try to stop." *I can't tell Brendon the truth and risk Zamir erasing his mind too.*

Brendon's expression became serious. "Listen, I know I've been teasing you about all this, but I'm really worried. Are you sure you're okay?"

Liam refused to meet Brendon's eyes. "I'm fine."

Brendon crossed his arms. "You are not." Before Liam could interject, he continued. "First, the monitor says you have high pain levels. Second, I can tell something's wrong. I've known you since we were teenagers; I can tell that you're hiding something."

Liam sighed. "Can I have some pain meds?"

Brendon scowled and handed it to him. "This has something to do with Commander Desson, doesn't it?"

"Listen, Brendon. There's some…complications, and I don't want to put you in danger."

Brendon seemed to soften. "Fine. I'm here if you need help, though."

"Thank you," Liam said, relieved that Brendon wasn't pressing any further.

"By the way, King Zamir asked to see you."

Liam froze, panic spreading through him. "Did—did he say why?"

"No. He just said it was important."

"I—I'll go now," Liam said and stood up, pausing when pain shot through him.

"Are you sure?" Brendon asked.

"Yes," Liam lied as he left.

Liam walked through the empty halls, fear clouding his mind. What could King Zamir want now? He had been able to resist one wipe, but what if he couldn't resist another?

Somehow, Liam knew he wouldn't be able to resist again—or take another bolt of the dark shadows. His body still trembled with cold from the first strike.

Liam reached the foreboding double doors, but before he could knock, King Zamir's voice spoke.

"Come in, Monroy."

The doors opened on their own, and Liam stepped inside. He walked up to the dais slowly, keeping his eyes on the ground.

"Monroy." King Zamir stared down at him. "How are you?"

Liam would've laughed at the ridiculousness of that question had he not been so afraid. "I'm fine, Your Majesty."

"What have you been doing today?" King Zamir peered at him from his mask.

It's a test. He's trying to see if my memories have been erased so I can't remember the records

"Nothing, Your Majesty," Liam replied blankly. "Today feels a bit foggy."

"Of course," King Zamir said smugly. "That will be all. Dismissed."

Liam nodded, forcing himself to keep a normal pace as he

left. Once the doors had closed behind him, he sighed and sank down against the wall, his head spinning.

Now that he knew the truth, Liam wanted nothing more than to teleport to Anise—abandon the Embleck Army—even join the Qor…but it was impossible.. King Zamir would find him and Anise…

Anise. Liam ached to talk to her, to tell her everything…but he couldn't. It would just pain her to hear it, and it wasn't like she could fix anything.

No one could fix this.

Liam sighed and tilted his head back to rest against the cold black wall. He had managed to trick King Zamir once…but how much longer could he survive like this?

CHAPTER 31

Anise dug through her bag from the jungle, searching for her hairpin. She shook out the blanket and turned the bag upside down but couldn't find it.

It must've fallen out during the crash. Anise sighed before getting an idea.

Liam? she transmitted. *Are you there?*

Yeah, I'm here. Is everything okay? His worried voice pierced her mind.

I'm fine, I just think I left my favorite hairpin in the jungle. Are you busy, or can you take me there really quick?

No, I'm not busy. Everybody has been in strategizing meetings all day,

Can you make me a portal? I'll come to you if that's

406

okay.

No problem. A second later, a swirling portal opened in front of Anise, and she stepped through.

Anise started, glancing around. She'd teleported into a small, dark room. Liam stood only a few inches away from her, looking slightly embarrassed.

"Where are we?" Anise said.

"In a storage closet."

"Oh, of course," Anise said. "Anddd…why are we in a storage closet?"

"Because I didn't want anyone to see us," Liam said as though it should be obvious.

"Okay…" Anise said. "Well, hello."

"Hi." Liam smiled, lightly placing his hands on her waist.

Anise hugged his neck, leaning in for a kiss. Liam wrapped his arms around her, pulling her close. The movement caused Anise to stumble forward, pushing Liam's back into the wall.

They met eyes, each fighting back laughter for fear of being heard. Liam closed the distance again, pressing his lips to hers. Anise ran her fingers through his hair, holding him close with her other arm.

"… and I think it may be in here." The door to the closet abruptly opened to reveal Brendon with Deven and Andrew standing behind him.

"Uh…" Brendon *clearly* wasn't expecting what he had just walked in on while Deven and Andrew stared in fascination.

"Sorry, Sir!" Brendon slammed the door shut. Vaguely through the door, he continued: "And that, cadets, is a lesson to beware of opening closet doors when your boss has a girlfriend. You should have seen the time when…" his voice faded away.

Anise flushed though she was fighting back a laugh. "Is he going to rib you about that?"

Liam sighed, though his face was just as red. "Yeah, probably for the rest of my life."

Reluctantly, Anise pulled away. "Why don't we go to the jungle now? Before anyone else needs some supplies."

"Excellent idea." Liam sliced a hole in the universe and pulled her through. Instantly, they stood in the balmy jungle.

Anise pushed her out of her face, already feeling the humidity's effects. "I guess we're just lucky it's not raining. Let's find that pin and leave."

"This is like searching for a needle in a haystack," Liam

remarked. "What does it even look like again?"

"It looks like a...well, like a hairpin." Anise checked in some bushes near the wreck, catching sight of a glimmer of metal.

"That's helpful," Liam said as he looked under a pile of debris.

"Aha!" Anise triumphantly held up the hairpin. She climbed around the wreckage and showed it to Liam. "See, it looks like a hairpin."

Liam barely glanced at it, his attention elsewhere. "You aren't wearing your gloves again."

"Oh." Anise shrugged one shoulder. "I...guess I...like the way I feel without them."

"I'm glad." Liam took her hand, kissing her palm. "I don't think you need them, and I'm happy you agree."

"Thank you." Anise smiled at him. "Are we ready to go? I'm burning up. Or melting. I doubt anything can burn in this humidity."

"No problem." Liam led them back through the portal, and they appeared in Anise's room.

"Thanks again." Anise walked over to the dresser and put down her pin, her attention catching on something sitting on her dresser. She picked up the rectangle package wrapped in simple brown paper, turning it over in her hands.

"What's that?" Liam asked, coming over.

"I'm not sure." Anise felt a circular bulge on the top of the package. "Maybe it's from Caiden?"

"Was it here when you left?"

"No," Anise said as she began to tear away the paper. "It's a journal." The brown leather journal's cover was cracking, but she could very clearly see a symbol emblazed on the front.

"Liam!" she exclaimed, and he leaned over her shoulder. "It's our symbol, the two stars!"

Liam touched the cover, surprise appearing on his face. "And look." He picked something up from the rest of the paper. "This is a compass."

Anise peered at the compass. The face had a white flower with seven petals engraved in it. "It's pretty, but I think it's broken. The needle keeps pointing northeast. Compasses are supposed to point just north, right?"

"True." Liam set the compass on the dresser. "What about the book?"

Anise carefully opened the journal to the first page. There was writing scrawled on the inside of the front cover, and she squinted at it. "'Diary of Princess Asteria of Lidica'!"

"How are you reading that?" Liam asked, stunned. "Those are ancient runes."

Anise did a double-take. The letters were indeed runes, but somehow they made perfect sense. "I don't quite know; maybe it's another ability. Can you read it?"

"I..I can, actually," Liam said.

Anise turned the page and found a drawing of the same flower engraved on the compass. "Look, it's labeled *Starlidica*. I've never heard of that." She glanced at the page to the right and stopped. "Oh. Princess Asteria was an artist."

On the page was an intricate pencil drawing of a handsome young man, simply labeled *Tarak*. Asteria had captured his quirky smile and mischievous eyes.

"What else is there?" Liam sounded slightly impatient.

Anise flipped again, finding a sketch of the compass with the words *follow the needle* written across the bottom of the page. On the right page was a drawing of what looked like the mouth of a cave.

"We're supposed to follow the compass." Anise continued to flip, but the rest of the pages were blank.

"You really think we should follow a possibly broken

compass into an almost unexplored area of empty space with only this princess's diary telling us where to go?"

"Yes?"

"Alright, if you say so." Liam shrugged.

"Thank you!" Anise kissed his cheek and leaped up. "I'll pack an overnight bag. And please take off your badges, but leave the cloak, just in case."

Liam dropped his badges on her dresser as she packed. Anise grabbed a change of clothes, some food from her tiny kitchen area, and her comm. She handed Liam the compass and tucked the journal into her bag.

"I'm ready."

"Then let's go." Liam took her hand, and Anise led him out the door.

Together they strode through the bustling halls of the base. Liam eyed each person they passed hesitantly, and Anise quickened her pace. The knowledge that someone could recognize Liam and reveal their secret put her nerves on edge—and it was at that moment someone did recognize them.

"Hey, you two, wait up!"

Anise whipped around in fear but quickly relaxed "Oh, Keisha."

"Hi." Keisha skidded up to them. "What are you guys doing *here*? Is something wrong?"

"We're just leaving," Anise assured her. "Everything's fine."

"Good…but be careful, okay?" Keisha said.

"Absolutely." Anise nodded before dragging Liam off again.

"I have a question," Liam spoke up. "How are we going to get there?"

"Oh." Anise paused. "Your ship isn't here, and mine is a one-seater. Caiden's can fit two, but I don't want to ask him. I guess we'll have to squeeze into mine."

"If you say so…"

Anise slowed as they reached the shipyard. It was busy as always, and she would prefer to go unnoticed. She gestured for Liam to follow her, putting a finger to her lips.

They crept along the outskirts, ducking behind ships if someone glanced their way. Finally, they reached her ship, parked on the far edge.

Liam peeked inside. "Yeah, that's kind of small."

Anise silently agreed. "You climb up first; I'm after you."

Liam climbed into the pilot's (and only) seat. Anise tossed her bag up next.

"Now what?" Liam leaned down to see her.

"My turn." Anise braced her foot on the side of the ship and pulled herself up. She sat on the rim for a moment, thinking.

"I think someone's coming this way," Liam whispered, scanning the shipyard.

Anise maneuvered into the ship and lowered herself onto Liam's lap, quickly closing the ship's domed top. She moved over slightly, settling on his left leg and leaving room for him to see.

"Am I blocking your view?"

Liam looked slightly stunned, his cheeks flushed red. "N-no…you're good."

"Good." Anise twisted back around and held up the compass. "Let's fly."

Liam took hold of the steering, locking Anise between his arms as he lifted the ship into the air, and they soared off.

They cleared the atmosphere, soaring in the direction the compass pointed. Liam set the ship on autopilot, resting his forehead against the back of her head. "What do you think we'll find out there?"

"I'm honestly not sure," Anise said, distracted by Liam's arms around her. Her back was pressed against his chest, and she could faintly feel the rhythm of his heart. "I hope it will give us some answers."

"I do too." Liam tucked his face against her neck, lightly pressing his lips against her skin.

Anise relaxed in his arms as the ship continued to soar through space, drowsiness settling over her. She drifted in and out of sleep only to be abruptly awoken by the ship jerking forward.

"Liam?" Anise pressed a hand to her forehead. "What's happening?"

Liam gripped the steering, scanning the console. "I—I don't know."

Anise glanced out into space, her eyes widening. They were quickly approaching a large area of the sky that had no stars. "Liam, what's that?"

Liam paled. "It kind of looks like a..."

"A what?"

Abruptly, the ship leaped forward again, and Liam wrenched the steering back. "Like a black hole!"

Liam strained to pull the steering, but the controls were locked into place as the ship was dragged into the black hole.

Anise's heartbeat pulsed through her ears, adrenaline pumping through her veins. Liam pulled the wheel back, and the ship abruptly jerked to the side. Liam's head struck the side of the ship, and he instantly loss consciousness.

Anise grasped the steering, but she couldn't move it an inch. Panic set in, thrumming through her body.

Liam groaned as he came to. "What happened...oh. Never mind, I remember."

The ship shuddered as it was pulled closer. Anise gripped Liam's arm. "What are we going to do?"

"I...don't know."

The stars slowly faded away and the sky turned solid black as the ship was pulled into the black hole. Anise turned away, burying her face in Liam's neck. He wrapped his arms around her, and she could feel his heart racing.

It seemed like an eternity before Liam inhaled sharply. "There's...stars! Anise, stars!"

Anise jerked her head up, her eyes flying to the growing circle of open space, sprinkled with shining silver stars.

"I don't think this is a black hole!" Anise realized. "I think it's a portal, like yours!"

"Maybe..." Liam leaned forward. "Look, I can see the

end!"

Anise held her breath as the ship soared out of the portal into beautiful, nebula-streaked space. Far in the distance, a small green dot began to grow.

"What is that?" Anise asked.

"I think it's a...a planet!" Liam exclaimed.

"Oh!" Anise pulled the journal from her bag as well as the compass. "Liam, the journal is signed by Princess Asteria of Lidica—that planet must be Lidica! And look, the compass is pointing right at it!"

"Lidica is supposed to be a rumor," Liam said in shock. "I've heard some say that you can only find Lidica if it wants you to find it."

"Really?"

"It's just a story." Liam pushed a button on the dash, finally able to move the steering.

Anise watched Lidica grow, and soon the ship glided through the atmosphere. Soon, she could see treetops rushing by beneath them.

As they flew, the compass in Anise's hand began to vibrate as the needle swung around and pointed due north, just the way it should.

"Liam, we need to stop here," Anise said quickly. "The compass went back to normal."

With a nod, Liam carefully lowered the ship and landed in a small clearing. Anise climbed from the ship, and Liam followed her closely.

"Look, now the compass is pointing east. We need to follow it." Anise turned east and began to jog, A call seemed to pull her forward as she increased her pace, breaking into a run.

"Wait!" Anise heard Liam call as he raced after her.

The compass in Anise's hand began to glow, its light encouraging her that she was going the right way. She wove through trees, continuing deeper into the forest—until the compass's glow faded.

Anise glanced up, her eyes widening. She stood before the massive mouth of a cave, though the jungle around her was so dark she could barely see.

Liam slowed to a stop beside her. "Refreshing jog."

Anise shot him a dirty look, struggling to catch her breath. "Look."

Liam scanned the cave, furrowing his brow. "It doesn't look like anything special."

"The compass is pointing inside the cave. We have to

keep following it."

Liam held out his hand. "Can I see the journal?"

Anise handed it to him, watching as he flipped to the drawing of the cave. "These are runes...*here is where all answers can be found,*'" Liam read. "Does that mean there's an answer about our connection here?"

Anticipation rushed over Anise. "Oh, I hope so."

Liam offered her his hand, and she accepted. "We'll find out together."

Anise took a deep breath. "Let's go."

CHAPTER 32

Carefully, Anise and Liam stepped inside the cave. The compass faintly glowed, giving them little light. The walls and floor of the cave seemed unnaturally smooth…almost like polished stone.

They didn't speak as the light from the forest faded away, and they were left in almost darkness. The air became moist and heavy the further they continued.

Anise glanced around the darkness. "Do you think we'll find anything soo—"

Her words cut off as the ground disappeared from beneath her feet. Anise screamed as she fell forward, hearing Liam's shout and bracing herself—

Abruptly, everything halted. Anise couldn't feel any ground beneath her…but she'd stopped falling.

"Liam?" she called, her voice shaky.

"Yes?" Liam's voice shook as well. "Where are you?"

"I don't know; it's too dark." Anise placed her hands on the surface she was on, shocked that she could push herself up and stand. "Keep talking."

"What should I say?"

"Anything." Anise felt her way around, heading to the right where she'd heard his voice.

"Anise Desson, you are the most incredible person I've ever met in my life. I am so lucky to know you, and you grace me with—oof."

Anise stumbled into Liam, gripping his shoulder before she fell. "You interrupted my speech!"

"Terribly sorry," Anise said, finding his hand and holding it tightly. The compass began to glow again, and Anise glanced up. With the light, she could barely see that they stood in a ravine.

However, they weren't at the bottom.

Anise's eyes locked on where she stood…on nothing. The bottom was at least another thirty feet down, and Anise hated to think about what would have happened if they had continued to fall.

"How—how are we doing this?" Liam stammered.

"Councilor Indu told me that sometimes new abilities appear when you're in a life-or-death situation," Anise recalled. "I think this counts."

"I'd agree." Liam glanced upward. "Do you think we can go back up?"

"I would think so." Anise closed her eyes, imagining herself levitating upwards. She grinned as she began lifting up, pulling Liam with her. Moments later, they were on the other side of the gorge, and they both released a sigh of relief.

"Well, *that* was terrifying."

Liam nodded. "I *never* want to do that again."

"Do you think that the rest of the cave has traps too?"

"Probably, but I have a suspicion that, somehow, our powers are connected to these traps."

"I guess we'll find out." Anise followed Liam as he continued deeper into the cave.

Slowly, watching for more traps, they continued down the path. Anise wasn't sure how far they had gone, but soon they reached an archway leading into a large room with a door on the far side.

"This wasn't made naturally," Liam said, running his fingers over the carvings in the arch.

"Then that proves that someone was here. We should keep going."

They stepped into the room, tensed for traps…but nothing happened. Hesitantly, Liam strode forward, but no traps appeared. Anise walked after him, watching where she placed her feet.

"I think it's safe, but—" Liam began as a rumbling sound filled the room.

A huge boulder fell from the ceiling, crashing down just inches from Anise's foot as other boulders began to fall, the sound almost deafening the pair.

"Anise, what about a shield?" Liam had to shout to be heard over the crashes.

"Right!" Anise lifted her hands, and a glittering white force field appeared over them. The rocks continued to crash down, but they couldn't break Anise's shield.

A few minutes later, silence fell over the room, and Anise waited, holding her breath.

"Is it over?" Liam asked.

"I think so." Anise dissolved her shield, waiting a moment. When no other threats appeared, he pair carefully navigated around the boulders until they reached the opposite door.

Liam clenched his jaw as he pulled the heavy door open. "This has to be solid stone."

Anise stepped through the door, and Liam followed her, the door closing behind him.

The compass light dimmed, leaving them in the dark. Liam tried to open the stone door, but it was shut fast.

"Great." Liam rested his forehead against the door. "We're locked in this room with no way out."

Stepping back, Liam colliding with Anise, nearly knocking her down. "Oh, I'm so sorry!"

Anise remained where she was, unaware of Liam trying to help her stand. Her eyes locked on a pinpoint of white light, shing through a tiny hole in the wall.

She peeked through the hole, her eyes widening as she took in the sight of a much larger room lit with white light...and it had a massive double door.

"Liam, look through here!" Anise exclaimed.

Liam knelt and looked. "You found our way out."

"But how do we get there? I don't see a door."

"Well, now that I've seen it, I know exactly where to teleport us to." Liam pulled free his sword.

They stepped through the portal Liam created and appeared in the large room. The splendor left Anise speechless for a moment as she glanced around.

"I think this is it." Anise brushed her fingertips across the carvings on the doorframe.

"I agree." Liam took a deep breath. "Are you ready?"

Anise's heart leaped, and she felt a little flutter of nervousness. "Yes. I'm very ready."

She took Liam's hand and squeezed it. He smiled at her, his own nerves showing through.

"On three," Liam whispered, "One, two, three!"

Anise and Liam laid their hands on the doors to push them open, but the second they touched the doors, they swung open by themselves.

The doors opened to a huge, round cavern. The floors were intricately carved with swirls and stars, and glittering inside the walls were thousands of tiny diamond-shaped crystals. The crystals looked like diamonds, each glowing like a mini star and collectively lighting the whole room.

In the middle of the room stood a stone pedestal, covered in runes and carvings.

"It's beautiful," Anise said in awe. Liam simply stared at it all, but she felt him gently squeeze her hand.

Anise read the runes across the pedestal: *"Here you can see all the memories of the galaxy; not the way they were seen, but the way they truly were."*.

A bright light abruptly shone from Anise's bag. She opened it and pulled out the journal, stunned to see the symbol on the front glowing brightly.

Anise carefully opened it, her eyes widening as she saw more pages had been filled with runes.

"Liam, read this." She held out the book, and Liam leaned over her shoulder as they read the entry together:

Dear Finder,

If you are reading this, then you have found my journal. Inside, I have written many entries on Lidica. This planet is magical, and I am lucky to call it my home. Now, since you are reading this, it means that you have found Lidica (a feat within itself!) and made it to the Star Caverns.

Since you have made it to the final cavern, I can only assume you are a Starlink. You may or may not know what this is, and I will explain.

Due east of Lidica are two stars, unlike any others. They orbit each other—the only stars that do so. Every three thousand years, these two stars ever so slightly touch. On the first day it happens, only one person will be born, and they will be the first half of the Starlink. Then, the stars will continue to orbit normally.

However, one year and three months later, they will touch again. Again, only one person will be born on this day, and they will be the second half of the Starlink.

Both members of the Starlink will be granted extraordinary powers. They will be able to transmit thoughts to the other, and each will have a single lock of blue hair. They may also have the symbol that is inscribed on this journal on themselves.

Also, the two members will share two powers. They will both have levitation and will be able to harness star energy and heal with it. Since levitation needs little explanation, I will move on to stardust energy.

Harnessing stardust energy is done by concentrating on the energy flow through the air and enhancing it. Stardust energy is exponentially powerful and is known as the most powerful healing agent. Starlidica is a flower that only grows here and contains a tiny, tiny portion of the stars' healing power.

Healing with stardust energy, on the other hand, is endlessly powerful. Stardust energy can cure everything but death. However, it can be dangerous. Healing with stardust energy has three stages.

The first stage is minor healing. It is easy and less draining. It works on minor injuries and has little to no after-effects.

The second stage is intense healing. This is harder and can leave the healer drained. It works on serious injuries, but the risk is much higher. The easiest you will get off is very tired and weak. The worst is losing your powers completely.

The third stage is for grave injuries and near-deaths. This stage is the hardest and will leave the healer weak and tired. The risk using this stage is the very highest. The least that can happen is losing all abilities. But, when this power is used, it is unfortunately not very uncommon for the healer to die.

Now that I've informed you of all the essential information, I'm sure you will use it well. Good luck, and I hope you find what you are looking for.

Signed,

Princess Asteria of Lidica

Silence fell over the cavern as Anise ran her thumb over Asteria's name, processing the information.

"Are...are you drawing the same conclusion I am?" Liam asked, his voice uncertain.

"That we're a Starlink?" Anise whispered.

Liam nodded. "This has to be it…right?"

Anise slowly closed the journal. "We're a Starlink."

"That's why our powers won't work on each other," Liam realized. "The other half of the link must be immune."

Anise's mind spun as she gently tucked the journal into her bag. "I…I didn't understand how much power I—we have access to. I wouldn't have guessed my healing could be that powerful."

"It's a double-edged sword, though," Liam replied. "It has grave consequences, remember? Imagine healing someone you love, knowing you'll never get to be with them.'"

"I know," Anise said softly. "But in some cases, it's worth the risk."

"I'd agree," Liam said, glancing at her.

"There's a few people I'd heal, no matter what," Anise admitted.

Liam turned to her, an oddly emotionless expression on his face. "What few people?"

Anise furrowed her brow at him. "People I care about. My brother, Keisha…you—"

"No."

"No?" Anise repeated. "What are you talking about?"

"I won't try to stop you from healing your brother or friends—but not me."

Anise stared at him, bewildered. "Why not?"

"Never mind." Liam's voice held the same emotionless tone. "Just promise that you won't heal me for anything that isn't minor."

"And why should I do that?" Anise protested.

"Anise!" Liam said, his voice sharp. "Just promise me."

Anise's first instinct was to argue—to demand a better reason. But it was so unlike Liam to be harsh...and she could see fear in his eyes, even as he tried to suppress it.

"I promise," Anise said finally, crossing her arms. *But I don't promise to keep that promise.*

Relief filled Liam's face, and he visibly relaxed. "Thank you. That's all I needed to hear."

"You promise me the same thing."

"I can't."

Anise watched in confusion as he turned away, slowly walking around the room. Something in the back of her mind felt unsettled by his refusal to make the same promise...

What is he afraid of? Anise followed behind Liam, wishing he'd tell her. "Liam, I—" Her words were cut off as she abruptly stumbled over a dip in the floor.

Liam was at her side in a heartbeat, neatly catching her. Anise steadied herself, looking up at him, but Liam's attention was locked behind her.

"Look what you tripped over," Liam said, releasing her and gesturing to the floor.

Anise turned, her gaze locking on the unusual dip, caused by...*handprints*, pressed into the stone floor. Oddly, they'd been set opposite from each other, so the right hand was on the left side.

"What are these?" Anise asked as Liam knelt beside them. "And what are you doing?"

Liam placed his left hand into the print. "I'm testing these. They have to do something."

Anise waited a moment, but nothing happened. "Maybe it needs...both halves of the link."

"Worth a try."

Anise knelt beside Liam and placed her right hand into the correct imprint. The cavern fell silent as they waited.

With a *whoosh*, a beam of white light shot up from the

pedestal, filling the whole room with a brilliant glow. Two of the crystals inset into the wall mimicked the glow as they hovered away from the wall, floating in midair.

"Are we supposed to take them?" Anise whispered.

"I think so." Liam reached out, touching the left crystal. It glowed in his hand for a moment before turning normal.

Anise shrugged and took the right crystal. It, too, glowed for a moment before turning back.

"What are we supposed to do with these?" Anise examined the crystal. "Are they supposed to do something?"

"I don't know," Liam admitted. "It seems like they're for us."

Anise dropped the crystal into her bag with a shrug as she stood. "I guess so."

Liam stood as well. "Should we go back?"

"Yeah, we don't want to be gone for too long. If people start looking for us…well, it wouldn't be good."

Liam walked over and tried to open the door. He frowned and pulled harder. "Um, we may have a problem. This door won't open."

"I'd call that a problem," Anise agreed, scanning the

room. "I'll look for a secret door. There's got to be a way out."

"I'll check over here," Liam said. Anise turned away, searching for any fissures that might hint at an exit.

Liam scanned the walls, only for the crystal in his hand to begin glowing again. He glanced back towards Anise before the crystal turned ice cold and everything turned to black.

CHAPTER 33

A cool breath of air washed over Liam, loud crashes echoing through the dark. A voice whispered, "Thirty-two seconds."

Abruptly, Liam stood in a crumbling, dark tunnel with only a tiny speck of light at the end.

Anise had fallen to her knees on the ground in front of him, terror in her eyes. Blood dripped from a cut on her head, and she reached a hand towards him. She screamed something, but the crashing sounds drowned her voice out.

White light shone around him for a second, then black. Pain filled his side, and the emptiness changed. It was colder, darker, and empty, with no light.

The voice whispered again. "Thirty-two seconds."

Abruptly, Liam was again standing in the Star Caverns, with

the crystal clenched in his hand. He inhaled a sharp breath, trying to shake off the strange feeling settling in his chest.

"Liam, I just remembered," Anise called, snapping him back to the present. "I feel like an idiot—you can teleport us back to the ship."

"Oh, of course." Liam slipped the crystal into his pocket and drew his sword.

Anise walked up beside him, wrapping her hand around his arm. Liam lifted his sword, created a portal to their ship, and they both stepped through.

They exited the portal, and Liam did a double-take. Instead of standing by the ship, they'd appeared before the oversized double doors of a crumbling castle.

Anise's eyes went wide. "Liam—where are we?"

"I...have no idea." Liam glanced around them. "I was trying to bring us back to the ship...but my portal brought us here."

The jungle had begun claiming the castle, thick vines covering every wall. Tree branches reached inside the castle, breaking through the walls.

"I wonder who lived here," Anise said softly.

"I don't know." Liam approached the large doors, pushing one open. The door creaked as it opened, and startled birds took to the sky. Anise stepped around Liam and into the castle.

"Look in here!" Anise's voice echoed from inside.

Liam peered into the castle. The doors had opened into a long hall with a throne sitting at the end. Light streamed in through dirty windows, and the holes scattered through the walls and ceiling.

"This place must've been the home of the royalty that ruled here," Liam remarked. "This place looks at least a thousand years old."

"Royalty!" Anise dug through her bag. "The journal belonged to a Princess Asteria. This must be her palace."

"Look, there's another door," Liam commented.

Anise strode over to the smaller door, pulling it open. Liam followed, and they stepped outside.

Liam glanced around at the expansive garden pathways. Any landscaping was long gone, but patches of huge white flowers grew, scattered among the flowerbeds. A cobblestone pathway wove deeper in the garden, and a large statue stood in the middle.

A low, crumbling stone wall surrounded the statue's base. On either side of the statue stood a large headstone, engraved in runes.

The statue depicted a young man with short curly hair, and

somehow, the sculptor had managed to catch a mischievous gleam in his eyes. His arm was wrapped around a beautiful young woman with long flowing hair and laughing eyes.

"*Empress Asteria of Lidica,*" Anise read from the stone on the left. "And *Emperor Tarak of Lidica.*"

"This is their memorial," Liam said softly.

Anise plucked a few of the large, white flowers, leaned over the fence, and gently laid the blossoms in front of each headstone. "Thank you, Asteria."

Liam wrapped his arm around Anise's shoulders as they stood, taking in the peaceful setting.

Anise broke the silence. "We should probably get back now."

"You're right." They turned and started back, only pausing once to take one last look at the statue.

"Look, the same flowers are here!" Anise said as they stepped back into the jungle. "These must be the Starlidica that Asteria mentioned in her journal."

Anise leaned down and picked a few of the flowers. Liam plucked an especially beautiful blossom and tucked it in her hair. Anise smiled at him as she gathered the last of her bouquet.

"What are you going to do with all those?"

"They're supposed to be good for healing." Anise bent over for another blossom. "I thought it might be a good idea to have a few, just in case." She stood back up and sighed. "This place is so beautiful; I wish I never had to leave."

Instantly, the words were on the tip of Liam's tongue. *We don't have to leave. Stay here, with me. We could finally be together.*

Liam bit back his words, forcing himself to remain silent as Anise returned to his side. He drew his sword and created another portal. This time, they stepped out beside the ship.

"We'll go back to the Qor shipyard, and I'll teleport back to base," Liam said as they climbed back into the ship.

"Alright," Anise said as she settled into his arms. Liam activated the ship, soaring into the sky. Silence fell over the ship, and soon Anise nodded off in his arms.

Liam glanced down at her sleeping face, feeling a flash of pain through his chest. The soft moments like this reminded him that he could never be with Anise. The secret they kept was dangerous enough now, but if they got in any deeper, it would be deadly.

Closing his eyes, Liam tried to ignore the ache pulsing through his chest. ...He desperately wanted their relationship to work, to find a way for them to be together...but he couldn't risk

Anise getting hurt.

It would be better to cut off their relationship before anything else happened. The longer it was, the worse the unavoidable separation would hurt.

Anise shifted slightly, and Liam gazed at her beautiful face. Instantly, he could tell cutting it off now would hurt him worse than anything he had ever felt.

Finally, Liam landed in the Qor's shipyard. It was dusk, and the shipyard was empty. Liam shook her awake. "Anise, we're here."

"Okay." Anise yawned as she climbed out of the ship.

Liam jumped down after her. "Here, let me teleport you to your room."

"Thanks." Anise yawned again as Liam created the portal. "See you." She leaned over to kiss him, but Liam turned his head, her kiss landing on his cheek.

Anise pulled back, her expression a mixture of confusion and hurt.

"Good night," Liam said, ignoring the deep pain throbbing between his ribs.

"Bye." Anise stepped through the portal.

Liam inhaled a shaky breath. His heart felt like it was tearing in two, but he had to keep Anise safe...no matter how much he hurt himself in the process.

CHAPTER 34

It had been two days since the visit to Lidica, each day without Anise feeling like an eternity. Liam longed to talk to her; to hear her voice.

Liam?

Liam started, taking a moment to make sure he hadn't imagined her voice. *Hi, Anise.* Against his will, he added, *it's good to hear your voice.*

Mhmm. Anise sounded doubtful. *Can we meet up?*

I don't know if that's a good idea. Liam rubbed his temples.

Let me rephrase: I want you to teleport to me. Now.

Liam debated with himself for a moment before creating a portal. He hesitated a moment before stepping through, instantly in Anise's room.

Anise stood with her arms crossed. "Pick somewhere private we can talk."

Liam shot her a glance, wondering why she seemed so incensed. He envisioned the ballroom he had taken her to for her birthday, creating a new portal.

They appeared in the ballroom, and Anise turned to him. "What's going on?"

"Nothing, really," Liam replied, struggling to continue a normal conversation as though nothing was wrong.

"When are we going to see each other again?"

"Are we going to?" Liam forced himself to ask. "We were supposed to find the truth about our connection, and that was it."

"What are you saying?" Anise's voice wavered.

"I'm saying…now that we know…we…don't need to keep seeing each other."

"What's wrong with you, Liam?" Anise placed her hands on her hips. "What's with the change? You're acting like you're angry with me."

"I'm not angry."

"Did you take a new potion?"

"No, I didn't," Liam said, feeling horrible as Anise's face fell.

"Did something happen?" Anise asked after a moment. "On Lidica?"

The strange memory the crystal had shown drifted through Liam's mind. He couldn't shake the feeling that the memory was warning him. The image of Anise's terrified face and the blood streaming from her head was present in his mind, and he hardened his resolve.

Liam knew he wouldn't be able to live with himself if Anise got hurt because he had tried to find a way to make this doomed relationship work.

Besides, if he told her about the memory, she would try to find a way around it. She would try to find a way to make it work...and she might get hurt in the process.

"No," Liam answered finally. "Nothing happened."

"Does this have something to do with you leaving the Embleck Army?" Anise's voice held a note of barely suppressed emotion. "I'm...I'm not trying to make you leave them."

"I know," Liam said quietly.

"Is there anything wrong with...me?" Anise's voice broke Liam's heart.

"No, of course not," Liam said quickly. "I...I just think that seeing each other...it's a bad idea."

"I don't believe you." Anise crossed her arms. "I know there's something you're not telling me."

"I can't...tell you."

"That's it?" Anise snapped. "You told me you never stopped loving me. Do you still mean it?"

"I..." Liam bit his tongue, tasting blood. *Of course, I love you! I love you more than anything!*

"Do you love me or not?"

Liam couldn't take it any longer, "*Yes*, Anise, I love you more than anything in this entire galaxy!"

Anise's eyes went wide.

"I love you, and it's terrifying!" Liam's voice broke. "I can't imagine a life without you, but I know that we can't ever be together!"

Anise remained still for a moment, her expression stunned. Liam's heart skipped a beat—*what if she doesn't feel the same? What if I just poured my heart out to her for no reason? W—*

Anise took a step closer to Liam before throwing her arms around him, hugging him tightly. Liam closed his eyes, returning the embrace.

"And why didn't you tell me that sooner?" Anise whispered,

her voice strained.

Liam glanced away. "I…I didn't want to say it…didn't want to make it real for us…"

"It's already real," Anise said softly. "Whether we deny it or not."

"I know." Liam's throat burned with emotion. "There—there's just no way this will work. If the Embleck Army finds out, they'll kill you, just to teach me a lesson and—" Liam's words caught, choked with emotion. "And I…I couldn't live like that."

"I'm sorry." Anise leaned up, pressing her lips against his.

This time Liam didn't turn away, but he instantly knew something was wrong. There was no hope in her kiss…no future.

It felt like *goodbye*.

Anise pulled back with pain in her eyes, and Liam knew she felt it too.

Anise pressed close against Liam's chest, and he wrapped his arms around her. "What are we going to do?" she whispered.

Liam tried to think of something reassuring to say, but nothing came to mind. "I don't know."

"Is there any way this could work?" Anise asked.

"I'm afraid not," Liam murmured. "It seems like

this…between us can only end with…with one of us gone. That leaves us with only two options."

"We could go to Lidica," Anise suggested desperately, one last attempt to make this work. "We could be together, and no one could find us."

"You know that won't work," Liam whispered. "You have your brother, your friends—you're a commander in the Qor! You have your whole life ahead of you. I couldn't let you give that up for me." *I'm not worth it.*

"What about you?" Anise's voice was choked with unshed tears.

Liam forced himself to smile. "I'll be alright."

Neither of them acknowledged the lie. Anise rested her head on Liam's shoulder, and he felt a tear soak into his shirt. He bit his lip until he tasted blood, holding back his own tears. *Come on. You have to be strong for Anise.*

"I—I'll bring you home," Liam forced out.

Anise nodded against his neck. Liam created a portal, and they appeared in her room.

Liam sheathed his sword, fighting back a wave of emotion. Anise hadn't moved from holding him, but now she slowly pulled away.

"I guess this is goodbye." Anise glanced up at him, tears shining in her eyes.

Somehow, Liam felt this was all his fault. "I'm...I'm so sorry."

"It's not your fault." Anise turned away, only to spin back around and kiss him again.

Liam's lungs seized, making it hard to breathe. He pulled back, cupping Anise's face in his hand. His gaze roamed over her, trying to memorize every last detail.

"I love you," Anise whispered.

Liam's heart skipped a beat. "You...what?"

"I love you," Anise echoed, her voice stronger this time.

Liam gazed at her in stunned silence for a moment. "*You love...me? Really?*"

Anise grasped his jacket collar, pulling his lips to hers. Liam wrapped his arms around her waist and holding her close. The kiss reflected the knowledge that these could be their last moments together.

Finally, Anise pulled back. "I do. I love you, Liam."

Before that moment, Liam hadn't known how three words could make him the happiest man alive and the most miserable at the same time.

"I love you too, Anise," Liam whispered, his voice hoarse. "I always have...and I always will."

Anise forced a broken smile on her face even as her eyes glistened with tears. She stepped away, slowly letting go of his hand. Liam let his hand fall to his side, trying to ignore the pain of his heart tearing in two.

"Goodbye, Liam," Anise said softly.

"Goodbye, Anise." Liam created his portal home. He glanced over his shoulder to get one last glimpse of Anise. She wrapped her arms around herself and they locked eyes for a single moment.

Anise dropped her eyes. Liam forced himself to step through the portal and entered his room.

Stumbling to his bed, Liam sank down on the side. The darkness enveloped him, pain pulsing through his body with every heartbeat as he closed his eyes, picturing Anise's face.

Liam's heart shattered in a thousand pieces as he finally broke down and sobbed.

CHAPTER 35

Anise sat on the edge of her bed, absentmindedly twirling her galaxy rose. Joffrey lay at her feet, watching her worriedly.

Three days without any contact with Liam. Anise wondered how in such a short time, he'd become so valuable to her.

A knock on the door startled Anise from her thoughts. Numbly, she stood and opened the door.

"Hey, Anise." Keisha stepped into the room, giving her an odd look. "Are you okay?"

Anise answered by bursting into tears. Bewildered, Keisha ushered her back over to the bed, taking a seat beside her.

"Honey, what's wrong?" Keisha put her arm around Anise.

"Liam and I agreed," Anise managed. "We decided not to see each other anymore."

449

"If you're this upset about it, it doesn't sound like you're in agreement," Keisha said.

"We are…it's just too dangerous," Anise said miserably. "He doesn't want me to get hurt, and I don't want him to get hurt. It can't ever work between us."

"That's not the Anise I know," Keisha said. "You're determined—if you want something, you find a way."

"But how?" Anise choked.

"There's always a way where things will work out," Keisha said. "If the Embleck Army is keeping you two apart, you have to find a way to stop them."

"The Qor has been trying to do that for years!" Anise replied. "How could I do that?"

"You're something special, Anise," Keisha said softly. "I have faith you'll find a way if you want to."

"I want us to be together." Anise wiped her eyes. "I just don't know how."

"You'll figure it out." Keisha smiled.

"Thanks, Keisha," Anise said quietly.

"Anytime," Keisha said. "Now, on another note. Councilor Indu sent me to get you."

"Why?"

"Assignment to scan our territory on Tironlay. Small group, you, me, Caiden, Tyler."

"Okay." Anise sighed. "Let's go."

Reluctantly, Anise followed Keisha down to the hangar. Caiden stood beside their ship, grinning when he saw her.

Anise forced herself to smile back. "How was the date with Lydia?"

"It was great." Caiden's grin widened. "Lydia's something else. She's smart, funny—and *so* gorgeous."

"I'm so happy for you," Anise said honestly, unable to help wishing her relationship with Liam could be that simple.

Caiden spent the entire trip to Tironlay telling Anise about his date with Lydia. He had taken her out to dinner, and then they had gone stargazing. Anise nodded along, barely listening.

Finally, the ship landed on the rocky planet's surface. Anise led Caiden, Keisha, and Tyler off the ship as they set up the scanners for life forms.

Anise glanced out over the natural rock bridge joining their territory with neutral grounds. It wouldn't be long at this rate before the Embleck Army took the last of the free territory.

With a spy on our council, we may not stand a chance to win this war, Anise thought, her emotions numb.

"Commander?" Tyler called. "You should come see this."

Anise turned to where Tyler pointed, her eyes locking on an Embleck ship that had been hidden behind a large boulder at her previous angle.

A group of soldiers exited the ship, and it appeared that they had spotted Anise's group.

Anise looked closer, and her heart plummeted when she recognized the man leading the Embleck soldiers.

Liam.

"Commander, what do we do?" Tyler whispered.

"Leave them to me." Anise began approaching the bridge.

"Anise, don't!" Caiden started after her. "Are you crazy?"

Impulsively, Anise activated a shield around the entire bridge, preventing her teammates from reaching her as she kept her eyes locked on Liam.

Liam stared at her shield before starting toward her, effortlessly stepping through it. Caiden growled in frustration, slamming his shoulder against the shield.

"Seriously?" he shouted at the shield. "How come he can go

through, but we can't? And what even is this thing?"

Anise tuned them all out, focusing only on Liam. He drew his sword, and she did the same.

Liam's lips quirked up in a tiny smirk. "Your move, Commander."

Anise struck out first, and Liam blocked her. He moved next, and she ducked. Liam spun around, and they clashed swords again.

The sharp clanking of swords filled the air as Anise and Liam fought. Anise used every technique she knew and channeled all her pain and frustration into her movements. This fight might only be for show, but for Anise, it felt like much more.

She was fighting someone she loved—someone who meant the galaxy to her. If it wasn't necessary to keep the Embleck Army from finding out about Liam's relationship, Anise wasn't sure how she would do it. She would do anything to keep him safe…even if it meaning she had to fight.

Finally, Anise pushed Liam back, letting her sword hang from her hand. Liam stepped back but didn't raise his sword again either.

"What are we going to do now?" Anise whispered. "We can't keep doing this forever."

"I'm afraid that there's only one option for me." Liam approached her, stopping only arm's reach away.

Anise's breath caught as Liam lowered himself to one knee and held his sword out, offering it to her. "I need you to finish this."

Exclamations and shouts came from each side, but neither of them was aware. Anise bit her lip as she reached for Liam's face, but he caught her wrist, bringing it down.

Gently, Liam wrapped her fingers around the hilt of his sword, allowing his hand to rest over hers.

"This can only end two ways, and I can't let anything happen to you. Without my abilities, the Embleck Armies won't be able to win. I am their weapon, and if you take that away… the Qor can win this."

Anise met Liam's eyes, full of regret and sorrow…but resigned. "It's okay. I've done horrible things, and I…" his voice broke, and he set his jaw before continuing. "Just finish this."

Tears burned Anise's throat, choking her voice. "Finish it?"

Liam nodded. Anise tried to keep her tears from slipping down her cheeks, but one stubborn tear fell anyway. Liam reached up, lightly wiping it away.

"Don't cry for me." Liam pulled his hand away, putting the

full weight of his sword into her hand.

Anise took a deep breath, feeling her hands shaking as she glanced down at the sword she held. Liam was right—she knew it. The Embleck Army was ruthless, and they would hunt him down. This seemed to be the only option.

But Anise saw *Liam* in front of her, his eyes tightly closed, braced for what was coming. She remembered his kindness when she was seventeen…his smile after she kissed him…the pain in his eyes when they'd decided to separate…

Anise gripped the sword hilt. She knew it was time to finish it.

For good.

"Finish it," Anise whispered, feeling her stomach lurch when he nodded again.

Anise took a deep breath, raised the sword, and pointed it at Liam's chest, ignoring the exclamations from both sides. Anise faltered as Liam opened his eyes, and they locked with hers.

Finish it.

Anise spun around and slashed Liam's sword through the air behind her. A portal opened, and Anise grabbed Liam's hand, jerking them both through.

They staggered into the ballroom, the portal closing behind

them. Liam turned to her in shock. "What are you doing? You had the perfect opportunity—"

"I can't kill you!" Anise interjected.

Liam reached for his sword. "Fine, I'll—"

"No!" Anise shouted, pulling it away. "You don't have to do this! Do you really want to die?"

Liam wouldn't meet her eyes for a moment, and Anise felt a stab of fear. *What will I do if he says yes?*

"For the first time in *nine years*…" Liam's eyes held a haunted air. "I have something—someone—to live for. I don't want it to end like this."

"It doesn't have to!" Anise dropped his sword to the floor. "You don't have to die. We can find another way!"

Liam clenched his jaw. "I don't like this any more than you do, but it's my decision."

"Well, it's a terrible decision!" Anise snapped. "I don't want you to die!"

"I don't want to die either!" Liam snapped back. "But I can't live another day in the Embleck Army. It's torture, knowing what I'm helping them do!"

Liam glanced down at his sword. "If I do this now, it's my

choice…but if I leave the Embleck Army, they'll just kill me anyway."

Anise shook her head. "Please, Liam."

"I'm sorry. I wish this could be different—that I could find another way." Liam took a deep breath. "But even if I could…I can't undo what I've done in the past. We could never have a life together. I'm a monster, Anise…and I can't change that."

"You're not a monster," Anise whispered. "And I love you for who you are."

Something shifted in Liam's eyes. A spark of hope seemed to flicker, and Anise let it grow in her heart.

"You shouldn't. I…I don't want to taint you. Everyone would shun you. I couldn't do that." Liam sounded as though he was trying to convince himself. "I've been to nearly every planet and only to destroy for the Embleck Army. The only person who loves me—and the only person I love— in this entire galaxy is you…and I'm so afraid you're going to get hurt because of it."

Anise took Liam's hand and held it tight. "I know that might be true, but I can't…I can't lose you. Especially not like this."

That tiny spark of hope in Liam's eyes seemed to flicker, and Anise seized her opportunity.

"I may be the only person who loves you…but isn't that

enough? If we could find a way to be together and stop the Embleck Army, would that be enough for you?"

Liam was silent for a moment. "More than enough. More than I could ever hope for."

Anise's heart swelled with love at the hesitantly hopeful expression on Liam's face. She grasped the collar of his uniform and pulled his lips to hers.

Liam sucked in a small breath of surprise before wrapping his arms around her waist and kissing her back.

"Isn't that enough to live for?" Anise asked softly, cupping Liam's face in her hand.

Liam took a deep breath. "…Yes."

Anise grinned and kissed Liam again. "Thank you."

"But…how is it possible?" The hopeful light in Liam's eyes dimmed slightly.

Anise stepped back and straightened her shoulders. "We can't be together because of the Embleck Army—so we need to take them out."

Liam stared at her, incredulous. "You—you think we can destroy the entire Embleck Army?"

"We can find a way to stop them. I can use my mind control;

you can teleport! We can find a way to make this work." Anise placed her hand on the hilt of Liam's sword. "This isn't the only option—destroying the Embleck Army is."

Liam glanced away. "It'll be dangerous. You know that, right?"

"I know," Anise said softly. "And I know that you want to protect me, just like I want to protect you. But I'm willing to take a risk...if you are."

Liam gently brushed her hair from her face. "I want to keep you safe, Anise...you're my universe. But if that's what it takes for us to be together...and I'm willing to take that risk with you."

Anise felt tears of joy in her eyes as she hugged him. "I love you—so much. We can do this. I know we can."

"There's one thing I have to do before I leave," Liam said abruptly. "I have to go back for Brendon."

"Let's take care of this skirmish on the bridge," Anise decided. "Then you can go back for Brendon, and I'll alert the Qor Council."

"Yes, Commander," Liam said with a smile.

Anise offered Liam his sword. "Are you with me?"

Liam smiled and accepted his sword. "Till the Galaxy's End."

They stepped through Liam's portal, appearing back on the bridge. The two sides were still on opposite sides of the bridge, seeming unsure of what to do.

However, once Anise and Liam reappeared, High Commander Ankor had an idea.

"Destroy them!" High Commander Ankor shouted at his soldiers from his ship. His magnified voice echoed across the canyon. "All of them!"

Anise un-sheathed her sword and turned to Liam. "Let's do this together."

Liam nodded. "Together."

Anise and Liam raised their swords and attacked the advancing androids. Anise dissolved her shield, and Caiden, Keisha, and Tyler raced to her side.

Caiden crashed into Anise and grabbed her by the shoulders while Liam held off the advancing enemies.

"Is *this* the boyfriend you've been hinting about?" Caiden exclaimed, gesturing to Liam.

"Maybe..." Anise replied with a sheepish look.

Caiden sighed but let her go. "I want more details after this."

"*Fine*, fine," Anise groaned, turning back to the battle and raising her sword.

The group lunged at the androids, attacking and quickly destroying them. The human Embleck soldiers advanced, and the real battle began. Anise glanced up at the ship where High Commander Ankor was barely visible in the window, an idea forming.

"I need you to get me up there!" Anise shouted to Liam.

Liam glanced up, catching sight of the ship. "Here!"

"Thanks!" Anise dodged a strike and leaped through, appearing right before High Commander Ankor.

"What in the—" Ankor started, reaching for the ray gun on his belt.

"Stop," Anise commanded him, raising her hand. He did as ordered, freezing on the spot.

"You will return to your base and tell King Zamir that High Commander Monroy and his squad were ambushed, and he was killed in battle," Anise ordered. "Understand?"

"Understood," High Commander Ankor said in a monotone.

Anise ducked back through her portal just as it shut. She landed behind Liam and got to her feet, watching the huge ship take off and fly away.

Turning, she realized her team was horribly outnumbered. She saw Caiden attempting to fight off three soldiers at once, and more were moving towards him.

Making a quick decision, Anise opened her mind to the energy field, pulled power into her mind—and threw it over the battlefield.

"STOP!" Anise shouted. *Please work…please.*

CHAPTER 36

Liam sidestepped the soldier attacking him and swung back, only to stop as the soldier froze, completely unmoving. He whipped around to see what had caused it, stunned when he saw.

Anise stood behind him with both hands outstretched, her eyes screwed shut in concentration.

It took him a second longer than it should have to realize—Anise was causing it. Liam watched in amazement as he came to the conclusion that her power was even stronger than he could imagine.

She couldn't just control one mind at a time. Or a dozen minds. She could control *hundreds*.

"Hurry," Anise managed. "I—I can't hold this for long."

"Everyone to the ship!" Liam ordered, heading for Anise.

"I'm here. Come on, I'll bring you back to the ship."

"No—not yet," Anise whispered, prying her eyes open. "I'm trying to erase what they saw."

"From all of them?" Liam replied in shock. "Can you even do that?"

"I have to try," Anise responded, squeezing her eyes shut harder before taking a deep breath. "It's done."

"Really?"

"Yes...I hope."

"Then let's go." Liam tried to pull Anise away, but she resisted.

"No, let the others get closer to the ship," Anise mumbled. "I can hold it a little longer."

"Anise, are you sure?" Liam placed his hand on her shoulder, worry tugging at his chest. Anise's form was trembling, and he felt his heart clench when she didn't respond at first.

Finally, Anise nodded. "Let's go now," she whispered—and promptly collapsed.

"Stars." Liam barely caught Anise, lifting her into his arms and rushing back to the ship before the soldiers came to.

Boarding the ship, Liam braced himself as it immediately

took off. He laid Anise down on a bench as Keisha rushed over to her side.

"What did you do to her?" Caiden exclaimed in an accusatory tone.

"Nothing!" Liam snapped.

"He helped me." Anise opened her eyes, smiling faintly. "I insisted on staying."

Liam gently took her hand. "Are you okay?"

"I'm fine," Anise said but winced when she tried to sit up. "Other than a pounding headache."

"So, now that you're fine—I must ask," Caiden began. "WHAT WAS THAT?"

"Uh…" Anise glanced at Liam. "This is Liam."

Caiden rolled his eyes. "I figured that out. What I meant was—why is he in our ship, how did you create that force field, and, WHAT IN THE GALAXY IS HAPPENING?"

"Liam's defecting from the Embleck Army," Anise said, and Liam felt a thrill go through his heart at the words. "When we were in the jungle together, we found out that we both have similar powers."

"So…you created the light shield?" Keisha asked in awe.

"Yes…" Anise admitted, flushing. "And I was the one mind controlling the soldiers."

Caiden looked like he was on the verge of a mental breakdown. "I—I—I…need to sit down."

Tyler popped his head in from the control room. "That was sick, Commander."

Anise laughed. "Thanks, Tyler."

"What are we going to do now, Anise?" Keisha said hesitantly.

"We're keeping our power and Liam a secret for now," Anise said. "I'm going to talk to the council about our next move."

"I have to return and alert Brendon," Liam said, . "I'm going to my personal house on Uribeck, and I'll have him meet me there tonight."

"Perfect." Anise pulled herself into a proper sitting position. "Liam, can I have the coordinates of your house before you leave?"

Liam gave her the coordinates just before he created a portal. "Are you sure you're okay with this?"

"I am." Anise nodded. "Now go. We're getting close to the base."

Liam saluted her casually and created a portal. When the swirling black circle appeared, Keisha shrieked, clutching Caiden's arm.

"It's fine," Anise reassured her friend. "That's Liam's power."

"If you say so..." Keisha looked incredibly doubtful, but she didn't argue.

"Bye." Liam stepped through his portal and vanished.

Caiden broke the silence first. "This is by far the craziest day I've ever had."

"Not for me," Tyler piped up. "The craziest day I've ever had was the day Keisha wore a shirt and jeans without makeup or jewelry or anything!"

"I was sick!" Keisha exclaimed. "And how is that crazier than—"

"No matter how crazy this is," Anise interjected. "We have to get a resolution. I'm going to speak with the council now."

"I'll come," Caiden volunteered.

"No, it's fine," Anise insisted. "I'd rather do it alone."

Caiden sighed. "Fine. Let me know how things work out, okay?"

"I'll contact you after the meeting," Anise promised.

The ship soon landed at the Qor base, and Anise briskly made her way up to the Councilors' offices, heading for Councilor Indu's.

"Commander Desson!"

Anise whipped around to see High Councilor Mills striding towards her. *Indu warned me about him. If he's the traitor…I can't let him know Liam's defecting.*

"Hello, Sir," Anise said pleasantly, keeping her guard up. "Is there something I can do for you?"

"As a matter of fact, yes. Can I speak to you in my office…privately?"

Anise's heartbeat jumped up. "Well, Sir…I'm in the middle of something at the moment."

"Please, Commander. It's very important that I speak with you right away," High Councilor Mills insisted.

Anise tightened her hold on the strap of her bag. "I'm sorry, but can I speak with you later? My task is of the utmost urgency."

High Councilor Mills seemed distressed but nodded. "Alright…please come speak with me the moment you're done."

"Of course, Sir."

Mills continued down the hall, pausing beside her momentarily. "Avoid the other councilors until we've spoken."

Anise nodded obediently. *As if!*

High Councilor Mills straightened, continuing down the hall. Once he was out of sight, Anise gave a little sigh of relief.

Ignoring his order, Anise hurried down to the next-to-last office door: Councilor Indu's. Maybe he could explain why High Councilor Mills was acting so strange.

Anise hesitated only a second before knocking on the door.

"Come in."

Anise opened the door and stepped into the office. Councilor Indu was looking over a stack of paperwork but stopped and smiled when he saw her.

"Hello, Commander Desson. How was the scan of Tironlay?" He glanced at his comm. "A bit short, wasn't it?"

"It was a little…strange," Anise admitted. "We made contact with an Embleck ship…and General Monroy."

"Stars—are you alright?" Councilor Indu stood, his expression worried.

"Yes, I'm fine," Anise reported. "But High Councilor Mills was acting strange. Do you know why?"

Councilor Indu pursed his lips. "Was he now? I'm afraid he knows we suspect him. If so, an Embleck Army attack could be imminent." He paused, scanning Anise. "But the Qor will have you to protect them, won't they?"

Anise tried to shake off the strange intensity of his gaze. He was worried, that was all. "Yes, of course. I'll put all my power into protecting the Qor."

"I thought so," Councilor Indu muttered under his breath. "But you said the scan was strange. How so?"

Any uneasiness Anise felt disappeared, turning to excitement. "General Monroy is defecting from the Embleck Army!"

Councilor Indu stared at her in shock. "He…he's what?"

"He's requesting to join the Qor's efforts to destroy the Embleck Army," Anise said in a rush.

"Really?" Indu asked, a strange expression clouding his face.

"Yes!" Anise replied. "The Embleck Army's most powerful soldier—on our side. This could be the key to winning the war!"

To her surprise, fury broke across Councilor Indu's face. "Foolish girl—you've ruined everything!"

"What do you mean?" Anise asked in shock.

"Years of planning and arranging this all— only for you to ruin it with your big blue eyes and pretty face!"

"How could my face ruin anything?" Anise asked, offended. "I don't understand."

Councilor Indu turned to her. "And you never will, will you? Guards!"

The door behind Indu's desk swung open, revealing a dozen Embleck soldiers. Before Anise could draw her weapon, the soldiers grabbed her by the arms and dragged her before Councilor Indu.

Anise's lungs seized, and she felt unable to breathe. *No— no, this can't be. Not Indu—*

"You—you're the traitor!"

"Of course; who else?" Councilor Indu smirked. "Even you never guessed."

"You were the one who told the Embleck Army I would be scouting in the forest!" Anise struggled against the soldiers holding her. "You wanted me to turn against Liam!"

Councilor Indu backhanded her across the face. "I knew the danger a Starlink could pose to the Embleck Army. Your hatred for each other was necessary." He shook his head in disappointment. "If only the *weapon* was more resistant to your charms."

Anise's pain shifted to fury, burning hot in her chest. "I didn't *charm* him to my side! He fell in love with me himself, and I love him. Your precious Embleck Army can't control him completely!"

"Oh, naïve girl," Councilor Indu chuckled. "We can control him in ways you will never know. He is mine…and so are you."

Fear pulsed through Anise's veins as she activated her mind control—but each of the soldiers' minds slipped from her hold.

"Your powers won't save you here," Councilor Indu said smugly. "Certain materials can be made into talismans…and used to resist the effects of stardust power."

Anise jerked her arm free, elbowing a soldier in the ribs. He dropped her arm, and she punched another soldier in the nose.

"Kill her," Indu snapped.

Anise drew her sword as a soldier lunged for her. She dodged the first strike, but another soldier's sword caught her arm, creating a deep gash in her skin.

"How could you betray us?" Anise snapped as she dodged another swing.

"Easily," Councilor Indu scoffed. "The promise of power is worth betrayal."

Anise slashed an Embleck soldier across the chest, but the movement left her open. Another soldier aimed a strike at her side, his sword slicing deep into her skin.

With a gasp, Anise spun away, struggling to lift her sword. She lunged for the last soldier, but her hit was far off target. The room started to blur, and her side throbbed as she felt blood running down her leg.

Anise twisted away from the last soldier and bolted from the room as more Embleck soldiers entered through the secret door. She tore through the halls, hearing the sound of pursuit.

Ducking around a corner, Anise watched the soldiers run

down the opposite hall. *What am I going to do? Nowhere is safe here—Indu will be searching for me. I have to get out—fast.*

Abruptly, Anise recalled the coordinates Liam had given her. The pain in her side increased, and she staggered to her feet, taking the back way down to the shipyard.

Anise reached her ship and climbed in. She opened her comm and glanced over the numbers, typing them into the ship. It lifted into the air, and Anise set it to autopilot.

The world drifted in and out of focus as Anise slumped in her seat, barely conscious. It seemed only seconds later that the ship was soaring through the atmosphere of Uribeck.

Anise pulled her thoughts together, forcing herself to sit up. Only blinding white snow was visible through the windows, though soon she could vaguely make out a dark building standing out from the snow.

Her ship landed, and Anise struggled to open the top. She swung her legs around, jumping down. Her feet hit the ground, and she stumbled, falling into the snow.

The sudden cold shocked Anise awake for a moment. She dragged herself to her feet and stumbled towards the blurry house shape.

"Anise?" Liam stepped out of the house, approaching her. "Is everything okay? What are you doing here?"

"I...um..." Anise trailed off, swaying in place. The world began to tilt sideways, the frigid cold biting at her skin.

"Anise!" Liam's voice carried a note of urgency, fear tinging the edges.

Anise tried to look at him, but her vision was too blurred to focus on anything. The horizon seemed almost vertical now, and her cuts were starting to sting abnormally. She took a deep breath of icy air, freezing her lungs as forced her brain to work for a moment.

"I need help," Anise mumbled. She tried to take a step forward, but the world started spinning, and everything went black.

CHAPTER 37

Liam raced forward and caught Anise as she slumped forward, limp and unconscious.

"Stars, Anise," Liam whispered, alarm pulsing through him.

Anise's body shivered violently in his arms, and Liam trudged through the thick snow, entering the house and slamming the door behind him.

Once inside, Liam laid Anise on the couch, ignoring the snow spilling across the floor. Her skin was cold to the touch, and the snow dusting her side was…

Red. Liam jerked off Anise's jacket, fear slicing through him when he saw her side, stained with blood. *How did talking to a councilor lead to this?*

Liam snatched a towel off the kitchen counter, pressing it against Anise's side. After a few minutes, the bleeding had slowed but not halted.

Bandages. Liam jumped up and found some bandages and silver to prevent infection. He poured the silver on a cloth and dabbed it over the cut.

The gash stretched from the middle of her ribs almost to her hip bone, but it wasn't as deep as Liam had feared. He carefully wrapped the bandages around her waist until red stopped appearing.

"Anise?" Liam gently shook her shoulder. "Anise?"

Anise showed no response to his efforts, and he noticed her lips had taken on a sickening blue tinge.

At that moment, the roar of a ship landing outside filled the room. Liam shot a glance out of the window—*oh no.*

High Commander Ankor left the ship, briskly walking up to the house. Liam glanced back to Anise—he had to hide her.

Just as Ankor knocked on the door, Liam scoopsed Anise up and shoved her limp form under the couch. He snatched up a blanket and draped it over the side to cover her, threw a pillow over the bloodstain, and raced to open the door.

"Ah, High Commander Ankor!" Liam ushered him inside.

"General Monroy." High Commander Ankor sounded disappointed. "I thought you were dead."

"No, I'm alive as ever," Liam said, resisting the urge to shove Ankor back out the door. "What brings you here?"

"Despite my…fears for your life, King Zamir said you were alive. I was given orders to come and check up on you."

"Well…uh…here I am," Liam said, his eyes locking on the corner of Anise's jacket visible from under the couch. "Anything else?"

"You see…" Ankor's voice seemed to fade away as Liam realized Anise's hum starting to falter. Panic seized his chest, making hard to breathe.

"…and so it will be finished next week." High Commander Ankor finally finished speaking, and Liam realized he hadn't heard a single word he said.

"That sounds fine," Liam insisted, leading Ankor out the door. "Thank you for calling!"

"General Monroy, I haven't finished," High Commander Ankor snapped.

"If you recall, *High Commander,*" Liam retorted. "I now outrank you—and I can inform you when you need to leave. I have very important business to attend to."

High Commander Ankor looked like he wanted to kill Liam for the reminder. "I see. Well then, I suppose I will report back to His Majesty."

"Excellent," Liam said, gripping the door handle. "Good evening."

"Evening," High Commander Ankor spat violently, turned on his heel, and stalked outside.

Liam slammed the door, pulling Anise out from under the couch. More color had faded from her lips, and her hum wavered, softer than it had ever been.

What am I missing? Liam held Anise a little tighter, his eyes locking on a deep gash on her arm.

However, it wasn't the cut that worried him. It was the tiny green droplets *around* the cut.

Oh, please—anything but that.

Liam wiped a drop onto his finger and breathed in the scent of iron and citrus. Fear stabbed at him when he realized what it was: imila, a plant synthesized to create a deadly toxic.

The Embleck Army. Liam clenched his jaw. *Their blades must have been laced with it.*

Liam laid Anise back on the couch, striding to his kitchen and pulling open a cabinet filled with his collection of poisons—

and their antidotes.

Opening the bottle, Liam found a cup and poured the dose into it. He returned to Anise's side, lifting her head and helping her swallow it.

Liam waited with bated breath, his hand gripping Anise's. However, it seemed he was too late. Anise's skin was deathly pale, and her lips had faded, turning completely blue. Her hum faltered once, twice—and stopped, lingering on the edge of the last note.

For the first time in his life, Liam had complete mental silence…and it was agony.

A moment passed before Liam's lungs began to burn, and he realized he wasn't breathing. He pulled Anise's body into his arms, panic rushing through his mind. *No—no, no, no! It—it can't end like this!*

Grief crashed over Liam like a tsunami, dragging him under. He sank to his knees, holding Anise's limp form as the sound of silence rang in his ears.

Tears filled Liam's eyes, spilling down his face. Slowly, he cupped Anise's face in his hand, barely noticing the way he began shaking.

He'd never felt a grief like this before—as though his soul had died, draining all the life from his heart and leaving behind only this suffocating, agonizing *grief.*

A sob escaped as the deep, *excruciating* pain pulsed through Liam's chest, and he buried his face in her hair as another sob broke free.

"I can't—I can't lose you, Anise," Liam choked out. "I'm not—not strong enough to do this without you."

Silent sobs shook Liam's body as he held Anise close, praying for a miracle—*it can't end like this. How am I supposed to live without her?*

Liam lifted his head, tears sliding down his cheeks as he caressed Anise's face, brushing her hair away and cupping the nape of her neck.

"I—I need you, Anise." Liam's voice trembled, barely audible. "Wake up—please." His voice broke. "*Please.*"

Deep grief washed over Liam, his mind overwhelmed by the silence without Anise's hum filling his subconscious. Tears continued to fall, and he didn't bother brushing them away.

Liam tore his gaze from Anise, his eyes locking on his sword lying on the table. *You're the only thing I'm living for— how can I survive without you, Anise?*

Glancing back at his sword, Liam held Anise closer, warring with himself—

A flicker of silver light caught Liam's attention, and he turned back to Anise, his eyes widening.

A soft silver glow formed beneath his hand, lighting the outline of Anise's cut before vanishing just as quickly as it appeared.

Liam glanced at her face, not daring to hope as he felt a faint flicker in the back of his mind…then a falter. Liam held his breath…

Anise's hum resumed, the sound soft and unsteady…but present. Liam's breath caught, tears flowing again, but now for a different reason.

With a groan, Anise shifted in Liam's arms. A moment later, she opened her clear teal eyes, looking up at him.

"Roy?" she whispered. "No…Liam?"

"Anise!" Liam's voice broke into a sob as he hugged her tightly. "You're alive!"

Anise wrapped her arms around his neck, her head resting against his shoulder. "Liam? You're here?"

"I'm here." The joy filling Liam's heart choked his voice. "I'm here, Anise. You're safe now, I promise."

Anise lifted her head, meeting his eyes. "The last thing I remember is falling in the snow. What happened?"

"I—I was about to ask you," Liam managed, dragging his sleeve over his eyes. "How did this happen? I thought you were talking to the council!"

Anise's face fell. "I…I did…and he attacked me when I told him."

"Who?" Liam fought to get his overwhelming emotions under control.

"Councilor Indu," Anise whispered. "He's the traitor…and he's allied with the Embleck Army."

"Anise..." Liam rubbed his hand over her back. "I'm sorry."

"It…it'll be okay," Anise mumbled. "I just…never imagined he would…"

"Indu…" Liam furrowed his brow. "I…remember that name. He's…I think he's Zamir's…son? Nephew? I'm not sure."

Anise dropped her eyes. "If he's related to Zamir…he's probably been betraying us for years. That's why the Qor has been unable to end this war."

"And he attacked you when you told him about me?" Liam asked, guilt washing over him.

Anise nodded. "There were Embleck soldiers…I got injured…but everything seemed…wrong. My vision got blurry, and I blacked out. What happened while I was out?"

"I…I bandaged you up," Liam said, abruptly choking back another wave of tears. "But the blades must have been laced with imila poison…I…didn't think you were going to make it."

"Oh…Liam…" Anise reached up, brushing away the tears glistening on his lashes. "I'm sorry. I didn't mean to scare you."

"Don't apologize," Liam managed, his voice hoarse. "I'm just…relieved you're alright."

Anise coughed, pressing a hand to her side. "And…how am I…alright?"

"I don't know," Liam confessed. "I thought…I thought I'd lost you. But there was a…silver glow, and you woke up."

"You healed me?" Anise said, her eyes shimmering. "Liam, I—that was so dangerous for you!"

Liam realized the truth in her words. "I…I didn't even think about that."

Anise hugged him tightly, resting her head against his heart. "Thank you."

"Anything for you, love," Liam whispered, lightly kissing her head. *Everything is okay. She's here now.*

As the emotions slowly wore off, Liam could feel a sense of exhaustion settling over him, but he didn't care. As long as Anise was alive, nothing else mattered.

Anise coughed again. "Can I have some water, please?"

"Of course." Liam stood and set her on the couch, pausing momentarily when a wave of dizziness swept over him. He held onto the edge of the counter as he walked into the kitchen.

As Liam was filling a glass with water, Anise's shriek echoed through the room. He nearly dropped the glass, quickly setting it on the counter before racing to Anise's side.

"What is it?"

Anise turned her hands around. "Look what you did!"

Liam stared at her hands in dread, wondering what he had done wrong...but they seemed normal. "What did I do?"

"You healed them!" Anise stared at her hands in awe.

Liam did a double-take when he realized what she meant. All the metal rings had disappeared from her left hand, and only one was left on her right middle finger. The severe scarring had faded, and some of the smaller scars had vanished completely.

"I...I did that?" Liam asked, stunned.

"Yes!" Anise glanced up at him. "I couldn't ever do that!"

"I don't really know how I did that," Liam admitted.

"I don't care how," Anise said. "Thank you."

"Well, you're welcome," Liam said, returning to the kitchen. "Here's your water."

Anise took a sip and nearly choked. "It's freezing!"

Liam shrugged. "Everything's cold here."

"I can tell." Anise brushed a clump of snow off her pants. "And why am I so dusty?"

Liam coughed. "I'll explain later. You can take a shower if you like."

"Will it be this cold?" Anise held up the offending glass.

"No, it'll be hot."

"Then, yes, please."

"I'll get you some new clothes," Liam added.

"Thanks." Anise tried to stand but wavered on her feet. Liam quickly supported her, and she smiled at him gratefully. "I guess I'm not ready for walking yet."

"No problem." Liam carefully guided her to his room,

helping her sit on the side of the bed. "I'll find you something to wear and make some dinner."

"Thank you," Anise said softly. "Really. This means so much to me."

"I'm always happy to help you." Liam smiled. "And if you toss your clothes out, I can get them washed."

"Okay, thanks." Anise returned his smile as she slipped into the bathroom. She cracked open the door a moment later and tossed out her leggings and ripped shirt.

Liam threw her pants in the quick wash but decided the shirt was a lost cause. He dug through his closet, pulling out a shirt for her to wear.

Returning to the kitchen, Liam turned on the soup he'd found in the freezer. Once Anise's clothes were done, he laid them out on the bed.

The soup was just starting to bubble when Anise emerged from the bedroom, wearing Liam's shirt with her damp hair falling in waves.

"I'm sorry I didn't have anything that fit better," Liam apologized.

"Actually, I like it." Anise smiled a little shyly.

Liam glanced over at her, abruptly struck by how

adorable she looked in his oversized shirt. "I think it's cute. You make it look much better than I do."

"See, I told you that you were charming." Anise wrinkled her nose at him as she sat down.

Liam set down a bowl of soup in front of her, and silence fell over the house as they ate. It felt like such a beautifully simple domestic scene that Liam had to remind himself they were both on the run, hiding from Zamir and Indu.

"Do you mind if I get some sleep?" Anise asked once she'd finished, pulling Liam from his thoughts.

"Of course not." Liam helped her up from the table. "You can sleep in my room."

"Oh, I don't want to push you out," Anise started, but Liam held up his hand.

"It's no trouble. I'll sleep on the couch."

"Are you sure?" Anise paused at the bedroom door.

"Positive."

Anise leaned over and kissed his cheek. "Good night."

"Good night." Liam returned to the kitchen and washed the dishes before settling onto the couch with a book.

Liam was halfway through his book (which was from the

Embleck Army library and dreadfully boring) when a faint shout echoed from the bedroom.

Shooting to his feet, Liam raced down the hall. He threw open the door and found Anise sitting straight up in bed with the covers clutched to her chest.

"What's wrong?" Liam asked, scanning the room.

"I had a nightmare," Anise said in a small voice. "About Indu. I'm sorry to bother you."

"You didn't bother me." Liam hesitated in the doorway.

"Can you come here?" Anise whispered.

Uncertainly, Liam approached, taking a seat on the edge of the bed. Anise pushed back the cover, crawling into his arms.

Liam barely breathed as she nestled against him, tucking her head against his neck.

"What did you need?" Liam whispered, but Anise ignored him.

Hesitantly, Liam moved over, resting against the headboard. Anise felt around the bed until she found the covers, pulling them up.

Warmth settled over Liam as Anise relaxed against him, her breathing settling into sleep. A feeling of peace and contentment washed over Liam, and he closed his eyes, allowing sleep to pull him under.

CHAPTER 38

Anise awoke the next morning, disoriented. She shifted, rubbing a hand over her eyes as she tried to remember where she was.

The events of the previous day hit her, and she sat up, glancing around. Liam was gone, leaving her alone in his room. Anise pushed off the covers slightly, instantly shocked by the cold air.

The bedroom door opened, and Liam leaned in. "Oh, good morning. I was just going to grab you some extra clothes in case you were cold."

"Thanks." Anise sneaked back under the covers as Liam rifled through the closet.

"This should work." Liam held up a dark gray jacket.

"Thanks." Anise accepted the jacket and shrugged it on. "Oh, that's much better."

"Are you hungry?" Liam asked, and Anise nodded.

"I don't have a lot here, but there's toast," Liam offered, helping her to a seat.

"That works for me."

They both sat at the table and ate in silence before Anise spoke. "What are we going to do now? We can't just stay here forever."

"I know." Liam sighed heavily. "I just don't know what to do."

"I don't either."

Anise's wrist comm began beeping, and she glanced down. "That isn't my normal ringtone. One moment."

"*Mayday, mayday!*" A voice erupted from the comm. "*We— Tironlay. Embleck soldiers—attacking us—requesting backup!*"

Anise paled, scanning the coordinates listed with the message. "That's Caiden. I—I have to go!"

"We can take my ship." Liam leaped up, quickly sheathing his sword.

Anise stood at the door, shifting impatiently as Liam took his cloak off the hook and fastened it around her neck. "Here, it's freezing out there."

"Thanks." Anise hid under the cloak as Liam opened the door.

A gust of freezing air swept in, and Anise wrapped her arms around herself with a shiver.

"It's so cold." Anise's breath was visible as she asked, "How do you live here? And how do you walk in all this snow?"

"I have practice," Liam said, not even remotely shivering. "Want some help?"

"Yes."

Liam carefully scooped her up and carried her to the ship. "My ship is a one-seater. You sit here, on the edge, and I'll get in first."

Anise perched on the rim as Liam climbed in from the other side. Once he was in, she dropped down into his lap and slammed the top shut.

"Does the ship have heating?" Anise peered at the various buttons on the dash.

"The blue knob," Liam said as he lifted the ship up. "And please push the white button for lightspeed."

Quickly, Anise pushed the white button, and the ship shot forward. Liam carefully navigated around asteroids and stars as they soared through space.

Anise chewed her lip, sick with worry about Caiden. *I just hope we're not too late.*

Soon, the gray surface of Tironlay zipped by beneath the ship. "We're clearing the atmosphere." Liam's voice snapped her back to the present. "The coordinates they sent are close to here."

Anise scanned the ground for several minutes before her eyes locked on a flash of color. "Look, there! I see them!"

"Landing." Liam set the ship down. "Let's go!"

Anise and Liam practically leaped from the ship, racing toward the skirmish. Anise's legs pounded against the ground, her breath coming short.

"Cay!" Anise shouted.

Caiden turned around and saw her. "Anise?"

Anise skidded up to them, standing before Caiden. Liam stepped in front of Brendon, shielding Anise.

"Anise, what are you doing?" Caiden snapped.

"Sir, what's going on?" Brendon addressed Liam.

"This is the day, Brendon." Liam placed his hand on

Brendon's shoulder "I'm deserting—and you're coming with me."

Brendon threw his arms around Liam, nearly knocking him over with the force of his hug. Liam returned the embrace, his expression full of warmth.

Anise turned to her brother, speaking in a hushed tone. "Caiden, we can't go back to the Qor."

"What?" Caiden looked incredulous.

"What are you talking about?" Keisha asked, stunned.

"Councilor Indu has been lying to us," Anise told them. "He's been serving the Embleck Army...and we think he's related to King Zamir."

Caiden's face fell. "No..."

Anise nodded silently, fighting back a flash of pain.

"What are we going to do?" Tyler spoke up.

"And what are we going to do?" Brendon added as he pulled away from Liam.

"You should come with me," Liam said. "You and your cadets...uh..."

"This is Deven, and that's Andrew," Brendon supplied helpfully.

"Yes, thank you. Deven, Andrew, and you should come with me."

"It would be our honor, Sir." Brendon bowed deeply, and Deven and Andrew copied.

"How did you even get here?" Caiden asked abruptly. "I thought no one heard my message."

"Councilor Indu probably had something to do with that," Anise said. "But I got it, so Liam and I came." She gestured at the ship.

"Wait." Caiden arched an eyebrow. "Is that the ship you took?"

"Yes," Anise said hesitantly.

"Isn't it a one-seater?"

"Yes?"

Caiden narrowed his eyes. "How did you both fi—"

"Well, now that everyone's safe, we better be going," Anise interrupted loudly.

"Where are you going again?" Caiden was temporarily distracted.

"We're going to go stop King Zamir and Councilor Indu," Anise declared impulsively. "Liam and I, that is."

"No, we're coming with you," Caiden said. Keisha and Tyler nodded.

"Us too!" Brendon added.

"You all should stay here where it's safe," Anise argued.

"We're coming, Anise," Caiden insisted.

Anise shook her head. "No, you're not."

"What are you—" Caiden started as Anise closed her eyes. "Anise, no—"

Anise reached out and locked onto each of their minds. "You will stay here until it is safe," she ordered and released her hold. Everyone remained frozen, staring at nothing.

"Come on, Liam." Anise forced herself to turn away. It was disconcerting to see everyone else so still, but it was for their own safety.

"I'm coming." Liam took one last look at their frozen friends before following her.

CHAPTER 39

Anise and Liam returned to the ship together in silence. They took their seats, and Liam lifted the ship into the sky. Anise sighed heavily and leaned her head back against Liam's chest.

"I know I did that for their protection, but it still feels wrong."

"I understand," Liam said softly as the ship soared out of Tironlay's atmosphere. "It always feels odd to read someone's mind. You know, to hear their private thoughts in your head...it's disconcerting."

The ship soared through space for a few minutes before Anise spoke again. "I told everyone that we were going to stop King Zamir, but how? Where are we even going?"

Liam's grip tightened on the steering. "We're going to Nockalore. That's where the Shadow Palace is—and that's where King Zamir will be."

"Are we crazy for trying to do this alone?"

Liam shrugged. "Maybe, but we have to. I won't be able to get the Embleck soldiers on my side, and you can't go back to the Qor now. Councilor Indu will be waiting for you, and—"

At that moment, Liam's comm buzzed.

"I'll get in for you," Anise said, taking it from the bag by their feet. She offered him the comm, and he activated it.

A harsh, garbled voice came through the comm, and Anise jumped. The language was like no other she had ever heard, and she couldn't make sense of any of it.

Liam, however, seemed to get the message. His lips thinned as he listened, his face paling.

"What is it?"

"King Zamir gave the order for final preparations…for the full destruction of the Qor. He will give the command to attack when each of the battalions confirms they're in position."

"Plan to destroy the Qor?!" Anise choked. "What plan to destroy the Qor?"

"I'm not sure." Liam seemed helpless. "They've been talking about something in all those strategizing meetings, but they never told me this much. They have soldiers waiting to attack the Qor bases around the galaxy."

499

Anise swallowed hard, fear swirling in her stomach. "The Qor is strong. We can fight back."

Worry shone in Liam's eyes. "Not if Councilor Indu has anything to say about it."

Anise's heart plummeted. Liam was right. The Qor might be able to win this battle—but only if their leaders wanted them to…

Councilor Indu would do everything in his power to prevent that.

"That's why the comms aren't working," Anise mumbled. "Councilor Indu shut them down. He's going to destroy the Qor."

"Not if we stop him first." Liam tightened his grip on the steering. "We have to. It's the only option."

Anise nodded, taking a deep breath. "You're right. We *can* do this. How long until the attack begins?"

Liam swallowed hard. "An hour minimum. It will take that long to get all battleships in position."

Anise chewed her lip. "We can do this," she whispered, staring out at the blurred stars. "We have to."

Silence fell as the ship soared towards Nockalore. They dipped through the atmosphere, soon flying above dark green trees. Anise scanned the forest, catching sight of the black towers of a palace rising above the trees.

"That's the Embleck Palace," Liam said quietly. "King Zamir will be in the throne room. But I don't know where the councilor would be—if he's even here."

Anise rolled her neck. "If he's here…I'll find him."

Liam glided the ship down, landing just outside the clearing. "We need to see if we can sneak in from here."

Anise carefully climbed down and crept towards the clearing with Liam right behind her. Liam peered through the brush and frowned.

"There's something wrong here." Liam walked out into the open. "This courtyard should have lots of guards and ships. I…I think they're expecting us."

Anise followed Liam up to the double doors, unease settling over her. Darkness seemed to hover around the palace, leaving a cold feeling in her chest.

Liam paused a the doors, turning to her. "I…I want to say, in case anything goes wrong…well, I want you to know that I love you. Everything will be okay in the end—I promise."

Nerves twisted Anise's heart, but she nodded. "I love you too."

Liam took hold of the black obsidian door handles and pulled. The doors glided open silently, and Anise stepped inside. The large, dark room was empty, without a single person visible.

Liam entered, approaching a second set of doors. "This is the entrance to the throne room. Are you ready?"

Anise nodded. *Here we go.*

Fearlessly, Anise threw open the doors to the throne room. King Zamir stood at a large table displaying a holo-map. He turned to them, his mask covering most of his face.

"Well, if it isn't my former apprentice. Coming to challenge me, are you?"

"We have come to end your reign," Liam stepped forward, Anise right behind him.

"Well, that's amusing," High Commander Ankor stepped into the throne room behind them. "Thinking you can defeat His Majesty, Monroy?"

Liam whipped around to face Ankor, pulling out his ray gun. "I think it's possible."

Ankor made a wide berth from them as he walked up to the throne. "Let me guess. You want to destroy us and take over the Embleck Army—and therefore, the galaxy."

"Actually, I'd rather take you both out and watch the Embleck Army burn." Liam kept his ray gun trained on Ankor.

King Zamir raised his staff and shot a bolt of black shadows at the ray gun in Liam's hand. Anise jerked Liam out of the way, and the ray gun clattered to the floor. The shadows wrapped around it and dragged it to King Zamir. He picked it up, setting the weapon on the table.

King Zamir turned to face them. "I would have thought that you would know better than to challenge me again, Monroy. After all, you didn't have advantageous results last time."

Anise glanced at Liam in confusion, seeing him flinch. "I told you last time. I have a reason to be strong now."

King Zamir chuckled. "What, you feel strong with your little link beside you?"

Anise asked the question before she could catch herself. "You know what a Starlink is?"

"Of course I do." King Zamir smirked. "I am a Starlink."

"A Starlink can only happen every three thousand years," Anise protested.

"Natural ones, perhaps," King Zamir said. "I was an exception. The two stars touched ever so slightly on the day I was born. I was gifted with a weaker version of star powers, but I had no link...until I discovered this crystal."

"After I discovered the truth, I started looking for ways to enhance my powers. Then, I found you two."

"What do we have to do with any of this?" Liam retorted.

King Zamir shook his head. "Oh, naïve weapon. You two have everything to do with this. After years and years of research, I found that the only way for me to increase my powers…is to take someone else's."

"Here's what is going to happen," Zamir said as he stood. "I will drain one of *you* and take your power for my own. You won't survive, but that only leaves me with fewer enemies."

"We'll never allow that to happen," Anise snapped.

"How adorable," King Zamir sneered. "You think you have a say in this matter. I will have your powers…and they will be his."

"Not. Liam."

"It will be him, though." King Zamir examined the crystal of his staff "Because he will volunteer instead of letting you get hurt."

Liam tensed and placed his hand on Anise's shoulder protectively before addressing King Zamir. "You should know— after all, I've been your cadet since I was a teenager. And to think I believed you wanted to help me—all that matters to you is power."

"Obviously—and don't try to put up a force field, Desson," he added as Anise raised her hands. "My crystal can unravel that faster than you can create them."

"Wait..." Anise stepped back. "How do you know I can make force fields?"

"Because I *know* you."

"That's impossible." Anise hissed. "I couldn't know you."

"Oh...but it is possible." A man in a black cloak stepped out from a door beside the throne. "He told me himself."

"Who are you?" Liam asked, inching in front of Anise.

"I'm the son of King Zamir," the man said. "Prince Ruven Indu."

"I think I would know you as Councilor Indu, wouldn't I?" Anise said harshly, stepping away from Liam.

"Oh, I don't think you would." Ruven pulled down his hood, and Anise stared in confusion.

Ruven Indu...*wasn't* Councilor Indu. He seemed about thirty, with black hair and gray eyes. There was certainly a resemblance...but Ruven wasn't the councilor.

"I think you would know someone else as Councilor

Indu," King Zamir said as he removed his mask. "Perhaps even...me."

Anise inhaled sharply, her stomach clenching as she stared into a familiar pair of gray eyes.

"Councilor Indu?"

King Zamir—Indu—smirked. "Now that you know, you might as well address me by my proper title."

"How..." Anise's mind reeled, and she stumbled back against Liam. "No...no, it can't be."

"Oh, it is." King Zamir smiled at her—the same way Councilor Indu had been smiling at her for years. "It wasn't easy, keeping a double identity—but it was worth it. I could keep up with both halves of your link and develop a relationship with both of you that worked to my advantage."

"You saved me from the Embleck soldiers on Ceran—but you were Embleck even then, weren't you?" A deep ache of betrayal settled into Anise's heart, fostering the slow burn of resentment.

"It was all an act to trick me. You said you thought of me as a daughter—and the sad thing is, I believed you. I thought I could trust you—but all you ever did was lie to me."

"Of course," King Zamir said with a shrug. "You were

simply a tool, the same as Monroy here. You'd be surprised what people tell you when they trust you."

Anise met his eyes with every ounce of the fury and pain in her heart. "I guess so."

King Zamir gave her that same smile again. "Originally, I planned to allow you to battle and simply drain the power of whoever won. But you—" King Zamir shot a glare at Liam. "You were too weak and started falling for her. And Desson here found herself unable to resist the opportunity to have someone heal her loneliness—and then fell too."

King Zamir shook his head. "Now you've simply made things more difficult. Not that it really matters. You see, I have gathered my army of loyal soldiers in this palace, and I have a comm right here."

"When I give the word, those soldiers will leave and attack the Qor bases—which are conveniently unguarded, thanks to Councilor Indu. Once the Qor is weakened, we shall destroy the capitals of each planet. I shall drain you two of your powers, you will die—and I will rule over the galaxy, unopposed."

"No," Anise whispered in horror. *I can't let this happen— we have to stop him.*

Anise, what's our move?

Anise's eyes darted around the grand hall, finally resting

507

on the huge obsidian pillars placed around the room. The pillars were starting to crumble around the tops, and Anise began to get an idea.

Can you distract him?

I'd be happy to. Liam slipped her ray gun off her belt before jerking it up and shooting at King Zamir.

Zamir casually blocked each shot with his shadows, sending them to envelope and dissolve each ray. Anise activated her powers, sending a force field into each of the cracks of the stone.

King Zamir pointed his staff at Liam and shot a blast of black shadows at him, knocking the ray gun from his hand before aiming at Liam.

Liam created a portal and leaped away, appearing on the other side of the room. Zamir somehow anticipated this and shot a blast that hit the blade of Liam's sword. The sword glowed black for a second, then became dull.

"That will remove your teleportation for a while," King Zamir said triumphantly.

Uh, Anise, I'm kind of in trouble here. Liam dodged the next blast with only an inch to spare.

I've got it. Anise sent her force field into the last cracked pillar as King Zamir turned to her.

"What are you doing, Desson?" King Zamir pointed his staff at her.

Anise closed her eyes, praying her plan would work—

—and expanded all her force fields.

Light exploded from each of the cracks in the pillars as they crumbled into piles of stone. As they fell, the ceiling began to crumble, crashes filling the room. King Zamir raised his staff, shooting a shadow directly at Anise.

Anise tried to dodge, but she could barely move after using that much power. The blast struck her shoulder, and she collapsed to the ground.

CHAPTER 40

"ANISE!" Liam ran to her side, taking her limp form into his arms.

Anise stirred slightly, opening her eyes. "We…we have to get out."

"Neither one of you is going anywhere." King Zamir snapped and pointed his staff at them.

Dragging Anise to her feet, Liam jerked them back as a huge section of the ceiling fell, blocking them from King Zamir. Another piece of the ceiling collapsed, and Liam jerked them both away.

Liam pulled Anise down the hall as the palace collapsed around them. He threw them through the doorway and into the foyer as the walls collapsed, trapping them in the crumbling room.

Panic pulsed through Liam's veins. Anise was too drained to create another shield, and the roof was coming down in a matter of seconds. Dust choked the air, and the sound of crashes echoed through Liam's ears.

It was at that moment that Liam realized this scene—he'd seen the future in his crystal…and now he understood what he had to do.

Stealing a moment to hug Anise, Liam wrapped his arms around her, shielding her head as he slammed his shoulder against the crumbling wall.

A large piece of the ceiling fell, and Liam realized he only had a few more seconds. Pain shot through his shoulder, and he knew it was broken.

Finally, the wall broke apart, creating an opening—and Liam pushed Anise through the gap, falling to his knees as the entire palace collapsed.

As the palace crumbled, Liam locked eyes with Anise. A sense of calm filled him, and he took comfort in the fact that the last thing he would see would be her.

"*LIAM!*" Anise screamed, throwing out her hand to create a shield for him. It disappeared into the debris as a stone struck her head, and everything turned black.

Anise groaned as she opened her eyes. Black spots danced across her vision as her head pounded, and she felt a stream of blood trickling down her forehead.

Reaching up with a shaking hand, Anise touched her wound and drew stardust energy into herself, healing the injury. When she took away her hand, the pain had ceased.

Anise carefully sat up, and her headache returned, though duller than before. Her mind felt fuzzy, rendering her unable to even think for a moment.

Liam.

Anise gasped and scrambled to her feet, pausing when a wave of dizziness hit her. The world faded out of focus and inhaled a series of slow, deep breaths.

Stumbling to the remains of the palace, Anise activated her power, levitating the stones away. *Please—please let him be okay.*

Hope rushed over Anise as she caught sight of the glow of her force field. Pulling another surge of power, she lifted away the last stones—and her heart plummeted.

A slab of the ceiling had cracked her shield; crushing Liam's ribs and scattering shattered pieces of light around his body.

Fear pierced Anise's chest as her legs nearly gave out. She staggered to his side, levitating the last piece away. Rich, dark red stained the rubble around Liam, his white shirt completely soaked through.

The last of her shield faded away as Anise lowered herself to her knees, a numb sense of horror settling over her.

Anise wrapped her arms around Liam, instantly feeling warm blood seeping through her shirt. She dragged his limp form away from the castle and rubble.

Stumbling to a halt, Anise lowered Liam's body to the ground, sinking down beside him. She braced her hand on the dirt, struggling to keep upright.

The ground under Liam slowly became stained red, but Anise couldn't move—couldn't think—couldn't *feel*—

Anise reached out with a shaking hand, brushing Liam's hair from his face, her eyes roaming over the gash across his cheek and the dull blue of his lips.

The first sob caught Anise off guard, her throat burning as a tear slipped down her cheek.

No—please, no—it can't end like this—it just can't.

Another sob broke free as the grief finally hit, overwhelming Anise. She'd never felt such a chilling, merciless *pain* before—it engulfed her soul; filling her lungs until she couldn't breathe.

Anise pulled Liam's body into her arms, holding him close. A tear dripped onto his cheek, and she brushed it away, shuddering as she felt the unnatural cold of his skin.

"*I—I'm so sorry,*" Anise whispered, her voice rough with tears. "*Liam—*"

Grief swept over Anise like waves, and she finally broke down, sobbing. Her lungs ached, her eyes burning with tears.

A faint glow broke through the storm, and Anise lifted her head as tears slid down her cheeks. The crystal from the Star Caverns had fallen from her pocket, glowing white.

Slowly, Anise reached for the crystal and picked it up. Instantly, white washed over her vision, and the scene shifted.

Anise stood in the courtyard of the palace on Lidica. It no longer showed the signs of the centuries, and the garden bed overflowed with flowers in every color.

Anise's attention caught on a sob, and she turned to the sound. A young woman held the unconscious body of a man, and Anise recognized her features as—

"*Tarak*," Asteria whispered, her voice choked with tears. "No, please, no!"

Anise shakily stood, glancing at the dagger on the ground beside Asteria.

Asteria released another sob, resting her forehead against Tarak's. Her hand gripped his shirt, stained red with blood.

Anise watched, a numb sensation settling over her. Asteria raised her head, eyes shining with unshed tears as she laid her hand over Tarak's wound.

A silver glow formed beneath Asteria's hand, lighting the garden around them. Asteria's energy visibly drained as color slowly came back to Tarak's face. He opened his eyes, looking up at her.

"Ria?"

"Tarak!" Asteria cried, throwing herself into his arms.

The world shifted again, and Anise found herself on the ground, surrounded by rubble and clutching the crystal.

I have to heal Liam. Anise vaguely recalled her promise to him before dismissing it. The idea of living without Liam—it

515

wrenched something in her heart. If she didn't at least *try,* she wouldn't be able to live with herself.

For a single moment, doubt pricked at Anise. *What if I'm not strong enough? What if I lose my power completely?*

Anise took one look at Liam's face, solidifying her resolve—she would heal him…no matter what it took.

Gently, Anise cupped Liam's face in her hand. "You promised me that everything would be alright in the end. *I'm holding you to that promise.*"

Taking a deep breath, Anise hovered her hand over Liam and summoned her powers. They rushed through her veins, and her whole hand tingled as stardust flooded her fingers. A bright silver glow formed beneath her hand, illuminating the entire clearing with silver light.

Stardust shone around Anise as she pulled more power from her core, a burning sensation beginning in her lungs. Something tugged at her subconscious, warning that this was too much power—

Anise ignored it, drawing more energy and pouring it into Liam. The glow grew brighter, silver shimmering through the air around them.

Dredging up the last of her strength, Anise released a wave of power, washing it over Liam.

516

As the final bit of her power faded away, Anise's vision blurred, and for a moment, her consciousness slipped away.

Anise pulled herself together as the world slowly came back into focus. Soul-deep exhaustion settled over her, a hollow void opening in her chest.

Please. Anise flexed her aching fingers and tried to create a force field.

Nothing.

Anise inhaled a trembling breath. She'd lost her powers—completely. The loss swelled in the empty cavity in her chest, but she fought back the pain. *It'll be worth it…if Liam's alive.*

Taking another shaky breath, Anise hesitantly touched Liam's ribs, feeling no sign of his injury.

Hope filled Anise's chest and she took Liam's face in her hands, searching a sign of life. His skin remained ghostly pale, and the seconds ticked by without him drawing a breath.

"*Oh.*" Anise's hope drained away, grief filling her. She'd lost her powers…and Liam.

"No…Liam, *please*…" Anise rested her forehead against his. "You promised me that you'd be with me till the galaxy's end." Her tears overflowed, spilling down her cheeks. "You *promised* me."

"Anise?"

Anise's head snapped up, and she instinctively scanned the surrounding area—only to realize she *recognized* that voice. Barely daring to hope, she glanced down at Liam.

Liam's beautiful emerald eyes gazed up at her, shining with awe and love as he smiled at her—his perfect, wonderful smile that made her heart leap with joy.

"Liam!" Anise shrieked, throwing herself into his arms and kissing him soundly. Liam wrapped his arms around her, holding her close.

"You're—you're here! You're alive!" Anise exclaimed as tears of joy dripped down her cheeks.

Liam reached up, brushing away her tears with his fingertips. "I'm here, love. I promise."

Anise buried her face in his neck, unable to stop shaking. Liam used his free arm to help himself sit up, holding her in his lap as he gently rubbed her back.

"It's okay, angel." Liam rested his head atop hers. "I won't leave you…I promise."

"You scared me," Anise managed. "I—I thought I was going to lose you."

"You didn't lose me," Liam whispered. "I'm right here, okay?"

Anise nodded, pulling back to meet his eyes as relief flowed through her. Any doubt she felt washed away—her powers were an insignificant price to pay, and she'd do it again in a heartbeat.

Liam tucked her hair behind her ear, a questioning expression on his face. "Wait...how am I here? The shield—I thought it broke."

"It did," Anise said, her voice thick with emotion as she wiped her eyes with her bloodstained sleeve. Liam's eyes went wide as he noticed the blood.

"I...stars. How did I...wait." Liam glanced at her, pressing a hand to his ribs as fear flashed over his face. "Anise— Anise, you didn't."

"I broke my promise."

A variety of emotions played over Liam's face. "Oh, Anise. Your powers..."

Anise smiled tearily as she placed her hand over his. "You're worth them."

Liam expression showed a mixture of shock and dismay. "I—I can't believe—Anise, I'm so sorry."

"Don't apologize. I'd rather live the rest of my life without power if it means I have you."

Liam gently cupped her face in his hand, tears shining in his eyes before he pulled her into a tight embrace. "Thank you—thank you so much."

Anise returned the hug, savoring the feeling of him. *Liam's alive. He's alive—and I love him.*

"I should be thanking you," Anise whispered against his neck. "You saved my life."

"Anything for you, angel," Liam replied as he pulled back, lightly kissing her lips. "I just wish there was a way...maybe..."

"Maybe what?"

"You gave me your powers—what if I gave you mine?"

"Liam, no," Anise protested. "I couldn't do that to you."

"Part of my power, then," Liam appealed. "After what you did—please, just let me do this for you."

"Is that even possible?" Anise asked, relenting slightly.

"Let me try," Liam implored her. "Please, Anise."

Anise hesitated. "If you're sure..."

Liam took her hands with a nod, closing his eyes in concentration. A rush of warmth filled Anise, and she watched as the same silver glow formed, sending a silver shimmer over her skin.

The void vanished, and Anise inhaled deeply, feeling like new life had been breathed into her. Liam released her hands, hope and exhaustion combine in his expression.

"Did it work?"

Anise lifted her hand, summoned her power—and a glowing shield appeared around them.

"It worked!" Liam hugged her tightly.

Joy bubbled in Anise's chest, filling the void as she held Liam close—just as a large ship landed on the edge of the clearing.

Before the engines were even off, the door flung open. Caiden jumped down from the ship, scanning the clearing. The second he caught sight of them, he began to run, calling Anise's name.

"Are you okay?" Anise checked.

"I'm fine," Liam assured her.

Anise jumped to her feet and ran to Caiden, colliding with him in a tight embrace.

"Are you alright—are you okay?" Caiden held her at arm's length, checking her for damages.

"I'm fine," Anise said, hugging him again.

"What happened?" Caiden asked. "It felt like I fell asleep, and when I woke up, you were gone!"

"I…may have used mind control so you wouldn't follow us?"

"Wait—seriously? Anise!"

"How did you get here?" Anise asked, changing the subject.

"Once your *mind control* turned off, we followed your ship," Caiden answered, crossing his arms.

"How did you know where I was?"

"I…may have had Jack access the tracking on your comm," Caiden admitted.

"Oh, Caiden," Anise sighed despite her smile.

"Hush," Caiden replied, though he was smiling as well.

"Anise!" Keisha ran over to Anise and enveloped her in a hug. "I'm so glad you're okay!"

"You too." Anise hugged her back. "And I'm sorry about the mind control."

"It's okay—as long as you don't do it again," Keisha said, narrowing her eyes.

"I won't," Anise promised with a laugh.

"What happened while we were out?" Tyler asked as he approached them.

Anise inhaled deeply. "Zamir is dead."

Caiden stared at her blankly. "Are—are you serious?"

Anise nodded, a grin breaking out on her face. "He's gone—it's over."

Caiden enveloped Anise in a bone-crushing hug. "You did it, Anise! I'm so proud of you."

Keisha and Tyler joined the embrace, and Anise felt tears pricking her eyes, this time from happiness. When they finally broke apart, Keisha dabbed at her eyes, while Tyler glanced around them.

"Where's Liam?"

"Oh—Liam!" Anise turned back, watching as Liam hesitantly stood. "He was injured, but I think he's stable for now."

"Tyler, help him up," Caiden instructed, and Tyler nodded.

The roar of another ship landing filled the clearing, and Anise glanced up at it, her eyes locking on the Embleck Army crest on the side.

Everyone tensed for a moment—until the doors flew open, and Brendon jumped down from the ramp.

"Brendon!" Liam called, breaking away from Tyler.

"General!" Brendon flew to Liam, nearly knocking him over with the force of his hug. "Thank the stars that you're alright!"

"We're free, Brendon," Liam said, his voice slightly shaky.

"I knew you'd figure it out, General."

"Actually…it's just Liam now."

Brendon grinned. "I'm glad to hear it."

Tyler shot a nervous glance at the Embleck soldiers as they helped Liam over to the rest of the group. As soon as they were in hearing range, Caiden spoke.

"Both of you are going straight to medical for a check. No negotiations."

"Fine," Anise agreed. "I definitely want Liam to get checked."

Caiden's eyes locked on Liam's bloodstained shirt, and he raised an eyebrow. "What happened to him?"

Liam shrugged. "Nothing much; the castle just fell on me."

Brendon did a double-take at Liam while Deven and Andrew stared. Caiden, Tyler, and Keisha whipped their heads around to see the pile of rubble that once was the Embleck castle.

"So—wait." Keisha gestured at the castle's remains, her brow furrowed. "You're telling us that all of *that* fell on him— and he's *alive?*"

"That's correct," Liam agreed.

"We'll explain it to you on the way back," Anise reassured them, taking Liam's arm as they boarded the ship.

CHAPTER 41

Their ship landed at the Qor base, and Anise held tight to Liam as they disembarked.

"Commander Desson!" Jack ran up to their ship, skidding to a stop and saluting Anise. "It is a relief to see you, ma'am."

"It's a relief to be back," Anise said with a half-smile. "Jack, will you request the presence of the Qor Council for me?"

"Yes, ma'am," Jack said, bowing before he turned and ran back the way he'd come.

A crowd began forming around them, hushed whispers rustling through the air. Anise took hold of Liam's wrist, pulling him along with her and keeping her eyes focused forward.

Abruptly, a Qor officer stepped in front of Anise, pointing a ray gun over her shoulder. "Commander, I order you to step away."

"What is the meaning of this?" Anise snapped. "How dare you—"

Liam's wrist was ripped from Anise's hand, and she spun around to see two Qor officers—one holding Liam's arm and the other pointing a ray gun at him.

"Lower your weapons immediately," Anise ordered the soldiers, drawing her own weapon, though she didn't raise it. "He poses no threat to you."

The first Qor officer jerked his head toward Brendon, Devan, and Andrew. "Cuff them."

Anise lifted her ray gun. "I order you to halt!"

"What is the meaning of this?"

Everyone turned as High Councilor Mills stepped outside, followed by Councilor Kyles.

"Who do we have here?" Councilor Kyles asked, glancing over the newcomers.

Before Anise could speak, Liam wrenched his arm free and addressed the Councilors. "Sirs, I am General Monroy of the

Embleck Army. This is Commander Brendon Grant and Cadets Andrew and Deven."

"I am High Councilor Mills, and this is Councilor Kyles," High Councilor Mills introduced. "Now, what brings these Embleck soldiers here?"

"She brought them, Sir," the Qor officer who had first threatened them accused.

"Sir, I can explain," Anise interjected. "I was attacked by Councilor Indu and discovered his alliance to the Embleck Army."

"It *was* Councilor Indu," Councilor Kyles said, stunned.

"Wait...you knew?"

"We had feared," High Councilor Mills reported. "That is why I requested a meeting with you so that I could warn you. But it seems as though Indu got to you first."

"I also learned—" Anise dropped her voice. "That Councilor Indu and King Zamir are one and the same."

Councilor Kyles flinched but nodded while Mills remained stoic.

"General Monroy rescued me when I was injured," Anise added. "He offered his loyalty and assistance to me, and we traveled to the Embleck palace to put an end to this war."

"Did you succeed in defeating him?" Councilor Kyles asked.

"Yes." Anise exhaled a deep breath. "King Zamir of the Embleck Army is dead, along with his son and most trusted high commander."

Cheers broke out around them, filling the shipyard. High Councilor Mills smiled, relief evident on his face.

"You are a hero, Commander Desson," Councilor Kyles said warmly. "We are beyond grateful for the service you have done, not only for the Qor, but the entire galaxy."

"I couldn't have done it without General Monroy," Anise said, taking Liam's arm and pulling him forward.

"We are grateful to you as well, General Monroy," Councilor Kyles said.

"General, what prompted your assistance in defeating the Embleck Army?" High Councilor Mills asked.

Liam glanced at Anise before speaking. "I regret my time spent in the Embleck Army. When Commander Desson offered me a chance to end their darkness, I was honored to assist her."

"I see," Councilor Kyles said, shooting a look at Mills. "And what did you hope to accomplish by this?"

"My intention was to destroy the Embleck Army," Liam reported. "Nothing more, Sir."

"Very well," High Councilor Mills said. "The Council and I will discuss our…options moving forward."

Anise activated her powers, reaching into the energy field and the councilors' minds.

Surely, General Monroy's actions are enough to grant him safety here. Without him, the Embleck Army would still be a threat.

"General Monroy, we will permit you to reside here for the time being," High Councilor Mills declared, his voice only slightly wooden.

A burst of exclamations and protests filled the air, but High Councilor Mills ignored them.

"If I may, Sir," Caiden began. "I request for Commander Desson and Monroy here to be admitted to the infirmary."

"We can't have Embleck soldiers parading around our base!" a Qor officer objected. "It's unheard of!"

"It will not be a problem," Councilor Kyles said, his voice slightly off. "Release the Embleck soldiers."

The soldiers protested momentarily, but they followed Councilor Kyles' orders.

"We will admit Desson and Monroy to the infirmary immediately," Mills decided. "The other Embleck soldiers will be given temporary quarters."

"Permission to assist, Sir?" Keisha volunteered.

"Permission granted," Kyles replied.

Keisha saluted before taking Brendon's arm and offering him a quick grin. "Let's go, shall we?"

Brendon's expression shifted from surprised to pleased, and he allowed Keisha to lead him and his cadets into the base.

"Thank you, Sir," Liam said formally. "We deeply appreciate what you are doing for us."

"Of course," High Councilor Mills said, his voice still carrying traces of Anise's…suggestions. "We can discuss appointing you a role here at a later time."

"I—yes, thank you, Councilor," Liam said, seeming stunned as he took Anise's hand.

High Councilor Mills smiled and glanced at Councilor Kyles, who raised an eyebrow. Anise felt like they knew something she didn't, but she pushed the questions to the back of her mind as she led Liam into the base.

Liam sighed heavily, fidgeting with the scrap of bandage in his hand. Three weeks in the infirmary had him discovering new levels of boredom.

Two of his ribs had healed incorrectly, and he'd needed an operation to fix the issue—which meant at least three weeks of recovery.

Anise had offered to use her powers to speed his healing process, but Liam had turned her down, not wanting to risk it after she'd lost her powers healing him before. His own power didn't feel strong enough to heal himself either, so he was left to heal the normal—*slow*—way.

"Hey."

Liam glanced up as Anise entered the room, a grin instantly appearing on his face. Out of the corner of his eye, he saw his heart rate on the monitor jump up.

Anise laughed as she walked over to him, holding a lunch tray. Liam flushed red as he accepted the tray from her.

"I brought lunch." Anise raked her fingers through his hair, brushing it out of his face. "Make sure you eat."

"I will." Liam scooped up a spoonful of the steaming hot soup and lifted it, only to gasp as the movement caused a stabbing pain through his ribs.

"Here, give it to me." Anise plopped down on the edge of the bed, taking the spoon from him and holding it to his lips.

"I don't need to be fed," Liam protested.

"Hush, and let me help," Anise ordered, offering him the spoon again. Reluctantly, Liam allowed her to feed him a few spoonfuls.

Anise stirred the soup as she spoke. "There's going to be a victory ball at the capitol tomorrow night. The Qor Council will be there, and we've each received invitations."

"I'm well enough to attend," Liam decided. "If you want me to come—"

"Of course! You were invited personally," Anise said as she fed him another bite. "The Council is presenting medals for the removal of Zamir. You'll have to be there."

Liam nearly choked on his food. "I don't think they meant me!"

"Yes, they did," Anise insisted. "In fact, they mentioned you by name."

Liam stared at her in shock. "What? Why me?"

"Why?" Anise shook her head. "Liam, you're being recognized as one of the two people who defeated Kind Zamir and brought an end to this war. Without you, I don't know if we would have ever won."

"But you were the real hero," Liam objected, dodging the soup she offered. "I didn't do anything other than—"

"Heal me from a deadly poison? Stand by my side to face Indu—Zamir?" Anise took his hand in hers. "Not even mentioning that you, Liam, sacrificed your life for mine. I wouldn't be here if not for you. Accept the reward for that, if nothing else."

Liam sighed. "It still feels wrong."

"It'll be fine," Anise corrected him. "Besides, with a little help from my…unique capabilities…finding you a place in the Qor won't be a problem."

"Anise, what are you—"

"Hey, Anise." Caiden stepped into the room. "The Council is requesting you."

"Oh, right!" Anise leaped up, jerking the next spoonful away from Liam and spilling it. "Sorry! Caiden, help him finish eating." She dashed out, leaving the two boys alone.

The tension rose rapidly without Anise's presence. Liam watched her brother warily. Caiden had made it clear he didn't approve of their relationship—it seemed every time Anise had stopped by, Caiden had appeared to pull her away, tossing Liam a dirty look as he did so.

Slowly, Liam ladled out another spoonful, ignoring the pain throbbing through his ribs. He stared at Caiden as if daring him to try and help. Caiden simply stood and watched, his hands twitching at his sides.

This process lasted for several minutes until Liam raised the spoon too far, inhaling sharply when pain shot through his ribs.

"Hey, why don't you let me help?" Caiden stepped forward, his movements oddly jerky. "Or at least let me get you some pain meds."

Liam set the spoon down, staring at him uncertainly. "I thought you didn't like me."

"I don't," Caiden replied, shoving his hands into his pockets. "And under any other circumstances, I wouldn't be speaking to Embleck scum."

"Good to know," Liam muttered, picking up his spoon again.

"I think having you and your soldiers on our base is insanity," Caiden added. "We should be having this conversation on opposite sides of a prison wall."

"I'd have to agree."

"And I don't have to like you," Caiden reminded him. "But Anise likes you—I'd guess as more than friends. She explicitly asked me to be nice to you...and I'm trying to appease her."

"I do care for her," Liam said a moment later. "I wouldn't hurt Anise for anything in this galaxy."

Caiden shifted his weight, seeming uncomfortable. "Anise...she told me what you did when the castle collapsed."

Liam glanced up. "She did?"

"Well...I don't think she told me everything," Caiden admitted. "She told me that you pushed her out of the castle and stayed behind..."

Caiden's voice broke slightly, and he paused. When he spoke again, his voice was quiet.

"Anise means more to me than anyone in this galaxy, and hearing how you were willing to give up your life to protect her…I still don't like you—but I am grateful."

Liam briefly met his eyes before looking away. "Anise is worth more than I'll ever be—she deserves better. We both know that."

Caiden nodded—a sharp, bitter jerk of his head. "She deserves someone who will give her the galaxy—not a soulless Embleck soldier."

Liam hid his flinch. "I know." *Angels deserve better than monsters.*

"But…" Caiden sighed heavily. "As much as I hate to admit it…*you're* the one Anise chose. She wants *you*…and I have to accept that."

Liam rubbed his fingers over his wrist. "I…I don't understand why."

"I don't either," Caiden retorted. "I'd expect someone— *anyone*—else. But it's you…so I'm offering to help."

Caiden held out the pain remedy, and Liam hesitantly accepted it.

"Thanks."

"Who knows, Monroy?" Caiden shrugged. "Maybe I'll warm up to the idea. For now, I'm willing to get along…for Anise's sake."

"I am too," Liam said, setting his tray aside.

Caiden lifted an eyebrow. "I'm not feeding you, though— that's where I draw the line."

"You'd better draw the line way before that," Liam countered with a faint smile.

Caiden relaxed slightly. "You know, Monroy…I might get used to you after all."

CHAPTER 42

The night of the ball had arrived, and Anise strode down the hallway towards Liam's temporary room now that he'd been released from the infirmary.

"Commander Desson!" Councilor Kyles called as he approached her. "Do you have a moment?"

"Of course," Anise said, turning to him. "How may I assist you, Sir?"

"The Council and I have been beyond impressed with your dedicated loyalty and service to the Qor," Kyles began. "Tonight, we planned to offer you an award...but now we had another idea."

"Yes?"

"We've all discussed and voted by majority," Councilor Kyles continued. "With Indu gone, we have a spot open on the Council. If you wish to take his place, it is yours."

Anise's mouth dropped open, and she quickly closed it. "But—I—I haven't been part of the Qor long enough to qualify for the Council!"

"We're all willing to make an exception for you," Kyles said. "Your abilities provide you with a status that cannot be earned in years, and you are invaluable to us."

Anise swallowed hard, her mind spinning. "Sir, I'm honored…"

"But?" Councilor Kyles looked at her knowingly.

"But…I'm afraid I don't feel ready for the position," Anise finished. "I will have to respectfully decline."

"I understand." Councilor Kyles said. "Serving the Council takes a dedication and commitment beyond what most people want. No judgment on you. I am confident that you could do it, but I fully support you staying where you are."

"Thank you, Sir," Anise said gratefully. "Also…has the Council spoken about…General Monroy?"

"Ah, yes…" Councilor Kyles lowered his voice. "Your…Starlink?"

Anise's eyes widened. "You—you know?"

"Yes, and I suppose that I should fully explain." Councilor Kyles said. "My brother and I have been studying Starlinks for decades. When you arrived with that blue in your hair, we knew you had to be one half."

"Your brother?"

"My adopted brother—High Councilor Mills," Councilor Kyles corrected himself. "We studied Starlinks and made progress, but we felt we were missing a key piece. Resources are scarce due to the rarity of the links and how long ago the last Starlink took place."

"Then, we finally found the journal of Princess Asteria in a museum, placed in a historical display. We sent for it, and the journal was placed inside a robot."

"You don't mean—" Anise began.

"Yes, the very one you returned to us. My brother decided you should have the journal since we knew you were part of a link—and it seems you found what you were looking for."

"I did," Anise said quietly. "Thank you—both of you—for everything you've done."

"Of course." Councilor Kyles offered her a smile. "If you're ever interested in joining the council, we'd be happy to discuss it."

"Thank you, Sir," Anise said. "Maybe someday...I will."

Councilor Kyles nodded. "I will see you at the celebration tonight, then."

"See you tonight." Anise saluted the councilor before continuing down the hall, soon finding herself outside of the room Liam was staying in.

Anise knocked on the door. "Liam?"

The door flew open, and Liam stood in the doorway, clutching a piece of paper as his eyes widened. "Oh—Anise!"

"Hey!" Anise stepped inside, glancing around the bare room. Liam shoved the paper into a drawer before turning back to her.

"It's nice here," Liam said, rubbing his thumbs over his fingertips. "I...I could get used to it."

"You should," Anise said with a smile. "Are you looking forward to the ball tonight?"

"Yes...I think so."

"How are your ribs?" Anise asked, glancing over him.

"Great." Liam opened his arms as if to demonstrate. "Just great."

Abruptly, Liam froze, clutching his side. "Oh—*oh*—" He stumbled backward, falling onto the bed.

"Liam!" Anise ran to his side, but by the time she had reached the bed, Liam had started laughing.

"You were so worried!" Liam laughed, his eyes dancing with amusement.

"Oh, *you*." Anise flicked his head with her finger. "Just for that, I insist you let me check."

"Fine, fine." Liam sat up, unbuttoning his shirt. "If you wanted me to take off my shirt, you could've just asked."

Anise flicked him again. "Oh, really?"

"How could I say no to you?" Liam teased her. "Now, see? I'm fine."

Anise gave him a once-over, examining the faint scar from his operation and another thick, messy scar from where she had healed him. That scar, however, was...

"Silver?" Anise cocked her head in confusion.

"It must be an effect of star healing," Liam suggested.

"I don't care—as long as you're okay."

"I'm perfectly fine now—I promise."

"Alright," Anise relented. "It's getting late. I'm going to get dressed, and I'll see you later."

"Good idea; see you later." Liam practically ushered her out the door.

Anise paused for a moment. "Is everything okay?"

"Everything is great," Liam said—too quickly. "Bye!"

"Bye?"

Liam quietly closed the door, leaving her standing in the hall. Anise shrugged, returning to her own room. When she opened the door, Joffrey raced over to her.

"Hi, Joffrey." Anise picked him up and stroked his ears.

"Meerooowworr." Joffrey arched his back.

"I know, I know." Anise dropped Joffrey off at his bed and went to her closet.

Keisha had insisted on taking Anise shopping yet again for dresses. Anise protested and argued, but Keisha wouldn't take no for an answer.

Anise took her dress from the closet, admiring the sleeveless bodice, with gold piping across the necklind, waistline, and hem.

The royal blue fabric shimmered in the light, falling to brush the floor.

A knock at the door startled Joffrey, and Anise rushed to answer. "Hi, Anise!" Keisha exclaimed as she nearly bounced inside. "Are you excited? Oh, I can hardly wait!"

"I am excited!" Anise replied. "And I love your dress!"

Keisha was dressed in a pale butter-yellow dress that perfectly complemented her dark, creamy skin. It had one bell sleeve and a long, loose skirt with soft pink trim on the hem and at the waist.

"I just adore it." Keisha spun around. "Anyway, I came so we can do our hair."

"Good idea."

The girls sat on Anise's bed while Anise twisted Keisha's dozens of tiny braids into a large bun at the back of her head and tied a butter-yellow scarf around it.

They switched, and Keisha arranged Anise's wavy red hair into a simple, loose style, leaving a few wisps free to frame her face.

"Perfect!" Keisha finally declared. "Liam is going to be speechless when he sees you."

"You think so?" Anise hesitantly touched her hair.

"Absolutely!" Keisha said as she put in a pair of pink earrings. "Now, hurry up. The ball is starting soon."

Anise added gold hoops to her ears and selected her sea glass bracelet. She added a turquoise necklace and slipped her promise ring on her right middle finger.

"I'm ready."

"Me too," Keisha agreed. "Let's go!"

"Actually, I'm staying here," Anise said. "Liam offered to teleport us."

'Oh, of course," Keisha said, checking the time on her wrist comm. "I better run before I make us late."

"Us?" Anise lifted an eyebrow. "Are you going with someone?"

"I am," Keisha whispered, a thrill of excitement in her voice. "I'm going with that cute Commander Grant—you know, he came with Liam."

"Really?" Anise exclaimed.

"Mmhum." Keisha leaned in at the mirror and applied some lipstick. "He's really sweet. We hit it off the day I gave him a tour of the base. He asked me to go to the ball, and I said yes."

"That's great!" Anise congratulated her friend. "Caiden told me that he's going with Lydia."

"Good for him," Keisha said. "Oh, this will be so much fun!" She checked her reflection one last time and hurried to the door. "I'll see you there!"

"Bye." Anise waved as Keisha closed the door.

Anise bit her lip, nerves settling over her. She would have to stand in front of hundreds of people and make an acceptance speech after getting her award…and it was also Liam's first time at a public event.

Forcing herself to stop pacing, Anise sat in her chair, thumbing through a book. Her mind felt far too scattered to concentrate, and she bounced her leg nervously.

Someone knocked at the door, and Anise jumped up, her book forgotten. She checked her reflection one last time and raced to open the door.

Liam stood outside her door in a formal, navy-blue Qor uniform with a perfect galaxy rose in his hand.

"Oh, Liam, you shouldn't have," Anise cooed, accepting the flower.

Liam's widened eyes locked on her, his gaze softening. "Anise…you're stunning."

Anise felt herself flush. "Thank you. Let me put this in water, and then I'll be ready to leave."

Once she had returned, Liam offered her his arm. "Shall we?"

"Yes, I think so." Anise took his arm, and Liam created a portal.

Anise gasped when she stepped inside the oversized ballroom. The white marble floors had been polished, and the glass ceiling showed thousands of stars twinkling brightly. Couples glided across the floor to the music, and the entire Qor Council watched the festivities from their balcony.

"It's absolutely splendid," Anise said in awe.

"So are you," Liam said, his voice hushed.

"Anise!" Keisha called as she approached them, Brendon at her side.

"Keisha, Brendon. I must say, you two make a lovely couple."

Brendon grinned, glancing at Liam. "Thanks. I have to say the same for you two."

"The next song is starting!" Keisha said, taking Brendon's arm. "Are you two coming?"

Liam offered her his hand. "May I have this dance?"

"You may." Anise smiled as she took his hand.

One dance turned into two, then three—until had lost track of all time, caught up in the joy filling her chest. Finally, High Councilor Mills stood and clinked his glass.

"May I have your attention, please?"

The dancing slowed to a halt, and Anise began slipping through the crowd and toward the balcony, Liam right behind her.

"Today, we celebrate the fall of the Embleck Army. This enemy has been present for many years, but now the galaxy is free, thanks to each of our soldiers."

Applause broke out through the crowd, drowning out his voice. High Councilor Mills waited patiently for silence before speaking again.

"Tonight, we honor the two soldiers who risked their lives to destroy the late King Zamir of the Embleck Army. First— Liam Monroy."

"Go," Anise whispered as Liam remained frozen beside her. "Liam, go."

Liam nodded once, taking a deep breath as he started up the steps. Anise watched, warmth washing over her.

Hating before High Councilor Mills, Liam saluted. Mills smiled at him as he turned to the crowd. "As many of you know, General Monroy once served the Embleck Army. Now he has defected, and he offered us aid at the height of our struggle."

High Councilor Mills handed Liam a bronzed medallion, placing a hand on his shoulder. Polite applause sprung up around the room, and a slight flush crept up Liam's neck.

Anise held her breath, hoping the councilor would continue. *Announce that he's been accepted into the Qor. We've accepted defectors before—please, Mills!*

Councilor Kyles stepped forward, holding a small badge in his hands. "Monroy, your selfless actions have spoken to the Council, and we have decided to offer you probationary rank in Commander Desson's squadron, proven you wish to continue serving."

Shock filtered across Liam's face as a thrill raced through Anise's body. *Yes!*

"Thank you, Sirs." Liam's voice held a faint note of emotion. "I will accept gratefully and swear my loyalty to the Qor."

Councilor Kyles offered Liam the badge, and he hesitantly accepted it. More scattered applause accented Liam's descent as he quickly strode down the stairs, stopping at Anise's side.

Anise didn't have a moment to speak with him before Councilor Kyles spoke.

"Tonight, we also honor a soldier I'm sure you know well by now—Commander Anise Desson."

Thunderous applause filled the room, and Anise felt her heart skip a beat. Gripping the railing, she climbed up the steps, stopping before the councilors. She wracked her brain for what she had planned to say in acceptance, but nothing came to mind.

"Commander Desson, you have served the Qor faithfully for nine years," Councilor Kyles began, pausing for another round of applause. "In that time, you have risked yourself countlessly and proven your loyalty to the Qor, and the safety of the galaxy has no bounds."

"Tonight, we present Commander Desson with a medal for bravery many years overdue." High Councilor Mills placed the medallion in her trembling hands.

"Thank you, Councilors," Anise said, the cool weight of the medallion feeling surreal as she heard clapping in the background.

"Due to your actions of bravery in bringing an end to the late King Zamir and the Embleck Army as a whole, the Qor

Military Council is pleased to present you with the rank of high commander."

Anise's breath caught in her chest. "I—I thank you, Councilors. This is an honor."

"It is well deserved," Councilor Kyles said warmly. "Thank you, High Commander.

A roar of applause hit Anise, the sound echoing through the entire ballroom long after she descended the stairs. She stopped before Liam, unable to contain her smile.

"Congratulations, Anise," Liam said, reaching for her hand. "You deserve this."

"Thank you," Anise said, giddy. "I can't believe it—a high commander!"

"May I offer a celebratory dance?" Liam held out his hand.

"High Commander Desson!" a woman called. "May I speak with you?"

"Can I take you up on that in a moment?" Anise asked.

"Of course," Liam replied. "Go ahead."

Anise went to speak with the woman, soon finding herself swamped with questions. Everyone wanted to know what she thought of her new position, how she defeated the Embleck Army—and, of course, dozens of questions about the Embleck soldiers.

Overwhelmed, Anise tried to answer each of the questions, but for each she answered, there were five more. It felt like she'd never escape a particularly insistent woman's questions about Liam when a hand tapped on her shoulder.

"Pardon me." Liam stepped around her with a smile, offering his arm. "Someone is asking for you, High Commander."

"Oh, I see. Excuse me." Anise placed her hand on Liam's arm and walked away with him.

"Who's asking for me?" Anise asked as Liam led her out of the ballroom's large doors and down an empty, dimly lit hallway. "Liam?"

Liam slowed his pace. "Nobody's asking for you. But you looked uncomfortable, and I thought you might like to…slip away for a moment."

Anise grinned, placing her hands on his shoulder and leaning up. "You know…I think I just might."

Liam placed his hands on her wrists, lightly tugging her arms down. He held her gently, and Anise noted a nervous energy around him.

"Can I make us a portal?" Liam asked, caressing the underside of her wrists with his thumbs. "Please?"

"Of course," Anise replied, trying to recalculate the situation. *I'm sure he's just noticed all the eyes on us. It's a lot of negative attention for him. He doesn't want us to be seen together and add to the gossip.* "Where do you want to go?"

"It's a surprise," Liam replied, creating a portal. "Close your eyes."

"Alright." Anise closed her eyes, a sense of uncertainty creeping over her. *Why is he being so secretive?*

Guided by Liam, Anise walked through the portal, only to halt abruptly. The ground shifted beneath her low heels, making it difficult to stand. A cool breeze lifted her hair from her neck, cooling the warm, humid air. A faint rushing sound filled her ears, and she tried to piece together what it could be.

"Where are we?" Anise asked.

"Open your eyes and see."

Anise opened her eyes, a thrill of joy instantly shooting through her veins. "Oh, *Liam!*"

Moonlight illuminated the beach, shimmering off the crashing waves. Thousands of stars twinkled in the sky, and the sand glistened silver. Anise quickly kicked off her shoes, burying her toes in the cool sand.

"Do you like it?" Liam asked hopefully.

"I love it!" Anise exclaimed. "Liam, you got to take me to the ocean after all."

Liam stepped forward, taking her hand. "I…I brought you here because I wanted to talk with you."

"About what?"

"About us."

Anise felt a wave of anticipation wash over her. "I'd like that."

Liam glanced at her hand in his. "Now that the Embleck Army is gone now…we're finally free. I don't…understand why you chose me, but I'm honored. You saved my life—you offered me a future—and I love you."

"I love you, too," Anise whispered.

"Anise, I knew the day we met that I was meant to spend my life with you," Liam said as he slowly lowered himself onto one knee.

Anise's heart pounded, her breath coming short as Liam reached into his pocket, pulling out a small box.

"I love you more than anything in this whole galaxy, Anise. I want to have a family with you—spend the rest of my life with you." Liam cracked open the box, revealing a sparkling ring.

"Anise, will you marry me?" Liam's shyly hopeful smile warmed Anise's heart. "Please?"

Barely able to speak, Anise inhaled deeply, her voice choked with emotion. "Yes."

"Yes?" Liam's face lit up.

Anise threw herself into Liam's arms, nearly knocking him over. "*Yes!*"

A grin broke out on Liam's face as he hugged her, tucking his face against her neck. Anise's heart raced, joy pulsing through her body. *I'm engaged!*

Leaning back, Liam took the ring from the box, and Anise held out her hand. Gently, Liam slipped the ring on her finger, and Anise tilted her hand as she admired the gold ring with a circle diamond and a smaller sapphire on each side.

"This is gorgeous," Anise said, feeling tears brimming in her eyes. "I love you."

"I love you, angel."

Anise grasped the collar of Liam's uniform, pulling his lips to hers. Liam wrapped his arms around her, burying his hands in her hair.

When they finally broke apart, Anise rested her forehead against Liam's, cupping his face in her hand. A few tears shone on his cheeks, and she knew her face mirrored his.

Liam inhaled deeply, unable to stop smiling. "I've been waiting on this moment for nine years."

Anise kissed a tear from his face. "And now we'll have the rest of our lives together."

"It's worth it," Liam whispered, his eyes shining with love. "I thought about you every day...and now...you're going to be my *wife*."

Wife. Anise hugged Liam again, unable to think of another way to convey the joy she felt overflowing in her chest.

A long moment passed before Liam spoke. "We...we should get back to the ball."

Anise made to attempt at moving. "I guess so..."

Finally, they stood, and Anise shook the sand off her skirt while Liam created a portal. "After you."

Anise stepped back into the hallway, Liam right behind her. "Is my hair a mess?"

Liam glanced at her, a slight flush coloring his face as he brushed a wisp from her face. "I think it's beautiful."

"That means yes," Anise said, reaching up to try and smoothen it.

"Anise!"

Anise spun around to see Keisha and Brendon approaching them, followed by Caiden and Lydia.

"Where were you two?" Keisha asked, but then her eyes fell on Anise's new ring. "Wait—Anise?"

Anise glanced at Liam, and he offered her a smile. Anise turned back to her friend, holding up her hand. "We're engaged!"

Keisha squealed, hugging Anise. "Congratulations! Oh, this is so exciting!"

Brendon embraced Liam, a smile on his face. "I'm happy for you, Liam."

"Thanks, Brendon," Liam replied softly.

Keisha stepped back, and Anise's eyes fell on Caiden. He stood silently for a moment before stepping forward and shaking Liam's hand.

"Congratulations. You have an incredible woman— remember that."

"There's no way I could forget," Liam said, placing his hand on the small of Anise's back.

Caiden nodded, a look of understanding passing between him and Liam. Anise slid her arm around Liam as Caiden took Lydia's hand.

"Come on! Let's go back to the ballroom for a celebratory dance!" Keisha called, pulling Brendon down the hall.

Anise took Liam's hand as they entered the ballroom. The next song started, and Liam pulled Anise into his arms as the music swelled.

"I love you," Liam whispered in her ear.

"I love you too," Anise replied as they swept across the floor, dancing under the stars.

EPILOUGE

Deep in the forests of Nockalore, a dark palace once stood tall. Now, only stones remained in its place as a reminder of what had once been.

"AH!"

A hand reached out of the Embleck Palace ruins, and a man pulled himself free. He rested his hands on his knees and coughed, trying to remove the dust from his lungs. Blood dripped down his face, clouding his right eye, and he held his injured left arm close to his chest.

Another man climbed free of the wreckage, scanning their surroundings. "They're gone, Prince Ruven."

Ruven shot him an evil look. "I can see that, High Commander Ankor."

"Should we look for your father, Your Highness?"

Ruven glanced at the wreckage. "…No."

High Commander Ankor reached into the ruins and pulled something out. "I suppose you will want this, then."

Ruven saw the item Ankor was holding and smiled. "The staff."

Ankor pulled it away from Ruven's reach. "Not so fast. I may not be able to use it, but I'm not giving it up so easy."

Ruven crossed his arms, deciding to humor the man. "Very well. What do you want?"

High Commander Ankor glanced at the staff. "I want power. I want to be in command and take orders from no one." Ankor saw Ruven's scowl and rephrased. "No one other than you, Your Highness."

"That can be arranged," Ruven said. "Anything else?"

Ankor clenched his fist. "Monroy. King Zamir favored him—only for him to betray us."

"The weapon *will* pay," Ruven said. "Now, hand it over."

High Commander Ankor handed him the staff. "What now, Your Highness?"

561

"Ankor, you will address me by my proper title. My father is dead, and *I* am king."

"Yes, Your Majesty."

Ruven twirled his staff. "We'll have to rebuild—take new recruits. But first..."

"What, Your Majesty?"

"First, revenge. Not only on the weapon—but on the commander who destroyed my army..."

"*Anise Desson.*"

ABOUT THE AUTHOR

Grace Walker has always been an avid reader, and she hopes to inspire a love of reading in others with her writing. When Grace is not reading or writing, she enjoys graphic design, cooking, and taking long walks on the beach.

STARDUST

Made in United States
North Haven, CT
15 September 2023

41596731R00310